"I wa   Valeria took
out a sliqud and put it in the crone's palm.
"Tell me more, priestess."

"I se   a
young bride. I see a sacred grove, laid waste. I see
a great battle—" The crone twisted the Seeing
Stone. "Ah. Great love, my lady. All-consuming
love, a love like a flame." But instead of smiling,
she looked puzzled, then frowned.

Mebde's hand began to tremble, as if she were
struggling to hold the stone steady. Finally she
cried, dropping it as if it were hot, and staring up
in horror, using her hand to clench at her blind eye.

"My eye!" She held out her other hand. "Here!
Take the coin back!"

"What did you see?"

Mebde shook her head as if clearing it, the
money clattering on the stones between them.
She looked at Valeria in sorrow. "Beware the one
you trust," the old woman croaked. "And trust the
one you beware."

Hadrian's Wall is an adventure story, a love story, and
a novel of action and ideas . . . full of romance
and intrigue and politics and plotting . . . Dietrich
has researched the period and the place
                   ll it seems real."

Books by William Dietrich

Fiction

THE SCOURGE OF GOD
HADRIAN'S WALL
ICE REICH
GETTING BACK
DARK WINTER

Nonfiction

THE FINAL FOREST
NORTHWEST PASSAGE
NATURAL GRACE

HADRIAN'S WALL
A NOVEL OF ROMAN ENGLAND

WILLIAM
DIETRICH

HarperTorch
An Imprint of HarperCollinsPublishers

This is a work of fiction. Names, characters, places, and incidents are products of the author's imagination or are used fictitiously and are not to be construed as real. Any resemblance to actual events, locales, organizations, or persons, living or dead, is entirely coincidental.

HARPERTORCH
An Imprint of HarperCollins*Publishers*
10 East 53rd Street
New York, New York 10022-5299

Copyright © 2004 by William Dietrich
Map by Virginia Norey
Excerpt from *The Scourge of God* copyright © 2005 by William Dietrich
ISBN: 0-06-056372-9

First HarperTorch paperback printing: March 2005
First HarperCollins hardcover printing: March 2004

HarperCollins®, HarperTorch™, and ❦ ™ are trademarks of HarperCollins Publishers Inc.

Printed in the United States of America

Visit HarperTorch on the World Wide Web at www.harpercollins.com

10 9 8 7 6 5 4 3 2 1

To Holly

Acknowledgments

This novel had complications on the way to its birth, including false starts, a somewhat bizarre research trip to Hadrian's Wall at the height of England's hoof-and-mouth disease epidemic, and initial submission that coincided with 9/11. I owe a special thanks to my agent, Andrew Stuart, for finding the book a home at HarperCollins, and to my editors Jeffrey Kellogg and Michael Shohl for improving the story and overseeing delivery. The many historians and archaeologists in Great Britain who have uncovered the island's Roman and Celtic past all deserve my gratitude. I'd particularly like to thank Peter Reynolds at Butser Ancient Farm, Lindsay Allason-Jones at the Museum of Antiquities at the University of Newcastle for her lecture on women at Hadrian's Wall, and historical reenactor Matthew Bunker, who shared his enthusiasm for the past over a pint or two and let me get the feel of Roman armor and weaponry. Only in England can you drink beer in a helmet and hardly draw a curious glance. Finally, I'd like to thank my wife, Holly, an ever-more-remarkable woman who believed in *Hadrian's Wall* from its conception. This is her book, too.

ROMAN BRITAIN

PROLOGUE

A.D. 122

The northern wind blew across the ridge *with a howl like an army of barbarians.*

The metaphor pleased the emperor, who considered himself a scholar as well as a soldier. A new balcony jutted from the wooden quarters that had been hastily erected for the emperor's entourage, and Hadrian stood on it now, adding the gale to his mental inventory of the empire. The long green blades of the grassy ridge that rose before him were combed flat by the weather, and sheets of rain lashed his raw fifty-room complex, drumming against timbers still pungent from their cutting and dripping into the rooms below where the braziers were inadequate. The climate clung to one's clothing and drove deep into one's very bones. Rather than dwell on this, it was better to look outward, into the teeth of the wind. A ravine to the right sheltered a stand of trees that crept up the defile like an advancing patrol, and the emperor's tactical eye followed it, noting how bitterly the branches shuddered at the crest. Not a place any man would wish to be stationed, he thought, but then that was true of all borders, wasn't it? By their very nature, borders were where comfort ended. Behind him the corridors of the complex rumbled with the tread of military boots, the sound echoing all the louder for the paucity of furnishings and carpets. Retiring governor Pompeius, Hadrian knew, hadn't had much time to prepare for the imperial arrival. At the emperor's own insistence, the imperial dispatches heralding his approach demanded maps and models, not luxuries. He wouldn't tarry here long.

Yet Hadrian had complimented his host for the ambitious timber construction at lonely Vindolanda. Half his life had been spent under a tent, so this was a relative improvement. "Happiness is tied to expectations, not belongings," he told the officers assembled behind him. "At the empire's edge, we expect less and so take more pleasure in little things."

A legate dutifully wrote the remark down.

"A man of your responsibilities deserves all that we can share," Pompeius replied loyally. The comfort of his own retirement, he knew, depended on the emperor's favor.

"A man of my power could have chosen to stay in Rome, governor. But I didn't, by desire and by necessity. Right, Florus?" The head of his plump poet and jester poked out of an enclosing cloak like an emergent and miserable mole.

"We rejoice to share your burdens, Caesar," Florus said with all the insincerity he could muster. "In fact, a verse about your heroism has just come to me."

The emperor's courtiers smiled in anticipation of some new slyness, and Hadrian's eyebrows mockingly arched. "Really? What a surprise to hear an offer of your wit."

"It comes to me unbidden, sire, a present from the gods. I call my verse 'The Plea of Hadrian.'"

"Then let's hear the god's wisdom, fat Florus."

The poet stood, dropping his cloak with a dramatic flourish and coming chest-high to the centurion beside him. He recited in a high, piping voice:

I don't want to be emperor—please!
To tramp around Britannia, muddy to my knees
Or be stuck in stinking Scythia, watching my purple
  ass freeze!

Florus bowed and plopped down, burrowing again into his cloak. The visitors roared, even as Pompeius flushed with shock at this sally about the imperial color. No one else seemed surprised at the satire. Hadrian's close companions shared the camaraderie of endless miles, rude quarters, and homesickness. No ruler had ever attempted to tour the entire empire before. A permissible joke kept them all sane.

"Write that down, too," Hadrian instructed the legate, smiling wryly. Then he looked out again at the sodden slope, suddenly impatient. "So let's get muddy to our knees, Romans. Let's see this high ground!"

The ruler was as restless as he was quick. In the last half hour he had dictated three letters, suggested terracing the hills for orchards and pasture to save the commissary money, reviewed and approved the execution of a legionary caught selling a cache of spearheads to the barbarians, and requested for audience that evening a centurion's concubine who had caught his eye. The officer was not wholly discontented with this demand: the woman would get a bauble for her favor, his own chances for promotion would improve, and the emperor would be warm this night and in a better mood tomorrow. In the meantime, Hadrian wanted to climb the hill.

"We *could* wait on the weather," Pompeius offered cautiously.

"Wait on the weather in Britannia?" The laugh was a bark. "I'm forty-eight years old, governor. Wait on the weather, and I might as well order my tomb."

"It changes quickly, Caesar."

"So does my empire. I've traveled from Persian parch to Briton bog. If I'd waited on weather, I'd still be in Syria, sunburned and bored."

The new governor, Platorius Nepos, had accompanied Hadrian from Germania after being picked as Pompeius's successor and had quickly learned his master's impatience. "I'll order the horses," he said.

"No. We walk." The emperor addressed the assembled officers. "We walk like the barbarians walk, to feel the lay of the land as they do and try to imagine what this proposed line of ours will look like, to them and to us."

The emperor set a brisk pace. He was tall, his face bearded to hide the pits and scars left by the acne that had plagued him as a youth, and he habitually went bareheaded, his dark Iberian hair curling in the rain. His fur-trimmed cloak flapped behind him like a bird's tail as he strode, his hounds dashing excitedly ahead after nothing. Generals, engineers, logisticians, architects, and centurions followed him up the muddy incline like a procession of ants. A few Praetorian cavalry rode ahead in protective screen, but otherwise there was no formality to this survey, and no pomp. Gray clouds scudded across the broad valley to the south, soaking it, while the ridge crest still hid the country to the north.

Pompeius was panting. "I'd expected to show the scale models first."

Nepos grinned. "Those he'll want at midnight. In daylight, he moves. When he ordered a palisade in Germania and Flavius balked at the cost in labor, Hadrian grabbed a spade and ax himself. The legion almost stampeded to get ahead of him. By the time he left, the first mile of log wall was already in place."

"His pace is quick."

"And his mind quicker. He wants to settle the world."

The Praetorians reined in abruptly at the crest. Hadrian paused below it, waiting in the lee of the hill to catch his breath and let the others gather around him. The rain was slackening to a blowing mist. The emperor squinted against it, seemingly immune to the cold. "Our empire stops at the dreariest places," he remarked to the huddled men.

There was dutiful laughter, but some looked uneasy at this confirmation of the rumored halt. "Not under Trajan, it didn't," one centurion muttered. Hadrian's predecessor had been a ceaseless expansionist. Trajan never stopped.

The new emperor, pretending not to hear this remark, turned and led the men up the hillside. At the summit the earth dropped away, and the wind struck them like a slap.

What had been a grassy hill on the south slope ended in an abrupt cliff of dark and rugged volcanic rock on the north. There was a sheer plunge of two hundred feet and then a wasteland of moor and lead-colored pond, undulating northward toward the smoky mists of distant Caledonia. In the pale light it was difficult to tell what was cloud and what was mountain. No matter. The view was magnificent, the rain stung, and the position was unassailable. The soldiers murmured their approval.

"This is the high point of a ridge that extends across much of the waist of Britannia," Pompeius explained. "You can see, Caesar, what a natural boundary it is. Inlets allow a port on both coasts. Flatter ground allows deployment of cavalry to the east and west. A road already runs in the valley behind us. Some forts and watchtowers—"

"A wall."

"Yes, walls, ditches—"

"A wall, governor, across the entire island."

Pompeius blinked. "The entire island?" There'd been no warning of this.

"A single wall to settle the governance of Britannia once and for all. Rome on one side, the barbarians on the other. This province has the most tiresome rebels since the Jews were scattered from Judea. A wall, Pompeius, to control trade, migration, smuggling, alliance, and civilization. A wall eighty miles long, built by Britannia's three legions."

"Even up here?" The governor looked warily over the edge of a precipice no army could climb.

"Even up here." The party's cloaks fluttered in the bitter wind, but the rain was thinning to spatters, and the panorama was sharpening. "I want the tribes to see a wall unbroken, filling ravines, crowning cliffs, and bridging rivers." Hadrian turned to Pompeius's successor. "Can you do it, Nepos?"

"The engineers have made some preliminary calculations," the new governor said, having had more knowledge than Pompeius of this idea. "The volume of stone is prodigious. Imagine a legionary carrying his own weight in rock. He would have to do so at least fifty million times. I estimate thirty million facing stones alone, Caesar, with rubble, clay, and lime mortar filling the thickness between. Such a project will require many quarries, timber for scaffolding, and a squadron of cobblers just to replace worn boots—not to mention tanners to supply the cobblers! The water alone to mix the mortar will require five hundred jars a day, and at least double that to slake the thirst of the soldiers. Most of it will have to be hauled up hills like the one we just climbed.

That means oxen, donkeys, and horses, and fodder for the herd. It will cost—"

"It will cost little." Hadrian was looking not at his governors but out across the northern landscape again. "It will be built by soldiers who have grown restless and need a project to organize their minds. And it *will* be done. Augustus said he found Rome in brick and left it in marble. I intend to defend that marble with stone."

"With all respect, Caesar, it has never been done," Pompeius had the courage to caution. "Not out of stone, for so long a distance. Not in all the empire."

Their commander turned. "Not in our empire. But when fighting the Parthians, governor, I heard stories of a wall far to the east, far beyond India, in the land where silk originates. The caravans say that wall separates barbarism from civilization, leaving both sides happier for it. I want that here."

The soldiers looked uncertain. Rome's army did not defend, it attacked. So the emperor caught the eye of the centurion who had muttered about Trajan, addressing the man as an equal. "Listen to me, centurion. Listen all of you, and listen well. Rome has been advancing outward for five hundred years, and all of us benefit from her glories. Yet conquest is losing its profit. I followed Trajan on his adventures in the East, and I know well how his battles were celebrated in every Roman city, from Alexandria to Londinium. What those who glorify my late cousin and guardian don't understand is that we conquered valleys but not the mountains above, nor the armies that still lurked there. We could not be defeated, but neither could we defeat. Is that not the case here in Britannia?"

There was no answer but the wind.

"I well know of the glorious victory two generations ago at Mount Graupius in distant Caledonia, far to the north," Hadrian continued. "I well know the courage of the Britannic legions that have never been defeated in standing battle. I know we've manned temporary turf and timber walls far into barbarian lands, ultimately beating every sally against them. But I also know that these barbarians don't submit like

Carthage or Corinth or Judea. As they have nothing to lose, a loss means nothing to them. Having no honor, they run instead of die. Having no true nation, they have none to surrender. They hide behind rocks. They haunt the mountains. They charge on horse or foot, hurl a javelin or fire an arrow, and then flee before the issue is decided. They are as weak as fog, and just as hard to bag. And most important, they inhabit lands we have no interest in! Here in Britannia it is cold highlands and peat bogs. In Germania it is swamps and trackless forest. In Scythia it is a desert of grass, in Parthia a kingdom of stones, and in Africa a wilderness of sand. Every mile our empire stretches into such waste means costly transport and vulnerable garrisons. I'll tell you what I learned from the great Trajan, centurion: that senseless conquest is meaningless conquest, because it costs more than it gains. Did you know that I inherited not just an empire, but a debt of seven hundred million sesterces? We have marched to the edges of the world, and it is time to defend what we have. Do you agree, centurion? Answer truthfully, because pleasing lies are as useless as costly victories."

The man swallowed. It was not easy to talk to an emperor, and yet this one, his hair wet and bright eyes glistening with intensity, seemed genuinely to welcome it. "A wall doesn't just keep the barbarians out, Caesar. It keeps us in."

"Ah." Hadrian nodded. "You're a strategist too. And you have more courage than many of my courtiers, centurion, to offer such opinion, and I congratulate you for it. So I tell you this: Rome has never waited for her enemies, or when she did—when Hannibal came down out of his mountains— the result was terrible. So this wall will have gates, and Rome's soldiers will march northward from them. Or rather ride—we need more cavalry, my generals tell me, to run the cowards down!" The assembly laughed. "The chiefs will never be allowed to forget our power, or to stop fearing our revenge. But at the same time, every barbarian will know that their own territory stops here, where civilization begins. Every chief will know it is easier to make peace with Rome than make war."

The racing cloud was fragmenting in the wind, and sunlight began to pick out parts of the ridge, lighting it with shafts of gold. The party stirred. The shift in weather seemed an auspicious omen. They tried to picture a wall snaking along the ridge, dotted with towers, buttressed by forts. They tried to imagine their long and bloody march finally coming to an end.

"We've conquered that which is worth conquering," Hadrian said. "In Germania the wall will be of wood, because our boundary is in a forest, and construction clears lines of sight. Here in Britannia, where it's too miserable for even trees to grow, we'll build of rock. Or turf, where there's no rock. We'll build and build, a manifestation of Roman power, and when it's done . . ." He looked past them to the south, slowly being settled. "When it's done, there'll be no more battle, and the world will have entered a new age. Let the barbarians have their bogs. We will have what's worth having." He turned to his governors. "Pompeius, your ideas have gotten us started. Nepos, finishing will be your monument."

The new governor nodded solemnly. "It will take a generation—"

"It will take three years."

The assembly gasped.

"Three years, legion matched against legion to measure speed, and at its end we'll have our barrier." Hadrian smiled. "Improvements will follow, of course."

"Three years?" Nepos nodded uncertainly. "As you command, Caesar. But I need the legions as committed to this project as if on campaign."

"This *is* their campaign, Nepos."

"Three years." The new governor nodded, and swallowed. "And how long is this line to last, emperor?"

"How long?" Now Hadrian looked impatient—much more so than he had with the impudent centurion. "How long, governor? As long as all my projects and monuments are to last: as long as the rock they are built on. This wall, Aulus Platorius Nepos, is to be built to last forever."

A.D. 368

The Dusk of the Roman Empire

PART ONE

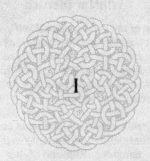

1

No one knows better than I just how big our empire is.

My bones ache from its immensity.

I, Draco, am frontiersman and bureaucrat, inspector and scribe. Men fear me for what I represent, the long reach of Rome. I have the ear of emperors. I make and break careers. I wear this power like armor because it's the only protection I have when making my unloved appearances and blunt reports. I carry no weapon but authority.

The cost of this power is exhaustion. When I was young, traveling Rome's borders to recommend a strengthened garrison here, a tax office there, my job seemed glamorous. It showed me the world. But I've walked, ridden, barged, and sailed for twenty thousand miles, and now I am old and weary, sent finally to this farthest place, my joints sore from its chill.

I have been ordered to northern Britannia to answer a mystery. A report on revolt and invasion, yes, but that is not all of it. I read again the dispatch ordering my mission, sensing the bafflement behind it. A senator's daughter, lost to the wilderness. Valeria, her name is, beautiful by all accounts, willful, adventuresome, discontented, the spark that ignited blood and fire.

Why?

The northern skies outside my window in the grim legionary fortress of Eburacum are gray and blank, offering nothing. I snap at my slave to add more charcoal to the brazier. How I miss the sun!

The tone of the plea I've received from the patrician

*Valens has more of the petulance and self-pity of the endan-
gered politician than it does the heartbreak and guilt of the
bereaved father. He is one of the two thousand senators who
burden today's Rome, clinging to an office that provides
more opportunities for greed than power. Still, a senator
cannot be ignored. I read again.*

> I wish for a public report on the recent barbarian inva-
> sion and a confidential addendum on the disappear-
> ance of my daughter. Rumors of her choice have
> strained relations with my Flavian in-laws and inter-
> rupted the financial partnership necessary to sustain
> my office. It is important that Valeria's reputation be
> restored so that her family can make claim to rightful
> estate. I trust you understand the delicacy of your mis-
> sion and the need for discretion.

*Retirement should have come long ago, but I am a useful
kind of man, loyal not to a ruler so much as the idea of Rule.
Loyal to stability. Longevity. That means I persist through
each change of emperor, each switch of state religion, each
reorganization of the provinces. I'm also kept as far away as
possible, out on the borders. An idealist can be usefully em-
ployed but never completely trusted.*

*I am here to interrogate survivors, which means I try to
find some truth in the web of lies, self-deception, and wish-
ful thinking that makes up human memory. Many of the best
witnesses are dead, and the rest are divided and confused by
what happened. They carry in their mood the stink of
Hadrian's Wall, the smell of burned timbers, unburied flesh,
and abandoned food pots that churn with squirming mag-
gots. The flies come by day and the wild dogs by night,
driven off by the desultory crew of sullen slaves, crippled
soldiers, and pressed Briton laborers working to repair the
damage. It is the stink of victory that in truth is a kind of defeat, of stability replaced by uncertainty.*

*How soon before the barbarians come back again, per-
haps for good?*

That too, the emperor and Senate want to know.

I have made a list of informants to interview. The hand-maiden. The cook. The villa owner. The captured druid. But I start with a soldier, direct and blunt.

The centurion on the field litter before me is named Longinus: a good record, his foot crushed by a battle-ax in the desperate fighting, his eyes dark with sleepless pain and the knowledge he will never walk again. Still, he has glory I can only envy. I question him.

"Do you know who I am?"

"An imperial inspector."

"You understand my purpose?"

"To do the bidding of emperor and Senate."

"Yes. And yours?"

"I'm a man of duty. It's all I've ever been."

"So you will answer any question?"

"When there's an answer I can give." *Crisp, unhesitating, to the point. A Roman.*

"Good. Now, you knew the senior tribune Galba Brassidias?"

"Of course."

"When he was promoted?"

"I brought the news to him."

"And when was that?"

"The autumn of two years ago."

"You were a courier?"

Longinus is no simple soldier. He understands I'm surprised that a ranking centurion had been assigned the mission of riding the post. "The news was delicate. Duke Fullofaudes, the commander of northern Britannia, sent me because I'd campaigned with Galba and knew him as well as any man could know him. A hard man, but a good soldier. Galba, I mean."

"What do you mean, 'a hard man'?"

"Cavalry. Not the kind to have at banquet. Not a conversationalist. He was a provincial from Thrace who lacked refinement, a superb horseman but never schooled. Solid but grim. The best kind to have on your right side in battle."

"Of course." *As if I truly know.* "And he took the news well?"

Longinus gave a pained smile, remembering.

"Poorly?"

"None of this will make sense to you unless you've served on the Wall."

It is a careful insult, an attempt to pretend at a vast difference between civilian and soldier. As if a breastplate changes the human heart!

"I have spent my whole life on the Wall," I growl, giving him a sense of the power behind me. "Rome's wall, from Arabia Petraea to your dunghill here. I have traded insults with the arrogant warriors of Sarmatia and sifted rumors of the distant hun. I have smelled the stink of Berber camels and eaten with sentries on the cold palisades of the Rhine, counting the fires of the Germans across the river. Do not think you have to tell me about the Wall."

"It's just that it was . . . complicated."

"You said you would answer any question."

He shifts, grimacing. *"I'll answer it. To be honest isn't simple, however."*

"Explain yourself."

"Life at the border is complex. Sometimes you're a sentry, sometimes an ambassador. Sometimes a wall, sometimes a gate. Sometimes we fight the barbarians, sometimes we enlist them. For outsiders like the woman to come in—"

"Now you are getting ahead of my questions. I asked for Galba's reaction to his superior's appointment, not his justification."

Longinus hesitates, appraising me. He doesn't seek to know if I can be trusted. How can you ever be sure of that? Rather, whether I can understand. The hardest thing in life, after all, is to be understood. *"You've been to the breach where the barbarians broke through?"*

"It is the first place I went to."

"What did you see there?"

The interrogation has been turned around. Longinus wants proof I can comprehend what he tells me. I think before I speak.

"A thin garrison. Sulking craftsmen. A cold pyre, nothing but bones."

He nods, waiting.

"The Wall is being repaired," I go on, betraying some of what will be in my report, *"but not with the same care as before. I measured the lime, and the mix is weak. The contractor is corrupt and the imperial foreman untrained. His superior died in the fighting. The mortar will dry to little better than hard sand and will have to be redone."*

"Will it?"

I know what he means. General Theodosius has restored rough order, but the treasury has been drained and authority is dissipating. The best builders are moving south. *"It should be redone. How well depends on good Romans such as yourself."*

He nods. *"You're observant, Inspector Draco. Realistic. Smart, perhaps. Smart to have gone to so many places and lived as long as you have."* The centurion has approved of me, I realize, and I'm secretly flattered by his approval. A man of action seeing value in me, a man of words! *"Maybe even honest, which is rare these days. So I'll tell you about Galba and the lady Valeria and the last good days of the Petriana cavalry. The patricians will blame him, but I don't. Do you?"*

I think again. *"Loyalty is the first virtue."*

"Which Rome did not repay in kind."

That is the question, isn't it? Everyone knows what soldiers owe the state—death, if necessary. But what does the state owe its soldiers?

"Galba dedicated his life to Rome, and then the influence of this woman took his command away," Longinus goes on. *"She pretended to innocence, but . . ."*

"You do not concede that?"

"My experience is that no one is innocent. Not in Rome. Not here, either."

Innocence is what I've come to decide, of course. Treason. Jealousy. Incompetence. Heroism. I pass judgment like a god.

Certainly Longinus is right about having to understand Hadrian's Wall. In all the empire no place is more remote than this one, none farther north, none farther west.

Nowhere are the barbarians more intractable, the weather gloomier, the hills more windswept, the poverty more abject. I listen, my questions sharp but infrequent, letting him not just answer but explain. I absorb, imagine, and clarify, summarizing in my own mind his story. It must have been like this.

II

The messenger would come at dusk, the signals promised, flags rising from tower to tower to race ahead of the courier's pounding horse like shadows in advance of the sinking sun. The waiting centurion read them from his fortress parapet with concealed exultation, his face its usual mask. At last! He said nothing to the sentry beside him, of course, but instead of descending to wait in comfort, he paced the watch-post impatiently, wrapped against the biting wind by the white ceremonial cloak of the cavalry. Twenty years, and these last moments were the hardest, he admitted to himself, twenty years and these last heartbeats like hours. Yet Galba Brassidias forgave his own impatience as he forgave his own ambition. He'd soldiered for this moment, soldiered in dust and blood. Twenty years! And now the empire was granting him his due.

The courier crested the horizon of a low hill. From long experience Galba could predict the remaining hoofbeats it would take to reach the fortress gate, just as he could number a sentry's steps before the turn. Using the faint rhythm of the approaching hooves as cadence, he counted out along the stone towers.

Against a northern wilderness, the Wall announced Roman order. It dominated its terrain, undulating along the crest of the ridge that separated Britannia from raw Caledonia and stretching farther than a man could run or see: eighty Roman miles. As such it was both fortification and statement. Its approaches had been shaved bald to allow clear arrow and catapult shot. A ten-foot-deep ditch had been dug at its base.

The Wall itself was thicker than the axle of a chariot and almost three times the height of a man. Sixteen large forts, sixty-five smaller ones, and one hundred and sixty signal towers were spaced along it like beads on a string. By day, the Wall's whitewashed stucco made the barrier gleam like hard bone. At night, torches in each tower created a winking boundary of light. Soldiers had manned the barrier for two and a half centuries, repairing and improving it, because the Wall was where everything began and everything ended.

To the south was civilization. Britannia's villas shone in the dusk like white echoes of the Mediterranean.

To the north was Outside: huts, dirt tracks, wooden gods, and druidic witches.

Opportunity, for an ambitious man.

His own fort, the fort of the Petriana cavalry, commanded a broad ridge. To its north was a marshy valley and rolling, empty hills, to the south a backing river and Roman supply road. East and west ran the Wall. The cavalry post was as squat and stolid as an oaken stump, the corners of its stone walls rounded for masonry strength and its interior jammed with barracks and stables for five hundred men and horses. Clinging to the bastion's southern side was a parasitical settlement of wives, prostitutes, bastards, pensioners, cripples, beggars, merchants, smiths, brewers, millers, innkeepers, taverners, priests, quack doctors, fortune-tellers, and moneylenders, all of them as tenacious as lichen and as inevitable as the rain. Their houses stepped down to the river in a crazed ziggurat of white stucco and red tile, an imitation of Rome. You could smell the manure, leather, and garlic from a mile away.

Hadrian's famous old wall was reputed to be the bitterest of stations. The wind howled off both oceans like the banshees of Celtic legend; the whores were as ugly as they were diseased, and the tradesmen as dishonest as they were disheveled. Pay went astray, dispatches were late, and recognition from Rome, when it came at all, was tardy and meager. Yet year after year, decade after decade, century after century, the damnable barrier prevailed. It worked as impediment, and it worked on the savage mind.

And its gates? These led to hardship and glory.

"A messenger from the Sixth Victrix!" the sentry standing stiffly next to the centurion now cried, identifying the legion of origin from the pennant the man carried. "A communication from Eburacum!"

Galba checked himself one last time. In preparation for this moment he'd donned his parade uniform: slave-polished chain mail atop a quilted tunic, golden neck torque and armbands of valor, a silver shoal of phalarae medals on his chest, and the long spatha sword of the Petriana cavalry, its blade coated with olive oil and its pommel gleaming where his thumb rubbed its gold. In his fist he held the vinewood staff of centurion command, his knuckles white. As usual it was frigid on the parapet, his breath fogging, and yet Galba felt no cold. Only the long-banked coals of ambition, now about to burst into flame.

"May the gods give you what you deserve, sir," the tower sentry offered.

Galba glanced at the man, flogged not long ago for falling asleep at this post. In the old army he'd have been executed. Was there any insolence hidden now? No, only the proper measure of fear and respect. None dared mock Galba Brassidias. He watched the man's eye glance nervously at the golden chain that Galba hung from two loops on his waist. The chain threaded a curiously high number of finger rings, made of gold, silver, iron, brass, bone, wood, and stone. They bore the design of every god and every charm. Forty of them now.

"Yes," the centurion replied. "May Rome give it."

The Petriana was not what it once was, Galba knew. Smaller by half. A mongrel of races and creeds. Marriage allowed to stem desertion. The barracks corrupted with bitching wives and bawling children. Most of the men were owed back pay and better equipment. Both, if ever received, would likely be lost to gambling debts incurred out of garrison boredom. Too many men were on leave, too many sick, too many lingering in hospital. The entire unit was short on remounts. It was a place run on habit and complacency.

All that would now change. All things would now become possible.

Galba straightened, the rings jingling at his waist, and held the sentry's nervous eye. "From now on, soldier, sleep on your watch at real peril." Then he trotted briskly down the tower stairs to claim his fate.

His victory had occurred the month before, on a cavalry foray to rescue the pigsties and lard lockers of Cato Cunedda: a neighboring warlord, smuggler, opportunist, and sycophant who pledged fealty to Rome whenever that fiction suited his politics. Word of a pirate raid by a band of Scotti, barbarians from the isle of Eiru, had sent Galba and two hundred men and horses on a near-killing pace through a long day and longer night, coming at dawn to the gray Hibernian Sea. Their greeting was a horizon of smoke and the faint wails of brutalized women and orphaned children.

The centurion called a halt well short of the combat, his troopers dismounting to stretch and piss as their weary horses pulled at autumn grass. With practiced deliberation they unstrapped the helmets tied to their saddles and unrolled the chain mail they'd bundled to keep down their sweat, donning both as they dressed for war. A belt and baldric held sword and dagger, their hasta spears were laid in the grass. Then they bit into bread and dried fruit, eating lightly in anticipation of combat.

"Shouldn't we break up the assault?" It was centurion Lucius Falco: capable, but too decent for his own good, in Galba's opinion. Falco was distantly related to almost everyone along the Wall because his family had served in garrison for six generations, and he thus had feelings useless to a soldier. In the old army the man would've been posted to a distant province where sentiment couldn't take root, but it was cheaper to leave officers in place these days. Such was modern Rome.

"We wait," Galba replied to the officers gathered around him. He sat in the grass and rotated onto his lap the scabbard holding his own sword, tapping the weapon's carved white hilt with rhythmic fingers. Rumor held that the grip was fashioned from the human bone of some particularly stubborn enemy, a tale the centurion did nothing to quench and had, in fact, started himself during a drinking bout through enigmatic hints and dour silences. Galba had long ago learned that it did no harm for a commander to inflate his reputation. He'd won fights with a glare.

"Wait?" objected Falco. "They're being skewered!"

"Listen to the wind," Galba rumbled. "By my ear a lot of the skewering going on is Scotti pricks into Cato's bitches, which simply seeds a bumper crop of barbarians for next summer. Meanwhile, most of our allies will get to a broch tower or scatter to the woods."

"But we rode fast through the night—"

"To set a trap. There's nothing more useless in battle than a tired cavalry mount."

Falco watched the smoke unhappily. "It's a hard thing to wait."

"Is it?" Galba's look took in all the officers. "For our barbarian ally to feel some pain and panic is not a bad thing, brothers. It reminds Cato how his pathetic cow-stealing, dirt-grubbing, pig-feeding existence would be even more hopeless if the Petriana cavalry weren't around to punish his enemies."

The decurions snickered.

"We're going to rescue him only after he's been robbed?"

"Watch and see if he's not happier for it, Falco! It's human nature to ignore prevention and appreciate a cure. We'll pick our ground for battle, and the wait gives the Scotti time to get drunk on Cato's beer, wear themselves empty on his wenches, and get winded carrying his loot."

"But to let them pillage—"

"Lets us kill them easier, and take it all back."

The blue-painted Scotti, tattooed and exultant, finally retreated toward their longboats at midmorning, the conflagration they'd lit so fierce that the smoke boiled like a thundercloud. The sorrow they'd brought lingered behind as a low keening; their booty weighted each warrior like a mule. The barbarians were drunk, blood-sated, and doubled over with looted prizes: grain, iron pots, woolens, scythes, jewelry, and several trussed goats and squealing pigs. Some of the prettiest wenches, sobbing and stunned, stumbled along with them, tied neck to neck by a rope. Most were bruised, their clothing torn to rags.

"There before you is today's practice, men," Galba told his cavalry quietly, riding up and down their hidden line. "Straw for your lance. Lubrication for your spatha."

He'd divided his command in two. Half still went to Falco, because he respected the man's ability as much as he was skeptical of his sympathetic heart. Now Galba's hundred came over the concealing hill two ranks deep, their upright lances a comb against the sky. The Roman shields were blood red and yellow, their chain mail rippled like gray water, and their helmets glinted silver in the autumn sun. They had the advantage of high ground and an unbroken, grassy slope. There were no trumpets and no cheers, their advance so quiet that it took some moments for the Scotti to even notice them. Finally there was visible shock at this sudden appearance of heavy horsemen on a hillside above and cries of warning. The livestock was dropped trussed in the grass. The female captives, now a distraction, had their throats quickly slit like sheep in a barnyard and fell like mown hay. Then there was a ragged formation of barbarian battle line and shouts of drunken defiance.

Galba gave them time to do it. "Easier to kill a Scotti in open combat than hunt him in the weeds." Britannia had been conquered by foot-slogging legionaries, heavy infantry that crushed every attack the frantic Celts could throw at them. It was held, like much of the empire, by cavalry. Once the barbarians had learned that they could not break the Roman legion, they turned to raid, feint, and ambush, relying on the lightness of their armor to outdistance pursuing foot soldiers. It was to the horse that Rome turned to run its enemies down, and to the horse-breeding provinces at the empire's periphery, such as Thrace, to find its cavalrymen like Galba. Both sides were in a constant race, the Celt to plunder and the Roman to block or catch him. With their hasta spear, three light throwing javelins, and long spatha sword, the cavalry could alternately break the barbarian line, harass it, or cut and chop in a general melee. Some army units on the Continent and to the east used heavily

armored cataphractarii and clibinarii, who carried their
heavy lances in two hands to break disciplined infantry for-
mations. In Britannia, however, such horsemen were too
slow, and cavalry stayed relatively light. War was a hunt,
and Galba was its master.

The ring and clang of drawn Celtic swords carried clearly
up the hill, the barbarians banging their shields to drum warning and fortify their own courage. The Roman mounts checked
at the rumbling, the animals remembering this noise and
knowing it meant battle. There seemed to be two leaders of the
Scotti war party, Galba saw: a redhead to the left, with drawn
sword and restless manner, and a great hairy blond lout of a
pirate on the right, lumbering in front of his men with shouldered ax. Both chieftains gestured and shouted and raised their
middle finger in what they'd learned was the Roman gesture of
contempt.

Galba rested his own sword across the twin front pom-
mels of his saddle in loose confidence. He'd ridden before
he could walk, killed before he knew any woman, and could
map his travels with scar tissue. Now came the anticipatory
moment he liked best in life, that frozen time when the
energy of warring men was coiled and almost breathless, the
immortal pause before the practiced charge. He looked
down the rank of men with whom he'd drilled and marched
and shot and slept and shit, professionals all, and felt an intimacy with them that he'd never felt with any female. Each
sitting high, his reins in the hand of his left shield arm, spear
shouldered, helmet tight, legs dangling loose until the kick
of the charge.

He loved war and what it could win for a man.

He loved the hunt.

"An eagle, tribune," a centurion commented.

Galba looked to where the man was pointing. The bird
was riding the morning's rising tide of air, wings dipping as
it rotated. The perfect sign.

"Look how the gods favor us!" he roared to his men. "A bird
of Rome!" Then his black warhorse, Imperium, jerked at his
nudge. "Forward!" Heels dug, and the Roman cavalry started
downhill with a sure, awful, accreting acceleration, the disci-

pline of constant practice keeping the line abreast and the
lances pivoting down in synchronization as steady as the drop
of a drawbridge gate. Their mounts quickened into a trot, the
very earth beginning to quake, and the men bent, shield high,
thighs tightening, each picking a target as the thunder of the
attack swelled until it filled their whole world. Against a more
disciplined enemy they would have formed a wedge or dia-
mond to pierce the line, but the Scotti were so disorganized
that the barbarians had left gaps, some backing from the
approaching Romans, others foolishly running ahead and
shouting challenge. The Romans would shred them with line
abreast. The cavalry didn't break into gallop until the last fifty
paces, so their line could remain even, Galba signaling the
final rush with a wave of his sword arm. Then their mounts
burst forward in the final sprint. Grass rolled underneath the
cavalry in a blur, clods of earth burst upward like sprayed
water, the pennants rippled in the wind, and each of the cavalrymen took up the cry of their ancestral homeland, of Thrace
and Syria and Iberia and Germania.

"For the standards of the Petriana!"

Arrows whizzed past like buzzing insects.

There was a great crash as the lines met, a scream of
horses and shout of men, and then the cavalry was over the
barbarians and past them, their lances left upright in
writhing, impaled bodies. The Romans slid free their long
swords and turned.

Galba's own sword had hit something solid in the initial
collision, coming up red and glistening. Now he sawed with
his reins, his horse's eyes rolling with the pain of the harsh
cavalry bit, and charged toward the blond giant with the ax.
The chieftain was whirling his weapon and singing a death
song, his eyes opaque with wonder at that ghostly world
he'd already half stepped into. "So shall I give it to you," the
Roman promised. He cut with his sword to parry the ax
shaft, used the heavy shoulder of his horse to knock his
enemy over, and then leaped from his saddle to finish the
pirate off. Strike fast, when they're down.

Yet the butted chieftain kept rolling and so Galba's grunting stroke missed and struck turf, sticking there. It was an

almost fatal mistake. The barbarian came up howling, covered in grass and dirt and the smoke and blood of his earlier pillage, his torso a topography of sinew, bone, and blue tattoo. When the warrior reared back to lift his ax, he was like some monstrous bear, and a newcomer to war might have been transfixed enough to let the Scotti strike.

But Galba was a veteran of a hundred fights and gave his opponent no time to set himself. Instead he saw opportunity. Yanking his blade clear in the time the Scotti took to raise his ax, he made a quick horizontal slash that opened the barbarian's stomach and then stepped smartly back as the ax whizzed by his ear. The shock of disembowelment caused the Scotti to let the heavy weapon thud all the way into the ground, and so the Roman swung again and heard an audible crack of bone as he took off the chieftain's hands. The Celt staggered, only dimly realizing what had happened to him, screamed to the gods who'd forsaken him this day, and held his bloody stumps to heaven. Then he crashed to earth.

Galba whirled for another antagonist, but his men had already made short work of the rest who'd dared stand, the bravest already dying or enslaved. The Roman horses were prancing over the corpses as if uncertain where to put their hooves, and there was that familiar battlefield smell of urine, dung, hot blood, and fearful sweat, as bizarrely intoxicating as it was repulsive.

Galba looked at his chipped blade tip. It was the first time he'd missed an enemy already down, and he couldn't make that mistake again. Grunting, he stooped and pried a severed hand off the ax handle to look for a ring. There was a fine golden one, he saw, with a red stone. Probably stolen from a Roman.

"I'll take this back, boy." He used his dagger to saw the finger off.

Victory!

"They're getting away!" a decurion shouted.

Galba stood and whistled for his horse, leaping agilely into the saddle and roaring his men into some kind of quick order. The redheaded chieftain had escaped and was leading twenty of his raiders into the trees toward the water.

"Let them run!" he shouted to his men.

The Romans pursued just out of bowshot, weaving through trees. As the barbarians ran they looked back at their seemingly wary pursuers and jeered, but Galba held his men in careful check. They came to a bluff in time to see the Scotti fling their weapons and helmets aside and spill like lemmings into the sea. The barbarians surfaced, wet and howling from the cold, and struck for longboats hidden among the reeds of an estuary.

"Hold and watch!"

The redhead who'd escaped turned in the water and taunted them in thick Latin, vowing revenge.

"Hold, I say!"

The Romans stood mute and winded, lining the bluff.

The Scotti reached the reedy water on the far side of the inlet, some managing to stand in the shallows and others thrashing for their boats. They shouted for the comrades they'd left behind, gasping explanations, and anxiously grasped oar holes to lift themselves aboard.

Then there was a Latin shout, Falco's command carrying across the inlet of water, and a row of helmeted heads rose from the bowels of the longboats.

More Romans.

Falco's wing had ridden around and already captured the craft, slaying their guards. Now they stood from the hulls where they'd been hiding and fell upon the unarmed barbarians trying to climb aboard.

Galba's plan had worked.

The red-haired one, half naked and weaponless now, saw the murder that was happening and thrashed his way to a muddy bank.

Falco himself rode the man down.

The bang and thud of weapons and the screams of the wounded echoed across the water for only moments and then it was done, the reeds stained red, bodies floating like logs.

"Come," Galba said. "We meet Lucius Falco on the other side."

The two wings of cavalry joined at the head of the inlet, the longboats already burning as fiercely as Cato's village.

A handful of captured warriors would stay with the Romans as slaves. Some of the booty would be returned to their client, others kept as tax.

One of them was the defiant red-haired chieftain: a rib cracked after being overridden by Falco's horse, head bloody, manner abject. In minutes he'd gone from conqueror to conquered, from lord to prisoner, and he stood trussed and naked with that dull expression of shock and resignation that comes from enslavement.

"I was hoping that one for my own, Falco," Galba congratulated.

"He's a bit of a badger. Even after riding over the top of him, I had to club with my dagger. He'll be trouble, perhaps."

"Or spirit. Get him home and make clear how things are."

Falco nodded.

"Let's find out who he is." Galba walked his horse up to the subdued barbarian. "What's your name, boy?" These Scotti were a last stubborn branch of those Celtic tribes the Romans had been fighting for eight centuries, their ferocity in battle and despair in defeat both as predictable as the tides. It might take a bit of whip and club to tame this one, but he, like them all, would submit. "What do they call you, stripling?"

The man looked up sullenly and for just one moment Galba felt chilled. It was a blackly baleful look he got, the captive thinking no doubt of the hearth and woman and horse he'd never see again, but beyond that there was something in his sorrow that seemed to give a glimpse of a dim and troubled future. Let Falco keep him, indeed.

"I am Odocullin of the Dal Riasta. Prince of the Scotti and a lord of Eiru."

"Odocul-what? That's more mouthful than a Sicilian sweetcake. Repeat yourself, slave!"

The man looked away.

Galba's hand went to the pouch at his side. He could feel the severed finger of this man's dead compatriot and the hard curve of the barbarian's ring. None ever ignored Galba Brassidias for long, and someday this carrot-colored Hibernian would learn that too. In the meantime, who cared what the captive was called by his own people? "We'll name you Odo, then," he pronounced, "and the cost of your defeat will be slavery in the house of the soldier who defeated you, Lucius Falco."

The Scotti still wouldn't look at his captors.

"Odo," Falco repeated. "Even I can remember that."

III

So Odo became houseboy to the villa of Lucius Falco, and Galba Brassidias, forty rings now jangling from the waist chain of his armor, burst from the base of the watchtower to receive his reward from Rome.

The courtyard of the fortress headquarters was lit with torches in the dusk, a turma of thirty-two men snapping to attention. "Straight ranks! Weapons high!" The butts of their lances banged smartly against paving stone. The courier who trotted through the barrel gate was another centurion, Longinus by name, his boots flecked with mud and the rim of his tunic sweaty.

The choice was reassuring. The duke wouldn't have sent a man of this rank unless he bore the message Galba was waiting for.

Longinus swung stiffly down, and his horse, hide steaming and muscles quivering, urinated in a great smoking hiss. The courier saluted. "Good news, commander!"

Galba's heart leapt. Yes!

"In recognition of your accomplished record, you've been named senior tribune of the Petriana cavalry!" His voice was loud enough to let others hear.

There was a rustle in the ranks. Senior tribune! The news would fly through the fort in minutes. Galba had gotten what every man expected, and confirmation would be received with both satisfaction and regret. The new tribune was as stern as he was able.

"Silence!" Galba shouted, in order to be able to shout something. He felt a flush of pride. Born a provincial, and now a Roman tribune. His eyes gleamed. "I'm unworthy of the honor."

"We both know the honor is long overdue."

Galba allowed himself a slight smile. False modesty was an affectation of weaklings. He lowered his voice. "For this long-awaited word I've saved Falernian wine, Longinus. Come into my new house and share it."

The man nodded uncomfortably. "My thanks for the offer." He hesitated. "However, there's more, tribune."

"More?" Galba's head was still churning with the new possibilities of command.

"Complications."

The soldier looked at Longinus uncertainly.

"Considerations."

Galba tried not to betray his unease. "I've waited twenty years for the news you've brought and prefer to savor it," he said slowly. "The rest can wait for the grape."

"Yes." Longinus's tone was quiet. "Inside would be best."

Orders were snapped, and the turma wheeled to disperse. The two senior men strode to the commander's house, its door swung open by slaves, their armor unhooked with silent efficiency, brass basins of warm water and towels offered to both. They went on to the warmth of the dining room and sprawled on couches in the Roman fashion. The vintage was as promised, transported in amphorae for a thousand miles and served in green glass with a painted frieze of gladiators battling around the rim. Longinus, parched from his hard ride, watered his and drank deeply. The new tribune sipped an unwatered serving and waited impatiently. "And this other news, centurion? Are we to start a campaign?"

The messenger shook his head, wiping his mouth. "It has to do with the command of this cavalry. This part of my message isn't as happy, tribune."

Galba hoisted himself on an elbow. "I've commanded as senior centurion already, since the transfer of the previous tribune. I've won a major action. Now I have his rank. The command is mine, isn't it?"

"Were it simply up to the duke, it would be. You know that."

Galba's eyes narrowed with that dark look men usually only saw in battle. He was being made a fool. "What are you telling me, Longinus, as you lie on my couch and sip my finest wine?"

"I'm sorry, but this part of the message isn't my choice to deliver. Rejoice in your promotion and new pay, Galba; you deserve it. But there are politics in Rome, of course, politics and more politics. A new alliance of families—and a position to be found for a new officer. A praefectus. He asked for the Petriana cavalry because of its reputation. He wanted this fort because word has reached all the way to Rome of what a job you've done. He wants to make his mark here. With you."

The new tribune sat up in disbelief. "You're telling me I'm promoted, only to lose command? I've worked my whole career for this command!"

Longinus looked at him with sympathy. "I'm sorry, it has nothing to do with you. It's simply preferment for an officer of the equestrian class. Unfair, I know."

"What politics?"

"The fellow is betrothed to a senator's daughter. It's as simple as that." He drank.

"Dung of Pluto!" Galba was a big man, but incredibly swift. He sprang, cuffed, and the wine cup flew away, shattering against the wall. A spray of red drops made a bright crescent across the mosaic floor. Then Galba loomed like a father over a child, immense and shadowy. "You're telling me that some Roman snoblet is taking away the Petriana— the unit *I* built—because he married some ranking bitch in Rome?" The question was a roar.

Longinus looked at his hand, stinging from the blow. "I'm only the messenger, Galba. And they're not married. Only betrothed."

He took a breath. "There's hope then."

"No. The wedding will occur here."

The new tribune sat. "I won't tolerate this insult. Take *that* back to the duke."

"I certainly will not. You're a soldier. You'll tolerate it because you must tolerate it. And you'll still be commander in all but name. This Lucius Marcus Flavius will serve a couple years and leave for higher things. The army remains ours."

"That Roman aristocrat will take my new house. My credit. While I do the work."

"So what else is new?" Longinus was becoming impatient. "Remember the way of things. Defy this Marcus, and you'll earn nothing but trouble. Flatter him, and he'll be of use. In the meantime, be grateful for what you have, like a well-deserved promotion—and that wine." He pointed with regret. "It was really quite good."

"Second place to a highborn dabbler who won't know one end of a spatha from another. Beaten by an arranged marriage."

"Never beaten in battle. Remember that."

The reply was bitter. "Beaten by a woman."

IV

Many Romans believe slaves are morally unreliable, but I, Draco, regard them as the most observant of witnesses. True, they will steal. Yes, they will lie. Of course they are lazy. They lack even the patient virtues of a domesticated animal. Yet a careful listener can turn this lack of character to his advantage. Slaves are shameless eavesdroppers and tireless gossips, their primary entertainment the foibles of their betters. You can learn a lot from a smart slave. And this one, before me, is one of the smartest.

She annoys me already.

Her name is Savia. Wet nurse turned substitute mother. Servant turned handmaiden, scold, and chaperone. Every highborn Roman girl like the missing Valeria should have one, and most do. Savia is, of course, a Christian, like so many of the lower classes, but unlike some, I cannot afford to be intolerant of naive beliefs in a peasant god and a happy death. I use every eye and ear I can recruit. A good Christian can be as upright as a good pagan, in my experience. Or as venal. There are scoundrels enough for all religions.

So. Savia is well fed and plump, despite her present incarceration, and was probably not uncomely a score of years ago. She would still feel warm enough in any bed, I judge. Now her hair is streaked with gray, her face has the paleness of incarceration, and her look is quicker and more direct than is proper. That intelligence, again: it cannot be hidden. She is a survivor, too, having passed through the re-

cent tumult entirely unscathed. Legend to the contrary, it is the rare slave willing to die for her mistress.

So I have this image of brutally efficient Galba, the frustrated subordinate, but that's hardly enough to explain the catastrophe I am investigating. Something more happened on Hadrian's Wall, something that led to incaution and treason, and it appears to have centered on the owner of this slave, the lady Valeria. I've summoned Savia from prison to explain her mistress so I can understand a woman who is no longer here. The slave, in turn, looks upon me as a potential rescuer. She abhors confinement and has protested it loudly. "I am of the House of Valens!" The soldiers laugh at her.

She sits now in my stone chamber, truculent, flustered, hopeful, wary, vain. She wants as much from me as I from her.

"You served the lady Valeria?"

She sizes me up, then nods with cautious pride. "For nineteen years. Fed her, wiped her, weaned her, and spanked her. Taught her to be a woman. And accompanied her all the way to Britannia—"

"For her wedding to the commander of the Petriana cavalry, Marcus Flavius."

"I saw it arranged in Rome."

"A political or a love match?"

"Both, of course."

I am dissatisfied by an answer so obvious that it's no answer at all. "You avoid my question. Did she love her intended husband?"

"It depends what you mean by love."

"Mean? By the gods, was her motive passion or politics?"

Savia looks at me speculatively. "I wish to help you, master, but confinement has confused my memory." Her eyes flicker around the room as quick as a bird, as if looking for a key to release.

"I've just brought you out of confinement."

"Only for this interview. I've done nothing to deserve that cell!"

"You were imprisoned because you aided an enemy."

"I was imprisoned because I saved my mistress."

I ignore that comment for now. "Still, you'll answer when I ask," I warn grumpily. I can, of course, have her flogged.

She refuses to be frightened, having sensed my lamentable sympathy for her gender and kind. "And I'll remember the past when I have a future."

"You will speak now or be beaten until you do speak!"

"And speak what?" she cries indignantly, as if it is I instead of she in the wrong. "The truth, or the cries of a whipped slave?"

I grimace. But I'm also amused, and struggle not to show it. She's watching me like a sly dog, knowing she is valuable property and a waste to feed in prison. Moreover, I need her story. So I employ silence. Nothing so prompts a companion to speak.

"I'm sorry," she amends. "It's horrid and dirty in my cell."

So I visibly soften, to soften her. "Then help me learn the fate of your mistress."

She leans forward. "I can help most if you take me with you!"

"I have no use for an old maid."

"Then take me and sell me! But it's better to keep me! Look at yourself. You're as old as I am. You should be retiring to a farm. You could use me there."

The last thing I need in the quiet of my life is this piece of spoiled baggage. Still, at the end of the day the horse will ride harder to the hay than to the whip. I pretend to consider this proposal. "I cannot afford another slave."

"The garrison would almost give me away! I complain too much!"

I laugh. "As if that is a recommendation!"

"I eat too much, too! But I can cook. Better than your servant does now, judging from your scrawny frame."

I shake my head, suspecting she's right. "Listen, impress me with the usefulness of your memory, and I will consider what you suggest. Agreed?"

She sits back. "I'm very useful."

"And you will answer my questions?"

"I'll try, inspector."

I sigh for effect, knowing full well why she'd like me to

buy her. A slave enjoys the status of her master. "All right, then. Back to it. Was the marriage a love match?"

She takes a moment to think this time. "It was a marriage of the upper class. Love is irrelevant, don't you think?"

"Yet not the usual dowry."

"It was the man who provided the coin this time, not the woman."

"Marcus needed a good posting?"

"He needed a new start."

"And Valeria's father needed money?"

"Being a senator is expensive. To entertain, to facilitate agreements—"

"You understand these things?"

She smiles. "I lived with Senator Valens longer than his wife."

"And became maidservant to Valeria."

"I instructed that child, as I said."

It is disconcerting, the pride of this slave. No doubt she'd once bedded Valens and was smug with the memory of coupling with a patrician. And Christians! It's their god that gives them their impudence. Their serenity can be infuriating.

"You lived with this woman daily," *I try again.* "Was she in love or not?"

"She barely knew Marcus. They'd only met once."

"Her reaction?"

"He was handsome. But old, to her eyes. Thirty-five to her nineteen."

"Yet she did not object?"

"She encouraged the union. She dressed for Marcus, charmed him, and promised obedience to her father's plan. The marriage rescued the senator and was a way for Valeria to get away from Rome. Marriage would please her father, let her escape her mother, and complete herself. Like all young women, she assumed either her husband would match her dreams or she'd teach him to do so."

Of course. Women think weddings the end of problems, instead of their beginning. "Why didn't the marriage take place in Rome?"

"The post was vacant, occupied temporarily by the senior

tribune Galba Brassidias. The army wanted the command settled, and Senator Valens was anxious for the money his daughter would bring. The promise was paid, promotion granted, and rather than wait for wedding preparations, Marcus was advised to take the risk of traveling in winter to assume office and clarify command. Talks were concluded in his absence. Valeria followed in March, as soon as the first ships could leave Ostia. Even at that, it was a rough voyage. We anchored three times on the coast of Italy before reaching port in Gaul. All of us were sick."

I nod. I hate the sea. "Then north through Gaul—"

"Tiresome. Bad inns, bad food, and bad company. The river barges were fine, but the mule carts wearying and tedious. It was odd to have the days grow longer and yet colder. And at the Oceanus Britannicus the sea sucked in and out."

"The tide."

"I'd never seen its like."

"It took Caesar by surprise when he first invaded Britannia." Why I offer historical trivia to this woman I can't say.

"I shouldn't wonder."

I plunge ahead, embarrassed by my own digression. "So you crossed the Channel—"

"We'd missed the naval galley and bought passage on a merchant ship. We were sick again, and afraid of pirates. The captain kept waving toward the white cliffs of Dubris, trying to impress a senator's daughter, but none of us cared."

"And came up the Tamesis to Londinium."

"It was all perfectly proper, as you can see. Except for her riding."

"Her what?"

"When crossing Gaul, Valeria became bored. She'd borrow a horse and go trotting ahead in a lady's manner, sidesaddle, accompanied by her bodyguard Cassius."

"A retired soldier?"

"Better. A surviving gladiator."

"And you did not approve."

"She wasn't so bold as to go out of sight, but a Roman lady doesn't ride a horse like some Celtic wench. As I told

her! But Valeria was always a willful child. I warned that she'd ride herself barren and be sent home in disgrace, but she just laughed at me. I told her she'd hurt herself, and she scoffed. She said her husband-to-be was a cavalry officer and would appreciate a wife who could gallop. I almost fainted."

I try to picture this bold and impudent young woman. Was she vulgar? Immature? Or simply impish? "She had learned how?"

"On her father's estate. He was as hopelessly indulgent when she was a child as he was strict after her menarche. Only I kept any control. She'd have played with wooden swords if her brothers hadn't refused."

"So she was in the habit of not doing what she was told."

"She was in the habit of listening to her heart."

Interesting. Rome's foundation is reason, of course. "I am trying to understand what happened here," I explain. "What kind of treachery."

She laughs. *"Treachery?"*

"The attack on the Wall."

"I would never call it treachery."

"What then?"

"I'd call it love."

"Love! You said—"

"Not in the way you think. It began in Londinium. . . ."

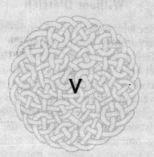

V

Roman lady!" the peddlers shrieked, lifting their trinkets up into the rain. "Look! The jewels of Britannia!"

Valeria had drawn her hood against the shouts and spring drizzle. Shadowed and thus shielded, she looked down in consternation and amusement at the little navy that had nosed to the bulwarks of her ship. River lighters and skin coracles surrounded the newly anchored *Swan* like a ragged noose, their grubby captains screeching offers to ferry the Roman passengers to the stone quay of Londinium. Briton women, their hair tangled and clothes sodden from the damp, held up offerings of wet bread, cheap wine, cheaper jewelry, and bared breasts. Children lifted palms to beg for coins, their fingers wiggling like the legs of an overturned beetle. Feral youths shouted advice on lodgings, brothels, and bargains. Dogs barked, a caged rooster crowed, her own captain cursed at the craft scarring his ship's side, and it was difficult to judge what was worse, the noise or the stink.

In other words, her tumultuous greeting to Britannia was as foreign, colorful, and marvelous as she'd hoped. One thousand miles from jaded Rome, and her life was at last beginning! Valeria glanced at the city across the gray water, imagining somewhere beyond it the distant Wall. Soon, soon: her wedding!

"Britlets," scorned the young man at her side, looking down at their besiegers. "*Britunculi!* Our soldiers called them that after the first battles. Naked, blue, screaming, undisciplined, and filled with bluster until they broke on a shield wall. After which they ran like rabbits." He shook his head. "These, apparently, are their progeny."

"They're offering help, dear Clodius." Valeria was determined not to let her own excitement be soured by the cynicism of her escort, a newly minted junior tribune putting in an obligatory year of military service. "Look how tall they are, how hairy, how pale, how gray-eyed, how bleached! I think they're wonderful." She was at the age when she enjoyed stating opinions boldly, as if trying them on for size. Nor was a senator's daughter impressed by the bright sword and reflexive snobbery of a young officer like Clodius, aristocratic by birth, prosperous by inheritance, and superior by that blissful ignorance that comes from inexperience. Knowing nothing, his type pretended to know everything, including what a young woman like Valeria should think and like and do. It was her game to put them in their place. "Look at the jewelry. There's Celtic craftsmanship there." She squinted playfully. "Of course, it's going green in the rain."

It *was* disquieting to have to choose a public ferry, Valeria conceded to herself. She could see the government barge still tied to its dock, its red enamel and gilt trim as brilliant as a flower in the gray-green riverscape. Had message of her pending arrival not preceded them across the Channel? Was her masthead banner of senatorial rank not visible from the city wall? Yet the *Swan* had anchored without a hint of official greeting.

None of her Roman acquaintances would have been surprised by this clumsiness. When told of Valeria's betrothal to an officer posted to Hadrian's Wall, their congratulations had been tinged with condescension. Marcus was rich, of course, but Britannia? Not a single university! Not a game worth reporting! Not a notable poet or artist or writer! The pitying concern had been careful, of course, and all the worse because of it. Some of the baths and villas were by reputation the equal of Italy's, her circle of maidens had comforted; it was only the rest of Britannia that was dark, wet, and filthy. And she was to live in a cavalry fortress? They'd all but shuddered at her fate, a sure sign of the decline of the House of Valens. But the money from Marcus's family would allow her father to sustain his senatorial career, while her own ancestral name would help her new husband's advancement. Let her silly friends sit in Rome! Her fiancé wanted glory. Valeria would help him get it.

"Why not enjoy our armada of suitors?" she gamely asked her escort. "Nobody would pay us this much attention in Rome." She dropped a coin, setting off a mad scramble that sent the lighters rocking. The anxious cries of the Britons rose louder.

"Don't do that, Valeria. They're leeches."

"It was only a brass coin." One of the natives had won possession by biting a companion on the ear. The ferocity of their greed surprised her. "My father says that Rome wins loyalty by generosity, not the sword."

"A balance of both, I'd say, each used with careful fore-thought."

"And I give too little thought?"

"No. . . . Just that your face needs neither sword nor money to earn loyalty."

"Ah, my gallant Clodius!"

Valeria was accustomed to such reactions from boys. Clodius, she knew, was already half in love with her. Her dark and liquid eyes were what first drew men's attention; a gaze of intelligence and will that allured and yet arrested, seducing strangers and yet making them wary. Hers was the magnetism of half girl, half woman, of bold curiosity and lingering inno-cence. It was advantage and burden that she'd learned to use and endure. The rest of her features reinforced the promise of her eyes. She had a southern beauty, her skin a cross of olive and gold, her hair a silken cascade of black, her lips full, her cheekbones high, and her figure as shapely as the carved wooden swan's head that arched over the tiller. Some specu-lated there must be Numidian blood in her dark, exotic looks; others opined Egyptian or Phoenician. She favored simple jewelry that would not compete with her: only three rings on her fingers and a single bracelet on one wrist, a tight and fine necklace at her throat, a brooch to hold her cape, and a golden clip in her tresses. Hardly any at all! Certainly none of the jan-gling ostentation of urban Rome, where women weighted themselves with gold like fetters. She usually dressed modestly and, with her handmaiden's coaching, could remember to stand demurely.

When she was excited, however, Valeria sprang and reached and craned like a boy. It was then that her male escorts would secretly groan at the curve of a hip, the swell of a breast, and wonder what her virgin enthusiasms might someday produce in bed.

The consensus aboard the *Swan* was that Marcus was a lucky bastard, and his father a sly one, to negotiate for a maiden of such station and desirability. Her parents must have been in extreme financial distress to let her go to the frontier, and Valeria dutiful to have agreed to it. None ever considered that the young woman wanted travel and adventure for herself, that she was well aware of her family's precarious financial position, and that she'd dressed carefully for shy Marcus because she was savvy enough to understand that her father's ruin would have been her own. Now she was saving them all: her father, her future husband, and herself.

The thought gave her a quiet thrill.

Valeria had been puzzled at her girlfriends' praise of her courage. It wasn't as if she were leaving the empire! Britannia had been a Roman province for three hundred years, and living on its border sounded more exciting than dangerous. It would be marvelous to live with rough cavalrymen and their magnificent horses, fascinating to see the hairy barbarians, and thrilling to stroll the crest of Hadrian's famous wall. She was eager to order her own household. Eager to learn of lovemaking. Eager to know her husband. His mind. His desires. His dreams.

"Like piglets at their mother's teat," Clodius muttered about the jostling boats. "We're at the utter edge of empire."

"This utter edge is home to the man I'm marrying," she reminded slyly. "The praefectus in command of your Petriana cavalry."

"My doubts don't include your future husband, lady, who we both know is a man of education, wealth, and refinement. But then he's Roman, not Briton, and deserving of the grace of one such as—I mean of equal stature—or rather . . ."

She laughed. "I know exactly what you mean, dear clumsy Clodius! How did an officer such as you suffer the ill fortune of not only being assigned to gloomy Britannia, but escorting your superior's betrothed across the Oceanus Britannicus!"

"My lady, I've enjoyed our passage—"

"We were all sick as dogs, and you know it." She gave a mock shudder. "Gracious! I hope I don't see such water again. So cold! So dark!"

"We were all thankful to enter the river."

"So get us the rest of the way ashore, tribune," a new voice suggested impatiently.

It was Savia, gazing longingly at the stone quay of Londinium. The handmaiden was the one bit of home Valeria had brought with her: nag, chaperone, and anchor. Savia knew Valeria's heart better than her mother did and cared more for propriety and promptness than Valeria did. The heaving sea had silenced the slave for two days. Now she was regaining her voice.

"I'm waiting for a ferry suitable to our station," Clodius said irritably.

"You're waiting the day away."

Valeria looked to the city. Londinium appeared civilized enough, she judged. Masts bristled from a thicket of lighters along a quay crowded with bales, barrels, sacks, and amphorae. Beyond the parapets rose the domes and red tile roofs of a respectably sized Roman capital, greasy smoke creating its own pall beneath the overcast. She could hear the rumble of urban commerce and smell the charcoal, sewage, bakeries, and leatherworks even from the water. Somewhere within would be baths and markets, temples and palaces. A long wooden bridge crowded with carts and couriers crossed the Tamesis a quarter mile upriver. On the river's southern shore was marshland, and in the distance low hills.

Such a gray place! So far from Rome! Yet the sight of it filled her with anticipation. Soon, her Marcus! She thought Clodius was making too much of the absence of the official barge, which was just the latest of the indignities any long journey inflicted on travelers. It wasn't as if her future husband could be on hand to greet them anyway. He'd be at his fortress, seeing to his new command. But within a fortnight . . .

"We simply need to be prudent," Clodius stalled. "Britons are coarse. A third of the island remains unconquered, and what we rule remains rude."

"Rude, or simply poor?" Valeria bantered.

"Poor from poor initiative, I suspect."

"Or by taxation, corruption, and prejudice." She was unable to resist the temptation to bait the boy, a habit her mother said was deplorable for a Roman girl of marriage-able age. "And these Britlets of yours prevented Rome from conquering their entire island."

It was supper-table talk picked up from the dining room of her father, and Clodius thought it slightly disreputable that a woman spoke so openly of politics. Still, he enjoyed her attention. "Rome wasn't stopped, it chose to stop, so Hadrian built his wall to fence away what we didn't want and keep what we did." He took on a lecturing air. "Don't doubt it, Valeria, this is a promising place for a military offi-cer like myself. Trouble gives soldiers a chance for glory. Marcus too! But I don't have to admire the cause of such trouble. By their very nature, Britons are rebel and rascal. The commoners, I mean. The upper class, I'm told, is acceptable."

"You seem quite the expert for a man who hasn't stepped ashore yourself," she teased. "Perhaps you should stay on the boat. I could tell my fiancé that Britannia wasn't up to your standards."

In truth, Valeria was apprehensive herself, her teasing a mask for her own anxieties. She was homesick, though like any good Roman woman she wasn't about to admit such weakness. She barely knew her intended husband, who'd seemed kind during their tentative meeting and quick betrothal in Rome but also big and quiet and, well . . . old. Certainly she'd never been intimate with a man. Never man-aged a household. Knew nothing about children. Was she ready to be a wife? Mother? Matron? What if she failed?

"Obey your husband," her father had instructed her. "Remember that duty is the steel that sustains Rome."

"Am I not to love him as well? And he to love me?"

"Love stems from respect," he'd intoned, "and respect follows duty."

It was the kind of admonition she'd heard a thousand times. Girls dreamed of romance. Parents plotted career and strategy.

Valeria looked up at the wet sky. Early April, the landscape an eruption of green, and still this cold cloud! Was it ever truly warm here? Come winter she'd see her first snow, she was sure of it. She was as anxious to get ashore as Savia was, and tired of waiting on Clodius. Why couldn't the youth decide? She saw another lighter and decided it was larger, cleaner, and better painted than the others. "Let's hire that one!"

Her request goaded Clodius to action, and with cries of disappointment, the little flotilla began to break up. The chosen lighter bumped alongside, a fare was negotiated, and there was confused bustle as sailors lowered her belongings into the bottom. Her trousseau was a mere cartload, given the expense of freight from Rome. Valeria's bodyguard Cassius lifted her down as if she were made of glass, plump Savia swayed down upon a rope, and Clodius took his place in the stern with the captain as if he knew something about piloting a boat. Then they made for Londinium's quay, the lighter leaning in the spring wind and an arrow of geese thrumming overhead, aimed toward the north.

Savia took heart. "Look! A welcoming sign from the Christ!"

"If so, they're bringing news of our arrival to my future husband."

Clodius smirked. "Don't they fly over everyone's head, and thus herald a dozen gods?"

"No. They appeared for our arrival."

They cut in and around other craft with practiced ease, a collision threatening at every tack and yet always narrowly avoided to cries of reflexive insult and hearty greeting. The shore was so crowded with craft that there seemed no opening to get ashore, and then a boat cast off and there was a glimpse of mossy stones and iron rings. The lighter pulled up into the wind and drifted neatly to lie alongside. A plank was laid and baggage slung. Valeria skipped ahead, Savia tottered across the plank in hasty reinforcement, and Cassius leaped the gap. Then the Romans were greeted with the kind of clamor that had besieged them on the *Swan* as merchants, beggars, and food vendors smelled money and class and surged forward.

"Sample the lamb of Londinium, lady? Sustenance after your long journey!"

She shrank from the crowding. "No, thank you . . ."

"Jewelry for the lass?" It was crude copper.

"I have enough."

"A flagon for you, tribune. . . . This way to the best lodgings. . . . Some help with your baggage. . . . No, I'm best for that!"

Cassius went first to plow like a bull while Clodius haggled with the lighter's master, who suddenly claimed a different understanding of his payment. Valeria and Savia followed the gladiator's lead but were wedged in a press of bodies. The Romans paused, uncertain where to go, while Britons struggled for a better view of the pretty young woman of high station. Women exclaimed, men pushed, and a thick odor of sweat, fish oil, and cheap wine washed over them. Suddenly Valeria felt dizzy.

"This way, lady!" A knobby hand closed on her arm, and she started. It was a plebe, coarse and gap-toothed. Her excitement was turning to alarm.

"Over here!" Another hand clasped her cloak, dragging her the other way.

"Let me go!" She pulled away. Her hood had been knocked back, and her hair was getting wet in the drizzle. Savia shrieked as someone bumped her. A child darted in, and there was a tug and rip. A brooch holding Valeria's cloak was suddenly gone, and it fell open, giving men a clearer glimpse of her form.

"Clodius!"

Her military escort was mired in a tangle of bodies behind. The Britons were laughing at them! A hideous looking man, red-faced and pockmarked, loomed. "Are you looking for a bed, fine lady?" He reached toward her, disgustingly.

"Leave us—"

"Give room!" Clodius shouted. "Which way to the Governor's Gate?"

"A coin first!" someone shouted. "A coin to show you the way!"

"Yes, coins, Romans! Coins for the poor of Britannia!"

Cassius smacked grasping hands away. In reply, a cabbage flew through the air and struck the bodyguard. The gladiator put a hand on his sword. An apple sailed past his head.

"Coins! Charity for poor islanders!"

"What a rubbish heap of a province," Clodius gasped.

"Pity for a people oppressed!" More bits of food flew at them.

"This is a scandal!"

And then, in deliverance, came a sharp cry of pain.

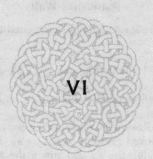

VI

Their siege ended as quickly as it had begun. The yelp had come from the rear of the crowd, the product of a whistling in the air that ended with a sharp crack. "Ow!" Then another smack and another, in remorseless rhythm, like harvesting wheat. The Britons were being parted by a military baton wielded with the cadence of a whip.

"Out of the way, dock dung! Get back from your betters!"

Their rescuer, Valeria saw, was a tall and heavily muscled Roman officer in chain armor and peaked helmet, his thick arms braided with tendons and nicked with scars. He had the shoulders and solidity of a bull. And the meanness of its temperament, too, it seemed.

"Offal!"

One beggar didn't scramble fast enough and was caught across the mouth, flung backward. Others retreated in fear as more Roman soldiers materialized, carving a path through the crowd with the shafts of cavalry spears, their lance heads black and broad. "Part, Britunculi! Get away from the Romans!"

"Brassidias!" The warning sifted through the assembly. "It's Galba!"

The sword at his side swung to the time of his baton strokes like a warning pendulum, and his stride had the powerful deliberation of a man fording a river. His physical strength was reinforced by a brutally handsome face: dark eyes, hooded lids, set mouth, and a broken and reset nose. The enclosure of Britons gave way, and when he turned to face them, none offered challenge.

So instead he swung to the Romans, offering no more approval of them. He had a full beard flecked with gray, an old wound leaving a crevice in its growth, and a complexion brown and leathery. A Thracian, Valeria guessed, backbone of the Roman cavalry. She saw in fascination that a piece of one ear was gone, and as if to balance this loss, a single gold earring hung from the other. Valeria found his masculinity and ruggedness disturbingly sexual. Embossed disks of courage were layered on his chest like a silver roof, his belt held a golden chain that threaded a curious number of rings, and he held his vinestaff tightly in both hands, as if contemplating snapping it. His eyes flickered disdainfully from one of the newcomers to another before coming to rest on Valeria, her cloak open, her hair half unpinned and cascading down, her garment wet. She straightened against a look that seemed to disrobe her.

His voice was gravel. "So what gaggle of Romans is this that disembarks in a sewer of Londinium and, faster than a cock can crow, provokes a riot?"

Valeria glanced around. With no gate nearby, where had this officer come from? She looked at the top of the city wall. Now there was a sentry peering down at them. Had he been there before? She opened her mouth to reply but was interrupted.

"I am Gnaeus Clodius Albinus, newly assigned junior tribune of the Petriana cavalry," the young Roman announced. "And this is the lady Valeria, daughter of the senator Titus Valens and the betrothed of my commander, the praefectus Lucius Marcus Flavius." Clodius was stiff with pride and indignation. "Our thanks for your help, soldier, but I must complain it's tardy. We'd expected proper reception. Instead we've had to find our own way ashore. Word of this indignity will reach the governor!"

"Indeed?" The tough-looking soldier inspected Clodius as well, with disdain. "You'll discover that the governor isn't here, tribune."

"Well, then, a senior commander."

"Who was expecting advance word that you apparently neglected to send. Who was waiting to provide the escort expected."

"Oh? And where is this elusive officer?"

A soldier snickered, his leader's eye silencing him. "Standing before you, junior tribune Clodius. I'm *senior* tribune Galba Brassidias, second in command of the cavalry to which you're reporting—and thus in command of *you*."

Clodius colored. "Tribune! I didn't realize . . ."

"Nor report, it seems."

"But I sent a message that our lateness required us to take a merchant vessel—"

"A message that obviously didn't reach us. Common sense would suggest waiting for a navy galley or, lacking that, waiting in your merchant tub for proper greeting. It's your impatience that has embarrassed Rome."

Clodius flushed.

"And when making an opposed landing"—Galba pointed to the slave Cassius—"don't rely on arena thugs."

The ex-gladiator's mouth tightened.

"Or women."

Someone in the crowd of Britons laughed.

"I don't think recriminations are necessary," Valeria said. Not liking the arrogance of this provincial, despite his timely rescue, her voice carried the sharp authority of her class. "We were unaware that docking at Londinium was considered an opposed landing, tribune."

Her reprimand made him appraise her anew. "It wouldn't have been, if you'd waited for me."

"And how long did you intend to make us wait?"

He smiled thinly. "I would have hurried had I known your beauty, lady." He bowed slightly, having apparently decided on caution. "And please, call me Galba. A pity that our acquaintance should begin so awkwardly, but I think we've all been taken by surprise. Marcus Flavius sent me here to escort you to the Wall. The noise of this rabble drew me."

"A remarkable coincidence."

"Fortunate." He looked around. "So let's get you to the governor's palace. He's touring in the south but left word to give you a night there."

Clodius spoke. "A lady requires proper transport—"

"Which I'm about to provide. Titus!"

"Yes, commander!"

"A litter for the lady Valeria!"

The man moved off at a trot.

"My apologies for this mob. If your tribune there had sent word ashore, we could have avoided— Your cloak is torn!" He looked concerned.

Valeria had clutched it around herself. "I was jostled by the crowd. A boy made off with a brooch."

"A what?"

"It was sudden. A small thing—"

Galba swung to the Britons and pointed. "Her."

A middle-aged woman screamed as two soldiers seized her and dragged her forward, anxious shouts rising. Galba drew his sword, the spatha rasping as it came out of its scabbard, and put its point under her chin. The blade gleamed dully in Londinium's gray light.

"A brooch is missing!" he shouted. "I want it back, and back now! Tell the thief who stole it to hurry, or I cut her!" A spot of blood appeared at the woman's throat, and she writhed, begging for time.

There was a commotion, a succession of cries. Someone small darted forward under the cover of the adults, and the gold clasp spat from the crowd's cluster of legs. Then the furtive thief ran madly away.

Galba glared at the others for a long minute and then dropped his sword, shoving the woman away. "Next time I slice off hands until I find the one that holds it!" Then he scooped the clasp up and presented it to Valeria. It was in the shape of a sea horse. "Your missing brooch. A horse of the sea. Appropriate for your new garrison."

She was shocked at his tactic. "You seize a woman at random, tribune?"

He slid his sword into its scabbard. "To get back what's rightfully yours."

"For which I thank you. But her terror—"

"I make clear what isn't tolerated so women are never terrified."

"Rome relies on the affection of her people—"

"You're not in Rome any longer, lady. Manners are

rougher in the provinces and worse yet on the frontier, as you'll learn. But these people won't bother you again." He raised his voice so the Britons could hear. "Count on it!"

She hastily pinned her cloak once more, hoping the brute didn't notice that her fingers trembled slightly. The mob began to break up as quickly as it had formed. "Well," she said, straightening as she tried to regain composure. "Let's see the rest of this rough Londinium, then."

"The litter hasn't arrived."

She took a breath. "And I haven't stretched my legs for two days. We'll meet it."

Clodius touched her arm. "Valeria, it's more appropriate to be carried—"

"And tedious to stay here." She started down the quay.

The party hastily formed around her, Galba and his cavalrymen to her front, Cassius and Savia to her rear. Clodius strode alongside, brooding and subdued.

"Well, that was exciting," she finally said to the young tribune as they threaded past piles of cargo, the wet pavement sparkling from the scales of landed fish. "Quite an introduction."

"Quite timely," he replied. "Your hero appears from . . . where? Was he waiting?"

"For what?"

"I don't know, but look there. Another prosperous party coming ashore, and I don't see them molested by a Briton mob."

"Galba's warning has spread, I think."

"Or his need for drama is over."

VII

Titus reappeared, leading a litter carried by four trotting slaves. Having made her point, Valeria allowed herself to be hoisted. Now that she had military escort, she felt the protection of the guest and the license of the tourist, and so she left the curtains open to see the place she'd come to.

The wall of Londinium loomed twenty feet high. A century ago the cities of the empire didn't need walls, so placid was Roman peace, but civil war and barbarian raid had eroded security, and so the provincial capital had been girdled. Their party passed through the Governor's Gate and marched into the city proper, the smells of urbanity immediately assaulting them. There was bread and sewage, perfume and wet laundry, the ammonia of the tanning shed and the sawdust of the carpenter. They passed a small forum, crowded with stalls, and then turned left on a narrow avenue toward the governor's palace.

The city was noisier and more crowded for its enclosure, human traffic jamming the streets. Here passed the litter of another fine lady, regal and powdered. The women gravely nodded. There went a proud magistrate, brisk and self-important, his clerk in tow. A juggler was earning coins with a flurry of tossed balls, a group of raucous sailors passed by in their hunt for a good tavern, and two matrons waved and gossiped at each other from adjoining apartments. A bed frame was being hoisted by a rope to a second-story window, strangers catcalling about its intended use. In turn, heads swung in curiosity to examine Valeria as she rode by. The attention flattered her. How many senators' daughters did Londinium see? She'd become someone special.

Britannia was not entirely foreign, of course. If the world was Rome's, Rome was the world. Here in Londinium were Roman streets, temples, porticoes, domes, and tenements, made exotic only by the polyglot accents of the usual ethnic rainbow: swarthy Syrians, blond Germans, dusky Numidians, arrogant Egyptians, quick Greeks, and earnest Jews. And class: slave and freedman, soldier and aristocrat, harlot and matron. The common Latin was heavily accented and corrupted, and other languages intruded. The lyrical Celtic tongue caught her ear, and she wondered if she'd have the time to learn it. Adding to the babble was the squawk of caged fowl waiting to be sold for dinner, the bleat of tethered goats, and the cries of bound lambs. There were shouting children, singing farm wives chanting the merits of their produce, wailing peddlers, shills touting the warmth of a tavern or pleasures of a brothel, and even an unkempt prophet of unknown religion, promising doom. The cries of gamblers, splash of water, and grunt of athletes sounded from a neighborhood bath. The urban noise was punctuated by the clang of blacksmiths, the rhythmic tap of cobblers, the thud of hammers, and the songs of weavers. Here was the glassblower, there the potter, and adjacent the butcher, just as she might expect, Latin signs promising bargains. There was the smell of charcoal fire and lamp oil, hot toast and frying eel, tanned leather and wet wool. Statues of dead emperors and generals were stained dark from rain, little gods of protection squatted protectively in entry alcoves, and phalluses jutted beside doorways for good luck. Only the tired paint and periodic empty, grassy lots gave evidence of what had been gossiped in Rome: that Londinium was tired, and shrinking in on itself. Commerce was retreating to Gaul.

"The city is grander than I expected," she said charitably, reaching from her litter to put her hand on Clodius's shoulder for balance. She enjoyed his jolt at her touch. "More important."

"Britannia once prospered from the wars on the continent," he conceded. "Trouble drove money to this place. Now . . ."

"If they could buy some sunshine, I think we'd be very comfortable here."

He squinted. "It will take more than sun. But Marcus will make his reputation, get a new posting, and move on."

"As will you."

"I'll certainly not let the mud of Britannia stick to my career. And then we'll be back in Rome, shopping for homes on the Palatine!"

"With memories of our adventures among the Celts!"

They came to the square that fronted the governor's palace. Pillars of imported marble supported the roof of a wide portico that sheltered soldiers, solicitors, and messengers from Britannia's rains. The palace's iron-studded oak gates, half open and guarded by legionaries, gave a peek of formal gardens and inner doorways. Lamps glowed in defiance of the day's gloom. Her litter stopped.

Galba was met by a servant, conferred, and came back. "Your arrival was unannounced to the household," he repeated. "Give me a moment to put some fire into them."

The rough officer seemed solicitous enough, Valeria decided, now that the shock of their meeting was over. He obviously belonged on patrol, not here, and was doing his best to chaperon a Roman lady. She should be polite. "You'll dine with us, tribune?"

"I'm a soldier, lady."

"Who must get at least as hungry as a young woman in this drizzle."

"My meal is with my men. I'll come later to secure your safety."

"That won't be necessary," Clodius said.

Galba ignored him. "You'll want a good sleep."

"What I long for are the baths!"

"So let's make sure the fires are lit to heat them." He bowed and trotted up the palace steps with his vinestaff tucked under his arm, shoulders broad as a doorway, medals jingling, harsh voice snapping orders. People scattered from his course like leaves.

"Quite in charge, for a provincial," Clodius said.

"I'm glad Marcus sent him, I think. Does he make you feel safer?"

Clodius looked at the other Roman soldiers, standing as patiently in the rain as hounds. "He reminds me that life in the provinces is never safe."

"We've just started poorly, that's all. Let's get you out of the wet." She climbed from the litter and let him escort her up the steps.

The portico was chilly and crowded, occupied not just by cloak-wrapped officials but by street vendors who had turned the outside of the palace into a small marketplace. Some merchants had food, others jewelry or woolens, and still more boasted enameled pottery. "Londinium," the pieces read. Valeria began to inspect them, Clodius trailing her reluctantly.

"What a quaint token of our visit! I'm tempted to buy one."

"And they're tempted to sell, no doubt."

"Yes, fine lady!" a vendor encouraged. "In honor of your journey!"

"We've baggage enough," Clodius said. "Pots enough. Buy one in the other direction, when you go home."

She picked up a bowl. "No. I want something to remember Londinium by."

"That's called a memory, and it weighs nothing."

"Nonsense. This is the kind of container where memories are kept." She gave the potter a coin. "For my trousseau."

The merchant beamed. "Festus is honored by your patronage."

Valeria gave the bowl to Clodius and picked up some cups. Here was some of the fun she'd been anticipating.

"And now comes a lady of generosity, I see!" crowed a voice from the shadows of the marble pillars. "A maiden of curiosity!"

The two Romans turned. Seated in the dimness against a pillar was an old crone with white hair and wrinkled skin, wrapped in a cloak and seated on a blanket. The bones of fortune were scattered before her.

"Yes," the old woman continued, "I see a woman on the brink of life!"

The pottery vendor was irked. "You may *hear* the clink of money, Mebde, but you can barely *see* past that crooked nose of yours—and you know it, you old witch!"

She swiveled her head in his direction. "I can see that you're adding weight faster than wit, Festus," she called back. "And trading the poor girl bad clay for good silver!

"What I also see," she continued, turning back to Valeria, "is a young Roman beauty on the way to her wedding and wishing, I suspect, to have her fortune told." One eye was as opaque as marble. Mebde lifted a stone disk, no bigger in circumference than an apple, and put her clouded sight to a hole in its center. "Would you like to know your future, pretty bride? Only one siliqua."

"A silver coin for a blind peek at fortune?" Clodius responded. "That's a steep tariff, old woman."

"Perhaps for you, tribune. Your future may be so short as to warrant only bronze. But the lady is willing to pay silver, I think." She extended a bony hand. "Come. Seek the wisdom of the oak."

"What's that curious stone you hold?" Valeria asked.

"A Keek Stane. A Seeing Stone. You get them in the north, where you're going. Through it I can divine the future."

"She's asking too much," Clodius insisted.

"No. Listen to how much she already knows about me."

"From city gossip! Word went ahead, as you said!"

"I want to hear what she predicts." Valeria took out a siliqua and put it in the crone's palm. "Will I be happy?"

Mebde brought the stone closer to her eye. "Oh, yes. And unhappy as well, I see."

Clodius groaned. "That could be the fortune of anyone in the empire."

Valeria ignored him. "Tell me more, priestess."

"I see the fire of torches to light the way for a young bride. I see a sacred grove, laid waste. I see a great battle—"

"By the gods, useless generalities. She's not even any good."

"Will I find love?"

"Ah." The crone twisted the Keek Stane. "Great love, my

lady. All-consuming love, a love like a flame." But instead of smiling she looked puzzled, then frowned.

"With my Marcus?"

Mebde's hand began to tremble, as if she were struggling to hold the stone steady. Finally she cried, dropped it as if it were hot, and stared up in horror, using her hand to clench at her blind eye.

"What is it? Is it about my future husband?"

"My eye!" She held out her other hand. "Here! Take the coin back!"

"But what is it?"

"My eye!"

"What did you see?"

Mebde shook her head as if clearing it, the money clattering on the stones between them. She looked at Valeria in sorrow. "Beware the one you trust," the old woman croaked. "And trust the one you beware."

VIII

It has been my experience that people are most positive about the things that are most unknowable. Ask them the best recipe for bread or the easiest way to plane a board, and they will hesitate, thinking carefully. Ask them about their standing with their peers or the direction of their lives and careers, and they will confess uncertainty. Yet ask them about the doings of the gods, or the likelihood of an afterlife, or the secret heart of a lover, or the monsters that inhabit lands they've never visited, and they will express complete conviction in even the most outlandish of beliefs. So it is with prophecies of the future. Improbable claims about the things that have not yet happened inspire the most devout certainty. Empires have turned on the mutterings of a priestess or the throw of bones.

I ask Savia if Valeria took the old witch seriously.

"My lady confessed she didn't sleep well."

"Because of the prophecy?"

"Because of everything. Excitement about our arrival and the wedding, of course. Distress from the trouble on the quay and the warnings of the fortune-teller, even though we all told her it was nonsense. The palace itself was an eerie place, half closed off because tax collections were short and the rest feeling empty because the governor was away. Lamps were few and shadows long. There were the strange sounds of any new house as we lay in unfamiliar beds. I was restless myself, listening to the cold rain on the tiles of the roof. I rose in the grayness before dawn and went to help Valeria bathe and dress her hair. What I found gave me yet another start."

"In Valeria's chamber?"

"Outside it. That scarred old soldier had displaced her bodyguard Cassius and was sleeping across the entry to her room, wrapped in his cloak on hard marble."

"Galba? I thought you said he went with his men."

"For supper, but then he came back. Unknown to us, he stayed to supplant Valeria's bodyguard. Galba said that Valeria's safety had been entrusted to him by his commander, Marcus Flavius, and that he had no faith in gladiators."

"Cassius tolerated this insult?"

"He was used to it. Soldiers have no respect for arena fighters—out of envy for their skill, I think. The slave retreated to an alcove, and Galba spent the night on the floor. An odd posting for a senior tribune, I thought."

"Yet Valeria didn't know he was there?"

"Not until I told her."

"She was displeased?"

"Flattered. In many ways she was still a child."

"Where was Clodius?"

"In a nearby apartment. Galba greeted him that morning by asking if his bed had been soft enough. There was male rivalry between those two, instant and instinctive. Clodius replied he could sleep on ground as hard as the senior tribune's, Galba said they might test that boast, and Clodius retorted he'd match him rock for rock, while reminding him it was their duty to keep Valeria comfortable. Galba said he needed no reminders from a soldier who barely needed to shave, and Clodius parried that Roman youth indeed defers to age." She shakes her head. *"It was not a wise way to begin."*

"And what was your opinion of this Galba?"

"That he'd assumed a familiarity with us he'd yet to earn."

I nod, knowing that slaves are jealous of familiarities. I ponder the tribune's action. Was he trying to win an alliance with the new bride? Supplant young Clodius? Mock the Romans? Protect from real danger? *"Not the easiest of nights."*

"*I distracted Valeria with talk of other things. We dressed her hair, brought out paints to make up her face, and tried our first Briton porridge, which the kitchen slaves said was defense against the damp. Then we discussed the hopes and fears any woman has. Until we landed in Britannia the wedding was like a distant promise. Now it was near. Who could know what Marcus would truly be like? The girl was a virgin. And more women die in childbirth than men by the sword. Marriage is the female campaign.*"

"*So you reassured her?*"

"*I instructed her.*"

"*You've never been married yourself.*"

"*No, but I've known more men than a wife ever will, willingly and unwillingly, from stubble to crotch and from love to lie. They're frightening at first glance and amusing ever afterward. As a proper lady she would lie with her husband only in the dark, without lamps, and never out of doors. But I've seen men in all places and all positions, as handsome as stags and ridiculous as dogs.*"

It is a crude kind of flirting, I suppose, and powerless on a man of my sophistication. Still, I shift restlessly. "*She was open to such instruction?*" I'm fascinated by this glimpse of female confidences.

"*I talked to her of the usefulness of fingers and of oil. Olive to help smooth things, vinegar to postpone children. Valeria listened avidly. I also stressed the importance of public appearance, regardless of what happens in private.*"

Of course. Romans will forgive any private transgression if a matron behaves with decorum and grace and obedience. Dignity for a Roman comes from the opinion of other people. The noblest goal is honor. "*You stressed propriety.*"

"*Never a public kiss. Never a public embrace.*"

"*And she agreed?*"

"*Did she ever agree with anything? She said she wanted a partner, not a master. I reminded what the philosopher said: 'Other men rule their wives. We Romans rule other men. And our wives rule us.' But always there*

*must be rectitude. A man too obviously in love with his
wife is a weakling."*

This is true, of course. The legions deserted Anthony in
part for his uncontrolled passion for Cleopatra. It is permissible to love, but impermissible to show it.

"All this settled her down?"

"I like to think so." She's enjoying my questions. It has
been my experience that all women thrive on attention, be
they slave or highborn. They are as unconfident as they are
vain.

"And you prepared to leave Londinium?"

"Valeria was anxious. It's bad luck to marry in May, and
the girl was too impatient to wait for propitious June, so she
hoped for a union in April. As did Marcus, meaning Galba
had been instructed to hurry us there."

"What was your impression of the senior tribune?"

Savia smiles, the smile of the Roman urbanite. "Proud,
but with the bluster that comes from being born a provincial. As a servant I saw through him more than the patricians did. He enjoyed our unease. It made him feel more
equal."

"You didn't trust him."

"He was obviously a competent soldier, and candid. He
said he'd been sent as escort because Marcus wanted time
at the garrison out of Galba's shadow, and that he himself
wanted a chance to ingratiate himself with his new commander's bride."

"You believed him?"

"Perhaps he was trying to make the situation work, in his
own way."

"Did Clodius accept Galba's leadership?"

"Clodius felt superior to the Thracian in everything but
military rank, and the Thracian felt superior to the Roman
in everything but birth."

"Not an easy way to begin."

"Galba couldn't show any resentment toward Valeria. So
he showed it toward Clodius, instead."

"And you rode north."

"No. We walked out of the city, Valeria in a litter."

Of course. Horses are prohibited in Londinium, as they are in Rome. Too much manure and too many accidents. "Your escort?"

"Eight cavalry. Clodius explained they were a *contubernium*, a squad that shares a single tent. They'd slept in garrison at the city's northwest corner and were waiting at a circus. Cliburnius the merchant had been elected to higher office from which to steal more effectively, and was rewarding his followers with games."

I do not comment on this cynicism. The knavery of Briton officials is well known. Corruption is rampant, intrigue second nature. Briton perfidy is as proverbial in the empire as Egyptian slyness or Greek arrogance. And any man elected had better provide for the mob. Still, Londinium is not as bad as its reputation. The streets are straighter than Rome's, the congestion less terrible. There is such copious water that the fountains run free, discouraging the gangs that fight to control the taps of the capital. The gutters run so copiously that the stink from shit and garbage is surprisingly small. The baths are packed—the only way to keep warm in this country, I think.

"They all wanted to watch Crispus in the arena," Savia goes on, "and the chariots of the Blue and the Green on the track outside. The wedding schedule made this impossible, so Galba told his men to meet us at the grounds, giving his soldiers a brief chance to mingle with the charioteers and see the exotic animals. Which led, of course, to the trouble with the elephant."

"The elephant?"

"We could hear its trumpeting a quarter mile away. Cliburnius insisted the slaves provoke its sound to remind the city of the day's competitions. The elephant was chained to a stake, and Galba's men were tormenting it for amusement, prodding it with the butts of their lances. Valeria, who has a weakness for animals, bounded out of her litter and demanded they stop. Immediately, the beast came at her."

I raise my brow.

"Somehow it got loose, and Valeria was trapped against

*the amphitheater wall. Then Galba was there with a torch
he'd ignited in a cooking fire, darting in front of the girl to
drive the elephant back."*

"I have seen an elephant kill a man," I remark, remembering a rampage in Carthage. The victim had been
grotesquely flattened. "Your mistress was rash."

"She has an impulsive heart."

"And Galba brave."

"So it seemed."

"Seemed?"

"It was Clodius who was suspicious afterward. Why had
the elephant escaped at that very moment? Why were
torches so ready at hand? We dismissed his complaints as
jealousy but now, looking back . . ."

"Valeria was not hurt?"

"Frightened and then rescued, twice in two days. She
found the experience exhilarating. Her eyes were wide, her
skin flushed, a lock of hair astray—"

"Fetching."

"Too much so. Galba told everyone we had no time for
circuses, saying Marcus wouldn't appreciate his men gaming while he was waiting for his bride. The soldier Titus said
he could understand his commander's impatience! The men
laughed, but I blushed. It was barracks talk, improper in
front of a lady."

"And Valeria?"

"There was an earthy honesty to these soldiers quite different from the gambits and wit of Rome. She thought it exotic and grown-up."

"So you finally exited the city."

"Not yet. Clodius picked a fight about religion."

"Religion!"

"Clodius wanted to show he was one of the soldiers.
We'd passed a temple of Mithras, closed at the emperor's
new order, and a couple men muttered at this sacrilege
against the soldier's god. So Clodius demanded of me why
Christian preachers don't bathe."

"Of you?"

"He knew I speak freely about my faith. He knew I'd

bathed myself. And he pretended not to know that public baths are a center for sexual vices and political intrigue. He said it was well known that Christian priests stink, which I explained is because they care nothing for this world out of preparation for the next. Then Galba reminded Clodius that Christianity was once more the state religion, with Julian's death and Valentinian's succession, which allowed Clodius to reply that Constantine converted originally only to seize the gold of pagan temples and—"

"Jupiter's ghost! All this, and you weren't even out of the city?" *Religion today is a topic as dangerous as it is heated. The emperor Julian tried to bring back the old gods, while Valentinian recognized that political power has shifted to the new. Here in Britannia the Christians remain a fanatic minority, but conversion can help a career. The only thing all sides share is intolerance.*

"Clodius wouldn't stop because of his jealousy. He called the Christ a slave's god, a weakling who counseled peace and was slain for it. He said Christians were tyrants, ending religious freedom. The litter bearers stumbled at these insults, almost spilling Valeria onto the pavement, and I don't think their clumsiness was a mistake. They were Christians and offended, some of them."

"This Clodius seems a fool."

"He was young and proud, which may be the same thing."

"Valeria was a pagan?"

"She was uncertain. Her parents worship the old gods, myself the new. She prayed to Minerva and Flora and Jesus without preference, even though I warned her that Christ tolerates no other gods."

"What did Galba say?"

"He ordered us all to shut up. He said religious opinion always makes trouble. As to the truth of a belief, he'd yet to see a god give a direct opinion on the matter. What good is a sign, he demanded, if a dozen believers interpret it a dozen different ways? It was Cicero who asked if all the dead of the battle of Cannae had the same horoscope. So Clodius asked the senior tribune what god he worshiped."

"And his reply?"

"The god Spatha. The Roman cavalry sword."

I laugh, despite myself. This man Galba is beginning to sound like the only one with common sense! Savia is offended I find the senior tribune's remark amusing, and I'm not surprised. One reason Christians are disliked so much is that they have no humor about their own righteousness. They invite mockery.

"What happened next?"

"We came to the city gates. There were horses for the men and a mule cart for Valeria's trousseau. Galba had suggested a carruca, with a couch to recline on, but she'd insisted on a swifter raeda, even though it meant she'd have to spend the journey sitting up. We watched the men vault into their saddles with full armor, one arm on the saddle and one on their lance to help boost themselves up. It's quite athletic. And so Valeria announced she'd prefer a horse herself, rather than be condemned to the bounce of a cart. Galba asked if she was as fearless of horses as of elephants, and she boasted that she'd ridden in a womanly way, legs to one side. Galba said it required trousers to grip a cavalry mount properly, and Valeria replied that men are born with many things but trousers aren't one of them and that anyone, man or woman, could learn to put them on. Galba laughed, but I was appalled, and Clodius took her by the arm and escorted her firmly to the cart. He, at least, had a sense of decency! The gladiator Cassius took the reins with me beside him, and Valeria was seated under a canopy behind, amid her trousseau. We had a fortnight more of travel, in mansiones and as guests of villas, the first belonging to Quintus Maxus—"

"Yes, I am interviewing him next. And this soldier Titus. They are waiting while I finish with you."

She looks at me. "Please, master, I've answered everything you've asked. Will you not take pity on me?"

"And do what?"

"Get me out of my cell."

"I'll speak to the commander about moving you because you've been useful. But I'm not ready to make a decision on your permanent fate. I'm speaking to many people."

She looks at me levelly. "In the end you'll want me with you."

I mistake this for further seduction. "In my bed?"

"No, in the wood, where Valeria has gone. Where you'll have to go too."

IX

The villa of Quintus Maxus, the first private residence that Valeria's party was to rest at in Britannia, was three days' journey north of Londinium. The road they followed was, in the Roman manner, a spear shaft thrust across hill and dale that sliced through ancient property lines and bridged streams, bogs, and wooded gullies. The highway was well maintained near Londinium, its tight-fitting stones cushioned with gravel and its stout puncheons rumbling like a drum. Grassy margins were cleared to the distance of a bowshot to discourage brigands, and the cavalry escort rode there instead of on the highway, to save the hooves of their unshod horses. But the farther Valeria's escort ventured from the capital, the more indifferent maintenance became. Holes went unrepaired, gravel was scant, brush invaded the shoulders, and frost heaved the stones.

Money, Galba told her as the cart jounced. There was never enough.

Contrasting to this Latin precision were the walls that marked the boundaries of Briton farms. These surrendered to topography and curved along the undulating terrain with the organic symmetry of cells. The result was a honeycomb, cut by Roman roads like a knife.

As an official party the wedding entourage had right-of-way over all but military units or imperial messengers. Private travelers, peddlers, wool merchants, cattle drovers, pilgrims, and hay wagons moved to the grassy swale as Valeria's procession passed, eyes peeking curiously at the woman on the high seat in the column's middle. A bright blue canopy shielded her from sun or rain, and a scarlet cloak was clasped round her neck. She sat straight, her dark hair lustrous at the margin of her hood, her eyes bright, her smile brave, her figure trim and rounded, her garments a display of Egyptian linens, Asian silks, and Roman embroideries. A senator's daughter! In rural Britannia, she was as exotic as a unicorn or giraffe. At Petrianis she'd be a kind of queen, she supposed. She smiled graciously and studied these people as they studied her, speculating on their quiet, secret lives. Did they envy her?

She looked forward to the hospitality of Quintus Maxus. She could learn from the province's aristocracy, and the manor owner would earn status by entertaining not just the future wife of a praefectus, but the daughter of a senator. His feast would be a display of his best because the empire was unified by ten thousand complicated alliances, where advancement revolved around family, friends, clients, loyalty, and long-owed favor. Every invitation was calculated, and every acceptance was strategic.

Galba was taciturn on the road north, brooking no dissent and joined to his horse like a centaur, his belt of rings jingling on his hip. While command came easily to him, companionability did not. He'd answer when asked but otherwise offered little conversation. This reticence made Valeria more curious, not less, of course. There was a peculiar restlessness to him, she thought, which left him brooding and mysterious.

"I'm told you're a Thracian, tribune," she prompted once as his constant prowling back and forth past their procession brought him alongside.

He looked wary. It was bold for a woman to initiate conversation. "I was."

"A long way from home."

"No." He took a moment to elaborate. "The Wall is my home now. You're the one who's a long way away."

So to him *she* was the outsider. Interesting. "What's it like in Thrace?"

"I left twenty years ago."

"But surely you have memories." Even as she said it, she realized how difficult it was to picture Galba as a child.

"Thrace is grass. Horses thrive there."

"A beautiful place?"

"A poor one. A frontier, like where you're going."

"And you a frontiersman."

"So it would seem." He was looking straight ahead now, as if to glance at her might reveal weakness. Galba, she suspected, was a man terrified of weakness. Perhaps, like many strong men, he was terrified of women.

"But you're a Roman as well," she went on, trying to draw him out. If she could understand Galba, perhaps she could understand Britannia. If she was to prevail in this province, she had to learn its mood. As a girl her studies had included little of the geography taught to boys, but she'd always been curious. Sometimes as a child she had hidden behind the tapestries of her father's dining room and listened to the men shouting opinions about lands, wars, and treaties in places she could scarcely imagine. Now she was beginning to see them for herself.

"I'm a Roman soldier. I've never seen Rome."

So she had experience that he did not. "Do you wish to?"

He briefly met her gaze, and for just a moment his eyes betrayed a look of longing. For Rome? Home? Friendship? Then he turned away again. "I wanted to once. Now, I don't think so. Rome, I suspect, would disappoint me."

She tried to tease him. "I thought all roads led to Rome."

"My Rome is the border, lady. My ambition is the Petriana cavalry. It may seem modest to you, but it's all I have."

She understood his meaning instantly, and felt guilty. He was escorting the cause of his own demotion! "And my future husband now has command. You must resent us." Was he loyal? Could Marcus trust him?

"Duty must never be resented, lady." It was a rote response. "Besides, fortune turns many ways." Then he galloped ahead.

Sometimes, when they stopped for the night at the public mansiones spaced every twenty-five miles, she caught him eyeing her from a distance. Just why was unclear. She was used to having men look at her, and Galba occasionally let his gaze linger enough to reassure her that he wasn't immune to her beauty. Yet his look was more complicated than that. It was as if he hadn't yet made up his mind about her. She'd become confident she could read the mind of the boys she'd flirted with in Rome, outguessing their strategies and manipulating their longings. But she couldn't tell if this grizzled, powerful man was intrigued by her or annoyed, impressed by her rank or dismissive of her gender and youth.

"That's just the way of him," the soldier Titus told her. "He looks at everyone with the glint of a hawk and the guile of a merchant. He's the kind with little he needs saying and less need of what others say. Don't be insulted; he's that way with everybody."

"The silences make him more formidable, somehow."

"Don't think he doesn't know it, lady."

"But is he really as fearsome as he seems?"

"Have you seen the rings on his belt?"

She smiled. "I can always hear him coming, like little bells!"

"Those are trophies from the men he's killed."

She was shocked. "You're joking!"

"Forty of them. If you want to understand Galba, look at his waist."

The original Celtic tapestry of meandering pathways and undulating fields had been drawn by a culture with no need for highways or towns, its patchwork a dazzling green. Pastures and grain fields were interspersed with small orchards, vegetable gardens, and wooded coppices of alder and birch. Larger woodlots filled hollows and crowned hills. At the junction of fieldstone walls were Celtic farmsteads, a cluster of oval or rectangular stone corrals enclosing two or three round houses with peaked thatch roofs. Here lived patriarch and matron, children and grandchildren, uncles and cousins, maids and midwives, all coexisting with pigs, goats, a milk cow, dogs, chickens, geese, and rodents in a trampled world of straw, manure, and planted flowers. The grays and greens of their world were punctuated by bright banners at the doors and hoisted weavings on the rooftops, adding blossom to the breeze. Sometimes the Britons themselves donned rainbow colors like Roman entertainers, as if to combat their country's gloom. From a distance they reminded Valeria of butterflies flitting on a velvet meadow, the reds, blues, and yellows quickening her heart.

These free farmers occupied just part of the countryside, however. Debt, sickness, conquest, or opportunism had put other Britons under the thrall of larger landowners, producing plantations of up to a hundred slaves and tenant farmers that were governed by a Roman villa. The result was an archipelago of Italian order in a sea of Celtic primitivism, or so Clodius saw the pattern.

"What amazes me is that the advantages of Roman life haven't been more widely copied," he opined as they rode along. "It's one thing to know no better. Quite another to live next to a superior way of life and fail to improve yourself."

He might as well have been talking to his horse, for all the attention the other soldiers paid him, but Valeria was bored. "Improve how, dear Clodius? By losing your farm to a Roman estate?"

"By adopting modern comforts. A leakproof tile roof. Heat. Glass windows."

"And a barracks of troublesome slaves. Steep debt. Ceaseless taxes. Long days and worried nights."

"You're no doubt describing our next host, Valeria, and yet you'll enjoy his comforts."

"I will, but I'll not pass judgment on his Briton neighbors until I've met some of *them*, and learned *their* lives, and understood *their* contentment."

He snorted. "What you'll meet are mud and fleas."

"Better to scratch than have a closed mind."

He laughed. "You're a rare woman to have such wit!"

"And you're a rare man to listen to it," she gave him, which seemed to please the youth. At least he paid her attention. The other men kept careful distance, giving deference but never presuming familiarity. She was to be protected but not approached.

Clodius was isolated as well. The young tribune had been pegged by the soldiers as an aristocrat posted for seasoning, and thus an officer who'd yet to prove himself. The highborn

Roman thought them crude, and they thought him priggish. So the aristocrat found himself befriending the dangerously disreputable Cassius.

The gladiator refused to be admired. "Don't flatter me, tribune. I entertained the mob, and they despised me for it. There's no glory in the arena, just blood, sand, and, if you're lucky like me, another form of slavery."

"Still," Clodius insisted, "you're an expert at fighting. What advice can you give?"

Cassius grunted. "Pain and fear are allies if you enlist them on your side. Strike first, without mercy, and you strike at the other man's will."

"Doesn't fairness demand that I give an opponent time to ready himself?"

"The graveyards are full of fair men."

As the party clipped north, the young woman counted the mileposts in boredom and studied the countryside with genuine curiosity. Rome did not just govern, it transformed, the power of its ideas enforced not just with the sword but with engineering, architecture, and agronomy. As traditional as Celtic homesteads remained, there were also rectangular and ordered farms, trim Roman towns of white stucco and red tile roofs, walled army garrisons with a gate precisely positioned in each of the four directions, counting houses, signal towers, post stations, pottery factories, stone quarries, and iron forges. Smoke from Roman industry rose into a scrubbed blue sky, and horizontal waterwheels turned tirelessly in the spring freshets. This was the world her future husband had come to defend.

It was late afternoon of the third day when they gratefully turned from the main road to enjoy the hospitality of Quintus Maxus. At last, the comforts of a proper villa! They passed through a break in a dike and proceeded down a poplar-lined lane through a series of orderly fenced enclosures, each field, orchard, and granary a testament to their host's accumulated wealth and epicurean taste. A stucco wall surrounded the villa proper, and when its gate swung wide, the garden drew a sigh of recognition from Valeria. Here were the familiar enclosing wings of a U-shaped house with garden and courtyard pool, roses and lilies, herbs and hedges, statues and stone benches. Under a shaded colonnade waited a somewhat portly Quintus, his head already reddened by the spring sun. Next to him was a regal and kindly looking woman who must be Calpurnia, Quintus's wife. "Come, shed your dust!" Quintus called jovially. "Fill your stomachs! Our home is yours, weary travelers!" The soldiers would have good beds this night, and all would use Quintus's baths, the women taking their turn after the men.

"It's Rome, even here at the edge of the empire," Valeria whispered to Savia.

"If the world is Roman, Rome is the world," came the proverbial reply.

"They have the taste of Italians!"

"Or at least their money."

The supper began at dusk. Quintus and his neighbor Glidas, a transplanted Gaul with dealings in both provinces, invited Clodius and Galba to join them on the dining couches. The matron Calpurnia and Valeria sat upright in chairs to one side as custom dictated, Calpurnia's sharp eye directing her slaves and the women entering and retreating from male conversation as was proper. The two ladies had become instant friends, Calpurnia eagerly dissecting the intricate braidwork of Valeria's hair because it mimicked the latest style of the empress, Valeria plying her hostess with countless questions about maintaining a household in Britannia. What foods did the province excel at? How best to keep warm through the seasons? How easy was it to import luxuries? What was the proper relationship between Roman master and Briton native? Did babes sicken unnaturally in the damp? How did highborn women keep in touch?

Oil lamps gave light and warmth to their gathering, and iron-mullioned glass shut out the evening's chill. The floor, hollow underneath and heated by a stoked hypocaust fire, had mosaics the equal of Italy's. There were rich tapestries, Italian marbles, and the dining wall bore a splendid fresco of Roman ships plying the Hibernian Sea. Valeria could almost imagine herself enjoying a banquet at Capua, but the splendor also unexpectedly made her homesick. How big the world was!

They began with an appetizer of eggs, imported olives, oysters, early greens, and wintered apples. Quintus raised his wine cup. "An opinion on this vintage, please, my new friends! I seek sophisticated judgment!"

"Most satisfying," replied Clodius generously after sampling, as determined to be polite in upper-class surroundings as he was dismissive in lower. "As good as any in Italy."

Quintus beamed. "Would my lady agree?"

Valeria sipped judiciously. While wines tasted little different to her, the Britons seemed to think her opinion important. "Excellent, dear Quintus."

"How delighted I am to hear you say that! You, so recently arrived from Rome!" He turned to Galba. "And you, senior tribune?"

"You already have opinions."

"Yet you're a famous warrior! I want yours!"

"I'm a man of the hard ground and rude camp."

"Of experience and forthrightness!"

Galba regarded Quintus over his pewter cup with faint annoyance, his mouth a line at its rim. For a moment it seemed he wouldn't drink at all, and their host began to look anxious. Then Galba bolted it. The suddenness of his movement caught everyone by surprise; the man had the quickness of an animal.

They waited.

"Briton," he pronounced. He tapped his cup with his thumb, and a pretty slave poured more. The tribune let his forearm caress her thigh, and she glanced at the soldier with interest, a sudden fluidity to her hip.

Quintus's face fell. "It's that obvious?"

"And no insult. But yes, no honest man would mistake this taste for Italy's." He kept his gaze from Clodius.

Their host looked morose. "Indeed! It's too wet in Britannia, too wet and too cold. If you can delay your journey, I'd like to show you my vineyard. The mildew—"

"I'm a drinker, not a farmer."

"This is from your own vines?" Clodius interjected. "No, it's really quite fine, dear Quintus! As good as any!"

Quintus was dubious. "Do you really think so?"

"I must have a second cup!"

Now the flirtatious slave came to the junior tribune. As she poured, he murmured in her ear, the swell of her breasts revealed by her low tunic. Then she slipped away.

The young Roman drank again. "I'm impressed by your industry."

Their host shook his head. "We're trying, but life in Britannia is daunting. The weather is bad and the tax collectors worse. I caught one the other day using a grain measure marked with the wrong number. He blithely admitted fraud, took his rightful share without apology, and then got his bite by adding a surcharge for 'administrative necessities.' He laughed at me—me, Quintus Maxus!"

"Protest to higher authority."

"I do! I complain to the magistrate, and nothing comes of it. I write the governor and get no answer. I try to see the duke and am told he has no time. I swear, every man with an imperial commission does nothing but sell smoke. A good wine can allow a man to forget many troubles . . . but we can't even make good wine!" He turned to his friend. "Glidas—aren't you building a Christian chapel?"

"I am," the merchant allowed.

"You find Christian prayers effective?" Valeria asked politely.

"I find public office ruinous. They've tried to make me consularis, but then I'd be responsible for road repairs I can ill afford. A friend has taken holy orders to escape obligation. I'm considering the same."

"Yet not every man in the province is dishonest," Calpurnia protested.

"No," Quintus admitted, "but something's gone wrong with the vintage of our society in Britannia here, just like this wine. The sense of citizenship is fading. Rome seems more distant."

"It's really quite acceptable, dear Quintus," Valeria insisted politely.

"Britannia?"

"The wine."

They laughed. Valeria blushed.

"It smells of the Briton bog," their host mourned, hoping for contradiction. "It tastes like cabbage and peat. A pig would trade it for puddle water."

"Nonsense," Clodius said. "Don't pay attention to our dour critic from Thrace."

"The senior tribune was courageous in his honesty."

"Or mistaken in his palate. Have him taste again." The youth smiled encouragingly.

"I've no need to taste anything," Galba grunted. "I said what I think."

"I challenge a more careful test," Clodius insisted. "Prove the consistency of your judgment."

The senior tribune frowned, but the others looked expectant, and so he waved impatiently at the slave, who'd returned. She refilled his cup, once more seductively brushing against him. This time Galba didn't bolt his drink but sipped it and then politely put it down.

"Quintus, I never said it was bad. But Briton wine is Briton wine."

"I should burn my vines," their host mourned. "I should break my jars."

"Except," Clodius interrupted mildly, "our military expert has just sampled not your wine, dear Quintus, but a superb and expensive vintage that *I* brought from Italy."

"What?"

"I had the slave girl switch them."

"I don't understand."

"My point is that our senior tribune can't tell the difference." The room was suddenly quiet.

"His opinion wasn't rude, but simply ignorant," Clodius blandly went on. "Your wine is quite good, Quintus. My apologies for our entire party."

Quintus looked alarmed. "I need no apology! I asked for an honest opinion!"

"You seek to embarrass me, boy?" Galba's voice rumbled like distant thunder.

"I seek the honesty you said you were giving."

Galba looked at Clodius in disbelief.

"Nor am I intimidated by your sullen scowls, tribune."

"Still," a flustered Quintus stammered, hoping to deflect what he feared might become a deadly quarrel, "I prefer imported to my own."

"Trade wheat for wine, then," Clodius said, as if he were governor. "Wool for linen. Lead for iron. Let every part of the empire concentrate on its strengths."

"And risk losing a year's cargo to storm or the next war," Glidas warned.

"What storm? What war?"

"The emperor is ailing. His heir is only eight years old. Wars of imperial succession are what I came from Gaul to escape."

"And escape you will. Imperial politics aren't decided in Britannia." Clodius didn't notice his own condescension.

"Constantine was proclaimed by his soldiers in Eburacum," their host reminded. "He went on to conquer the empire. And it's not that invading troops will come *here*. It's that Britannia's legionaries are drawn off to fight *there*, in Gaul and Iberia. And when they go, the Picts and the Scotti become restless. The Franks and Saxons raid."

"Raid where?" Valeria asked.

"The coast. Or the Wall, where you're going."

"By the gods, that's frightening talk for a woman betrothed!" Clodius objected.

"Yes, Quintus," Calpurnia scolded. "Frustration with your wine is no reason to threaten danger to a pretty bride. She'll be safer with the Petriana than in Rome."

Quintus looked embarrassed. The last thing he wanted to do was offend a senator's daughter. "Of course, of course. I exaggerate. It's just that Rome ignores our problems."

Valeria smiled in forgiveness. "The Roman energy you're seeking has come back in my Marcus," she promised.

"Well said! Every man should have such loyalty! And before you're even married!"

"The gods know that few men earn it *after* the wedding," Calpurnia said.

And with that they laughed, Quintus clapping for the main course in relief.

"Please, I don't intend to scare you, Valeria," their host went on. "This is a good place you've come to, and a good man too. I just talk without thinking at times."

"It's his most tedious habit," his wife said gently.

"But the barbarians are getting bolder and the garrisons weaker."

"The Wall stands," Clodius said grandly. "Sleep well behind it, Quintus."

"I appreciate your reassurance, young tribune. But I mean no disrespect when I point out that you've yet to serve in the north."

"True." Clodius speared a dumpling. "In military matters, as opposed to wine, I defer to our senior tribune." It was an attempt at truce.

Their host turned. "And you, Brassidias, who has served on the Wall: Are you as sure as your young officer here that the garrison can hold, should civil war break out?"

Galba had been speculatively eyeing the slave girl waiting in a corner. Her little conspiracy with Clodius had made him want to possess her even more. Now he turned reluctantly back. "For once I agree with the junior tribune," he said slowly. "The issue is never numbers, Quintus. It's fear, generated by Roman will."

"That's exactly what I'm questioning! Roman will!"

"No, you're questioning *my* will. And as long as I will it, no barbarian tribe will threaten Hadrian's Wall. *My* will creates their fear. *My* will sustains the empire."

X

I dismiss the landowner Quintus Maxus from my chambers and review my information with unease. It is but a short step in today's empire from candor to treason, and I realize that my report will have to tread carefully. How much can I blame on the characters of this story? How much on the empire itself?

The truth is that this woman Valeria came to Britannia at a particularly troubled time, and that the key to understanding what happened might be not just her but aging emperors and the dispatch of legions. How much do we control events, and how much are we controlled by them? As my own years grow longer, I argue increasingly for fate, and for blind reaction to trends so enveloping that we fail to notice their significance at the time. The world is changing, and I am disturbed by that change. Disturbed most of all that I can't quite put my finger on what is different. The soldier Titus comes next, and I hope that in his military simplicity he can see what I cannot. That he can explain the strange final episode of the woman's journey northward to meet her future husband.

Larger mysteries remain. I've detected a peculiar restlessness in the empire. Is there something about the human spirit that defeats satisfaction and prevents contentment? Rome provides peace, commerce, and tolerance. Yet there is this strange yearning among the empire's subjects for something intangible and inexpressible, a dangerous freedom that invites chaos. Part of it is this restless longing for religion, this back-and-forth favoritism between the old gods *and the crucified Jew. Part is a childlike rebellion against authority. Part is real difficulty with taxation, debased coinage, and cynical corruption.*

Now there are no truths, only opinions, and not just rightful birth but, under the Christian creed, an unseemly equality. As if patrician and slave can ever share the same paradise! Is it any wonder that disasters occur? Yet I must be careful how I couch my conclusions. Rome seeks fault in individuals, not in Rome.

Perhaps the problem is Britannia itself. It is too distant, too foggy, too ungovernable. Its northern third has never been conquered. Usurper after usurper has arisen here. The Britons themselves remain crude, intractable, argumentative, and ungrateful. One shudders at what will happen if they ever break loose of their soggy island and create empires of their own. One wonders if the Britons would have been better off left to themselves: ignorant, forgotten, and penned by cold water.

I am investigating only one incident. But as I talk to these people, I'm beginning to wonder if Rome should be here at all.

XI

The party was six more days reaching Eburacum, headquarters of the Sixth Victrix Legion. Despite her impatience, Valeria was grateful for a day's relief from the sore tedium of the mule cart. She'd never realized travel was so slow and terrible! Waiting at Eburacum was the pleasure and admonition of a letter from her mother. It had been mailed after she'd left Rome, carried by imperial post, and had now overtaken Valeria's own slow progress.

To my obedient daughter Valeria:

Two weeks have passed since you left to join your future husband. Already your absence seems like two years. The house is quieter without your mischief, and emptier than I would wish. Even your brothers miss you! I pray to the gods to keep you safe, and long for the day of your return to Marcus. Is it cold in Britannia? Have you kept your health? I told Savia that she must be your mother now, and I hope her common sense is helping you sustain decorum. Such a long journey! I grieve at its necessity, even while I am proud of you for making it.

Your father's career has been saved by this alliance, and he sends you goodwill. Your friends are astonished at your courage. I mourn that I cannot see you in your bridal gown, when I know you'll be beautiful. Yet my heart is glad at the thought of it! Valeria, make us proud by devotion to your new husband. Marcus is a good man, an aristocrat of duty and pru-

*dence. His honor is your own, and your reputation is
his honor. Obey, respect, and stay loyal. You are of the
House of Valens! Never forget that, even on the farthest frontier . . .*

Dutifully, Valeria wrote back of her own health and good
spirits, but what more could she say? She'd yet to see her
husband, let alone marry him! Valeria had been trying to live
up to Roman ideals for as long as she could remember, and
she didn't need reminders now. Savia was nag enough. She
felt already married to stuffy tradition, a thousand-year stale
crust of history, famed battles, proverbs, cautionary fables,
and overlapping religions endlessly repeated, in the most tedious ways, to instruct citizens how they should behave.
Rome worshiped its own past. Would her husband too lecture her on Roman virtues? And would she in turn torment
her own children?

Probably. But right now she didn't want rectitude. She
wanted strong arms.

Galba met briefly with Duke Fullofaudes, conferring on the
administration and mission of the Petriana cavalry and receiving dispatches for delivery to the fort. He emerged and
announced to Valeria and Clodius a change in plan.

"We're going to have to add a couple days to our journey.
We have to go to Uxelodunum, at the western end of the
Wall."

Valeria protested. "But I've been traveling for more than a
month!"

"Remounts have been imported from Hibernia. The duke
wants me to collect them for the Petriana."

"I thought our mission was to deliver Valeria," Clodius
objected.

"So it is. But with new horses, as well."

"I don't agree with this detour."

"I don't care if you do."

"I'm a tribune too, Galba."

"In name. Not yet in deed."

"My duty is to the bride of our commander!"

"And her duty is to come with me."

Clodius brooded and grumbled as they continued northward and now westward, their pace always set by the trundling cart. "He should take us to the fort first and then go get his damned horses."

"What choice do we have?" Valeria responded. "Wasn't this an order?"

"An order we neither heard nor read. An order that contradicts the one sent by your future husband. An order that fits Galba's needs more than your own."

"But how does this detour suit him, Clodius?"

"He's a border man! Bribery and graft. It's the same the empire over. Are we going to Uxelodunum simply to get horses?"

"How suspicious you are!"

"And why not? He takes over my mission to escort you, makes himself your rescuer, and drags you with him to get his remounts." Clodius leaned closer. "The other night I caught him sneaking out to confer with some ruffian or tramp."

"Sneaking out?"

"I went to relieve myself and heard Galba's graveled gargle. He was talking to some hooded Celt, and when I challenged them, the man slipped away. Brassidias was all bluster, claiming he was getting intelligence from one of the Areani, a spy from the north. They sell information for money."

"What's wrong with that?"

"Why not inform me? Teach me? Include me?"

She looked to Galba, riding a hundred paces ahead. "He does things alone."

"So why plague us with his dour presence in the first place? We were doing fine until he came along."

Here it was, Valeria thought: male rivalry, instinctive and ridiculous. Boys quarreling for meaningless status, and shedding blood for reasons forgotten an hour afterward. It was worse when women were involved. "Marcus sent him so we could become a partnership."

"Some partner. He treats us like children. We should

leave his tedious expertise and go directly to your future husband." He looked at her again and then dropped back to ride, like Galba, alone.

As they made their way north, native villages began to thin and the countryside steeped into rolling, windswept hills. Grain and vegetable fields faded away and were replaced first by pasture and then by open moors and marshes. Lakes dotted the landscape so thickly that northern Britannia looked like a table set with pewter, vast clouds of ducks and geese winging in to rain upon the water like spring hail. Between rainstorms the sky was a scrubbed blue, clouds towering overhead like ruins of white marble. Squalls swept across gray horizons, rainbows signaling a breakthrough of sun. Twice the travelers came upon small groups of deer that bounded away into thick forest. The presence of these wild beasts exemplified the difference the travelers were experiencing as they journeyed north. There were woodlots still, the trees young and orderly, but also large brooding tracts of arboreal wilderness, peasant woodmen chopping at the periphery like ants against a tangled garden.

And still there was no sign of the Wall.

"How much time would we save if we didn't accompany Galba and went straight to my Marcus?" she finally asked Clodius a day later.

He looked at her with new confidence. "At least two days."

They came the second afternoon to a small tollhouse and watch-post on a broad hill called Bravoniacum. A grassy track branched north from the main road and disappeared into forest. It pointed in the direction the Wall must lie.

As they watered the horses, Clodius announced to Galba, "We part here."

The tribune squinted. "What? Who parts?"

"I and the women. There's no need to drag Valeria a hundred miles out of her way. I've studied the maps. Petrianis is but a day's ride north of here, through that wood. My orders, from the signet ring of Marcus himself, were to escort her, not horses. I'll take her there myself."

Galba smirked. "You don't know the way."

"I'll find it."

"You couldn't find your ass by yourself."

Clodius remained cool. "This cart slows you down. Ride ahead for your horses, and you'll reach the fort of the Petriana when we do. We'll both sleep in proper beds a night or two earlier." He tried to give his voice authority. While Galba had the higher rank, Clodius had the surety of birth.

"The lady requires protection," the senior man said.

"Which she has from Cassius and me. Lend me a guide, if you wish, but leave me to finish my task while you finish yours."

Valeria's heart was hammering. She longed for a swifter end! "Yes," she spoke up. "I want to go with Clodius."

Galba looked at her impassively. So: she'd chosen the boy. The other cavalrymen were giving their own imperceptible nods. All were tired of this slow escort. This was a chance to save everybody time.

"If you take her down that track," Galba warned, "it's your decision, not mine, junior tribune."

Clodius nodded. "A decision I'm comfortable making."

"It's my choice as well," Valeria said.

Galba considered them. Then he spoke carefully. "So be it. I'll give you Titus as guide."

Clodius nodded. "This makes the most sense, I think."

"Prove to me that it does." Galba conferred a moment with the soldier he was to loan, clapped him on the shoulder, and then mounted. "We meet in Petrianis!" The decision made, he seemed newly energized. His men sprang on their horses as well, as if released from a dull lesson. Free of the trundling cart, the cavalry galloped. In moments, they were gone.

"Good riddance," Clodius whispered as the rumbling faded.

The women turned to look at the lane they would follow into the forest. Suddenly their group seemed much smaller and the wood much bigger, its canopy shimmering with spring's green. Valeria hoped the Wall was truly nearby.

Clodius pointed. "We go that way, Titus?"

"Aye, tribune," said the soldier. "A bit of woods, and we're home."

*   *   *

They set off down the track at dawn the next morning. A few
rude Briton farmsteads gave way to rough pasture, dotted
with sheep, and then pasture devolved into unkempt moor
and boggy marsh. Birch, aspen, and willow grew along a
meandering stream thick with rushes, their road following
its course. There was a wall of new leaf, a hole like a tunnel
where the lane led, and then they were swallowed by the forest. It was dimmer and cooler inside the wood.

Valeria leaned out from her cart's canopy to look up into the
trees. They seemed as old as time, and after the deliberately
open shoulders of the Roman road, she felt submerged. The
forest light was green and sallow, pressing with the weight of
water, and the gnarled trunks were fat as towers, their roots
sprawled outward like the legs of a lizard. Limbs entwined in
an obscenity of embrace. Some trees were straight, others
leaned ominously, and all of them creaked to a low moan of
wind. The trees of the woods of Italy were smaller and more
regularly spaced, paths broader, and intersections marked by
temples. Britannia's woods seemed primitive and unexplored.

The straight highway she was accustomed to had been
replaced by a winding track paved with the previous autumn's
leaves, giving no clear view of what lay ahead or where they'd
come from. Her cart jounced and tipped as it rumbled along,
occasionally bogging in mud until Cassius pushed it out.
Insects spun in whirling clouds above stagnant water. Birdcall
slowly faded. The deeper into the wood they traveled, the
damper and danker and quieter it became. They were all quiet,
the primary sound the creak and jingle of leather harness and
the rasp of axle.

It was with considerable relief, then, when they finally
came to a place where the track forded a clear stream, the
watercourse providing a welcome wedge of open sky. Titus
and Clodius dismounted to water their horses while Cassius
and the women climbed down from the cart. Bread, fruit, and
cheese were shared. They nibbled quietly.

The walls of the enclosing forest formed a green pit, its
escape the sky. White clouds scudded across the top of the
clearing like a fleet of boats seen from the ocean's bottom.

Green willows overhung the stream like bowing servants, their drooping tendrils brushing the water. Valeria decided to explore under the branches of one, letting the vines close behind her to form a tent. A forest house! So obese its trunk, so arching its branches! The willow's roots plunged down into the water, and she balanced on one, looking into a clear pool for signs of fish. A shape did dart through the water, and its quickness gave her a quiet thrill. So free it seemed! Swimming where it chose. Diving as it wished. Not trapped, as people were, in an itinerary of schedule and alliance and jealousy and marriage.

The thought startled her. How odd to think Marcus so close! He seemed farther away than ever.

There was a snap of brush, and the soldier Titus appeared, cutting through the willow's overhang after relieving himself. He stopped uncertainly, surprised and embarrassed to encounter Valeria so near.

"Isn't this a grand canopy, Titus?" she asked, hoping to put him at ease. "Like being in my mother's skirts."

He looked uneasy. "I've never heard the willow thought of that way, lady."

"You don't feel cozy here?"

"No Briton would think so."

"Really? And how do they think of willows in green Britannia?"

He looked down. "Briton children are warned not to fall asleep at the willow's twisted feet, lest they be seized and pulled underground. The roots drag them under if the trees aren't appeased."

She looked at him uncertainly. "Surely you don't believe that."

"I haven't seen it, lady." He pointed upward. "They also say hair can become ensnared and maidens hung helpless off the ground. It's just a tale. Still, I don't stay too long under one. The Celts worship the willow god with blood."

"Blood?"

"Life's essence for Esus, the woodman's god. The Celts believe he demands human sacrifice for safe passage. We Romans have ended the practice, of course, but my friend Servius once saw a human skull in the crook of a willow."

Valeria's eyes were wide. "What did he do?"

"Crossed himself and fled. He's a Christian."

"Surely that was from many years ago."

"Perhaps, but the old ways are coming back, I'm told. Life is less certain, and belief is less proven. People are turning to any god they hope might help. I scoff at none and respect the places of all."

He was just an ignorant soldier, of course, and she knew she shouldn't take his barracks stories too seriously. Still, as they moved out from under the willow, Valeria wondered just what she *had* seen in the water. Any deep forest could be haunted by mares, or ghosts, of the dead. Had she seen some kind of spirit in the water?

Valeria told Clodius what Titus had said.

"Like the black forests of Germania," he replied slyly. "Quiet as a tomb, and so cushioned by pine needles that you can't hear your own footsteps. Just dark trees, straight as pillars, and then suddenly from behind . . . the enemy attacks!" She started, and he grinned at her. "Varus marched in with three legions and never returned, you know. When relief arrived, all they found was a trail of bones."

"That was three hundred years ago."

"And Rome has never tried to conquer those forests since."

Now Valeria imagined unseen armies of huge blond Germans slipping from tree to tree, picking out an Italian head like hers to offer to their dark and bloody gods. "Perhaps we should go some other way," she suggested. "Go around this wood instead of through it."

"It's too late for that; we'd have nowhere to stay." He turned. "Right, soldier?"

"Aye, tribune." Titus was standing on the lane with his horse's reins in his fist, looking down the leafy tunnel.

"How far to the end?"

"I don't know. The track is longer than I remember."

Clodius looked too. "Do you sense trouble?"

"No. But I watch most where I can least see." He listened a moment more and then, abruptly, he mounted. "Come. Let's hurry. We don't want to be here at night."

So they set out once again. Valeria suddenly wished Galba were there.

The forest they reentered seemed older and stiller than ever. The stream wound away from them, taking away its noise, and so they were alone with the clop of hooves and the creak of cartwheels. A mile passed, and then another. The wood seemed to have no end.

Finally they reached a place where the road straightened enough that they could see several hundred paces ahead. They all strained to glimpse the light in the foliage that would signal a conclusion, but no, the way ahead seemed darker than ever. Then something moved lightly in the gloom, like the step of a deer.

Titus's hand went instinctively to the hilt of his cavalry sword.

"What is it?" Clodius asked.

The soldier whispered. "Men, I think."

There was another furtive shape in the shadows. "Probably woodmen. I'm going to ride a short distance ahead to learn their business. Follow as quickly as you can." Titus kicked and abruptly took off down the lane at a gallop, leaning forward, and then swerved into the trees where the shadows had gone. They heard him shouting, calling to the strangers, and then it was quiet again.

They waited a moment, uneasy at this desertion, and then Clodius trotted his horse to the front. "Let's move smartly, then," he said. "Cassius, stay alert."

The gladiator twitched the reins, and they followed the trace as before, the mud more visible where the hooves of the cavalryman's horse had scattered the leaves. Everything was still again, as if Titus had vanished.

"I'm uncomfortable with him leaving us alone like this," Valeria complained. "Titus is the only one who knows where we're going."

"We're going where the road goes," Clodius replied. "Our guide is simply trying to surprise trouble, rather than be surprised by it."

"But what trouble?"

The young tribune glanced aside at the enclosing forest. "None that I can see. It's peaceful in here, don't you think?"

"Too peaceful," Savia said. "In Rome it's never quiet, and never dark.".

The carts crested a low hill and then descended into a dark hollow. Where was Titus? It was as if they'd been abandoned. Surely the trees would end soon. . . .

Suddenly there was a birdcall, quick and vibrant. Clodius straightened. "Hear that?" Another trill, answering the first. "It's been a while since we've heard birds. We must be near the edge of this wood—"

Then there was a snapping of branches overhead, a rain of leaf and twig, and something big dropped in front of the startled mule. The animal jerked, Savia screamed, and Valeria grasped instinctively at a pole of her canopy, wishing for a dagger. Something was terribly wrong.

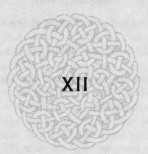

XII

By the gods!" Clodius shouted, turning his horse. "Thief!" And the forest erupted.

A second assailant dropped to knock the Roman from his mount before he could even draw his blade, the two crashing into the underbrush and rolling over and over. When they ended, the assailant was on top, his knees pinning the tribune's shoulders and his knife at the stunned Roman's throat.

The gladiator Cassius leaped to grasp his spear, only to find two archers aiming arrows at his heart.

More brigands rose from the bushes or dropped from trees and formed a hedge of sword and spear, their eyes fierce, their faces bearded, their clothes earthen-colored, their weapons huge.

In an instant, the Romans were taken prisoner.

"Resist, and you die," the first man warned as he stepped around the mule to examine the two women clutching each other.

His movements were like a panther's. Who was he? Tall and hideously disguised, Valeria thought, his long hair tangled and his face—while clean-shaven in the Roman manner—painted half black and half green. Leaves were caught in his hair and his boots, and the Briton trousers tucked into them were dark with mud. What gave him humanity were startling blue eyes that revealed an alert, confident intelligence. A long barbarian sword was slung across his back, and a knife almost as long as a Roman gladius hung on his belt, but he had not bothered to draw either. He wore no armor. His tunic, half opened, revealed a tanned chest ridged with muscle. His voice was quiet, his Latin educated.

"You're a long way from home, fine lady."

She looked hopelessly for help. Clodius was pinned on his back, his assailant astride him. Cassius was having his wrists bound, a brigand murmuring in the gladiator's ear. Savia was staring wide-eyed at a spear point aimed at one of her pendulous breasts. Tales of bloodthirsty gods and creeping barbarians had come true in an instant.

"But you've brought your things, I see," their chieftain went on, rifling through the baggage as if he owned it. His knife came out to slit her bundles. There was a cascade of golden jewelry. A hand mirror. A vial of perfume. An onyx figurine of a rearing horse. Woolen socks, a game board, a cookbook. Her linen shift, embroidered for her wedding night, lifted mockingly to display its translucence. Finally he stopped in puzzlement.

"Pinecones to a forest?" They'd tumbled from a cotton bag. Valeria sat straight, looking away in humiliation.

"Leave her be, or you'll be crucified to the crows, you barbarian bastard . . ." It was Clodius, his threat choked off as his captor's dagger pressed against his throat.

Their leader's gaze flickered. "Kill the noisy one."

"No!" The plea escaped from Valeria before she realized it. "Don't harm him!"

"Ah." The painted man held up his arm to stay the execution. "She speaks! And to beg for another! Is this weakling your lover?"

She was shocked. "Certainly not!"

"Your brother?"

"My military escort!"

"Hardly an escort worth having."

She glanced around, yearning for Galba's ominous presence. "Listen. Roman cavalry are nearby and are returning soon. If you kill us, they'll hunt you all the harder. Just take what you want and go."

The brigand pretended to consider this. "And what is it you think I want, here in my forest on the soil of my ancestors?"

"This is Rome's forest," she retorted, more bravely than she felt. "Near my home, not yours."

"Really? And what home is that?"

"The home of the Petriana cavalry."

He seemed unimpressed. "Well, this forest is the home of Dagda, the great and good god who walked here long before any Roman saw it. Dagda still tends it for my people and dislikes all trespassers. The forest gives us all we need, and so there's nothing of yours I really want."

"Then let us go."

"Except, perhaps, these pinecones." He held one up. "Curious."

"Those are stone pine from the Mediterranean, brought as a present to my future husband."

"And why does he desire forest litter?"

"He's an initiate of Mithras. Those cones are burned for protection and immortality. They're sacred to Roman officers."

"Immortality?" He seemed intrigued. "And who is this future husband of yours?"

"Marcus Flavius himself, praefectus of the Petriana cavalry."

The man laughed. "Praefectus! Then he has more men than I do, and I have need of more protection than him." He hauled the bag of cones out of the cart. "I'll keep these for myself, and leave everything else, I think"—he looked around, as if considering—"except . . . yourself." His eye came to rest on her. "A Roman beauty to grace our tribe." He winked at the other men.

Valeria drew her cloak around herself, clutching the sea-horse brooch.

"You understand my invitation?"

"I'd never go with a barbarian like you! I'd rather die! If that's what you want, then kill me and be done with it."

The barbarian laughed. "Kill *you*? Besides these pinecones and their gift of immortality, you're the only thing of real value here."

She looked wildly around for a weapon or avenue of escape. Her rape would not just be hideous in itself; it would annul her betrothal and ruin her father's and fiancé's careers.

The bandit looked over at Clodius. "Offal of Rome! We're going to borrow your horse!" Then he whistled. Another barbarian appeared, leading Titus's horse as well. Valeria groaned. Was the soldier already dead?

"The lady and I will make our departure sitting down," he announced to the others. Then he turned to Valeria. "I hear you like to ride, lady."

"That's not true."

"Which horse do you choose, you who wishes to gallop?"

"I have no such wish! I can't ride a horse!"

"I'm told you admire the animals and dream of riding them like a man. Which will you ride with me to my castle in Caledonia, my fort upon a hill?"

"I'll hunt you with dogs if you take her, Britlet scum!" It was Clodius again, lifting his head out of the dirt. The man kneeling on his chest growled and drew his dagger lightly over the tribune's throat, tracing a line of blood. The young tribune winced, his head falling back in frustration.

"Speak again, little fool," the chieftain warned, "and Luca will take off your head."

Clodius opened his mouth and then closed it.

The barbarian reached to grasp Valeria's forearm, his grip like iron, and hauled her off the cart.

"I'm not dressed for riding," she pleaded, hating the way her voice was breaking. Where was her courage?

"We Celts have a remedy for that." Without warning he jabbed his dagger at her legs, and her stola and tunic were rent in two, exposing her knees and a glimpse of her thighs. The cool air kissed them. "There, Celtic trousers. Now climb up there."

She felt faint. "Please kill me instead."

"Climb up, or I'll put your slave over a fire and roast her heart! I'll skin your young escort there until he screams for his mother!"

Valeria looked at him in horror.

"Ride with me, and I let the others go!"

Shakily, she grasped two of the four horns of Titus's saddle. The animal was immense, and she realized that in the past she'd always been boosted upward. How to climb aboard? As if reading her thoughts, her abductor grasped her legs and bottom and swung her upward with the most casual indecency, plopping her between the horns as if she were a child. "Push your butt against the two horns behind you and tuck your thighs under the two in front," he instructed.

"I know what to do," she muttered. She felt humiliated, her legs splayed like a man's. Yet she also felt more secure. No wonder the cavalry rode so confidently! She could feel the animal's rough hair against her bare calves and smell its warm heat. It twitched uneasily beneath her. Letting go with one hand, she fingered her own hair at her shoulder, feeling her brooch.

Her abductor vaulted up onto the mount of Clodius and grabbed Valeria's bridle. "We meet where we planned," he told his men. They nodded. Savia was bawling, Clodius cursing impotently. The barbarian began to lead the woman away.

Suddenly Valeria kicked her mount hard, and the horse bolted ahead to prance alongside its companion. Her abductor looked at her curiously. She'd stealthily unhooked the brooch holding her cape, and now she let the garment slide off her shoulders like a sheet, the folds catching a moment on her mount's tail and his eye distracted by its seductive drop. Leaning forward as if to speak, Valeria suddenly jabbed, plunging the sea-horse brooch into the flank of the brigand's stolen horse. The animal reared, screaming, and in an instant the arrogant barbarian was thrown, landing on the ground in a tangle of weaponry. Even as he scrambled up, clawing for his sword, Clodius's frightened steed crashed away. Meanwhile Valeria jerked Titus's horse around and charged back to the lane, riding over a man who tried to block her and thundering madly ahead toward the promise of the distant fort, expecting an arrow in her back at any moment. The lane twisted, and she was gone.

"Morrigan's damnation!" The barbarian's sword was out but useless as he watched Valeria gallop away, his expression furious but grudgingly respectful. "That woman has the fire of Boudicca and the guile of Cartimandua." It was a compliment to compare her to the Celtic queen who'd led a bloody revolt against the Romans and another who'd saved her people by wily collaboration. He looked at his men. "It was a smart trick, and a brave one."

"She's gotten away," the one called Luca complained.

"We'll pursue on foot. The Attacotti have the endurance to run down a horse."

His men groaned.

"Chances are she'll spill."

"What about the others?" a companion asked.

"With the girl gone, we'll tie them and take them—"

"No!" cried Savia.

Then there was a birdcall again, sharp and urgent. The barbarians froze. They could hear a low rumble of approaching horses.

"Romans, Arden."

There was no hesitation. The barbarian whistled just once, and the brigands melted into the trees, vanishing as quickly as they'd appeared. Only their leader hesitated, stooping to scoop the sea-horse brooch from the mud. Then he too was gone. Only a rocking of disturbed branches showed where the Celts had been.

Savia remained still as a statue, shocked by the sudden turnaround. Clodius reared up from the dirt to fumble for his sword and then stopped in humiliation.

His captor had stolen it.

Valeria had left them all behind, pounding down the track in fear and exultation, breathless at the power of the animal under her, the horse's muscles rolling like the waves of the sea. She felt guilty at leaving the others but knew she was their only hope: she must find help! And then suddenly her mount stumbled and she was flying through the air, landing so hard that the wind was knocked out of her. She tumbled over and over before fetching up against a log.

The idiot steed had thrown her.

The horse got to its feet, saddle askew, and limped off with a snort and an accusing look, as if it was her fault.

Now the barbarians would catch her.

But then there was the sound of approaching hooves from ahead, many of them, and she stood shakily, as filthy as her would-be abductor. Dazed, she saw the dull glitter of armor and weapons through the leaves and slowly recognized the purposeful rhythm of Roman cavalry. Far more men, in fact, than Galba had left with, pounding hard to save her! She swayed with emotional exhaustion, relief and joy overtaking her. Two leading scouts pulled up and shouted their bizarre discovery of this bedraggled figure. Next came a trumpeter and standard-bearer, then the officers. . . .

"Marcus!"

She ran down the track past the Roman scouts, all decorum forgotten, legs half bare, her cloak gone to reveal the shape of her shoulders, her stola torn and covered with mud, twigs the only decoration in her hair. In the saddle ahead was the tall praetor, resplendent in a mail lorica of golden leaf, a traditional crested helmet on his head and a red cape rippling behind, the very picture of Roman military bearing.

Lucius Marcus Flavius sawed on his reins in shock, his white mount skidding to a halt and his cavalry bunching behind him. "Valeria?"

"Brigands, Marcus! They might kill the others!"

"By Hades and Gethenna!" a familiar voice cursed. "I leave that young fool for a day—" Galba! Waving his arm, the senior tribune led a contingent of men around the couple at a charge back toward the cart.

Valeria tried to grasp Marcus, reaching for his leg, but before she could do so, he dismounted and unhooked his cape to cover the girl, acutely aware of the curiosity of his remaining horsemen. Her disarray was bewitching, the beauty of her body apparent. Then she was wrapped, the enclosure of the cape like a heated blanket, and Valeria sagged with relief. Savia will be scandalized, she thought, but I'm going to lift my face until he kisses me. Yet Marcus

wouldn't comply with her wish. Instead, he held her by both
shoulders.

"What are you doing alone?" By Jupiter and Mithras, he
thought, his intended bride was as dirty as a pig girl and as
lost as Ulysses. He was embarrassed.

"A barbarian tried to steal me!"

"A barbarian?" He still didn't comprehend what had
happened.

"Bandits, Marcus! They made us prisoner but I stabbed
his horse and rode off. Clodius tried to save us, but—"

"Who?"

"My escort! A new tribune!"

Marcus remembered the name from dispatches. "And
where is this escort?"

She pointed. "Where Galba went!"

Finally he understood her urgency and remounted; then
looked down in confusion. She lifted her arms. After hesitating a moment, he swung her up behind him, and her hands
circled his waist, breasts pressed against the hard armor of
his back. For the first time since leaving home she felt truly
safe. Then they pounded back down the lane the way she'd
come with thirty more men around, swords unsheathed,
ready for an enemy. When they pulled up at the cart,
Clodius was standing alone, unarmed and forlorn.

"Where are the bandits?"

"They fled into the forest."

"It was Valeria!" cried Savia, appearing from a hiding
place behind the cart. "She unhorsed the thief!"

Marcus glanced over his shoulder, still not compre-
hending.

"I stabbed his horse with my brooch pin," Valeria
explained again.

"They ran when they heard your horses," Clodius added
gloomily. His clothes were filthy, his scabbard empty, his
neck red. The blood from his wound had dried like a bib on
his bright new chain mail, baptizing the armor with a red-
dish brown stain. "They took nothing but a few pinecones."

"Cones?"

"Stone pine, Marcus!" Valeria said. "For the ceremonies

of Mithras. I was bringing them to you as a present, but the barbarian decided they would protect him—"

The praefectus shook his head. "Cones. By the gods."

"They must have slipped through as traders," a centurion suggested. "Or over the top at night. A bribed sentry, perhaps. It was a bold gamble."

"A gamble for what, Longinus?"

"Loot, I suppose."

"They wanted the lady Valeria," Clodius said.

"My escorts were willing to die before that happened," Valeria interjected. She didn't want the men punished. "Brave Clodius had his throat cut."

"Brave who?"

The junior tribune saluted in pained embarrassment. "One-Year Appointed Tribune Gnaeus Clodius Albinus, reporting for duty, praetor."

"By the horns of Mithras, it gets worse and worse."

Clodius bowed his head. "This is not how I imagined us meeting, praefectus."

"Nor did I. Well, welcome to Britannia, junior tribune. It appears you've had quite a reception."

Clodius stood stiffly. "Let me remount, and we'll see the reception!"

"So I'd hope. And your horse?"

He glanced around, immediately miserable again. "It ran away."

Someone laughed. A sharp glance from Marcus silenced it. Then the praefectus glanced again at the woman behind him. "Go to the cart and repair your clothing." It wasn't a suggestion, it was an order. She slipped off the horse's rump and went to Savia, who'd retrieved Valeria's cloak and now bundled her in it.

"And for the sake of Mars, find something to bandage your throat, tribune," Marcus growled. "You're dripping like a gutter." Clodius retreated to comply.

There was noise, a crash of branches, and Galba and his troopers came bursting out, horses lathered, men cut from vine and twig, their leader furious and frustrated, glancing at Valeria with disbelief. He saluted. "No sign of them, praefectus."

"No sign?" Marcus looked at one of the mounts. Titus was sitting behind a trooper with a rope bound around his wrists, face turned away. "Who's that man there?"

"One of mine, ambushed. We found him unconscious and bound."

"And these brigands? Are they smoke that vanishes?"

"They're quick, and they know this wood, I think. Every trail and every hole." Galba looked at Valeria again. "My apologies, praefectus. I thought us almost home and had orders to collect those remounts. If I'd insisted your lady stay with me—"

"It was my decision to hurry, not Galba's," Valeria corrected. "Nor Clodius, nor Titus. I simply yearned to see you and insisted on the quickest way."

Marcus scowled. "Yet all of you were surprised. And if Galba hadn't met my exercise near the Wall and told me you were near, we might not have rescued you at all."

"Fortune played with us this day," the senior tribune observed grimly. "Ill and then good. If gods exist, then perhaps they're at war with each other."

"It was the one true God who saved us," Savia spoke up. "I was praying."

Marcus ignored this. "But why Valeria?"

"For ransom," Galba said. "A wealthy husband-to-be, a senator's daughter. I wouldn't have thought any man so bold or foolish, but this rogue must be both."

The praetor nodded glumly. It was no secret in the province that his family was rich. Every man credited it for Marcus's appointment to the Petriana. "Galba, how far did you hunt?"

"No more than a quarter mile."

"Then we'll run them down yet." Marcus turned to the troop of cavalry behind him. "Decurion! Half to the right, half to the left! Now, into the trees! Find them!"

The Roman horses plunged gamely into the forest, but it was hard going. The animals stumbled on the uneven ground, branches swatted at the rider's helmets, and brush caught on weapons. They looked, and sweated, for hours, but had no better luck than Galba had. The Celts had disappeared like mist before the sun.

The bodyguard Cassius, gladiator and slave, had disappeared with them.

XIII

Of all the spectacles of human existence, a wedding is the most public and private of ceremonial contracts. It is that rare moment in Roman life where a display of affection is allowed and even encouraged, and yet the true emotions of the principals remain hidden behind a veil of ritual and revelry. A Roman wedding is always a mixture of love, strategy, breeding, and money, and a Roman marriage is a mysterious combination of companionship, alliance, selfishness, and separation. No outsider can understand its complexities. As for sex, well, that is always simpler with one's slaves.

Yet it seems that if Valeria is to be fully understood, then her relationship to her new husband is crucial to that understanding. Perhaps this makes me a voyeur, but I'm a voyeur in quest not of sexual titillation but of high truth: the political consequences of betrothal. At least that's my justification. I'll confide in these private pages that it's the unraveling of the human heart, not the frailties of empire, that really sustains my odyssey. So I'm human. What of it?

My informants in this matter are two. Valeria's handmaid Savia was as shamelessly curious as I am, and eventually won from her mistress a bride's assessment. Savia comes back to my interrogation chamber in a mood of tentative triumph, sensing how necessary she's become to my investigation. She still hopes I'll buy her. She tells much of what I am about to relate.

The other that I interview is the centurion Lucius Falco, the veteran who fought with Galba. He lent his modest villa for the wedding and became a temporary confidant of Marcus. There's some interesting nobility to this soldier, I sense, a quiet belief in happiness and justice that some would judge admirable. Others, naive.

There is no requirement in Roman law for a wedding ceremony, of course. Even custom often dispenses with formal ritual. Yet Falco tells me that he and his wife were eager for the union to be formalized in their home, located near the fort of the Petriana on Hadrian's Wall.

"Why?" I ask him, to judge the honesty of an answer I already know. Like the other soldiers I'm interviewing, Falco is a practical and stoic man, his military bearing giving him dignity and his legionary ancestry giving him pride. Of mixed Roman and Briton blood, he is the son of a son of a son of soldiers of the Sixth Victrix—each generation following the next into the legion as the army strains to maintain its numbers, each retiree adding to the estate his family has established in the lee of the Wall. This history gives him a sophistication I can make use of; he understands the mix of dependency and resentment that swirls on both sides of the barrier. He knows how permeable a Roman border can be.

"My wife urged that we host it in order to be polite," he replies to my question. "Lucinda is sympathetic to officers' wives on the Wall. It's a male world, lonely for highborn women, with brides strung out along eighty miles of stone and mortar. And a wedding is as daunting for a maiden as it's longed for."

Not as candid an answer as I would like. "You'd also attain social prestige by hosting the wedding of a commanding officer," I suggest.

He shrugs. "Undeniably. My family's house has been pressed into duty for generations. We've given shelter to the good and the bad: to inspectors like you, to military contractors, to magistrates, to generals, and to their wives, mistresses, and courtesans. It's the Bite."

The Bite, I know, is what soldiers such as Falco pay their commanders to be kept at the Wall and not sent overseas. The bribes also buy leave to tend to crops and animals.

Playing host to the parasites of officialdom is a way for an officer to ingratiate himself.

"You didn't resent this new commander?"

"I had good relations with Galba and expected the same with Marcus."

"You didn't have to choose between them?"

"I try to stay on good terms with everyone. A man advances only as fast as his friends allow it."

"I appreciate your candor."

He smiles. "Lucinda had another motive. She said cavalrymen have the patience of a battering ram and the delicacy of an elephant. She wanted to befriend Marcus's new wife and give her encouragement."

"You agreed?"

He laughs. "I complained how much it was going to cost!"

"Yet the wedding was an investment."

"Lucinda told me Marcus might ride to my rescue one day. I told her that on the night in question, Marcus would be too busy riding his new bride!"

"And her response to that?"

"She hit me with a spoon."

I shift restlessly, considering how to get to what I really want. "Your wife is not highborn herself, is she?"

For the first time Falco looks at me warily, as if I might know more than he assumed. To judge what my informants tell me, I have to know something of who they are, so I ask ahead. "She's a freedwoman," he says. "My first wife died, and Lucinda was my closest slave. We fell in love . . ."

"Not so extraordinary these days. A love match, I mean."

"I consider myself a lucky man."

"What I'm after is the degree of love between Marcus and Valeria, the mood you saw on their wedding night."

"Wedding night! That's the least typical of all the nights of a marriage. And yet we could all see that Marcus was nervous . . ."

XIV

The wedding of Marcus and Valeria began in the long blue twilight that reigns in the spring of Britannia's north. Clouds blew away to leave the sky as clear as a river pool, the first evening star glowing like a welcoming lamp. The lights of the villa of Falco and Lucinda were lit in reply, candles flickering among hanging garlands and oil lamps throwing a wavering blush. Slaves hummed songs of merriment in anticipation of a banquet of such excess that there'd be delicacies enough even for the field hands to share: chicken in fish sauce, pork with apricot preserves, milk-fed snails, stuffed hare, salmon in pastry skin, lentils and chestnuts, onions and leeks, oysters packed in seaweed, and shrimp hauled in brine barrels from the coast. The kitchens steamed and smoked with grouse, pigeon, stewed lamprey, and haunches of venison. There were platters of olives and cheese, sweet cakes and sweetmeats, boiled eggs, pickled vegetables, and dried figs. Flasks of honeyed mead glowed like amber, while Briton beer and Italian wine filled flagon and cup. Some of the food had to be imported, given the paucity of imagination of Britannia's cooks, but Marcus and Falco had spread enough coin to quiet any grumbling about Roman snobbery. So much money, in fact, that it ensured a steady stream of well-wishers and gifts to the villa door.

An aristocrat's honor was the honor of his neighborhood. The alliance of Marcus and Valeria promised to elevate the status of not just the Petriana cavalry but also the adjoining village. A senator's daughter! Even the natives coveted an invitation.

The loan of his villa had given the centurion Falco a tentative familiarity with his new commander, of course. Marcus had money and position, and Falco had experience and local ancestry. Each could appreciate the usefulness of the other, and the centurion tried to cement a relationship as they dressed.

"So what's your feeling about ending bachelorhood, praefectus?" Falco asked conversationally as Marcus carefully folded and draped his ceremonial white toga, the Roman muttering about the intricacy of patrician dress. "Are you gaining a companion or losing freedom?"

Marcus frowned at himself as he tilted one of Lucinda's face mirrors this way and that. He disliked ceremony and was uneasy being the center of attention. Both, unfortunately, came with his new command. "You're the married one—you tell me. I've gained this posting and a new chance. What Valeria will become remains to be seen. She seems sweet enough."

"Sweet! By the gods, she's beautiful! Eyes like a starry night, skin like the blossom of spring, the curves of a Venus—"

"You'd better not let Lucinda hear such poetry. She'd be jealous."

"She was jealous the moment that nymph rode in on her mule cart, looking better after ambush than other women after their bath. I envy you this wedding night."

Marcus shook his head. "Thank the gods it's even occurring. That thief half stripped her. To almost lose the girl near my doorstep, and with it my appointment . . . what near disaster I escaped! Can you imagine the fury of her father? The outrage of mine? I've come a thousand miles to make my reputation, not squander it."

"You'll have your revenge. Galba's informants are offering gold, and barbarians will sell their own mothers. Meanwhile, you have a more delicious conquest."

Marcus's polite smile betrayed unease. The truth was that he was awkward with men and shy with women. Females had always seemed utterly mysterious, frequently frivolous, and deliberately unpredictable. Moreover, he'd never had a virgin. "I know little of young women," he confessed.

"That will change tonight."

"It's not that I'm not looking forward to her. It's just—"

"You're a good horseman, no?"

"You're the cavalryman to judge that."

"Women are no different than a horse. Slow and gentle is the best way. At the least the result is children. At the best, love!"

"Yes, love." Marcus looked pensive. "The plebes marry for it, you know. The Christians attribute it to their strange skinny god. For people of my rank it's not so simple. I'm not sure I understand the word at all."

"You don't understand, you feel."

"She's so beautiful that it's . . . daunting. The fact that we don't know each other, I mean. And when I said I don't know women, I meant I don't know about living with them. What to do after the bed."

"Here's the secret: they pretty much take care of themselves. Like horses, again. And they'll take care of you, if you let them."

"You compare everything to horses."

"Horses are what I know."

"And now, for me, a woman." The groom stood straighter, mentally rehearsing his entrance. "I betrothed to get this posting, Falco. I could live in Rome on my family's fortune, wanting nothing, but that's not my destiny. My father made his fortune in salt but longs for martial honor. I want to prove myself. It was her father who suggested this union—"

"Favored by the gods, as I said."

So why did he feel such misgiving? Because in truth he was a scholar, not a soldier. The tribune he'd supplanted, this gruesome Galba, had seen through his martial pose and golden armor in an instant. He felt uncomfortable amid these rude people. Marcus feared the woman would find him out too, and mock his quiet nature. But if she could help him instead . . . "Valeria *is* sweet, if somewhat headstrong."

"She seems to have a lively intelligence."

"She half-suggested a Christian priest! It's her maid's influence. I told her I'll not have a cult that pretends to eat their god. Centurion Sextus serves the shrine of the garrison's spring. He'll do well enough."

"And she agreed?"

"She seemed to want to please."

"Obedience is a good sign."

"Yes." He hesitated. "I changed her mind, I suspect, but not her heart. Do you know that she told Galba's soldiers that she wished she could ride like a man?"

"We've all heard of her courage."

"She could have broken her neck, and she came to me looking like a harlot. My mother never rode. Nor my grandmothers."

"So thank the Fates you're not marrying them! These are modern times, praefectus. New ideas are abroad in the world. Wait until you meet some of the wild women of the north: I've seen them fight, curse, plow, bargain, command, spit, and piss."

Marcus grimaced. "That's why I want a bride who's a proper Roman, centurion. I didn't come a thousand miles to wed a barbarian. I came to defeat them."

The banquet hall was on fire with light, its banked candles as thick as the glint of sun on a ruffled lake. The air was heady with the scent of spice, wine, male oils, and female perfume. And yet Valeria, in the traditional wedding gown of white with saffron veil, dominated the gathering as a jewel dominates its setting, her long dark hair a swirling river beneath its golden, translucent net. Her tresses had been braided into six parts and parted with the silver spearhead of Bellona, sister of Mars, and three curls fell past each cheek, in the manner of the Vestal Virgins. Her sandals were yellow and her waist cinched by an intricately knotted golden cord that only her husband could untie.

Valeria found to her surprise that she wasn't as frightened as she'd feared. The groom was still a stranger but a handsome and earnest one, she judged, who'd been solicitous after the initial confusion of the ambush and compliant with her wedding plans. He seemed a bit stolid—his tolerance of tardy deliveries had pushed the date of their union to early unlucky May, despite her best efforts—but then he was a man of learning who said belief in bad luck was silly superstition. She looked forward to knowing him, while shivering slightly at the prospect of lovemaking. Would it enchant? Would it hurt? She wished he'd been bolder in their embraces so far—more experience would reassure her—but his shyness also made him less threatening. If he'd done nothing yet to ignite the kind of love that the druidess had forecast in Londinium . . . well, that would come.

Lucinda had tried to explain it. "Men don't talk as openly of their heart, but they feel as much as we do. You'll see his moods and learn to read and direct and love him."

"Like you and centurion Falco?"

She laughed. "I'm still getting him in harness."

"So love comes?"

"His nature is to protect you. You'll teach him to hold you as well. And when he does—" The matron smiled. "That's when the pair of you becomes stronger than iron against all the cares of the world."

The simple ceremony came first. Sextus, a good-natured and simple-spoken veteran of the Wall, did a creditable and diplomatic job, calling on his spring's goddess to let the couple's happiness well upward like a fountain. In deference to the varied beliefs of all those present, he asked for all the other gods—Christian, Roman, and Celtic—to join in blessing the union.

Marcus stood stiffly during the recitation, as if afraid of making a mistake. Valeria was appropriately demure but stole glances at her new husband. When he took her right hand in his to promise fidelity, the firm grip was more suggestive of a treaty or business agreement than a touch of love, but when he took her left, it was with a gentle touch that he slipped a ring on that fourth finger that physicians teach leads with a nerve directly to the heart. The ring bore a sculpted intaglio of the goddess Fortuna: luck, perhaps, to counter her fears about the wedding's timing. Finally he lifted her veil, and she gave her new husband a tremulous smile. And that was that, because, as was proper, he made no move to embrace or kiss her yet. That must wait until the end of the feasting. Valeria was led to a banquet couch where, on her wedding night alone, she'd be allowed to recline at supper like a man.

"And now eat and drink so that your joy might become theirs!" Sextus concluded.

The party obeyed with gusto.

There was song from the lute and pipes, games of wit, and poems of love. A village maiden leaped upward to dance a vigorous jig with the speed of swallow wings, kicking and twirling to the thump of ancient drums. The music was primitive and simple, but the song was so primeval that it seemed like blood pumping to Valeria's heart, an echo of a wilder world. Was that what it was like beyond the Wall? She felt superior, as reigning lady of the fortress and its civilization now. Yet what must it be like to be as free as this wild Celt, dancing and drinking and catching men's eyes . . .

From duty comes devotion, and from devotion comes love . . .

Slaves slipped in and among the guests like wraiths, refilling plate and goblet, furtively nibbling themselves, and secretly smiling at the growing drunkenness of the guests. One slave in particular was tall and well muscled but noticeably clumsy, with the feral look of a recent captive. What defeat, she wondered, had led him here? Had he left his own wife behind?

The wounded Clodius, reclining on another couch, also studied the awkward servant, but with ill humor. While most of the assembly was boisterous, the young tribune was uncharacteristically quiet. He'd watched the brief ceremony that gave Valeria to her new husband with a tight smile, and now he watched the slave to keep his stare from fixating on the young bride. She reclined on her wedding couch like a ripe golden apple, her skin smooth and flawless, her dark eyes bright and triumphant, her hair like a bolt of Asian silk, and watching her was a kind of exquisite torture. Wed to a wooden man who seemed embarrassed even to have Clodius on his staff, a praefectus who had more appreciation for his office than for the woman who'd given it to him . . .

Clodius also sat well away from Galba, who, he suspected, was laying the blame for the ambush on him. By the gods, it hadn't been *his* decision to get those remounts! And yet it was he who had stumbled into a Celtic ambush, and he who had been made a fool of. Word of how he had greeted his commander, stripped of sword and mount, had swiftly made its way through the fort. One turma of soldiers had snapped to attention before him with red lines painted across their throats, grinning like idiots.

Never had he endured such humiliation.

How long this single year would drag! The few Roman girls at the party were plain and boring provincial brats, giggling and dull, while the Celtic lasses were rudely independent and, in any event, beneath his station. None came close to the beauty of Valeria. Worst of all, his neck wound ached where the bandit had cut it, forcing him to wear a humiliating neckerchief to hide the cut.

What he *could* do was drink, and he did so industriously. He imbibed his wine as if parched and soon was observing the wedding party through an alcoholic haze. Everyone seemed to be having fun, which made his own gloom worse. Even the slaves seemed to be enjoying themselves, except the big one who kept dropping things. "Who's that slave over there, the tall and clumsy one?" he croaked irritably to a merchant named Torus. "The oaf looks like a mule in a pottery shed."

The Briton looked where his seatmate was gesturing. "That's our grand Scotti prince, I'm told. Captured by Falco in recent battle. Odo, I think his name is."

"A prince cleaning food scraps?"

"It was Galba who set the trap for him."

"Ah, yes, Galba. Our premier strategist." Clodius looked across the room. The senior tribune sat in the shadows quiet and alone, sipping little, never looking at the bridal pair, and ignoring attempts at conversation. "Our unconquered warrior. Except when allowing my throat to be cut."

"It was a barbarian who cut you, not the senior tribune. Probably some other hotheaded buck just like you, or that Eiru slave there. All of you out to end life at its beginning, when the real purpose is to enjoy it to its end."

"Yes. Like him." Clodius drained his cup. "Brother in arms to Britlet scum." He reached for a fig, eyeing Valeria morosely, and as his arm extended, he accidentally knocked over the flagon of his seatmate's drink. Before he could right it, beer foamed off a slate table in a white cascade. He looked at it numbly while heads swung to the clatter. Damn them for noticing.

"My opinion of Briton beer!" Clodius shouted.

A Roman laughed. Encouraged, the young tribune reared up and swayed unsteadily, making the assembled guests titter in anticipation. The tribune's scarf caused a whisper of explanation.

"In fact, my opinion to date of bastard Britannia!"

There were hoots and catcalls. "Beer takes you to the same place as wine," insisted an annoyed Torus, watching as a slave girl mopped the mess. "More cheaply and with heartier taste." Several guests applauded, and the merchant signaled for another cup. Odo was pushed forward.

"Really?" Clodius slurred. "Well, may I offer an observation on the matter penned by the emperor Julian when he was stationed in Britannia? I find his wisdom appealing."

"Yes!" shouted the assembly. "Recite the pagan emperor's critique!"

Odo bent down beside Clodius to refill Torus's flagon.

"The title is, 'Of Wine Made from Barley,'" Clodius announced. The other Romans laughed. Their disdain for crude northern drink was well-known.

"Who made you, and from what?" Clodius recited, hoisting his neighbor's refilled cup for display and looking at it as if baffled. *"By the true Bacchus, I know you not."*

There was snickering, a clap, and cries of disagreement. *"The wine smells of nectar, as the poet wrote."* Clodius cautiously took a sniff. *"But this beer, alas, smells of goat!"*

Laughter, and applause. Encouraged, Clodius bowed. Then, impulsively, he tilted the beer goblet and dumped its contents over Odo's head.

The slave went rigid. The laughter faltered. Odo stared straight ahead at nothing, blinking his eyes against the sting.

Clodius looked down at the slave's wet head and smiled

with amusement. "Little Celt! You don't like your nation's drink? Or are you hoping I'll pour you more?"

The slave knew better than to risk an answer.

Clodius waited, daring the man to respond, and then jerked the goblet toward the slave's face, making Odo flinch as he was spattered with the last drops. "I don't think our Scotti prince agrees with Roman taste, comrades. Perhaps he's too good for us."

The room had gone quiet.

Suddenly the slave shook his head, spraying Clodius and Torus with beer.

Clodius exploded with rage. "Damn you!" The tribune flung the goblet, and it banged against Odo's head. The slave staggered.

Now the bullying had gone too far. Falco jumped up. "By the code of Mithras, lie down, Clodius! You're drunk!"

Clodius turned, still swaying. "On the contrary, dear host, I'm not drunk enough. Half of what I've imbibed has leaked out of this Celtic hole in my throat." He pointed to his scarf and laughed at his own joke, a quick bray.

Galba was watching the little drama with intent interest.

"Lie *down*, tribune." Now it was Marcus, his voice flat with warning.

Finally realizing that he'd crossed the line of propriety, Clodius gave the groom a truculent salute and did what he was told. "As you wish." He plopped back onto his couch.

There was a long moment of awkward quiet. Then the pipes and drums started up again, Torus was given a cloth to finish mopping himself, and the buzz of conversation resumed. The merchant moved angrily away from the Roman officer.

Falco came over. "Odo, you're excused for the evening," he said quietly to his slave, who was bleeding from a cut on his forehead. The Scotti gave a curt nod and left. The centurion watched him go and then leaned close to the young patrician. "That's just the kind of foolishness that keeps trouble brewing in this country," he scolded quietly. "You don't have to drink Briton beer, tribune, but don't mock it, either. Or my slaves. Or my household."

"My would-be tutor Galba says we must rule the island by fear," Clodius muttered. "I meant no ill will, but I've been in Britannia little more than a month and am already sick of it."

"And have you asked yourself where Galba is, dolt?"

Clodius looked across the room. The senior tribune's place was empty. "Indeed, where is his sullen face?"

"Galba's as anxious not to call attention to that near-disaster in the forest as you seem anxious to commemorate it. He knows it was mere luck that got Valeria away from those brigands. Now you've reminded everyone else! So Galba told me he was going outdoors to spend this night with his men, organizing a guard of honor to restore his own. Don't think our commander won't notice his contrition."

"Galba? Contrite?"

"He's paying penance for both of you."

The young tribune glanced around, suddenly deflated. Everyone was avoiding his look. "I've paraded my shame, haven't I?" he said gloomily.

"Just give the province a chance to work, Clodius. Give the garrison a chance to come together."

"The soldiers don't like me."

"They don't like you because they're not convinced you like them."

The tribune looked miserable. "I want to *be* them."

"Then act like them. It's the end that counts, young officer."

Clodius stood and swallowed, looking ashamed. "I apologize for my boorishness. I'm drunk, and you're right, I've not earned my opinion of Britannia. I too am going to spend this night in the dark and somehow set things to rights."

"To rights?"

"To somehow, like Galba, reclaim my honor."

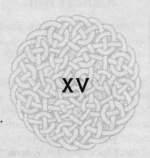

XV

Bride and groom at last came together at feast's end. Marcus rose, tipsy himself by now, and crossed the room to where Valeria lay on her banquet couch, her eyes bright with anticipation. Lucinda, playing the traditional role of protective mother, bent to grasp the young woman's shoulders as if reluctant to let her go. The praefectus, painfully self-conscious at this ritual play, grasped Valeria's hand and pulled as if to abduct her. She sat upright, but Lucinda's arms encircled the young woman as if in protest. The groom seemed momentarily perplexed.

"Grab her, you donkey!" someone yelled. "Surely your sword is stiff enough by now to win victory!"

Valeria couldn't help but think of the firm grasp of the horrid barbarian who'd hauled her off her cart.

"Don't yank her! Scoop her!" another suggested.

Grinning uncomfortably, Marcus bent and put his arms around Valeria's waist and under her knees, hoisting her off the couch as Lucinda's grip obligingly fell away. The crowd roared approval, and Valeria put her arms around her new husband's neck, lifting her face. The praefectus pecked her.

"By the gods, Marcus, she's not your sister!"

"Let's take you home," he whispered. She hugged him tighter.

The chariot in the villa courtyard was garlanded with spring fern at its rim, wild roses twisted around each spoke. Two white horses, their harness punctuated by silver coins and their backs warmed by bright red blankets, waited to pull. A bonfire crackled in one corner, and a dozen cavalrymen sat on their horses in full armor, their lances pointed at the sky. Their ceremonial gilded helmets included a full face mask of Apollo, each golden visage identical to the next. The effect was formal and eerie, black holes marking where their eyes gazed out.

Marcus set his bride's feet on the chariot floor and stepped up beside her, tenderly fastening a long fur cloak of Briton fox across her neck. His composure having returned—now that he was at a distance from his audience and half shielded by the dark—he raised his arm in salute to the wedding guests pouring outside. "My thanks for your blessing!"

"Talassio!" the guests cried in response, a wedding salutation inspired by the name of the Sabine bride that Rome's founder had kidnapped.

"To long union!" some added.

"To a long night!"

"To a long spatha—and a receptive target!"

Valeria flushed. Now she would become a woman.

An officer shouted command. "Turma . . . to the right . . . ho!" It was Galba's voice, his face as invisible behind the mask as his emotions. What must he think about this marriage that sealed his demotion to second? And where was Clodius? Had he fled?

The cavalry escort rode out of the courtyard smartly, lance heads bobbing, and Marcus let the chariot follow at walking pace. Guests tagged behind, each plunging a torch into the bonfire and then holding it aloft to form a chain of dancing flame. They sang drunkenly and called forward to the newlyweds with more ribald advice and jokes. It was three miles to the gate of the fortress, and as the procession traveled, it began to lengthen, stragglers dropping back from wine, age, or the need to relieve themselves. Still, it was a river of fire that crossed the arched stone bridge and entered the village of square-cornered Roman houses that stacked high toward the looming walls. Whitewashed stone gleamed in the night, and watch fires atop the guard towers beckoned. Far up the lane the fortress gate glowed with more torches, a portal of red, flickering light.

There were five hundred men in Marcus's cavalry, and

they'd been turned out on foot for this moment, all wearing the helmets of Apollo and lining both sides of the village lane that led to the gate. Native Britons pressed at their back, anxious to see the beautiful bride of a commander whose fortune affected their own and jostling with each other for the best view. As the chariot passed, the soldiers' lances tilted inward slightly, forming an arbor of ash and iron. Then, as the butt of a decurion's lance came down on the paving stones to mark rhythm, the soldiers cried "Talassio!" in concert, the chant booming from mouths invisible behind their metal masks. The helmets gave the cry an echo, as if issuing from a cave.

Galba's turma of thirty-two cavalry clattered into the fort's central courtyard and again formed a ceremonial line, the chariot rolling up before them. The wedding guests streamed in behind like an exultant mob, torches bobbing. Valeria looked around curiously. The headquarters building was straight ahead, she saw, its grim facade pierced by an entry that led to an inner court and colonnade. To its left was the hospital; to its right her new home, two stories high and aglow with light, slaves dutifully waving colored streamers from its windows. Fir boughs garlanded its eaves, and flower petals were scattered on the paving. Still, there was no mistaking the utilitarian architecture of the military residence: stony, solid, practical, austere. She swallowed. Here was to be her new life.

Marcus jumped from the chariot and lifted his wife down, releasing her waist as if it were hot.

"Kiss the lips of our Venus, Marcus! Kiss so we can enjoy it!"

The fortress commander ignored them.

"He's waiting to kiss more than that inside!"

The couple walked past Galba's solemn patrol to their front door, where Savia waited with a bowl of oil. Valeria dipped her fingers as tradition demanded and anointed the entry, carefully drawing oil along its frame to ensure good fortune. The bride dribbled some drops on the threshold and then, after hesitating, brushed oil on the tip of the carved

stone phallus that jutted to one side of the entrance. The
crowd roared approval.

Marcus opened the door, revealing a shimmering aurora
of candles and lamps, and moved to ceremonially block Valeria's entrance as tradition required. "Tell me your forename, stranger," he commanded, his voice carrying to the
spectators beyond. It was the ritual request.

Women had no forename, and so in accord with the
Roman wedding custom she used his. "Wherever you are
Lucius, there shall I be Lucia," she replied clearly. And now
at last he swept her up again and, arms strong, eyes proud,
carried her over the threshold and into her new life.

Marcus set his bride down. Their new home had a Briton
plank floor, but its interior walls were reassuringly plastered
and painted in the intricate and colorful Roman geometric
manner. Her new husband made no move to take her cloak,
and so Valeria finally unhooked it and gave it to him, letting
him drape it over a stool. Savia and the servants had disappeared, she saw. Marcus looked relieved at the privacy, the
public ordeal over, but still he was uncertain what to do.
"Would you like a tour of my quarters?" He was not accustomed to the pronoun *our*.

"Tomorrow, perhaps." She was trembling slightly. How
handsome her husband looked! But also old and remote and
formal, like a statue. He was a quiet man, she realized, and
would never have the dramatic instincts of a Caesar or the
eloquence of a Cicero. Yet didn't that make him deeper,
more honest, and less vain?

"Of course," he said, as if to apologize. "Would you like
some wine?"

"I'm already heady, and in danger of floating away."

"I need a cup." He led her up a short flight of steps to the
dining room and poured himself one. Flowers had been scattered on the central table, and behind there was a mural of
some epic Britannic battle, legionaries surmounting splin-
tered chariots and Britons cowering at their feet. Shields,
spears, and animal horns decorated the walls, jutting like the
doorway's phallus. "It's a masculine kind of place," he said

apologetically. "My most recent predecessors weren't married. It will change with your things." He pointed at some rusting weaponry. "Those are trophies the Petriana won in combat. My goal is to add my own."

"How long has this house been here?" It was something to say.

"Two hundred years, maybe longer. The ghosts of commander after commander must walk here, in a long scarlet line."

"Ghosts?"

He smiled. "A figure of speech. What I really mean is the tradition of the army. I've inherited that, and now you have, too. The cavalry is the best paid and most highly trained, and needs the quickest and bravest men. None from the softer trades, like weaving or fishing. We look for carpenters, stonecutters, wheelwrights, blacksmiths—"

"I'm tired, Marcus."

He looked concerned. "Would you like to sit?"

"We should go to bed." It was a gentle suggestion.

"Of course."

The wedding chamber was small, as in all Roman houses, to conserve the heat of its occupants. There was a single high window of colored glass, a chest, a small table, and a single chair. Spring apple blossoms had been scattered on their bed, and incense gave the room a sultry smell, but its military plainness couldn't be hidden.

"The slaves have done with it what they could," he said.

The two stood awkwardly. Could they teach each other, as Lucinda had promised? Valeria's expectations of marriage had never really extended beyond the ceremony. Now they had a whole lifetime together! She felt intoxicated and dizzy. Marcus was looking at her in a new, strange way, and she was thrilled and frightened to realize that he finally seemed to desire her. And still he seemed frozen.

The oil lamp sent their shadows dancing.

"You're a very pretty girl, Valeria."

She lifted her chin. "Will you kiss me, Marcus? I've come so far."

He nodded and gently reached out. They kissed more

deeply this time, his beard exhilaratingly rough—so different from the furtive kisses of the boys she'd known in Rome—and his scent of wine and some deeper man-musk earthy and powerful. She shuddered slightly as his powerful arms went around her, drawing her closer, and kissed him ever more hotly, enveloped in the folds of his toga and dimly feeling his body beyond. Married! Everything was different now.

They broke, gasping.

"Ah, Valeria." He studied her face. "I remember when I saw you in your father's atrium in Rome, so young, so exquisite. You conquered me in an instant! Then so wild and ragged in the forest. And now here you are, so soft again, on this hard frontier."

"Now we're here together."

"Yes." He stroked her cheek. "You've given me a chance at glory."

"We'll share that glory, and together we'll make our name."

"You must warn me if I hurt you. You must tell me what you enjoy."

She nodded dumbly. She didn't know what she enjoyed.

He untied the ceremonial knot that held the waist of her gown, revealing the bridal linen shift that the barbarian had rudely fingered, its weave fine enough to reveal the swell of her breasts, the slight curve of her belly, the delta of her secret hair. Then he moved to the oil lamp, dousing it, and it was completely dark. Valeria felt brief panic. She wanted to cry for him to wait, that she wasn't ready, but it was too late for that, wasn't it? Could he hear the hammering of her heart?

"Take off your bridal tunic."

She nodded to indicate that she'd heard and then realized he couldn't see her. "Yes." She took out the last pins, and it fell to the floor. Her body prickled at the cool air.

She could hear the rustle of his own garments being discarded and the creak of the rope webbing of the bed. "Come, lie beside me."

She shuffled forward until her shins felt the edge of the

woolen blankets and stooped, feeling the feather mattress
until she touched his leg. Her hand jerked away.

"It's just me."

Venus, give me strength, she prayed. He already thinks
me an idiot. She crawled forward to lie on the rich mattress
and felt his heat as he came near, his strong hand reaching
to touch her arm and stroke her side. It helped calm her.
"Please, kiss me again."

He did so, tenderly at first and then harder, more anxiously, and slowly moved atop her. He was heavy, and she
could feel this real phallus against her thigh, hard and hot.
She half wanted to touch it and half wanted to push him
away. So she did neither, waiting to see what would happen.
His hands moved over her breasts, and he kissed one of them
too, and then his powerful leg levered apart her thighs.

"I'm frightened," she whispered.

"It will be over quickly."

He was breathing hard, pushing insistently. How could she
ever accommodate such invasion? She wished they could
kiss more first. She clung to his broad back, her fingernails
unconsciously biting. Suddenly, there was sharp pain.

"Oh!" She realized she'd cried out.

Now he was impossibly deep, but instead of feeling worse
it began to feel better, wet and full. She relaxed a bit. Marcus
was moving again, breathing hard, and they rocked as he slid
back and forth. She lay obediently, listening to the creak of the
bed, trying to inventory what she was feeling. It was not so
much good or bad as confusing. . . .

Suddenly he stiffened. Had she done something wrong?
He grunted, a half-cry. Then he collapsed on top of her,
exhaling.

He lay like a dead man, sweaty.

"Marcus, are you all right?"

He hoisted his head. "Give me a son, Valeria."

Then he rolled off her.

She was shaking. "Will you hold me?"

He took her into his arms. So this was what all the fuss
was about! Valeria felt amazed, and a little betrayed. The

bed was wet, her husband keeping his own hips away from hers. She still wondered what he looked like.

"I love you, Marcus," she finally said. Her confidence was returning. She was a woman! She gripped him. "Now I want to learn all about you so I can be a good wife. All your thoughts, all your secrets. And everything about Britannia as well."

He breathed against her. "Why are women so inquisitive?"

"We care about our men."

He was quiet for a while. Then: "And I care for mine. No secrets tonight. Dawn comes early in a fortress, and I have to see to my troops."

"Your soldiers? Can't you give tomorrow to me?"

"There's much to do. That surprise in the forest, for one."

She cuddled closer. "What can you do? They're gone."

"Galba is investigating, and he won't rest. He's a raw provincial, rough as bark, but I'll give this to the man: he's a soldier." Marcus was quiet a moment. "What a near thing that was! What if I'd lost you less than a day from my fort!"

"You saved me! You and Galba together!" She curled deeper into his arms. "How did the barbarians set their trap?"

"They must have spies. But so do we."

She lay there thinking of the green, aqueous forest and the wild men who dropped from trees. So sudden, and yet so planned. She thought of their chieftain's good Latin and his cocky boldness. "Marcus?"

"Hmmm?" He was near sleep.

"I wonder how the painted man knew I wanted to ride a horse."

"Your gladiator, perhaps. He betrayed you."

She nestled even deeper. "Beware the one you trust," she recited.

XVI

The first thing Valeria decided about married life is that she didn't feel very married. She slept until noon, exhausted by the previous day's excitement and the night's apprehension and unsatisfactory fulfillment, and woke in a bed half empty and cold. As he'd warned, her new husband was gone. The house was quiet.

She swung her legs onto the floor of the sleeping chamber and felt its chill on the soles of her feet. The blossoms on their bed had browned and fallen to the floor, her wedding ribbons curled among them. The smell of incense had given way to the musty dampness of wet stone. The one tapestry, she saw now, was nothing but a woven replica of the red-and-yellow shields of the Petriana. She shivered. Perhaps summer would eventually come and bring some warmth to Britannia, but so far the lengthening days of spring carried a memory of winter and the dank breath of the northern sea. She'd have to learn to dress warmly, as the Britons did.

Valeria went to the chamber door and called for Savia. The older woman came eventually but without hurry, sleepy and cross. Hadn't Savia slept in as well? Pushing Valeria aside, the maidservant made a brisk and businesslike inspection of the bed, clucking approvingly at the blood.

"Now you're a woman. When you bear your first child, you'll have consummated your marriage. But you haven't started yet, I hope."

"You know I don't want a child in this fortress. I'll wait until we're home."

"Did you use the vinegar?"

She nodded, embarrassed. "Don't tell Marcus. He wants a son." She was anxious to change the subject. "I thought my husband would stay with me today."

"He's married to his fortress as well as to you."

"But the day after our wedding?" It was the only day in which Roman custom permitted daytime lovemaking. "He could at least spare a morning."

"You've wasted that morning asleep! And he has five hundred men to attend to. It's his duty to concentrate on the Petriana, and yours to concentrate on him."

"I was wondering how long it would take you to remind me of duty, Savia."

"Roman duty won you this house, this post, and this province. You've got an entire lifetime to see your husband, and if you're like any other wife, you'll get sick of him long before it's over. Now stop feeling sorry for yourself and come to the baths."

The house, Valeria saw, was built around a barren central atrium open to the sky, giving the domicile four wings. The courtyard drank in pale Briton sunlight but had no fountain or plantings to soften its stone. The baths at the rear were more encouraging: a privy above the burble of a piped underground stream with its sponge on a stick to wipe oneself, a fountain of clean washing water, a steam room, and hot and cold plunge baths. Mosaics of dolphins and waving kelp were laid with crude but colorful Briton craftsmanship. Valeria descended into the hot with a sigh and the cold with a gasp, climbing out with her pores shut and her skin goose-pimpled. The physical shock had washed away some of her strange gloom. She was married! It was both accomplishment and relief. Surely, now things would begin.

"You look as if you just awakened yourself, Savia," she observed as her maidservant dried her.

"Rather I was awakened at dawn by banging pots and splashing water," the slave replied. "Your new staff rose perversely early to impress you. I got up to scold the cook, Marta, and she said *I* was to answer to *her*. She's a Saxon by birth, as obstinate as any German, and as haughty as an Egyptian. I could barely understand her accent."

"I'll make clear the order of things," Valeria promised. "And you and I must learn to speak and understand Celtic, or they'll be chattering about us like magpies."

"It can be as difficult to command a household staff as a ship of pirates!"

They laughed, having heard a hundred stories to confirm the proverb. Valeria donned her linen underclothes, put on a long tunic, and then pulled over it her woolen stola and fastened it with brooches. How sad to have lost the sea-horse one, a present from her mother. She slipped on socks before her sandals and felt swaddled as a baby. What a sight she'd be in Rome!

"But before I organize the staff, I want to clear my head, perhaps with a tour of our fortress. Can you send for an escort?"

She nibbled on breakfast as she waited.

It did not entirely surprise her that Clodius was the one who eventually answered her summons. He bowed in the atrium. "It seems I've been sent again, my lady."

"Thank the gods," she joked. "My husband has already abandoned me!"

"No man abandons beauty like yours. Rather, he's been abducted by duty. We've received word that there may be news about the ambush. Galba is being sent to get it by helping a barbarian chieftain in a cattle dispute. He's riding with a hundred men."

The realization that Marcus had the power to send a hundred soldiers off into the wilderness gave Valeria a quiet thrill. Here was a tiny flexing of that vast power that reached all the way to Rome. "My husband has been busy, hasn't he?"

"And sends me as poor substitute in his place. I confess I suggested the assignment myself. It's a way for making up for my boorish poetry at your wedding."

"Oh, that's entirely forgiven and forgotten!"

"It's the oaf who is last to forgive his own clumsiness, I'm afraid."

"You were brave to defy those barbarians!"

"Brave, but helpless." He touched his neck. "I allowed us to be surprised."

She didn't contradict him. "Does it hurt?"

"I'll have a scar."

"Which will soon be covered by a Celtic torque of valor!"

They went outside. The flower petals of the night before had been swept from the courtyard, and men and horses were gathering there for the expedition. The cavalry animals weren't fine-boned steeds but shorter, shaggier, more stolid beasts, obviously bred not just for speed but for endurance. They snorted and whinnied, nipping at each other. Each was loaded with equipment for a short expedition: water skin, food bag, holstered throwing lances, cooking utensils, and tarps. The prelude to attack was often a great rattle, as necessary baggage was set aside before a charge.

Soldiers' heads swung to look curiously at the woman who was the reason for this expedition, their expressions not unfriendly. Valeria was novel, beautiful, aristocratic, and newlywed, and this foray was a welcome break from post routine.

Galba was waiting at their head. "Good hunting, senior tribune," Valeria greeted. "I understand you ride to help one of our allies."

"Rufus Braxus would swell like a toad to hear you call him that."

"He's a chieftain?"

"He'll tell you he's a prince of the Novantae tribe, sire of nine sons, keeper of three wives, lord of a timbered hill fort, commander of eighty spears, and blood-bound to five high families. I'll tell you he's farmer, merchant, shepherd, drover, smuggler, cheat, and thief, who uses Roman money to carve a bigger stink-hole than he could by himself. As a result he's loud, ignorant, blasphemous, boastful, vain, sly, and lazy."

"In other words, a Briton," Clodius said.

"Aye, junior tribune, a Briton. A Celt. A barbarian. He helps us with word of the tribes farther north, and then tells them of Roman intentions. He's a border man, as close to an ally as we get in these parts. Now his neighbor, Caldo Twin-Axe, has stolen twenty head. Braxus promises information if we help get them back."

"Is such theft common?" She was fascinated by this glimpse of border politics.

"Braxus no doubt stole the same cows himself the season before. It's their sport."

Decurions reported the men ready; Galba bowed his good-bye and began shouting orders. The line of assembled troopers began to uncoil, making for the barrel arch of the north gate. A legionary standard, cavalry pennants, and dragon-head banners jutted into the air. As the column moved, the open heads of the dragons filled the fabric behind, inflating it, and so the cavalry rode out of the fortress with the bodies of serpents writhing above their helmets.

"They're so imposing," Valeria said.

"Which is why they ride forth," Clodius replied. "To show our power. Come, let's watch from a tower."

The buildings of Petrianis were packed ten feet apart. The junior tribune pointed out the granary, the saddler's shed, and the hospital as they passed. "Good doctoring is the most powerful recruiting tool the army has." Beyond was an armory, noisy with working soldiers. German recruits were hammering dents out of old armor. Syrians were shaping and fletching arrows from aspen, yew, and pine. Numidians were sorting river stones that would be fired from slings or catapults. The armory had a pungent smell of metal shavings, olive oil, and animal fat, used to combat rust.

"Because of the ambush, the post is sharpening preparations," Clodius explained.

She was taken aback by the industry. "I didn't mean to start a war. I fought them off with a brooch pin!" Since he grimaced at this unintentional comparison, she searched for another question. "How did they know we'd be in the forest?"

"Our journey was no secret, and our progress slow. I made a bad choice."

"It was at my insistence, Clodius."

"We shared the mistake."

"Perhaps we've all just had bad luck."

He shook his head. "I think things happen for a reason."

Behind the armory were the stables of the cavalry, and

they decided to pass through inside. The animals snorted and whinnied as the pair walked by the stalls, some begging for a treat, and Valeria's heart quickened. "I'd like to pick one to go riding," she said. "Ride fast again, like in the forest. That white mare, perhaps, with the gray forehead."

"A good eye. See how she's got the chest and legs for speed? Wide nostrils for stamina? And the mane falls to the right."

"Is that important?"

"All Roman soldiers must be right-handed, so their shields are uniformly on the left to maintain formation. A horse's bare neck lets a cavalryman's shield hand rest on its muscles and guide the horse while he fights."

"You sound quite the expert."

"I've read the classic advisories, from Xenophon to Virgil."

"I hear the Celts have women who ride. Women who are warriors!"

"Which makes us the Roman and they the barbarian," he jibed.

There were long heaps of fodder near the fortress wall, the hay roofed with tile for protection against flaming arrows. In one corner was a kiln and clay. Adjacent was a blacksmith shop, next to that a glassworks, and beyond a carpentry woodshed perfumed with wood chips.

"It seems less a fort than a factory," Valeria remarked.

"It has to be, at civilization's end. The army has taught the world. A full legion employs architects, surveyors, plumbers, doctors, stonecutters, glass fitters, coppersmiths, armorers, wagon makers, coopers, and butchers." He grinned. "My dreams of martial glory have been tempered by my duties managing manure."

They mounted to the top of a tower, Clodius guiding her around a wooden ballista and its rack of darts and pointing north. "Out there, Valeria, is the end of the world."

She looked. There was a ditch directly below the wall, pools of rainwater at its bottom. Then a steep slope beyond to a valley, all shrubs and trees chopped away to preserve a clear field of fire. Nor could there be surprise: the view beyond seemed endless, a rolling panorama of moor and wood and fen and ridge and ponded water, as clearly seen as if she were a bird. Wisps of smoke marked a few crude farmsteads. She could still see the line of Galba's cavalry, riding north, lance heads glinting in the sun.

"How did the ambushing Celts ever cross this barrier?"

"That's what Galba hopes to learn from Braxus."

She looked back at the fort and the roofs of the village clustered beyond. Then the river, and beyond that the villa where she'd been married. What a little empire a praefectus governed! She turned to sight along the Wall itself, a bony crest that stretched as far as the eye could see. "Like the back of a dragon."

"A poetic description," Clodius complimented. He was standing quite close, perhaps closer than proper now that she was married, and yet his torso gave her some protection from the breeze and so she was secretly glad of it. He was trim, rather handsome, and solicitous in his eager way. Clodius was like a brother, she told herself, and Marcus still remote, like her . . . father.

She was shamed at the sudden comparison that had come unbidden into her mind.

"It's designed to intimidate as much as block," Clodius went on. "Any barbarian realizes the army that built this bulwark represents a power beyond their imagination."

"We're safe, then."

"Life is never safe. It's the possibility of death that defines life."

"You sound like Galba," she teased. "Are you acquiring his grimness?"

"His realism." He touched his throat.

She turned around, taking it all in. "This fortress is grim like your soldier's philosophy, isn't it? It has the feel of a prison."

"It doesn't lock us in. Only others out."

"So I want to see this wild world of yours, Clodius. I want to go riding!"

He was watching her carefully, trying to mask his attraction. By the gods, if he were Marcus, he wouldn't leave her alone for an instant, let alone the first day of their married life! He was guilty at his fascination, but escorting her was like rubbing a wound, exacerbating it and yet soothing it at the same time. Now he kept his voice carefully flat. "With your husband's permission, perhaps."

"South of the Wall, to be safe." She gave him an impish smile, trying to seduce his support. "A test of your defenses."

"Yes. A test." He swallowed. "And if they do test it, they learn of a wall of a different sort." He took a breath. "Come. The Petriana isn't really about horses. Or stones and mortar."

They descended to the eastern half of the fort. Here were the barracks, long and trim. She could smell wood smoke, baking bread, male sweat, and oil for flesh and weapons. A cat lolled by one doorway, and crude graffiti decorated a whitewashed wall. In another entry the wife of a soldier watched them pass, a newborn suckling her breast.

Soon that might be her, Valeria realized, or at least her hired wet nurse. How unready she felt to have children! Yet it could happen at any time, despite her precautions. Her life had changed overnight. So many changes that she felt, for a curious moment, as if she were looking at herself from outside, assessing her life's new peculiarities from a distance.

Against the eastern wall was a small training ground enclosed with a low wooden palisade. A turma of new recruits was being drilled by a frog-throated decurion who seemed capable of cursing in three languages. The probatios looked tired, confused, and awkward in their armor, their forearms bearing a fresh red welt.

"What happened to their flesh?" Valeria whispered.

"The military tattoo. Officers don't bear them."

"I saw one on Galba."

"Evidence of his humble birth."

"Does it hurt?"

"I suppose, but pain is a soldier's companion. The tattoo discourages desertion and helps identify pulped remains after battle."

It was sword practice, and the drillmaster picked out one of his recruits. "Brutus!" he barked.

The man jerked, clearly unhappy at being singled out.

"Step forward!"

The new soldier hesitantly complied. He looked uncomfortable in his stiff new armor and walked as if weighted. His superior pointed to one of a score of heavily scarred wooden posts that had been inserted into stone holes in the training courtyard. "There stands your enemy! Attack with your sword!"

The man obediently marched forward with heavy oval shield, lifted a blunt-edged Roman gladius, and began hacking at the wood with vigor, his companions laughing good-naturedly at his effort. His blows echoed from the fortress walls like the ring of an ax.

"Now, for cavalry practice the men ride in the meadows outside," Clodius murmured. "It takes a year to make a good horseman and a lifetime to make a good cavalryman. But basic soldiering skills begin here."

As chips flew, the man began to sweat and his strokes to falter. "His training armor and weapons are twice normal weight," Clodius explained.

"Don't give up now, Brutus!" his companions called. "We need more kindling for the barracks!"

Grimacing, the soldier kept swinging, but his assault had turned to dispirited labor. Finally the decurion raised his arm. "Enough, dull-wit!"

The soldier stopped, arms hanging like ropes.

"Tired?"

There was no need to nod.

"No matter, because you were a dead man twenty strokes ago. First, you let your shield arm drift to your left, making a target of your chest and belly. Second, you were chopping high like a barbarian, inviting a sword point into your armpit." He raised his own arm in demonstration and looked at the other recruits. "Forget the gladiatorial nonsense of fancy arm and footwork. This is war, not the arena!" The decurion crouched, sidling forward. "Now, a barbarian looks fearsome with his long overhead stroke, but in the time he takes to swing, a Roman will kill him three times. Why? Because a Roman doesn't stroke, he stabs—from below, like this." The decurion thrust, and the young man recoiled. "You go for the abdomen. You go for the balls. Stab in . . . and up! I don't care if your blue-colored Pict is seven feet tall, he'll squeal and go down. You'll be standing on his great gaping face, smelling his blood and shit, while you do the same trick to his brother. Thrust!" He showed the move again. "That's the Roman way!"

The men laughed.

"I get queasy just listening to it," she whispered.

"Decurions like that made us masters of the world. He's the real Hadrian's Wall."

"Men like Galba." She understood some of the hardness of Galba Brassidias then. Understood his dour nature. Most Romans never met anyone like him, and never knew who kept their lives so placid.

They walked back toward the commander's house. An older soldier was standing near the training stockade with his arms stretched out, a centurion's vinestaff balanced on his wrists. "Galba's discipline," Clodius whispered.

"Galba's world," Valeria murmured. "A man's world. So odd to see no other highborn women within these walls."

"Invite Lady Lucinda for company. Or wives from the other forts."

"I will."

"And don't hesitate to ask for me, as a friend."

"I appreciate that, Clodius."

"I almost let you be captured once. I won't again."

"Tribune!"

They looked ahead. Marcus! Valeria's first instinct was to run, but he looked stern, even unhappy. So she stopped to wait for his approach, earning a brief nod of approval at her circumspection.

"A pleasure to see you again, bride. My apologies for not having more time today."

"Clodius has been showing me your fort."

"An assignment he was sly enough to ask for." He turned to his subordinate. "I wish to talk to you in private, Clodius Albinus. Falco is here."

Clodius looked depressed. "Is it about the banquet?"

"The young tribune has already apologized," Valeria

spoke up. "The wine made him foolish. Please don't be harsh."

"This isn't your issue, wife."

"I'm sure he'll have more kindness for British beer!"

"This has nothing to do with beer, either."

"But what, then? Why bother him further?"

Marcus was annoyed at her persistence. "It's the slave, Odo."

"Odo?" Clodius didn't understand.

"The one you poured beer on."

"What about him?"

"He's been murdered."

XVII

This man-boy Clodius has not impressed me, from every description I've had of him. "You seriously suspected him of murder?"

I put the question to the centurion Falco, owner of the dead slave, unsure if this bizarre detour has anything at all to do with the real mystery I'm trying to unravel.

"Clodius had impressed no one—except, perhaps, Valeria. They were close to the same age and both newcomers. She bewitched him, I think, which made the other men think him an even greater fool. So yes, the rest of us suspected him."

"Tell me how this came about."

"My slave, Odo, was found dead the morning after the wedding, killed by a table knife thrust to the heart. His head was still sticky with the beer that the buffoon had poured on it, and we all knew Clodius was angry at the Celts for marring his throat. Odo was Scotti, a recent capture, and fighter enough that he hadn't entirely learned a slave's humility. The young tribune was drunk, unhappy, and unable to avenge himself. We thought he might have killed in frustration."

"What did Clodius say in his own defense?"

"He said that he was ashamed of what he'd done to the slave at the banquet and had no reason to harm him further. If anything, he argued, Odo should have more resentment toward Clodius than Clodius toward him. Which of course made us think that perhaps Odo had attacked Clodius. The boy had no alibi. He'd left the wedding in disgrace and hadn't been seen the rest of the evening."

I study Falco. He seems a fair but practical man. His decency has a foundation of iron. "You cared for this slave?"

"I valued him at three hundred siliqua."

"So you wanted the culprit punished?"

"I wanted the culprit to pay me for my loss."

"What did Marcus decide?"

"Nothing, as usual." Falco stops, realizing he has finally betrayed something useful. His glance shifts away as he remembers unhappy times.

"The praefectus was an indecisive man," I clarify.

The centurion hesitates, weighing his loyalties, and then remembers how many are dead. *"The praefectus was . . . careful. We learned eventually that he'd made an early blunder as a junior tribune in campaign against brigands in Galatia. Later, he'd been unfairly caught up in the stink from the sexual scandal of a superior. He'd mismanaged a business of his father's. He'd learned caution, and it's but a short step from caution to fear."*

"I'm told he was bookish."

"His library filled two carts. Not at all what we were accustomed to."

"Galba, you mean."

"The senior tribune could be rash, but decisive. The two had different styles."

Different styles. A unit responds to a commander like a team to the rein, and so his personality becomes the personality of his men. Accordingly, it troubles soldiers whenever there's a switch, and it takes them a while to settle under the new hand. If they ever do. *"How well did they work together?"*

"Awkwardly. The first time I saw Galba in the baths I counted twenty-one scars on the front of his body and none on his back. He had a chain or belt of rings—"

"I've heard of this chain."

"Marcus, in contrast, had never seen real battle. It was even more uncomfortable after our commander's marriage to his inquisitive bride."

"The men did not like Valeria, either?"

"They appreciated her beauty, even when it made the garrison restless with longing. But yes, she made us uneasy as well—even Lucinda was taken aback. Valeria roamed the

fort like a decurion. She was curious about the natives and demanded that a kitchen maid teach her and the Roman slave woman the Celtic tongue. She absorbed it like a child, and asked about things that are no business of women."

"What things?"

"Warfare. The mood of the men. The organization of the Petriana. Firing a forge, straightening an arrow shaft, the sicknesses of soldiers. Her curiosity was boundless. Marcus couldn't silence her. He was embarrassed but confused by her, I think, and the men didn't like it. It was no secret that she was the reason for Marcus's command."

"And Galba?"

"The quieter he was about his resentment, the plainer his frustration. He was the one man who knew how the fort worked, and everyone looked to him for instruction and direction. Even Marcus. Yet the Roman made a point of countermanding the Thracian to establish his own authority. We were a cavalry with two heads."

I frown, recognizing the situation from problems I have investigated before. There is nothing more fatal than disunity of command. "The duke did nothing?"

"He was stationed at Eburacum, and it took time for the situation to reach his ears. Then he was distracted by events on the Continent."

He means the succession, which I will get to in my own good time. I want to get to the heart of matters before it. "Did these difficulties affect the Petriana as a whole?"

Falco ponders. I am asking him not about individuals but about the performance of his unit, of the eagle standard to which all good soldiers give their ultimate loyalty.

"The strain made us too eager," he suggests. *"None of us were happy with the situation, and all thirsted for change. There's opportunity in conflict. Some men fall in battle, but others rise. Careers demand a certain amount of chaos."*

Chaos. I've spent my own career trying to prevent what ambitious men long for. Men seed their own disasters. "All this was in the background when you discussed the murder of Odo?"

"Yes. For Galba the murder was an opportunity."

"To use against Clodius?"

He smiles thinly. "Brassidias thought further ahead than that. He'd recovered the cattle of Braxus and, as a reward, took information from a Celtic spy—a man named Caratacus."

"Caratacus!" That is the name of a Briton rebel from the earliest days of the Roman occupation. He was betrayed by his own people, taken to Rome in chains, and glibly talked his way out of his own execution.

"Your reaction was Marcus's own. The name has undoubted power, which is probably why the rogue chose it. It was an alias for a rather mysterious figure with experience in the empire. A deserter, a disowned aristocrat, an escaped felon—we weren't sure which. He'd set himself up as a chief in the north and sat in the highest councils of the Picts and Attacotti. It was he who told us the druids were rising again."

"The druids?"

"Wise men and magicians of the Celts. They've always urged resistance to Roman occupation. We annihilated them in the initial conquest, but never entirely suppressed them in the north. We feared their reappearance."

"Reappearance where?"

"The oak is their sacred tree. There was a grove well north of the Wall where they were supposed to be secretly gathering."

"So Galba urged the attack on the grove that started all this trouble?"

"Galba was too clever to urge anything. He set the bait for Marcus and Clodius."

"How?"

"This Caratacus said the druids were behind the attempted abduction of Valeria. When Marcus asked why, Galba explained that the priests might be bringing back human sacrifice. In olden days they'd put victims into gigantic figures made of wicker and set fire to the effigies, forecasting the fortune of battle by the writhing of the victims."

I grimace. "By the gods!"

"Galba told this, waited, and let young Clodius propose the attack."

"But how could he know Clodius would do that?"

"It all went back to the murder of Odo. Galba had already argued that if we couldn't solve this mystery, we'd simply eliminate it by ridding ourselves of Clodius. He proposed we place the young tribune with another legion. While pretending this was an act of charity, he knew it would cripple the boy's career. No one cares about a dead slave, of course, but they do care about a Roman who can't hold his emotions in check. Who can't hold his wine, or keep from spilling beer. Clodius would have left the Petriana not so much with the stain of failure, from which any good Roman can recover, but with the stain of losing self-control, from which recovery is impossible. Marcus wouldn't agree."

"He was fond of the young tribune?"

"Hardly. The boy was a boob, in Britannia for a year's seasoning. The rumor was that his new wife interceded on Clodius's behalf."

"You believe that?"

"Who knows? Certainly the whelp hung around her like a puppy."

"A puppy, or a tomcat?"

Falco laughs at my joke, which is not meant as a joke.

"So Galba proposed Clodius be transferred. What did Clodius say?"

"He was furious, of course. He disliked the Petriana cavalry until faced with the possibility of leaving it. Yet Galba wasn't so much making an enemy as setting Clodius up to make the suggestion."

"Of attacking the grove. Of avenging Valeria's ambush."

"You have to understand that Clodius represented everything that Galba resented: birth rank, preferment, arrogance, snobbery, incompetence, and even a measure of charm. The young tribune was actually somewhat likable in his eagerness, and when he wasn't drunk, he had manners. Even wit. Galba was forever serious because he couldn't forget his own humble beginnings, and he hated himself for it."

"He wanted to pick a fight?"

"They both knew that Galba would win such a fight so

easily that it was almost meaningless. Galba didn't want Clodius's life, he wanted his pride. He wanted to push Clodius, and through him Marcus, into failure. Make Galba the rescuer of success."

"By getting Clodius to propose the attack. An attack that was dangerous."

"Risky. Action that might stamp out rebellion can also ignite it. We were trusting the word of one rogue, Caratacus. Galba said he was willing to lead the attack, but he wanted the order in writing. This irritated Marcus, who felt the senior tribune was failing to support him. So he decided to lead the strike himself, with Clodius."

"Which Galba intended all along."

"He'd gotten the result he wanted."

"To force a battle?"

Falco smiles thinly. "To be alone with the bride of Marcus Flavius."

XVIII

It was near dawn, time to strike. The grove of the druids was in a fog-shrouded hollow, the tops of the great oaks emergent islands in a gray sea. What secrets were hidden there? There was no sign of human movement. The guide who'd brought them here, a sour Celt of evasive manner, had taken their gold and slipped away in the night. Now a single wisp of smoke rose above the wood.

Marcus would look like a fool if there were no priests in the trees.

There'd been liberating joy when he began this expedition. He'd lain with Valeria the evening before his departure, anxious to test her fertility by seeding a child. He'd enjoyed their intimacy but didn't linger, as brisk and forthright in conjugal duty as in reviewing unit lists or a tally of provisions. Valeria had wanted more, like any woman, so he'd held her for as long as he could spare and then left to sleep alone so he could rise without disturbing her. It was so strange to be married! He wasn't used to lying all night with another person or having them constantly about, wanting to chat about everything and nothing. The girl asked a thousand questions, offered opinions he'd never asked for, and was even learning the barbarian tongue from the household slaves, which he considered undignified. Sometimes she'd even ask what he was thinking!

So it was a relief to don bright armor and gallop with his men. He'd ordered in Rome a lorica of the Eastern kind, each scale shaped and veined like a leaf and faced in gold, giving an effect far bolder and more resplendent than the gray and oily chain mail worn by men like Galba. Yes, it was ostentatious, calling attention to his wealth, but Marcus couldn't resist its splendor. It marked him as the commander! He'd dressed without his slaves, his armor over padded tunic, his belt and baldric holding sword and dagger, and his greaves strapped onto the banded leggings so necessary in this cold place. His high-crested helmet forced him to duck through the doorway as he emerged beneath the last stars to joke roughly with his centurions. When the assembly was ready, he'd led the way out the northern gate to a pink flush of dawn, riding hard through a long day and longer night to take the druids by surprise—and feeling better for it, despite the ache in his muscles. How freeing a campaign was! All the tedium and minutia of lists and logistics, petty rivalries and inadequate budgets, nagging repairs and missing equipment, could be momentarily left behind. In the field he was the spearhead of a military establishment that reached all the way to Rome. He was the bearer of tradition dating back a thousand years. A million Romans had marched and died before him, and so when he was tight in the saddle, sword slapping his thigh, reins gripped in gloved hands, Homer's muscles twitching beneath his own, the air fresh and the horizon beckoning . . . then he was brother to them all!

But now the long hours were catching up to him. The fog increased his doubt.

"We're sure this grove is the root of our troubles?" he asked the centurion Longinus, who lay on the crest of the ridge next to him.

"So our spy said. We're never sure of anything in life, praefectus."

"I don't want to attack the wrong people."

"Right and wrong aren't easily sorted north of the Wall. The tribesman who befriends you one day will slit your throat the next, and the tribe that pledges allegiance in summer will attack in winter. It's all blood feud, cattle raid, and magic to them. If druids are there, though, they're Rome's enemies: enemies for all time. They hate and fear us because we rob them of power."

"I know all this. I just want to be certain."

"Certainty is for the dead." The centurion was impatient. None of the soldiers liked following a man who was indecisive. It created fear.

"I read they can foretell the future," Marcus remarked. "When he was just a soldier in the ranks, Diocletian once tried to shortchange a barmaid, and a druidess in the tavern chided him for being cheap. He joked that if he ever became emperor, he'd be more generous, and she scolded him for his jest and predicted he *would* become emperor—but only after he'd slain a boar."

"So he went on a hunt?" Longinus had never heard this story.

"He forgot the prediction. But before he assumed the purple, he had to kill the prefect of the Praetorian Guard. The man's name was Aper: the boar."

Longinus laughed. "Maybe she was just lucky. If your druids are really so prescient, we'd see them running from the trees!"

So Marcus rolled away from the edge of the ridge and stood straight, a glittering, vengeful angel. As always, early morning in Britannia was crisp, the May grass high and green, the trees exploding with leaves. Everything was wet and silvered with dew. The cavalry had left their lances crisscrossed in the grass because they'd be useless in the trees, and they created a Euclidian geometry on the hill. It seemed a day for poetry, not war. But if Marcus were to prevail in his ambitions, he must prove himself on the Wall, and to do so would require action like today's, delivering a message that was clear and unmistakable. Here he would avenge the insult to his bride. Here he would prove himself to Galba Brassidias. To his father. To his uncles. To his young wife.

Would Clodius do his part?

"Let the boy command one wing," Galba had privately advised. "He'll either win or be killed, and solve the problem either way."

It was the kind of brutal judgment the senior tribune seemed to make with ease. There seemed no philosophy to Galba, no hesitation, no remorse. No depth, no complexity.

Yet the man exercised an influence over the soldiers that Marcus envied.

The praefectus waved, and they mounted, the horses snorting at this prospect of action, the rasping of drawn swords giving the praefectus a chill like fingernails drawn across a slate tablet. The automatic obedience to his orders still surprised him. No wonder Galba loved it! Longinus had suggested penetrating the grove on foot, given the difficulty cavalry had in dense forest, but Marcus was expecting a rout and a chase. Burdened by heavier armor, the army had long learned how useful the horse was in chasing down barbarians. The enemy, in turn, had learned the wisdom of skulking in forest or rock fields, where a cavalry charge couldn't overrun them. So be it: the druids would simply be either herded onto open ground, or trapped in their grove. Woods could be threaded. The Petriana trained weekly on negotiating thick ground.

"Signal to the other wing," he ordered. "Set the trap."

A pennant waved from the crest of their hill and got its answer from the opposite side of the vale. A signaler pressed his lips to the long lituus horn, using his free hand on the back of his head to push his lips against the metal with the necessary force, blowing with cheeks inflated. Its call echoed across the valley, low and warning, and birds flew up from the trees. Then they started down the hill, their rumble fracturing the morning's quiet. It was a slide of dun and silver, a jingling half-moon of men closing around the grove of oak, and as they thundered down the hill the sun broke from the horizon and lit the top of the mist with golden fire, like a promise of discovery. From within the forest another horn sounded, low and warning.

The Celts! The barbarians must be there as promised.

The Romans crashed through the edge of the wood and slowed, the trees dividing them like a sieve. Men lost sight of all but their closest comrades as they walked their mounts through the forest, pushing toward its center. Under the canopy it was still gray and foggy, the trees like ghosts. Mounts awkwardly skidded into gullies thick with the previous year's leaves and scrambled up muddy banks. As they penetrated, the cavalrymen began to lose any sense of direction, simply urging their horses forward in line with the sound of their comrades, wending this way and that on faint game trails—and indeed, their intention was to flush human game. They tensed and waited for a cry, an arrow, or the crack of branches signaling attack from above, but none came. The forest held its breath.

Marcus pulled up a moment to study the trees, his helmet heavy on his forehead. The oaks were huge, their limbs twisted as if in arthritic misery, their girth greater than the columns of Rome. They seemed so old as to be immune from time. There was power in this wood, and it fed barbarian boldness.

The trees themselves were his enemy.

From his right there was a shout and scream, cut short. A kill! He gripped his own sword tighter, but no challenge came. The wood ahead remained empty. He glanced to each side, his men cursing at the slapping branches and insulting each other as mounts stumbled. It was reassuring to hear the obscenities.

Suddenly a fugitive broke like a startled quail and darted away, a decurion whooping and galloping in pursuit. The quarry was agile, but the chase was short: a weaving horse, a stumbling Celt, and then the Roman running the barbarian into a tree, leaving his sword to pin the fugitive's torso so violently that its handle quivered from the impact. The man thrashed like a fish for a moment and then hung still. He was gray-haired and robed, Marcus saw. A druid? The decurion trotted back and dismounted to wrest free his weapon, and the body fell to the forest floor. Then the Roman wiped his blade and remounted.

They pressed on.

The cavalry reached a ditch, broad and old, its bottom black water. It curved left and right, appearing to make a huge circle around the center of the forest.

"Sacred water, praefectus," Longinus said. "Look, a dike."

On the far side of the ditch was an earthen berm that also formed a circle. If the Celts were going to resist, it would surely be here, at the boundary of their holiest trees. But no, there were no defenders. There was no one at all. The horsemen splashed through the still water and rode easily up and over the grassy earth of the inner ring. Their rank tightened.

The oaks within this circle were even more ancient and mammoth, their trunks as thick as a village hut and their roots writhing across the ground like a nest of snakes. In crooks and hollows were wooden and stone and clay images, crude and grotesque.

"Who are they?" Marcus murmured to Longinus.

"Celtic gods. There's Badb the crow and Cernunnos of the horns." They rode slowly on, the man pointing. "Blood-drenched Esus. Thunderous Taranis. Flowing-maned Epona. That one is the great Queen Morrigan, of war and horse and fertility. These are all gods from the beginning of time."

There were hanging garlands of fresh and dried fruit, necklaces of bone, and concoctions of shell and wood and tin that tinkled in the slight breeze. A rack of antlers was tied to one limb, the horns of a bull to another. Shafts of sunlight were beginning to shine through the boughs now, burning the mist, and beyond the huge trees was a grass meadow studded with standing stones. The monoliths shone with morning dew.

Marcus's skin prickled. He felt he was being watched by something white, and so he urged his horse forward to look more closely. The object he had sensed was nestled in the dead and hollow heart of an ancient tree, gleaming as if rubbed and staring at him with twin pools of permanent night. He swallowed. A human skull.

"Who dares violate the sacred grove of Dagda?" a high voice now challenged in Latin.

The praefectus yanked to swing his horse's head around and walked it to the clearing. A frail figure was waiting amid the standing stones, thin and longhaired and leaning on a dark wooden staff topped with a carving of a raven. The druid was unarmed and wearing a white robe, as slight and insubstantial as a dried leaf, and showing no fear at the enveloping hedge of Roman cavalry, huge and hulking in their mail and helmets, swords gleaming at rest on the front two horns of their saddles. Marcus slowly recognized that the challenger was actually a woman, a priestess, who looked as old as the trees she tended. "Who commits murder in the sacred wood?" she called thinly.

Her head was oddly tilted as she spoke, as if blind.

"Not murder, but war," Marcus replied, raising his voice so his men could hear. "I am Lucius Marcus Flavius of the Petriana cavalry, hunting for bandits who ambushed my bride. We've word that their orders came from this grove."

"We know nothing of this ambush, Roman."

"We've word that it's the work of the druids."

"That word is false. Go back where you belong."

"This *is* where I belong, witch!" Even as he said it, he didn't believe it. The mist seemed to swallow his words.

She pointed south. "You know better than I that Rome ends at your wall. It was your soldiers who drew that line across the earth, not us."

"And your followers who violated that line, according to spies among your own people." Where were the rest of the Celts? He could sense them, waiting and unseen, but even as he twisted to see, he could find no one. "Give up the trespassers, and we'll leave."

"You know there's no trespassers but you," she insisted. "Can't you feel it?" She paused to let them hear the silence, oppressive and ominous. His men shifted nervously. Those who were Christians crossed themselves. "In any event a man's life is not mine to give, nor yours to take. The people of the oak have souls as free as wolves and elusive as the wind. They belong to the trees, rocks, and water of this island."

Marcus was becoming impatient. Yes, they belonged to the land, and that was precisely the problem; under proper civilization, land belonged to people. "If you answer to a tree, then that tree will come down," he proclaimed. "If you commit crimes for a rock, then the rock must be shattered. If you sacrifice to water, then that water must be drained." He turned to a decurion and pointed to the oak with the skull. "Chop that one down unless she gives us what we came for. Burn it, and the trinkets that hang on it."

The soldier nodded and jumped off his horse, beckoning

several men to follow. They untied axes that had been secured to their saddles and advanced to the tree.

"You're marking your own doom, Roman!"

He ignored her. "Smash the skull first. I don't like it looking at me."

One of the Roman troopers swung. There was a sharp crack as bone shattered into a spray of splinters. The skull's lower jaw dropped as if in surprise.

"That's what I think of your gods, witch! They've no power against Rome!"

She raised her staff.

There was a shriek, and Marcus realized it had come from one of his men. He turned and saw that the soldier had an arrow jutting from his back shoulder, punched through his mail. Blood was welling from its shaft. Then there was a buzz in the air, like fat sizzling on a barracks skillet, and a rock banged against the head of a second man, taking his helmet off. His horse neighed as its rider lurched sideways, his face broken and his nose spraying blood.

"Barbarians!" his men cried. "Ambush!"

The Celts came from ahead and behind, darting through the standing stones and surging over the encircling embankment. Unable to withstand a Roman charge, they ran crouched to get at the cavalry from underneath. They fired arrows and slung stones and flung spears, without armor and without shields: half naked, painted, and howling. Where had they come from? They were wild as animals and desperate as gladiators, swinging swords and so heedless of their own danger that for a moment it seemed the trapping Romans had become trapped.

Yet even as Marcus and the Roman horse wheeled and sidestepped awkwardly against them, swords high and hooves thrashing, another lituus sounded.

This was the battle he'd craved. And Clodius and Falco were coming.

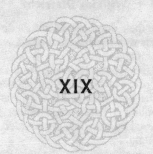

XIX

There was a wild barbarian rush, and then Marcus's men and their attackers swirled together in a clash of spear and sword, locked in fierce struggle. Despite their surprise, the Romans had the advantage of height, horses, and armor. They kicked to override the Celts and chopped down at them. Agile barbarians in turn ducked under the mounts and stabbed upward, or danced around tree trunks, using them as shields. As wounded horses went down, their stunned riders were hauled off their saddles and hacked without mercy. Hooves in turn kicked and trampled the barbarians.

A rock buzzed by Marcus's ear, exciting him and hitting nothing, and then he leaned and swung, the edge of his sword striking an attacker between shoulder and neck and the shock of the strike felt up to Marcus's elbow. The Celt grunted and fell, Homer dancing across him, and Marcus's spatha was finally bloody. The praefectus looked wildly around for another target, yanking his reins to haul the mount around. An arrow thumped and quivered in a tree just two feet from his head. His heart hammered.

A Celt cried out "Marroo!"—"Kill!"

It was another druid, Marcus saw, this one a younger and taller male, standing on the dike and directing barbarian fire at the praefectus, or *dubgall*: invader. Marcus ducked as another arrow whizzed by.

"Get their priest!" the Roman roared in reply. Here was the source of attack, he guessed, a wizard of war. Destroy their leadership, and the barbarians would submit. The druids thought they could win in their grove of oak, but their magic would be their doom. At Marcus's direction troopers began to cut their way toward the druid. Could they capture and interrogate him?

"Kalin!" As the Romans closed, someone pulled from behind, and the priest abruptly vanished, even as more Celts emerged from the trees. One rammed a spear into the breast of a horse, toppling it backward. Another had his unprotected skull cleaved by a spatha, the bearded face exploding in a spray of blood.

Had Marcus's contingent been the only Romans, it would have been a near and desperate fight, the numbers nearly equal. But even as the combat intensified, there was another Roman horn and a great approaching rumble like the swell of an earthquake. The strategy had been to push the Celts through the wood and into Clodius's waiting contingent on the other side of the forest, but the youth, hearing sounds of battle, decided not to wait. The rest of the Roman expedition had plunged through the far side of the grove and now burst across the clearing and charged into battle, surprising the barbarians as the Romans had been surprised.

Now the cavalry outnumbered the enemy two to one.

Young Clodius rode at their head, taut and anxious as a bird, his sword raised high and vengeance in his heart. Celts were trampled under, screaming defiance as they died. The junior tribune got one, slashing at his back, and narrowly avoided the spear thrust of another. Then he spotted a new target and pursued. "A wiiiiiitch!"

The blind druidess was groping her way through the standing stones with hand and staff. A big bearded warrior jumped from behind a stone to block Clodius's gallop, but the Roman expertly swerved and swung and clipped the barbarian on his chin, lifting off half his face. Even as the man's great sword spun harmlessly into the air and his body staggered, the junior tribune was on top of the crone, chopping her down like straw and then wheeling to make sure. His horse pranced as he stabbed down once, twice. Then he charged back, his blade red, his face flush. "Revenge, Marcus! Revenge for my throat!"

The distraction was almost fatal. There was a grunt that

made the praefectus instinctively duck, and a spear sailed over his head. He belatedly tried to pull his mount around to meet the man coming from behind, and then Clodius's excited horse spilled into them both and the Celt was knocked backward in a tangle of hooves, his bones cracking under the trampling. The young tribune swung at this barbarian too, viciously, and stove his head in.

"They're running!"

The surviving barbarians were dashing away into the trees, the Romans struggling to control their plunging horses and give pursuit. One Celt had pinioned a trooper to the forest floor with the man's own spatha, the soldier screaming and kicking under the press of the blade until his commander charged by and took off the assailant's head with a single swing. It bounced across the forest floor like an errant ball, picking up a coating of leaves and dirt, and came to rest with a vacant expression.

The melee was spreading out, the pursuit difficult in the tangle of trees. Marcus reined up at a cluster of men. A circle of Romans had formed around an oak, trapping a defiant Celt like dogs around a bear. Now the wounded chieftain had tied himself upright to the oak, a rope around his chest, and was taunting them with curses in thick Latin. "Come match swords with Urthin, Roman dogs! Come perish with me!"

The Romans slashed at him like a pack of wolves, but he parried the Romans again and again, his sword stinging as he lashed out. "Watch while I die on my feet, not my knees, legion scum! Come, are you afraid of an old man?" One Roman wanted to hurl a spear and another to club and enslave the defiant Celt, but a decurion stayed both and stepped forward to fence, slashing expertly and silently to open up wounds and drain the man of his defiance. Soon the bleeding barbarian was leaning against his rope and heaving for breath, his strength leaking away with his blood. "I bleed, but you piss, Romans," he gasped. "You piss in fear of Urthin." Then his eyes began to glaze. The Roman stabbed him a final time, and it was over.

The soldiers ran on, whooping in the hunt. Marcus didn't

follow, staring at the body hanging against the rough bark. Why hadn't the Celt surrendered? What kind of people tied themselves upright? Marcus looked at the great shaggy body with a sudden foreboding. No wonder Hadrian had built his long, rocky wall.

The Romans, meanwhile, were shouting triumph. Dead and wounded Britons littered the grove. The praefectus trotted among them, peering down. Several were women, he saw, as frenzied in their assault as the men. What barbarism!

The cavalrymen silenced any who still groaned, making methodical stabs.

Finally, all was still.

"It was a trap, Marcus!" Clodius gasped, his sword wet and his eyes bright. The boy was trembling with release. "The spy was right but wrong, too!"

"A trap we turned on them. Form up your men, junior tribune."

A circular line of horsemen was organized facing outward. A trooper next to Marcus grinned and pointed at his commander's bloody sword. "You've lost your virginity this day, praefectus."

"It seems so." The rough compliment pleased him. Blood spattered his clothing, there was a roaring in his ears, and his muscles quivered from tension. He was cold from sweat and hot at the same time, and above all exultantly alive. "Forward! Steady advance!"

Like an expanding ring from a stone thrown in a pond, the Romans rode up and over the dike, across the watery ditch, and into the surrounding trees, hunting for survivors. Where were the rest who'd attacked them? The Celts were once more as elusive as smoke. How did they disappear so quickly? How did they run so fast?

After a few hundred paces Marcus put his arm up and the line of horses halted, the animals blowing. Then he sat a moment, considering what to do. Longinus rode up. "Why are we hesitating?"

"Where did they come from, centurion? Not behind the ridge, or we'd have seen them when we rode in. How did they get around us?"

"They're animals. They don't move like we do."

"No, we've missed something. They came too quickly and vanished too easily." Marcus made a decision. "Dismount!" The command echoed up and down the line. "Search the ground back toward the dike. Carefully!"

The troopers were reluctant to walk, feeling more vulnerable on foot, but did as they were told. They began leading their horses back toward the central grove, scuffing at the carpet of old leaves. Suddenly a man stumbled, his ankle caught, and Marcus gave his reins to a decurion. "Probe with your sword," he ordered.

The soldier's spatha sank into the earth, sawing at air. "It's a hole."

The Romans knelt, throwing aside a leaf-covered wicker frame concealing a tunnel. Tree roots jutted from the soil, and its bottom was utterly dark.

"That's where they came from, and maybe where they fled," Marcus said.

The soldier made the sign of the cross. "Like demons. Devils."

"Or worms," Longinus growled.

"How can we get at them?"

"Maybe we could use fire. Smoke them out."

Marcus shook his head. "It's almost certainly a burrow with more than one entrance. Besides, we've killed enough. The real danger isn't surviving Britlets but the grove itself. This is the source of their boldness. If we destroy it, they'll lose courage."

"Destroy how?" asked the soldier.

Marcus looked up at the dark canopy. "By burning. Not these holes but the entire forest. Longinus, bring the men back inside the dike. Half on watch in case they attack again. The other half I want destroying this place. The trees chopped down, the stones uprooted, the dike leveled. We'll switch the teams every hour. I want this grove obliterated. Do you understand?"

"If we start to do that, they may crawl out and attack again."

"So much the better." Their praefectus had a new crispness. "We'll beat them again."

There was no attack, however. The surviving barbarians either stayed hidden in their dark tunnels or crept out of the forest. The only sound was the ring of axes and the crash of trees. The largest and oldest were like iron, so the officers ordered their bark girdled and dry brushwood heaped around their bases. The forty enemy bodies were layered with more wood to form a pyre, their witch hurled onto its top.

The five Roman dead, were wrapped in their cloaks and slung over their horses for transport back to the fort. Another dozen Romans were wounded.

The troopers dug to topple the standing stones but soon gave up. Their rock roots seemed endless, extending to the bottom of the earth, so they contented themselves with urinating on the monoliths and scrawling obscenities. The encircling mound was leveled in several places, but as the day went on and the scale of the work became apparent, Marcus ordered a halt. Nobody wanted to spend a night in the forest.

When the sun dipped below the valley ridge and the sky flushed red, the praefectus ordered the fires lit. "Junior tribune, it's your honor. You've proved yourself this day."

Clodius nodded tiredly, took a dry branch for a torch, and walked to the pyre of barbarian dead. Before he lit, he paused to examine the druidess he'd killed, and after studying her withered face he turned away with a troubled look before finally thrusting the torch home. The funeral construction began to burn, its inky smoke roiling into the sky. The soldiers held their noses and backed away.

Felled trees were lit, and then the mighty standing oaks. Fire licked at their feet, and then, as the branches dried, the blaze leaped into the crown and the sacred trees exploded, their blackening limbs looking like the outstretched arms of crucified criminals. The heat grew so intense that the Romans had to retreat to the half-ruined dike. Smoke and sparks wafted over their heads into the main forest beyond and started new fires. The air danced and became choking.

"We'd better leave," Clodius said. He'd taken a neck torque from a warrior he'd killed, wiping it clean and putting it on to cover the scar on his own throat. Despite this trophy he was subdued.

The praefectus nodded. "Yes. We've done what we came for."

The Romans rode out of the burning forest and up to the grassy ridge beyond, pausing at its crest. It was dusk now, the first stars coming out, and the glowing pillar of smoke rose into a cobalt sky as a warning to all the tribes of Caledonia. Here was the price for threatening a bride of Rome! The central part of the grove throbbed red as a furnace, its standing stones like blackened teeth in a mouth of coals.

"You thirsted for revenge, Clodius, and now you've had it," Marcus said. "Does it salve your wound?"

The youth touched his neck. "It's not that I feel better, it's that I finally feel nothing." He hesitated.

"Nothing?"

"The witch. I don't feel proud riding down an old woman."

"You faced brave warriors as well. She was the ant queen behind them."

"Perhaps." He watched plumes of sparks fountain into the night sky. "When I went to light the fire, I had a shock of recognition."

"What do you mean?"

"I'd seen that face before, I think. Seen *her* before. In Londinium, on the steps of the governor's palace. She was a blind old fortune-teller."

"Fortune-teller!"

"She made a forecast that disturbed Valeria. I can't remember what it was."

"And you as well?"

"She said I might not live long enough to justify a coin."

"Surely you're mistaken. A beggar seer all the way up here?"

"It makes no sense, but I could swear it was her."

Marcus put his hand on the boy's shoulder. "Memory plays tricks when we're exhausted. Be proud of the duty you've done this day. Rome will read of your courage!"

"Killing isn't what I expected, praefectus. It leaves a taste like copper."

"Then let's go home to wine."

They rode southward in a long, weaving line, the Romans wrung out. Gray cloud ran across the stars.

Falco brought his horse up alongside his commander's in quiet companionship. They rode in silence for a time, the veteran centurion watching Marcus carefully. Finally he spoke. "You're not smiling, praefectus."

Marcus turned to look again at the glow behind them. "No philosopher can be happy about such destruction, centurion. The praefectus in me ordered it, the husband in me desired it, and the soldier in me accomplished it, but the poet in me regrets it."

"And the Celts?"

"They know they brought this on themselves. I feel regret, but not guilt."

"Which is my feeling as well."

Marcus looked down the long rank of tired cavalry. "And there we have young Clodius, blooded and satiated, proving himself a Petriana but still accused of murdering Odo. What should we do about that?"

Falco watched the new hardness in his commander's face, realizing what his answer was supposed to be. "Does it really matter? The man was a slave, praefectus."

"It matters to his owner."

The centurion bowed his head. "Who can afford the loss."

"And his commander can afford to reimburse him."

"Thank you, praefectus. I'll let the issue drop. I only mention that the killing still matters to the Britons we rule. They want to see Roman justice."

Marcus pointed back toward the burning valley. "Then let them come here."

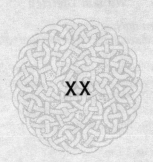

XX

The kitchen slave Marta is prettier than the vague description I had from Savia. I should not be surprised by this disparity: the two women were rival powers in a single household and looked at each other with competitive eyes. Marta has none of the refinement of a free Roman woman, of course, but she's blond and buxom and has an unusually trim waist and fine hip for a cook, with blue eyes and generous mouth and a look adventurous enough to awaken any number of appetites—including mine. In other words, I suspect she made her way by more than merely cooking, and thus has old jealousies that might be put to use for my report.

She remained in the fortress household during the attack on the grove by Marcus and Clodius, so I am curious what she saw during that time. Curious whether there was more to this Galba, who stayed behind, than mere ambition.

Marta steps into my interrogation room as if onstage, conscious of her looks. She is a slave, Saxon, and thus as coarse as she is proud, but she's also used to drawing the glance of her betters. Slaves, owning nothing, fall back on wit, muscle, and beauty. Accordingly, I keep my gaze disciplined while I explain my purpose. Then:

"I understand you served in the household of Lucius Marcus Flavius, praefectus and commander of the Petriana cavalry?"

"I did. As I serve his successor today, Julius Trevillus."

Another survivor, I think. Armies march, empires topple, and slaves serenely persist. "You were the cook?"

"I commanded the house staff."

"Except for the maidservant of lady Valeria, the slave Savia."

Marta shrugs in dislike, saying nothing. She's wearing a simple wool work-stola fastened by a copper brooch in such a way as to give a glimpse of her breasts and the valley between. It makes me wonder which lover gave her the brooch.

"You were satisfied working for the praefectus and his lady?"

"They did me no harm."

"What was their relationship?"

She looks at me as if I'm simple. *"Married."*

"Yes, of course, but how close were they? As people? As man and woman?"

She laughs. *"They were married! Familiar but formal, like any highborn couple. Stiff as statues, that's what aristocrats are. Cold as marble. The Romans work at it. Marcus was decent enough but more scholar than soldier, dull as a scroll."*

I take this metaphor as evidence she's illiterate. *"He wasn't interested in love?"*

"What do you mean by love?" Her smile is a little wicked. *"His sword wasn't just for her scabbard, if that's what you're getting at. A praefectus is a busy man, but he's still a man. Like you."*

"So you lay with him." I know how common this is.

"Like any master, he sampled his property. But it was for relief as much as pleasure, if you understand the difference."

I nod, gloomily conceding that Marta too knows the difference, and knows entirely too much about those she serves. A slave is the most complicated of belongings. Owned and yet owning, subservient and yet vital. Many are mirrors of their masters, as vain or clever or base or indifferent as the Romans who bought them. They know us intimately, learn our weaknesses, and flatter, cajole, and abide. In ancient days Oriental slaves died with their owners, and what a splendid system that must have been: their master's secrets died with them. In these modern times, slaves have become outrageously expensive, truculent, proud, and indis-

creet. So difficult is it to find a good slave that some landowners are actually experimenting with freed labor. This is what we've come to! And as I muse about their abject class, I think of Savia again, whether her comfort as companion would be worth her trouble as slave. . . .

Scolding myself for letting my mind wander, I come back to it. "And you knew Galba Brassidias as well?"

"He was the senior tribune."

"No, I mean, did you know him personally? Lie with him as well?"

"I did." There is no embarrassment in her answer.

"And was he good at showing his *interest?*"

A smile again. "Galba was a man of strong appetites."

"He liked women?"

"He desired them."

Of course. These distinctions are important. "Did he desire more than you?"

She knows where this is going. "Undoubtedly."

"And acted on it?"

"He was a man who acted on everything."

I take a breath, finally getting to the point. "And did Galba desire the lady Valeria?"

She laughs again, short, sharp. A sardonic smile, a bitter-sweet memory. "You could warm yourself by his heat. And as she made herself the little queen of the Petriana, all of that energy turned on her."

My guess is confirmed. This emotional Galba, this womanizing Galba, doesn't sound like the enigmatic senior tribune that others have described. "And yet he concealed this from others."

"Galba concealed everything from others."

And by so doing, I ponder, concealed it even from himself. Lied to himself. And was tormented by his twin desires to possess Valeria and destroy her. This is my theory, anyway. "I'm told she was very beautiful."

"The most beautiful woman most men at that post had ever seen." There's no rivalry or regret in that statement, simply an expression of fact. No slave is going to compete with a senator's daughter, and Marta knew it.

"I've been interviewing soldiers about the time that Marcus and the Petriana attacked the druids in the grove. He left Galba in command of the fort."

"Yes. He wasn't just dull, he was stupid." It's an arrogant observation for a slave to make, but she senses I value candor. Besides, she's probably had sex with half the surviving officer corps and has allies I can merely guess at.

"Did Galba visit the lady Valeria while Marcus was leading the strike on the druid's grove?"

"He did, inquiring about her health and how well she was settling in. It was unusual for him to do so, for he cared little for the feelings or opinions of others. It was also amusing to see him less commanding: more human, out of his armor and away from his men. She was cool, properly reserved, but when he told Valeria that he'd found her a horse, she changed from Roman matron to excited girl. He said he was planning to canter between the fossatum and the Wall and invited her to come along."

The fossatum, I have learned, is the ditch and dike and road behind the Wall to the south. The space between, a bowshot wide, is the military zone. "She agreed?"

"Immediately. Galba was shrewd. He'd found Valeria's weakness."

"Her weakness or her desire?"

"They're the same thing, don't you think?"

XXI

I'm having the senior tribune to supper, Marta."

Valeria's eyes were bright, her skin pink and shiny, her hair curled at its edges from the sweat of her ride. Her breasts were still rising and falling in visible animation, not from shortness of breath but from excitement.

It amused the cook because she knew how the senior tribune could ignite a woman. It wasn't Galba's looks, it was his intensity.

"Your husband is still on campaign, lady?" Marta asked innocently.

"Yes." Realizing his omission sounded improper, Valeria elaborated. "I'm hoping to improve relationships with the senior tribune. Galba has been generous to us, and now I wish to be generous to him."

"Of course." Marta gave a slight bow. "Something ambitious for supper, then. A hot sauce for roast venison, perhaps. Sweet wine cakes."

"Yes, and those peas you make."

"Vitellius. With the essence of anchovy."

"Exactly. All of it served with a good wine."

"I think you enjoyed your outing, my lady."

In truth the ride had been magnificent. Galba had shown her how to handle the harsh cavalry bit and allow her body to bind itself to the saddle, flowing with its rhythm. Then they'd ridden very fast, he on his black stallion Imperium and she on the white mare she'd first spotted in the stables and dubbed Boudicca, after the Celtic warrior queen. Because Hadrian's Wall commanded the high crest of this part of Britannia, the space between it and the fossatum dike and ditch undulated with the topography, dipping precipitously into narrow gaps and steeply climbing the next promontory. They'd galloped this hilly course like the wind, plunging recklessly down one slope and surging up the next, her horse's muscles rippling under her thighs with equine power. It was an exhilarating pounding that had left her breathless. Galba, saying little, had kept a watchful eye, pointing out hazards and leading her through thickets she wouldn't have dared thread through herself.

His company had been flattering. The ride had been release.

Now she'd return the favor and, in doing so, help smooth her husband's path. It was no secret that Clodius distrusted Galba and that Marcus was uncomfortable with him, male pride getting in the way of friendship. As a woman she might make peace among all three. Certainly she amused Galba. She could turn this to advantage!

Valeria took a long bath, letting Savia sponge her vigorously as she tried to plan what they might talk about. Galba was too masculine to be much of a conversationalist. Too provincial to be a sophisticate. Yet he was also a warrior who could perhaps be enticed to share some of his past adventures. Share his thoughts about the Petriana. Perhaps she could reform the fort! It wasn't just pleasure to invite him to supper, it was duty.

"I don't like him," Savia said. "He's been rude to Clodius and difficult for your husband. And now, the instant Marcus is gone, he takes you riding?"

"He's a man of the frontier," Valeria said as she dressed. "We're in his world now. We have to understand men like Galba."

"There's nothing to understand. Men live on impulse, which is why they require women. We give them some sense."

"I don't think my husband is a man of impulse."

"Galba is. Be careful you don't confuse him."

"How can I confuse him with simple politeness? Really, Savia, you make every encounter more difficult than it has to be."

"It's you who are complicating things, not me. He's a killer, Valeria."

"A soldier, subordinate to my husband."

"You're naive."

"No, I'm a woman and a Roman matron and more than a little tired of your incessant opinions! Now hand me my stola and tuck in your tongue."

The thought of enduring her maidservant's frowns throughout the evening annoyed Valeria, who was hardly the girl she'd been in Rome. Savia simply couldn't bear the fact that her charge had grown up! Accordingly, she ordered her maidservant to take a basket of wine cakes to Lucinda in repayment for her generosity during the wedding. Then she attended to her own jewelry and makeup.

The senior tribune was punctual, arriving at the twelfth hour, when the sky is red to the west. Galba too had bathed, shedding his armor for a tunic of bright blue. He was clean, rugged, and slightly awkward, a combination that Valeria thought endearing: the rude trooper doing his best to keep company with a daughter of Rome! So strong. So male. So disarmed.

Marta brought them boiled mussels as an appetizer, then lingered so long that Valeria had to pointedly dismiss her. Galba, typically reserved, gradually let his hostess prompt him to talk about the nature of horses and the skills required to govern five hundred men. Valeria was politely asked in turn about her plans for the household, the reported ease with which she was mastering the Celtic tongue, and changes she had brought. The tribune noticed that a flowered tapestry now covered the bloody mural.

"You're interested in my domestic campaign, tribune?"

"This house was mine, briefly."

She looked at him sympathetically. "Of course! How strange it must be to go back to your quarters in the barracks."

His look was enigmatic. "I'm at home out there."

"This house will be the garrison's home, not just mine, tribune. We will have many dinners. I want to make my husband's officers feel comfortable here."

He looked at her evenly. "That's very generous."

"It's the least I can do."

Supper was served. Galba seemed entertained simply by watching Valeria eat, the nibble of her lips, the pearl of her small teeth, the liquid of her eyes. She enjoyed his attention. The wine relaxed her, the company excited her. "Tell me your impressions of Britannia," he finally invited.

She approved of the subject. It wasn't time yet to discuss relationships in the fort. "It's a beautiful province, of course."

"So are most in the empire." He wanted something more interesting.

"It's a curious combination of the rustic and refined. At Lucinda's villa you can find products no different than Rome's. A mile away, a Celtic farmstead hasn't changed for a thousand years. Britons are grumpy one moment and lively the next. Even the weather shifts mood. It's fascinating."

"Not dull, after the glories of the capital?" He took another bite of venison.

"I've seen those glories and feel more alive here. Clodius said it's the possibility of death that defines life."

"Did he?"

"The ambush made me appreciate life more, I think. Isn't that curious?"

"And now you're being avenged."

"Yes. By my husband and Clodius."

"By two hundred men. To make you feel safe."

She shrugged. "I feel safe already. Safe with you."

He laughed. "A suitor would not think that a compliment. Nor a warrior."

"Which are you, Galba?"

"A guardian. A wall."

"The Wall is everything to you, isn't it?"

"It's my life. Not as grand as a senator's, but the Petriana is my core."

"I don't think you're quite the rogue you pretend to be. Not the dangerous man you pretend to be. Not the provincial you pretend to be. Do you ever pretend, Galba?"

"Everyone pretends a little. But I am what I am."

"That's what I like about you. You pretend less than the boys of Rome."

"Part of being a man is to stop pretending, lady. Pretense is useless on the battlefield. Weak men who pretend to be strong get killed."

Did he mean Marcus? "You're not a weak man."

"I'm an able one who needs only the right connections to go far."

"Of course you are!"

"Who needs only the right partner to achieve great things. Emperors have started from beginnings as humble as my own."

"You mean a patron?"

"I mean an alliance. Between the two brightest people on this post."

Was this the opening she was seeking? Marta brought the cakes, and they were quiet while she served them. Galba was watching Valeria carefully, impatient at this interruption.

"Is it lonely for you, Valeria?" he began again after the slave left. "Being so far from home?"

"I have Savia, of course."

He snorted.

"But she nags. She can't see that I've grown up. She treats me like a child."

"And you're a woman."

"Of course."

"With a woman's needs."

"Yes. Though I know I live in a masculine world now. Society here is so different than in Rome! I have to make new friends. Have new experiences."

"And you're adventurous."

"I want to know what life is all about. I've been too sheltered."

"Experiences like our ride today."

"And this supper! I'm enjoying our conversation."

"My poor company?"

"I'm enjoying your company, too."

"And I yours. I can give you more experience, Valeria."

She looked at him with amusement. "Can you, tribune?"

"I can teach you what the world really is, not what poets imagine it to be. How to impose your will on it. Just like you can teach me about Rome."

She laughed, nervous now, but a little thrilled. "What an instructor you must be!"

"I can teach you what it is to be a woman."

"You, a man?"

"I can teach you what it is to be a man."

Valeria looked at him uncertainly, confused as to what they were talking about. He was looking at her with an expression of frank equality, and it disturbed her.

"I can teach you about men and women." Suddenly Galba reached with his powerful arm around her neck to grip her shoulder, and pulled to kiss her. The action was as quick and practiced as a sword stroke, and before she could resist or exclaim, his mouth was on hers, his beard against her skin, his breath and tongue insistent.

It frightened her, and she jerked her head back, pulled free her arm, and slapped him awkwardly. It was hardly more than a tap because of her fear and confusion, and it produced only a sardonic grin.

"Please stop," she whispered.

He bent to kiss her again.

So then she reared away from him in earnest, spilling her wine cup and knocking over her chair as she pulled upright. "How dare you!"

He stood too. "Indeed, I'm a man of daring. You've never known one, Valeria. Let me show you what real men are like."

"I've just been married!"

"To a man who is never around, or half absent when he is here. He's at least a day's ride away, and your maidservant is off with Lucinda. Stop dreaming about life and experience it. Seize opportunity, or your life will be filled with regret."

"What opportunity?"

"To be with a real man and soldier who could win you a real empire, not just this rude fort."

She stepped back until she pressed against the tapestry on the wall, still sensing the dreadful mural behind it. Her indignation grew with her embarrassment. How could she have miscalculated so disastrously? "You've misunderstood my invitation. By the gods, you're just a common soldier! You dare make an advance on the newlywed wife of your commander, a praefectus of Rome?" She drew herself up, trying to be haughty but her voice breaking. "A senator's daughter, a woman chaste and loyal? You've mistaken an offer of friendship for an offer of another kind!"

"Don't pretend you didn't expect that. Or welcome it."

"Certainly not! Do you think I'd ever be physically attracted to the likes of you? That I would be intimate with someone of your station?"

"You impish flirt!"

"I'm sorry that you misinterpreted my invitation."

"I misinterpreted nothing."

"Now I must ask you to leave, and not return unless my husband is present."

She thought herself too good for him, this preening bauble? Galba's fury was growing. "You asked if I pretend, and the answer is no, Roman girl. I'm an honest man and thus incomprehensible to someone as false as you. You play at outrage? I know your kind. By the gods, you can be sure I *won't* come back to this house, with your husband or without him. Everyone knows that your favored birth is the only cause of Marcus's appointment, and that the two of you combined couldn't survive a day on the Wall without the protection of men like me."

"What arrogance! Get out of here!"

He stepped back, the distance between them suddenly yawning. "I'm going, to leave you to your loneliness. But someday, when you really grow up, you may indeed want a real man—and when that day comes, you'll have to come to me, not me to you, and then we'll meet in the stables, not here."

"How *dare* you speak to me like that!"

"How dare you toy with me at your table."

"I despise you!"

"And I laugh at your pretensions."

She broke into tears and fled.

Galba looked after her, an inner pain of defeat flickering across his face, and then he kicked angrily and overthrew their table, crockery shattering on the floor and red wine spilling across the mosaics. Marta, who'd come to the door to witness their fiery exchange, darted back into the kitchen. The senior tribune began to stride toward the entry hall in fury but then checked, turned, and looked back at the kitchen with a glower. The slave bitch had heard it all! He was boiling, and needed release.

So he stamped back in that direction and burst into the hot chamber. All the slaves but Marta scampered like rabbits. Her face was red from the heat of cooking, her tunic unpinned to the cleavage of her breasts, her arms bare, and she looked at the soldier with fear and triumph as he charged, sweeping her up in a crush of arms and plopping her down on the chopping block, food knocked aside, his hand ripping open the front of her tunic, her apron up around her waist, her thighs shouldered apart.

Marta was grinning fiercely. "This is what you want, Galba. This is what you deserve. Not a highborn girl, but a woman!"

He ravaged her like an animal, his roar of fierce lust echoing through the commander's house like a taunt, and Marta's own cries carried even farther, drifting down the corridors and echoing in the drafty rooms. They penetrated finally to the sleeping chamber where Valeria lay alone, weeping.

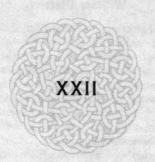

XXII

I would like to be surprised by this tale, but I'm not. I have made too many reports about the things people do or say in the heat of passion. "He seems injudicious," I observe mildly to Marta.

"He'd exercised so much power over base women that he mistook his opportunity with Valeria. Or was so frustrated that he was willing to take a risk."

"You thought him foolhardy?"

"Men should know their station."

Of course! It's interesting that slaves are more conscious of proper station than any of us. I wonder if any of this disaster would have occurred if all involved had simply accepted the duty and conformity that sustains the empire.

"Still, quite risky in the commander's house."

"He still thought of it as his house, inspector. And he was reckless from envy. This issue of command was eating at him. He also knew she'd never breathe a word of this to Marcus; he'd calculated in advance that her embarrassment would be greater than his own. But he also knew he was finished with her and finished with her husband. He'd gambled, and lost. He'd let his shield drop and been stabbed to the heart."

"And went to you."

"He was a stag in heat, and I his substitute."

"You endured it."

"I enjoyed it."

I shift uncomfortably, never quite accustomed to the bluntness of slaves. "Did they see each other again before Marcus came back?"

"Of course. Petrianis is a cramped place."

"How did she react?"

"She was cool, but not as outraged as she pretended. His advance repelled but fascinated her, I could tell. Not that she welcomed it, but she couldn't help but be flattered. Curious. I know she heard us crying out as we coupled. Galba was a man of passions her husband didn't have. He was a stag, and she was like a fly to a spider. He sensed this, and it tormented him. Tormented her. We laughed at both of them. With my class, these things are much simpler."

She wants me to envy her, and I do, in a way. *"Nothing else happened?"*

"Galba let it quietly be known that he'd solved the murder of the slave Odo."

"What evidence did he have?"

"He wouldn't say. Not yet, anyway."

I dimly begin to see it now. *"And then Marcus came back."*

"Bloody and sated and full of his own righteousness, hardly seeing anyone else around him. Valeria and Galba pretended nothing had happened, of course, but Marcus was strutting too much like a rooster to notice anyway. That fool Clodius was even worse, having stolen a tribesman's neck torque to cover his scar and pretending to be the new Achilles. These were men who'd played at war and loved it. They'd seen the fires of the spring festival of Beltane before their raid, assumed they were some kind of tribal war signal, and credited themselves when the fires went out! It's no wonder they lit a real fire."

"Did Clodius come around to visit Valeria?"

"Yes. She put him off for a time out of confusion and embarrassment, but they were nearly the same age, and friends. He could sense her desire."

"Were they lovers too?" Any question seems within bounds with this Marta.

"I don't think so. They liked the tension more than the release. Flirting more than fucking." The slave shrugs, the ways of her betters incomprehensible to her.

"And what happened then?"

"Real trouble started. Marcus had committed a sacrilege by burning that grove. It was just what Celtic leaders wanted. The Petriana had a patrol chased. A sentry was shot through by an arrow under a full moon. There were reports of brigands slipping through the Wall. The praefectus hadn't cowed the tribes, he'd aroused them. The duke called him to Eburacum to give account. And that's when Galba threatened to arrest Clodius."

"He what?"

She smiles and nods, enjoying being able to surprise me with the miscalculations that humans can make. Except, what if it was no miscalculation?

"With Marcus at Eburacum, Galba was once more in charge of the garrison. He pretended to make friends with Clodius, complimenting the youth for his performance in battle. He ordered him to inspect the Wall to the west and then swing north to the spring of the Celtic god Bormo, to meet one of Rome's agents and learn the mood of the tribes. The boy was flattered. Once he was gone, the senior tribune met with the centurion Falco, who'd owned the slave Odo."

"Yes. I have been interviewing Falco."

"Galba claimed he'd found one of the centurion's wedding table knives secreted in the junior tribune's chamber. He said Clodius was also hiding a Celtic bracelet that had been worn on the wrist of the slave. He said the youth should be confronted."

"How do you know this?"

"The steward Clio, who serves at headquarters, told us. Nothing is secret in the fort of the Petriana." She smiles again, enjoying my discomfiture. If post slaves know the results of officer conferences, so, I suspect, could any enemy. This is a point I should make in my report.

"Falco," Marta goes on, "said he'd been asked by Marcus to drop the matter. But Galba insisted an unpunished Roman murder would be used to incite the tribes. Formal charge, and formal compensation, might demonstrate Roman fairness."

"And blemish the young Clodius's career."

"Galba said the grove assault had been a mistake and

*that his doubts about Marcus had been confirmed. He said
the line officers should act against Clodius before Marcus
returned because aristocrats try to shield each other. Since
the youth was north on reconnaissance, he could be arrested
with a minimum of disruption. The boy had won some loyalty. At the shrine of Bormo, he wouldn't have protection
from his men."*

None of this makes sense to me. "Falco had already been
promised compensation by Marcus. Why would he agree to
this plan?"

"Oh, but he didn't, we learned later. He said a slave
wasn't worth disruption and that they must wait until Marcus returned. Falco was no fool. He feared Galba was plotting mutiny and wouldn't have it. But all that was of no
matter."

"No matter? Because Galba was going to act alone?"

"Because no arrest was ever intended. The entire idea
was a sham. Galba caught Clio listening to the proposal and
sent him away before Falco could make his objection. He
knew the slave would eavesdrop and knew just how much he
wanted Clio to hear."

"I don't understand."

"Have you ever watched a street magician, master?"

*I'm annoyed at her manner, of teacher to slow-witted
pupil.* "Yes, yes. What of it?"

"Do you know how he does his trick? He persuades you
to look at one hand while he does his mischief with the
other."

"What does that have to do with the arrest of young
Clodius?"

"Galba was a magician."

"I don't know what you mean."

"There was never to have been any arrest. His talk with
Falco was intended only as slave gossip, designed to reach
the ears of the maidservant Savia through the eavesdropping
Clio. And through her to Valeria."

Suddenly I see it. "He didn't care about Clodius at all!"
Galba had seen the girl escape her abduction. Watched his
rival marry her. Failed to undermine that marriage by se-

ducing her. But her husband had blundered by attacking the druids, and if Galba could eliminate the source of Marcus's political influence . . .

"The young tribune was of no real importance to him," Marta says. *"But Valeria had scorned and humiliated him. She was naive enough to believe any plot. Rash enough to leave the fortress. Brave enough to warn her young friend of an impending arrest that was never to have happened. Fated enough to go to a new world."*

XXIII

I can't get *up* there," Savia decided.

"Then don't come at all!" Valeria hissed.

The slave glared. "And how would you feed and dress and bathe yourself? Or what would I tell your husband when he asks where you've gone? Better to get lost in the wilderness with you, torn apart by wild animals, than explain your absence."

"Then stop complaining about Athena, who's as tame and plodding and placid a mare as you could want, and mount her." They were whispering in the garrison stables, not daring to risk a light. "Come, I'll give you a boost."

"She's too big!"

"Don't you imagine she's thinking the same about you?"

Savia finally clambered up, moaning softly as she did so, and Valeria mounted Boudicca, the white mare she'd ridden with the presumptuous Galba. The tribune had revealed his base character at their dinner, and so it had come as no surprise when Savia whispered he was planning treachery against poor Clodius. Now she must outwit and outrace him! Nudging her mount, she led the way past the headquarters building to the north gate, threading through the tightly packed buildings. It was midnight, the fort quiet, a faint illumination provided by a half-moon. Sentries were silhouettes against the sky.

The duplicarius in charge came out from the sentry house. "Lady Valeria?"

"Open the gate, Priscus. We go for a Christian service. We're meeting our church at the moon's crest."

He was wary. "You've become a Christian?" There'd been no rumor of this.

"Like our emperor."

"But I've seen no other worshipers."

"My slave is to prepare the site."

He slowly shook his head. "You need a pass, lady."

"And who am I to apply to?" She drew herself up. "I, who am of the House of Valens, a senator's daughter, a commander's wife? Do I ask the governor? The duke?"

"I'm not certain, lady—"

"Perhaps you think I should send to the emperor himself for permission to go through his wall and pray to his God? Or wake senior tribune Galba?"

Priscus hesitated. She had a lifetime of practicing the imperiousness of her class, and he a lifetime of surrendering to it. To make an enemy of a commander's wife was foolish. He signaled the gate open. "Let me send an escort—"

"We can't wait for that. We've no need of that." She kicked her mount, and it started ahead through the archway, her slave's horse instinctively following. "Don't bother others about our prayers. We'll be back by dawn!"

And with that they were across the embankment that crossed the ditch and trotting down the hill, Savia bouncing fearfully on her saddle as her horse broke into a trot.

The duplicarius watched uneasily. Something wasn't right. He turned to his companion. "Rufus, rouse three others and follow her. Make sure she meets no harm."

"It will take us a while to saddle, decurion."

"No matter. You'll catch them, judging from the jiggling rump of that fat slave."

Valeria stopped on the open moor and looked back at the Wall. It was the first time she'd been north of the barrier. Its undulating, crenellated crest stretched east and west as far as she could see, each tower marked with torches like a chain of lighthouses, the stars cold sparks above their fire. The whitewash glowed in the moonlight like wet quartz. It looked impregnable from this side, its approaches shorn clear, farmsteads forbidden within a mile of its ditch. How strange it must be to come from the north, ignorant and unwashed, and see its regal length for the first time!

"It's lonely out here," Savia said gloomily.

"The tribes are somewhere. Asleep, we hope."

"I think this is a very bad idea."

"And I think we're going to save our friend Clodius. I've seen the true nature of Galba Brassidias, and it's necessary to warn our young tribune."

"His true nature?"

"He's a very arrogant, very incautious man."

They rode on, Savia bouncing in her unfamiliar saddle and muttering misgivings. It was frightening to ride north beyond the Wall's protection, Valeria readily admitted to herself, and eerie to be out at night. Every wooded hollow seemed a possible haven for wolves or bears. Every rise threatened to hide skulking barbarians.

Yet as they rode mile after mile without incident, the thrill of the night's freedom began to infuse her. She was finding her own way! Never had she experienced such freedom. She felt like a bird or spirit, gliding like a ghost over a silvery landscape of lunar-lit dew. No one was watching her. Judging her. Coveting her. Envying her. Resenting her. What if they simply kept going?

Savia had no sympathy when Valeria expressed this idea. "I don't feel free, I feel hungry," the slave said. "And what are we going to do when we get there?"

"Send poor Clodius to the duke, where this preposterous accusation can be laid to rest. It would also amuse me to see this arresting posse of Galba Brassidias net us instead. I'd have no hesitation in telling him exactly what I think of him!"

Savia looked reproachfully at her young charge. "I warned you, lady."

"We'll say nothing more about *that*."

So they were quiet for a while. Then the slave spoke again. "But what if Clodius did kill this Odo, and didn't pay for him?"

"Savia! How can you think such a thing of our companion, a man who tried to save me in the forest?"

"Save you? He couldn't even stand up."

"And had his throat cut for his defiance. Marcus said he fought well at the grove. Galba has been unfair to Clodius since we stepped ashore in Londinium."

"I'm afraid of Galba's soldiers."

"I'm not."

The last mile was the most intimidating, the track to the spring of Bormo leading down into a wooded glen. The gloom under the trees was much deeper in the night, the path hard to follow. As they picked their way through the murk, they heard a distant rumbling of horses, as if someone was following. Galba already? "We must hurry!"

They trotted recklessly ahead, narrowly missing low branches, and finally Valeria heard the murmur of gently falling water. The spring! They came at length into a small clearing in a circle of silver elm, the moon overhead and the world turned white. On the far side of the glade was a Celtic shrine devoted to the water god Bormo. Carved on a rock cliff was the voluptuous representation of a nymph, the spring's fount the creature's mouth. Water tumbled down a carpet of wet moss to a wide dark pool, ripples marching in rank across it. Moonlight reflecting off gold and silver coins on the pool bottom like another sky of moons. Flowers, small items of clothing, jewelry, and tokens of a person's life—a comb, a knife, a chariot whip—had been left in hopes of improving the efficacy of prayer and curses. Beyond, in the trees, was a small Roman temple. Horses were tethered there.

"See the mounts? It must be Clodius."

"This is a pagan place," Savia murmured. "An evil place."

"Nonsense. Can't you sense the water god?"

"No, these gods are dead, killed by the Christ, and demons have taken their place. We shouldn't be here, Valeria."

"And we won't be if you hush and let me deliver our message!"

The temple was a simple square building with domed roof, a porch, and pillars before its door. Valeria called with a loud whisper. "Clodius!"

No answer, so they knocked. "Clodius, are you in there? Open up! Soldiers are coming!"

Again, no answer.

And then . . . "By the gods, it's you!"

They whirled. The young Roman had crept behind them, his spatha unsheathed, his cloak bunched around his left arm as makeshift shield.

"Clodius!"

"Valeria?" He looked at her in bewilderment.

She ran and pecked him on one cheek, then danced back. "I found you!"

"What are you doing here in the middle of the night? I almost attacked you! I thought I heard the murmuring of men, not women."

"We came to warn you. Galba Brassidias claims to have found a murder weapon and intends to arrest you for the murder of the slave Odo. His men are approaching."

"What? Are you certain?"

"Ride to Eburacum and demand true justice from the duke."

The youth lowered his sword. "What evidence? Falco said the matter was settled."

"A bracelet from Odo in your room. A knife from Falco's own dining table. Maybe some other things."

The tribune scoffed. "Put there by Galba Brassidias, I'll wager. He's wanted me gone from the beginning."

"So make *him* go. Get the duke to transfer him to Germania."

"I'd need Marcus to support me."

"He will! You're both of the same class."

Clodius listened to the distant rumble. "You rode out here by yourselves?"

"The slave Clio whispered the secret to brave Savia here. When she told me Galba's plot, I knew what we must do."

Savia gave a tremulous smile, trying to live up to this new reputation for courage.

The junior tribune turned and spoke into the dark. "Sardis! We must flee!" Another man, a narrow-faced Celt,

emerged like a wraith. "This is one of our informants,"
Clodius explained. "Barbarian raiders are about. It's not safe
out here. You two better come to Eburacum with us."

"No, Savia and I will just slow you down. Go while we
mislead Galba. He can take us back to the fort."

"She's right, tribune," Sardis said. "Better to flee alone if
we're to . . ." Suddenly the man jerked, cut off in midsen-
tence, and then lurched sideways as if drunk. Valeria
strained to see in the moonlight. Something was protruding
from the front of his throat. The man gave a curious gurgle.

It was the point of an arrow. Savia screamed.

"It's Galba!" Clodius spat. "Quick, inside the temple!"

As they moved, a staff snaked out from the underbrush.
The young tribune tripped, sprawling, and silent men
sprang. One stamped on his hand, and the spatha came free.
More men blocked the door of the temple, and still more
came from behind. They were bearded, their skin blackened,
their swords unnaturally long. The women whirled in shock
and confusion. These weren't Romans! Even as Valeria realized that the man holding Clodius down was the one called
Luca, the barbarian who'd cut him in the forest, strong arms
snaked around her from behind. She heard a familiar voice
in her ear, speaking Latin again. "This time we'll ride
together, lady."

It was the man who'd tried to abduct her before! She
twisted, trying to kick backward, and he squeezed and
laughed. "I'll keep your hands from your brooch this time.
You'll not prick my horse again."

Other barbarians had seized Savia and were gagging her
squeals. The approaching horses were drawing nearer.

"Who's coming?" one of the men demanded of Valeria.

Her captor turned his mouth to her ear. "Did you bring an
escort, lady? Speak honestly and quick, before Luca cuts
your Roman friend."

The barbarian once more held a knife to Clodius's throat.

"It's Galba Brassidias," she said, "come to arrest
Clodius."

The Celts cursed.

"I thought you said the Thracian wouldn't come here," Luca complained to his leader in Celtic. Valeria's tutoring in the language from her servants let her eavesdrop.

"Galba?" the chieftain repeated skeptically. He chose Latin again. "I think you're mistaken, lady, which means you're either fool or liar. It's somebody else, looking for you in the dark."

She squirmed, trying to get enough freedom to bite or scratch. "My husband is commander of the Petriana!"

"And a hundred miles away."

How did the barbarian know that?

"Let's move, Arden," a man urged in Celtic again. "We've got what we came for."

"I want their horses, too."

"Gurn is already fetching them," a female voice said from the dark.

"What about this one?" Luca asked. He was sitting on Clodius, holding his head to the ground by his hair.

"I'll not kill a man when he's already down. Clout and leave him."

The man struck Clodius on the head with the hilt of the dagger, making him slump, and then kicked him, hard, to make sure he was out. The Roman didn't move.

Then their leader swept Valeria up as if she were no heavier than a cloak, flipped her upside down over his shoulder, and began leading the pack deeper into the trees at a quick trot. He jumped. "The vixen is scratching me!"

His men laughed quietly.

A boy appeared with the Roman horses, even as they could hear new Romans cantering into the clearing.

Valeria screamed. "Help! We're being stolen!"

The sound of pursuit swerved at her cry.

"Plug her noise," Arden said with exasperation, and someone ripped her hem for a gag. But even as he moved to fasten it, there was a crashing ahead, and another shout. "Over here!" a Roman called. "Barbarians!"

It was Clodius, risen from the ground and circling around to save them!

"I thought you knocked him out," the leader called Arden muttered.

"He must have a head like a helmet."

"I'll silence the bastard," another Celt said, notching an arrow. Yet even as he did so, a Roman javelin sailed out of the dark and struck the archer squarely in the chest, knocking him backward. His arrow flew harmlessly up into the moonlit branches, rattling as it passed, and the archer fell on his back, impaled, the shaft erect as a standard.

"You Britlets won't get away again!" Clodius was charging, sword up, head bloody, vengeance in his eye. It was as magnificent as it was foolhardy, and so unexpected that he was almost on top of the barbarian leader before the Celt could react. Arden was forced to drop Valeria like a sack of wheat, stunning her, and desperately claw for his weapon. Clodius would run him through! Yet honor made the tribune pull up short of a kill. "Draw and die, brigand!"

Surprised at this reprieve, the chieftain did so. Then a clash of steel, sparks bright as the blades slithered across each other. Even as rough barbarian hands reached to gag Valeria, she could hear the shouts of other Romans dismounting and plunging into the trees. Their leader didn't sound like Galba at all. It was Rufus, the soldier at the gate.

"Clodius!" Valeria gasped. "Wait for help!" Then the gag caught her mouth.

His sword rang. "I'll not fail you this time!"

The Celt crouched low, sidling to one side in the manner of an arena swordsman. There was skill here, the Romans could see. Clodius darted forward but was parried, the long swords repelling the combatants from each other, their song sharp in the night. And then again, and again, the clash of metal.

"Finish him, Arden," one of the Celts hissed.

"The lady is fond of him," the leader said, breathing heavily.

"Finish him before he dooms us all!"

Valeria lifted herself to run, but a boot caught her in the stomach. She went down again heavily, the wind knocked out of her, stars dancing, breath clogged, the distraction diverting the barbarian leader's eye. It was enough! Clodius leaped, sword whistling in a long overhead stroke. Now he would avenge his ambush!

And yet the counterreaction was instinctual and instantaneous. The Celt ducked under the descending blade and lunged forward, his own sword stabbing through the Roman's stomach and out his back before either man knew consciously what was happening.

Clodius froze, his expression not of pain but utter surprise, as if something inconceivable had happened. His weapon left his hand and stuck in the ground.

The graveyards are full of fair men.

Then the Celt butted the Roman with his shoulder, knocking him backward, and as he did so his sword slipped from the Roman's torso to shine in the moonlight, its blade slick with the young tribune's essence. Clodius was dead before he hit the ground.

Yet now came the other Romans, Rufus and three companions, weapons out, unsure what they'd stumbled into but anxious for battle. They were running silhouettes in the dark. "Put the sword to them!"

Bowstrings twanged and arrows buzzed. The other Celts had set themselves ready, and the Romans ran into a volley. There was almost no sound, just the quick thwack of missiles striking armored flesh, and then the four would-be rescuers toppled like puppets with their strings cut. They hit the ground and lay still, each bearing two or three arrows.

The Celts ran forward and severed the Roman necks with a howl of triumph. Great gouts of blood blackened the shadows.

The Celtic leader wiped his own sword on the grass, sheathed it, and strode back to Valeria, scooping her up in his bloodied arms. She felt hurt, winded, sick, and faint all at the same time. It had all happened so fast!

"If your friend there had let us go, all of them would still be alive now," he said. Then he carried her through the trees and threw her over the front horns of his saddle, mounted, and gave his horse a hard kick. "To Tiranen!"

His men gave a cry of shrill agreement. "Tiranen!" They

mounted themselves, swords raised in triumph, Savia captive as well, their whoops an echo across the glen, the spring of Bormo still serene under the moon. Then they rode north, away from the Wall, and deep, deep, into the barbarian night.

PART TWO

XXIV

The barbarians had taken the riderless Roman horses, and so, just a mile from the spring, Valeria and Savia were freed of their gags and seated on their own mounts to enable better speed. Their wrists were tied to the saddle horns, and the reins attached by rope to other riders. The dead soldiers' horses and Clodius's steed followed in train behind, the Celt who had died draped across one saddle. There were eight surviving warriors, Valeria counted, seven of them raffish-looking men and the eighth, shockingly, a woman. Her waist-long hair was braided and tucked into her baldric to tame it in the night wind, while a yew bow and quiver of feathered arrows was slung across her back. The female had the same arrogant ease as the men, riding with confident expertise.

It was frightening, this perversion of nature. But fascinating, too.

Their chieftain commanded with a quiet surety different from the stiff formality of Marcus or the sternness of Galba. The barbarian didn't demand obedience so much as expect respect, and his ragged warriors gave it to him, even while joking about his choice of route or his eye for pretty hostages. They followed no obvious course, trotting along a track here and leaving it there, cutting across moonlit field and moor and woodland with casual certainty, all of Caledonia the color of bleached bone. Savia was mute with fear and clinging miserably to her jouncing saddle, while Valeria grieved silently for poor Clodius and desperately tried to puzzle out what had happened. What was this chieftain doing at the sacred spring? Why had poor Rufus ridden up, only to be killed? Above all, where were they going, and what would they do with her when they got there?

They descended at dawn into the dimness of a wooded hollow to rest and water the horses. A tether tied the captive women to a tree. The barbarians looked curiously at their prisoners in the light as the Romans looked at them. The one called Luca was a compact, strongly muscled man with long hair and mustache in the Celtic manner, wearing nothing but trousers and cloak and seemingly as impervious to weather as a greased legionary tent. The barbarian's chest was bare, his face and arms smeared with charcoal to help hide him in the night. The woman wore similar trousers but also chain mail over a leather jerkin, her breasts slight and bound flat and her limbs long and sinewy, like the toughness of young willow. Despite the mannishness of her garb, she was blond and rather pretty, but the men treated her with wary distance.

"Brisa, give them some food and water," their leader commanded in their native tongue.

The woman nodded and went to the stream. The decision that their female member would tend the captives, not a male, seemed somewhat reassuring.

Savia wrinkled her nose as she ate some of the sharp cheese offered, but Valeria refused, her appetite gone. Both women did drink from the offered skin of water. Then they waited, apprehensive and desperate for some opportunity to escape. The warriors made no move to molest or help or even watch them; their initial curiosity satisfied, they now paid no more attention to their captives than dogs.

The barbarian leader squatted alone by the stream, carefully washing his face and arms and apparently lost in thought. Valeria viewed him speculatively. She'd escaped from him once and was determined to do so again. Arden, the men had called him. He wore a sleeveless tunic that left free the powerful arms that had gripped Valeria, yet he too seemed oblivious to the dawn chill. It was interesting that he cleaned himself, contradicting her image of the northern barbarians as little more than unkempt cattle thieves. Maybe he was trying to wash his blood from his hands. No doubt he felt satisfaction at killing Clodius and capturing Valeria after his earlier failure. But how had he known she'd be at the spring? How did he know Galba?

Eventually the leader stood and strode to his prisoners with the stride of a man accustomed to covering many miles, then dropped into a squat before them. The water's transformation of his appearance was surprising. Washed clean of dirt and paint, the barbarian was actually rather handsome: unexpectedly so, like a hero among jackals. He was beardless in the Roman manner, though stubbled this morning. His long hair was tied behind him, his nose straight, his expression firm, his eyes that bright, disconcerting blue, his gaze bold, his manner calm.

Valeria hated him.

"We're going to sleep here a few hours before moving on," he told them in Latin.

"Good," she replied with more confidence than she really felt. "It will give time for the Petriana to catch you, and flog you, and hang you from that tree."

Her abductor looked up mildly at the limbs. "There'll be no alarm yet, lady. We'll be on our way again before the Petriana is much out of bed."

So he was overconfident. "You've condemned yourself by seizing a commander's wife and senator's daughter," she insisted. "The entire Sixth Victrix will come looking for me. They'll burn Caledonia to ashes before they give up."

He pretended to consider this. "Then maybe I should chop off your pretty head now, send it in a basket, and save them the trouble."

Savia moaned, but there was nothing in his manner to make Valeria take this threat seriously. If he wanted to kill them, they'd already be dead. "I have influence," she tried. "Let us go now, and I'll stop the pursuit so you can get away."

He laughed and put a hand to his ear in mockery. "This pursuit you keep talking about? I don't hear it!" He bent close. "You're my guarantee there'll be no pursuit, daughter of Rome, because if there is one, it will be your death warrant, not mine. You're hostage for our safety, and if the cavalry finds us, then you and your slave here will be the first to die. Understand? Pray that your new husband forgets about you."

Valeria looked at him, trying to mask her disquiet with an expression of contempt. She didn't believe for a moment that no rescue would come. And she didn't believe he'd kill her when it did. He wanted something from her, or he wouldn't have come again. For just that reason she had to get away.

"Do you understand what I'm saying?" he persisted.

"You murdered my friend, Clodius."

"I killed a Roman soldier in fair combat that he didn't have to seek. He was a fool the first time I met him, and had his throat marked in warning. Men who are fools with me a second time don't live to regret it."

She had no answer for that.

"We can't sleep on the dirt!" Savia protested instead.

Arden looked at her with interest. "Now here's a practical objection. And where would you sleep, slave?"

"This is a Roman lady! In a proper bed! Under a proper roof!"

"Why? Grass is as fine a bed as there is, in summer, and the sky the best roof. Rest easy. We'll not disturb you."

"It's too chilly to sleep!"

He grinned. "Cold enough to keep down the insects and the snakes."

"Savia, be quiet," Valeria muttered. "We'll cuddle together with our cloaks in the mud where his kind prefers to live."

"What do you mean to do with us?" Savia persisted.

The barbarian considered them solemnly. Then he smiled, his teeth as bright and clean as his scrubbed skin. He didn't display any of the ignorant squalor Valeria expected, and in fact had a rather annoying sense of self-satisfaction and apparent pride. Perhaps he was vain. Primitive people often were, she'd heard.

"For the lady here, I intend to take her home and teach her to ride, in the Celtic manner."

His meaning was unclear. "If you touch me, my ransom will be less."

"As for you," he said to Savia, "I intend to free you."

"Free me?"

"I don't like slaves, Roman or Celt. They're unhappy, and I don't like unhappy people. They're unnatural, because all other creatures run free. So when you're in my hills you'll be a slave no longer, woman."

Savia sidled closer to Valeria. "I'll not leave my mistress."

"Perhaps not. But it will be your choice, not hers."

The slave couldn't help asking it. "When?"

"Now." He stood. "You're still captive, but not a slave. You're tied up as a free woman under Celtic law, and thus are the equal of your mistress." He walked away.

Valeria watched him angrily. "He's very arrogant. Pay him no mind."

"I certainly won't." Yet Savia watched Arden go with some regret, and felt guilty at her own longings. "Being free under him is more frightening than being slave under you," she finally offered. "It's an empty promise he made."

"He's a brute and an animal and an ambushing murderer, whatever he says about fair combat," Valeria said. "The cavalry will come, you'll see, and all these terrible brigands will hang. If they sleep, we might slip these bonds and reach the horses—"

"I can't outride these barbarians!"

"You will, or you'll stay here to mop out their pigsties. Or worse." She glanced around. "Those cavalry mounts are closest and . . . oh!" She gave a little cry, staring at the nearest picketed horse.

"What?" Savia said, turning.

"Don't look!"

So of course the slave did. What she saw were four Roman heads, gaping and sightless, tied with twine and suspended from the four horns of the saddle. Whenever the horse shifted its feet, the heads rocked in unison, as if to give a mournful shake of warning.

By late morning they were moving again, riding ever farther from the Wall. Valeria had been unable to sleep and felt increasingly exhausted. Her body was sore from the kick she'd received, the long ride, and the hard ground. Her refusal of food had been a mistake. Yet no one offered her anything more or even bothered to look at her. She wasn't used to being ignored, and that annoyed her as well.

In the daylight she began to get a better sense of the barbarians' country. They rode a few fragments of old Roman roads, long abandoned after the retreat from Caledonia and recognizable principally for their straightness. Yet their general direction was more circuitous, as if to confuse both hostages and any pursuers of direction, so for the most part they followed the meandering cattle tracks and game trails that doubled as human pathways. There were no towns and few fences, the farmsteads scattered so widely that livestock grazed free. All the homes were Celtic in style, the squat round huts topped by conical thatched roofs, but they seemed meaner and poorer than the habitations south of the Wall: lower to the ground, stained by the smoke of peat, and with more rubbish in the side yards. Chickens roamed, dogs barked, naked children played in the doorways, and each habitation stank of smoke, cooked meat, hay, manure, and leather. Yet a few paces away were fields of grain, meadows of high green grass, and flocks of sheep and prancing ponies.

Their abductors never stopped. Maybe this Arden was more frightened of pursuit than he pretended. They rode into a snarl of hills, the ridges cutting off distant vision and any sense of progress, their gallop occasionally setting off an avalanche of sheep as they breasted a flock. On and on they cantered, even the Celts beginning to slump, and just as Valeria felt so dizzy, sick, and weak with hunger that she feared she might tumble from her saddle, they finally paused for evening. She was in a daze. Her home and her Marcus already seemed impossibly far away, the Wall lost in a blur of hard riding. The stabbing of Clodius was like an unreal nightmare. The country ahead looked steadily higher and more rugged, its farmsteads degenerating into grubby hovels and its fields giving way to raw moor. She was being swallowed by the wilderness.

Their camping place was by a stream in a grove of pine,

brown needles forming a cushioning carpet. The horses were picketed once more, a fire was built, and the smell of cooked meat and porridge made Valeria's stomach twist with anxious longing. Brisa brought them cheese again, and this time she accepted it eagerly, gobbling like a wolf. A skin of some kind of liquid was offered, and she squeezed it to release her first taste of acrid, foamy beer. It was awful but she drank anyway, sensing the nutrition in its dark grain. Thoughts of escape had been replaced with sheer exhaustion.

Then the Celtic woman strung her longbow, notched an arrow, motioned for Valeria and Savia to get up, and pointed to her crotch and some bushes.

"You don't have to be crude." Valeria spoke for the first time in Celtic. "I understand your tongue."

The woman was instantly wary. "How does a Roman know the language of the free tribes? You've never been in our country."

"I've been learning from the Celts at Petrianis."

"Why? Are you a spy?"

"I wanted to understand your people."

"You learned from your slaves, didn't you?"

"My helpmates."

"Your captive dogs, whipped and shorn of pride. They are Celts no more." Brisa glanced at Savia. "Does this woman know our tongue?"

"Enough to answer you," Savia said.

She considered them. "I admit that it's a novelty to meet Roman girls less stupid than the donkeys that pull them about. I've never seen one who cares for anything but her own comforts."

The savage pretended to superiority! "If you'd rather, we can try your Latin," Valeria said to put her in her place.

She motioned them to move. "You can piss," she allowed, "but if you run, I'll kill you."

The women did their business and then went to the stream to wash as the barbarian leader had. The water was shockingly cold but also restorative, jerking Valeria from weary fog to harsh, all-too-vivid life. How grubby she already felt, just a day removed from her daily bath, her combs, and her table of paints! She mourned her imagined appearance, her hair unfixed, her clothes stained, her jewelry left behind in her reckless thirst for adventure. It wasn't comfort she craved, but simple decency. She must look as rustic as the Celtic woman sitting silently behind her . . . except in truth the woman didn't look all that plain but was strangely compelling in her warrior garb, a bright necklace of silver at her throat and bracelets at her wrists. A baldric and belt held a short sword, her mail had a sheen like raindrops on a window, and the laced boots that reached to her calves were of doeskin. Her cloak was a deep green, and she displayed the same animal grace as the man Arden.

"What are you doing here?" Valeria asked her bluntly.

The woman understood what she meant. "I'm Brisa, daughter of Quint and a warrior of the Attacotti tribe. No man has yet won me, so I ride with the men."

"But you're a woman."

"What of it? I can shoot straighter than any man here, and outrun them too. They know it, and fear and respect me for it. When my brother was killed, I took his armor and sword. We Celtic women aren't soft and stupid like you. We go where we please and do what we wish and lie with who we want to."

"Like animals."

"Like free women of choice. We fulfill nature's demands by openly lying with the best men, while you Romans commit your adultery with the worst. You boast of how superior you are, and then chain yourself with fear and custom and hypocrisy. I wanted to see this wall of yours, and now I've seen it and am not impressed. I could scale it in a heartbeat."

"And be arrested just as quickly."

Brisa snorted. "I haven't seen you Romans catch one of us yet."

"It isn't natural for a woman to dress like a man," Valeria insisted doggedly.

The Celt laughed. "I'm dressed for war and riding! What isn't natural is to dress without sense, like you do. Maybe those men over there, the ones dressed like me, are dressed like women! Have you considered that?"

This Celt was turning everything around! "How did you learn to shoot?"

"My father taught me, as my mother taught me weaving. I could teach you, if we decide not to kill you." It was a matter-of-fact offer, as if the precariousness of her future was obvious enough. "To shoot, at least. We'll see if you can hit anything."

Valeria eyed the bow, secretly intrigued. "I don't even know if I could draw it."

"You pull each day, and each day you can pull it a little farther." Brisa sprang up, enjoying this opportunity to boast. "Here, I'll show you." She pulled off a bracelet. "Take this and walk twenty paces back toward the pine where you were tied."

Valeria hesitated.

"Go on, I won't hurt you. But I might hurt your companion here if you don't do what I say." She nodded toward Savia.

Valeria took the circular bracelet and began to walk back to the tree.

"There! Stop and turn!"

She did so.

"Now, hold the bracelet out at arm's length. . . ."

Valeria lifted. Before her arm had steadied, the Celt pulled and shot. A puff of wind kissed the captive's fingertips, and the shaft sang through the bracelet and hit the pine beyond. It was so sudden that the Roman heard the arrow hit wood before realizing what had happened.

She dropped the ring as if it were hot. "You could have killed me!"

Brisa walked over and scooped up her bracelet. "I didn't touch you, but I can put my arrow through any Roman's eye, so don't quarrel with me until I've taught you to do the same. *If* Arden lets you live." She shouldered her bow. "Which I suspect he'll do, from the way he looks at you. Come, the food smells ready. You need meat on those bones of yours if you're going to stay warm in the north."

The food and the fire were restorative, and despite her apprehension, Valeria felt a drowsy relief. The barbarians gath-

ered around the flames afterward to sing and boast. None
bothered to post a watch. No rescuers appeared. Instead, the
captives had to hear their enemies crow, each in turn, about
their prowess in the ambush. To these ragged people the
mere deed was not enough, it seemed, but only took on true
importance in the retelling. They were as vain as children.
"The Romans understand our tongue, brothers," the woman
told them. "Let's remind them of what they have seen."

Brisa boasted that shooting through the neck of the Celtic
spy had been "like threading a bone needle in a lightless
room." Luca recounted how he'd tripped the Roman tribune
with a stick shoved out from the bushes. The warriors guf-
fawed at the memory of Clodius's awkward sprawl. A Celt
named Hool bragged that his second arrow at the Roman
soldiers was notched and drawn before the first had even hit
home. The stripling named Gurn claimed to have stolen all
the Roman horses before their riders were dead.

Only the chieftain Arden stayed quiet, declining to retell
how he'd killed the Roman tribune with a bold and desperate thrust. Instead he studied Valeria across the fire, as if
speculating what to do with her. As the eating ended and the
warriors rolled themselves up in their cloaks, swords alongside, he came around to sit by her. She stiffened warily.

"I saw what Brisa did with her arrow," he said quietly.
"Don't be afraid. We're warriors, not thieves. You're a prize
of war and will be kept safe."

"But there's no war."

"There's been a war ever since your husband burned our
sacred grove. He united the tribes as no druid could have."

"That was because you attacked me before! The ambush,
in the forest!"

"The druids had nothing to do with that."

"That's not what our spy told my Marcus."

"Told Marcus? Or told Galba?"

"They wanted to burn me in a wicker cage."

He smiled. "You know nothing of what's going on. But
there are men in your cavalry who know the truth."

"Which men?"

He wouldn't answer.

She studied him curiously. He'd killed Clodius, true, but his bearing and words suggested he wasn't a simple savage. His look was thoughtful, his manner almost courtly, his bearing slightly Roman. "You don't have the beard or the mustache or the manners of a Celt," she said. "Your Latin is fluent and your swordsmanship trained. Who are you?"

"I'm of my people."

"No. You're something more."

"You seem very confident in your judgment."

"You don't conceal yourself as well as you think."

He smiled. "Roman aristocrats judge and rank people as surely as a Briton hound trails a badger."

"There, you see? You know too much about Roman aristocrats!"

He laughed. "You're my prisoner! I should be asking questions of you!"

"But you act as if you know all about me. It's I who am in your power, and who doesn't know her fate. Why have you taken me, and what are you going to do with me?"

He thought before answering, studying her features in the fire like a trophy long sought. "I'm a Caledonian of the Attacotti tribe," he said finally, "with a long bloodline among the tribes of the north. But yes, I know something of Rome." He raised an arm, revealing a tattoo. "I enlisted in your army."

"You're a deserter!"

"I'm a free man, come back to help my people remain free. I enlisted to see this Roman world of yours and learn enough to beat you. I'm a patriot, lady, fighting against the suffocations of your world."

His conviction was maddening. "I was wrong in my guess," she said. "You know nothing of Rome."

"It's you, pampered and highborn, who knows nothing. How much do you know about the commoners who groan to feed your kind?"

"I know more than you think! My father is a senator with feeling for the poor."

"Who sent his own daughter to the edge of the empire for enough coin to maintain his office. And so now you sit captive and cold, with a deserter and murderer and traitor like me, while he gives speeches and takes bribes a thousand miles away."

"That's not fair!"

"It's the morality of a poisoned empire."

"We brought the world peace!"

"By leaving it a wasteland."

"Yet you don't fear my husband's revenge."

"My fear is why you're alive. Your safety is our own. Our doom is yours."

Valeria drew her cloak around herself, pondering. It was odd being outdoors at night, the fire's warm fingers caressing the front of her, the night's cold teeth biting at her back. With no roof overhead, the dark emptiness yawed above like a pool she could fall into. "There's something more," she said with sudden certainty. "Some other reason you hate Rome and have made me captive."

He stood up. "I need to sleep now."

"But you haven't even told me your name yet."

"It's Arden. As you know."

"Yes, but what other name do you go by? What's the name of your clan?"

His response was so quiet she almost missed it. "I go by Arden Caratacus. Caratacus the patriot." He gave her a quick look and then stepped away.

Valeria watched him disappear into the shadows. Arden Caratacus: Galba's spy.

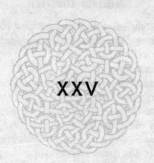

XXV

The dungeon of the legionary fortress of Eburacum was
hewn out of foundation rock by captive Britons some three
hundred years ago. The prison, when its oak and iron door
is swung open, has the encrusted odor of blood and tears of
all that time. Stone steps, worn down in the center from the
ceaseless tramp of hobnailed boots, descend into lamp-lit
gloom. Even I, who have interviewed countless prisoners in
the meanest of cells, hesitate. The Roman sentry beckons impatiently. I follow, my footfalls returning to me as echoes,
and I wonder what it must feel like to be dragged down this
stone staircase and hear the door slamming ominously
above for the last time, cast into darkness and lost forever to
sunlight.

Up to now my informants have been brought to me. This
one, the Celtic priest Kalin, I must visit myself. The soldiers
fear him and will not risk allowing him up to the surface.
He's a druid with claim to ancient magic and prophetic vi-
sions, and so is chained deep to keep his powers buried.
Most of the garrison would prefer to see him dead, but I've
ordered him kept alive. These druids, these relics from the
past: Were they instigators or victims? Will the barbarians
come again?

At the bottom of the steps is a dank tunnel much like a cat-
acomb. The air inside feels heavy, and it stinks of the smoke
of oil lamps. A feeble cone of light from the narrow ventila-
tion shaft at the tunnel's far end shows cavities gated with
iron bars. Behind these sit the dungeon's inhabitants, dispirited men that if not executed will simply grow crazed. The

guards say you get used to the smell and the sorrow, but I
don't believe them. Dungeon duty is considered punishment.
Despair grinds at a man.

"This way, inspector."

I wonder what infraction won this soldier, this day, the
task of being my guide.

We walk down the passageway past the deserters, traitors,
murderers, and madmen, the rapists and politically ill-
favored, all those banished to underworlds such as this. At the
very end is Kalin. The druid's brown robe clings to him like an
old dry husk. The druid's spirit is gone, I think. I hope he is not
already insane. But no. A moment later he recognizes our
presence and moves toward us, in the tentative way of a beaten
dog. His chains rattle when he does so.

"Open the door," I command.

"It's safer to speak to him from out here, inspector."

"And less useful. Lock me in with him and leave us
alone."

The cell door clangs shut behind me and I listen to the
rap of boots fade away. I cough, trying to ignore the druid's
stink. When we're caged like animals we become animals.
Kalin unfolds himself from his corner and stands waver-
ingly, his wrists weighted with shackles. His eyes are
sunken, his lips cracked, his hair a greasy tangle. The
bravado with which he led barbarian armies has left him, of
course. Dangerous? He seems broken enough.

"Is it over?" he whispers.

He means death. "No." I disappoint him. "I am Inspector
Draco, come to explain the recent uprising against the Wall.
I need to understand what happened."

He looks at me dully. "Understand? I'm here. I've lost."

"Of course you have lost. But the emperor desires permanent peace. He wants to understand your people."

"My people?"

"The Celts. The druids. The tribes. The ones who choose
to live as barbarians. We seek neither to conquer you nor
fight you. That is why the Wall was built. We wish only to
maintain our border. So: why did you attack us?"

He blinks. It occurs to me that it might be difficult for him to remember beyond the nightmare of his incarceration. Then: "You attacked us."

"You mean the incident at the grove."

He doesn't like my choice of word. "Your 'incident,' Roman, slew the high priestess Mebde and burned the sacred oak."

"The druids were inciting the tribes."

"That's a lie. We care nothing for politics. We simply worship wood and rock, stream and sky."

This is the lie, I know. The druids wield as much power as barbarian chieftains and guard their influence zealously, plying on the superstition of their followers. Spirit, magic, and capricious fortune dominate the Celtic world. Their wizards and witches are all. "And yet you were there to direct the ambush at the grove, I am told. It was a trap for the Roman cavalry, was it not? A trap set by Caratacus to either massacre the Petriana or provoke the tribes. And you helped later to assault the Wall."

"You asked why. The answer is that it is you who started the trouble, not us."

"Except that the wife of the Roman commander, Marcus Flavius, was nearly abducted on the way to her wedding."

"I know nothing of that."

"Yet you met the lady afterward, at the hill fort of Arden Caratacus, after a second abduction succeeded."

"So?" *His tone is guarded.*

"I am interested in this woman. I am trying to understand her role in what happened. My theory is that if the tribes hadn't tried to steal her, perhaps none of this would have ever occurred."

He smiles thinly. "You think a single woman can cause so much trouble?"

That's my question—remember Troy!—but his skepticism makes me hesitant. "I want to know what became of her."

Kalin, pinned like a brown butterfly to our rock wall, shakes his head. "If you want reason for events, look to the gods, inspector. Look at what you Romans have done to the *sacred places. Look to Taranis and Dagda and Morrigan. Hear them in the summer thunder and the winter winds. You're a plague upon the land, you Romans, with your crowded cities and arrogant engineers. But the old gods are rising again."*

Brave words for a man shackled in a hole, I think. "No, Kalin, it is your gods who are dead. Sometimes I think even Rome's gods are dead, replaced by this Jewish usurper. Maybe all the gods are dead, and men are alone in this world. In any event, I know Rome will endure as Rome has always endured."

He shakes his head doggedly. "I see it coming. I see your end."

It's his blind conviction that chills me, his certainty in the face of all reason. The generals are right. It's extermination of his kind, not conversion, that's the only solution if civilization is to remain safe. "And yet you're conquered, and I'm among the conquerors."

He squats. "So kill me and be done with it."

Here he gives me the opportunity to enlist him. "No, I have ordered you kept alive. I honestly want to understand these gods of yours, and something of this Roman woman you took. This Valeria. I don't understand what the tribes wanted with her."

"You'll keep me alive if I tell you this?"

"I will do my best."

"Existence in this burrow isn't life."

"We fear your magic, wizard."

"My people don't build dungeons. We let every man live in the open air. If he's a transgressor, then his clan must make payment to the clan that was sinned upon. If he's defiant, we cast him out. If he returns, we sacrifice him. But cage him? That's cruelty."

"You are not among your people."

"I want to go back to my people."

I'm quiet a moment. "I will confer with the duke if you will help me." *There's no chance, of course, but I need Kalin's hope.*

"You'll do more than that." *Suddenly his smile is dis-*

turbingly confident. "You're wrong, Inspector Draco. My gods are not dead. Last night the full moon hung above the shaft and whispered to me from her milk. Then today you've come. It's a sign that what I say is true. The gods speak through you. You're a messenger of fate."

This is so obviously insane that I know better than to say so. "But I will not speak to the duke until you help me," I go on. "Until you tell me why this woman was abducted."

"You're obsessed with her, aren't you? Like Caratacus."

"And who is he?"

"A Celt turned Roman soldier, come back to our side with sorrow and revenge in his heart. This senator's daughter could bring ransom. She was a hostage to control the cavalry of her husband. She bought us time while people found their courage."

"So she was a strategic asset," I sum up. "That's why this Caratacus risked capturing her a second time. Yet how did he know she'd be at that spring?"

"Galba promised she'd be there."

Here we have it, at last. "Brassidias was a traitor, then."

"Was he? Giving Valeria to Caledonia actually kept the peace. Her capture left her husband impotent. Her abduction promised to preserve that truce you say Rome desires."

"Galba used her for peace?"

"Galba understood the Wall in ways that his commander never could."

"And Caratacus was Galba's agent."

"Arden was no man's agent, and no man's dupe. It was he who suggested trying a second time to capture the woman, not Galba."

"But you said Caratacus wanted revenge, not peace."

"I say the motives of Arden were as transparent as those of Galba were complex. The rest of us could see it in his eyes and his manner."

"What? What was he after?"

"Not just what the woman could do for us, but the woman herself, of course."

Why am I surprised?

"Don't you understand what happened?" Kalin asks. "He'd been ensnared by her during that first ambush in the forest. The capture had nothing to do with war or revenge or Roman plotting. He simply couldn't rest until he won her for himself."

XXVI

As Valeria's abductors rode up a grassy hill to the earth-and-wooden fort that crowned it, her eyes desperately sought escape. Surely cavalry patrols were searching for her right now! Not only did she need rescue, she had information vital to the Roman cause: that Galba's informant was, in fact, the brigand who'd first ambushed her. Just what this meant she wasn't sure, but Marcus needed to know that the agent who'd told the Petriana about the druids in the sacred grove actually seemed faithful to the barbarian side. Either that, or he was a scoundrel who played each camp against the other. Why? Was this Arden trying to foment a full-scale war? By capturing a senator's daughter, he'd surely taken a dangerous step toward one.

She looked toward the tall and arrogant man riding ahead of her, his unbound hair falling in a mane to his shoulders, his sword strapped across his broad back, his arms bare and brown and corded with muscle as he gripped the reins of his stallion, his neck revealing the glint, when he turned, of a golden torque of valor. His manner seemed careless now that he was back in his own country, and that was good. His confidence would be his undoing.

The chieftain's fort crowned the hill like a tonsure, circling its crest with a ditch, earthen dike, and low palisade. The crude enclosure protected a large, timbered central building, a dozen round Celtic houses with peaked thatched roofs, and pens and corrals for livestock and horses. Twin wooden towers flanked the gate, warriors on the platform of each blowing horns of welcome as the raiding party rode the winding path up the slope. More barbarians crowded the fort's log parapet, yelling and jeering.

The climb gave a grand view of the country they'd just ridden through, and Valeria looked back across the gray hills to the south. The world looked wild and disturbingly empty, a haven only for barbarians and beasts. She imagined for a moment she saw out there a flash of armor from pursuing horsemen, pounding to her rescue, but then admitted it was just the reflection of the sun on distant ponds. She imagined she saw the white of the Wall, but admitted it was only low, distant cloud. She did notice that at the base of the hill were more houses, a ramble of grain fields, and an enclosure for horses. Could she steal one and ride away on her own? Or would they lock her in a wicker man, the flame kept ready for her husband's approach?

The Roman aristocrat glanced down the line of horsemen to poor Savia, hoping her maidservant might have ideas that had eluded her. Yet the slave didn't return her look, having slumped into despondency. If Arden's promise of freedom had encouraged the woman, Savia gave no sign. Even her complaints had ceased.

Valeria had never felt so hopeless.

Arden Caratacus, in contrast, rode like a prince, his fist lifted to the whoops of men and cheers of women, savoring his triumph like a general of Rome. They called to him from his fort.

"You've brought us a Roman kitten, I see!"

"Did she not stick your horse this time, topple-bottom?"

"Does she fuck as well as she fights?"

"How much gold can we squeeze with this one?"

And then howls and shouts as they rode between the two towers.

"Where's your husband, my pretty? Has he lost you?"

"Rome must be ripe for robbery to give up the likes of you!"

"This is what Romans get for burning sacred trees, tyrant bitch!"

The fortress courtyard was a bog of mud, straw, and manure, a trampled forum in which dogs leaped, horses pissed, and children screamed and scampered. Cooking smoke drifted from the buildings, and flies orbited a dung pile. As the mounted warriors swung down into the mire, the mob streamed off the earthen dike to greet them in an exultant tide. Valeria and Savia stayed stiffly mounted, disdainful of the filth and fearful of the host of alien blonds and redheads who crowded around. While most of this enclosure was drab, the clothing of both sexes was a complicated pattern of browns and bright colors, Valeria noticed, all checks and stripes and diamonds. Their jewelry was heavy and ostentatious, their weapons oversize, their hair a deliberate cascade of curls. There was no subtlety or stoicism among them; all was for display. The women were as boisterous as men, rude and coarse-tongued, and their children wrestled and punched and squealed. Most in the crowd were young, and all were fit, so why didn't they have energy for simple paving? The place was a sty, and not one of these Celts had the breeding to even notice. Males were pummeling Caratacus in welcome, and females were giving him hugs and lewd kisses, all of them exultant at the capture of an aristocratic Roman. She was a trophy.

Only one woman didn't share the mood of triumph. She searched the riders' faces with growing dismay and then ran wailing to the shrouded body of the Celt that Clodius had killed with the javelin, throwing herself against the horse that bore the corpse and sobbing sorrow to her gods.

Arden glanced in sympathy but made no move to comfort. Death was the warrior's fate, and everyone knew it.

Instead, he raised both arms to quiet his rabble. "I've brought you guests!"

They howled anew, buffeting the Romans with taunts. "Take the fat off the one and fit it to the bones of the other, and you'd have a single decent captive, Arden!"

"Does the regal one like to gallop?"

"Give me the other for my barn! She's got the butt of my horse, the udders of my cow, and the pout of my prettiest sow!"

Valeria sat straight, determined to maintain aristocratic indifference. *You are a daughter of Rome!* Secretly, she feared she was about to be raped.

Caratacus motioned for quiet again. "And as guests of the

clan of Caratacus, tribe of the Attacotti, land of the Caledonians, these women are to be treated as you'd treat your mother or sister. These captives are weapon and resource if treated well; useless if foolishly harmed. I say to them now that I guarantee their safety with my own heart and arm—and if any trespass against them, then they have trespassed against me." He glanced around in challenge. His warning briefly subdued the crowd.

"And trespassed against me," another rough voice added. Valeria felt a shock of recognition at the sound. Cassius! It was her bodyguard, who'd disappeared at the ambush. "I protected her once, and I'll do so again," the ex-gladiator told his new clan. "I had no quarrel with the girl when I ran to freedom." He shouldered his way to the front of the crowd, more thickly muscled than any of them, now a great Celtic sword at his side.

Arden nodded and went on. "I've freed the fat one named Savia, but she'll work in the Great House as she worked for Rome. Eventually she'll choose her own future. The skinny one is called Valeria, and she's going to tell us more about her husband and his men. Don't insult her, for she's a great lady in the city of Rome."

They hooted in derision, laughing at their great lady.

"No, listen!" Arden protested. "We can learn from her!"

"Learn arrogance and corruption and crushing taxation!" one man shouted.

"Learn treachery and ruthlessness!" added another.

"Valeria will learn from us in turn: the pleasure of life among the free and proud Attacotti!" At this they roared approval. There was promise and a glint of humor in his eyes as he looked at her then, as if he knew her heart and understood her fears. She found it disquieting that he believed he could understand anything at all about her, and disturbing to find herself grateful for his small charities. This man was her husband's enemy and friend's killer. "She'll live among us and become one of us."

"And which bed will she share, Arden Caratacus?" one woman cackled.

He looked solemn. "Whichever she chooses, like any

Celtic woman. She'll begin in the Great House as guest, and have her maid for company if the freed woman Savia agrees."

Heads turned to the maidservant.

"I'll not leave my mistress no matter what you proclaim," Savia said, her voice quavering but her words unexpectedly brave. "I, too, am a woman of Rome, and I still serve my lady." She stiffly got off her horse, legs buckling for a moment, and then walked unsteadily to help Valeria dismount as well. The two women stood in the mud and held each other against the tall people who surrounded them, the men powerful, the women lovely and haughty, the children curious and impudent, their dogs pushing to sniff and whine.

"I'm terrified of being alone with these savages," the slave whispered.

"They've freed you, Savia."

"I'm terrified of depending on myself."

The rectangular Great House dominated the hill fort like a forum's temple or a castle's keep, its forty-foot height and two-hundred-foot length evidence of more sophisticated construction than Valeria had expected the Celts could produce. Its pillars were made of intricately carved pine, birds riding curved vines that climbed in swirls up the length of each column. Beams ended in the sculpted and painted heads of dragons and unicorns and gaping gods. Painted moons and stars were scattered across the tall door. Pictured horses, sinuous and galloping, circled the otherwise gray and weathered wood of the building's periphery as black-and-white abstractions. It was as intricate a construction as her trousseau chest from Rome, and infinitely larger. How had these rude people built such a thing? How had they even dragged the trees?

Inside, high windows under the building's eaves let in a crosshatch of light from glassless openings that could be shuttered against storms. Smoke had stained the interior dark, but in compensation the side aisles and rafters were decorated with bright banners, woven tapestries, painted shields, and crossed spears. Horns and heads of trophy animals were mounted on every pillar. Underfoot were rush mats to catch the courtyard mud. The long oaken tables smelled of wood, smoke, and beer.

It was here that the clan of Arden Caratacus gathered each evening to eat, boast, sing, and plot. Here that legend and druidic lore was passed on, generation after generation. Here that information was traded, gossip spawned, lies told and challenged, quarrels settled, flirtations started, children spanked, games played, cups filled, dogs fed, and cats left to hunt mice in the alcoves.

Wood-paneled sleeping cells opened off the communal hall. It was to one of these that Brisa, the archer, and Cassius, the escaped slave, led Valeria and Savia.

"Since you don't have man or family, you'll sleep here," Brisa said. The chamber had two wooden sleeping platforms piled with wool fleece and furs, a copper basin to wash in, and a scrubbed board floor. There was a tapestry of a fantastic forest, woven in rainbow colors, a table with a bronze hand mirror, and a shelf with rank of candles. The wax smelled of berries and the sea. It was plain, but clean.

"Are you going to lock us in?" Savia asked, peering from the threshold.

"There's no need. You've nowhere to go."

"Can we lock others out?" Valeria asked.

"None will bother you."

"I sleep nearby," Cassius said, "and I'll protect you as I did before. Don't fear, lady, you're safer here than on the streets of Rome."

"Not very reassuring, Cassius, after your desertion in the forest."

He bowed his head. "That wasn't meant as insult to you. I know how Roman soldiers mock gladiators, and I'd no desire to live among them. I was dreading the Wall."

"These people treat you like a prince, it seems."

"I'm free, lady, and not just by being my own master. I'm free in ways hard to explain. You'll understand in time."

Savia sniffed. "It's a rude and primitive place you're free in, Cassius."

"And you, too, woman. Arden told me what he granted you." She blushed.

"What's going to happen to us?" Valeria asked.

Brisa shrugged. "Only the gods know that. The gods and the druids."

Valeria felt apprehensive at mention of their priests. While Marcus had tried to keep the ghastly tales from her, slaves kept nothing secret. She'd heard the rumors of human sacrifice. "I've seen no druids here," she said with faint hope. "Only that cocky thief who brought us here, this Caratacus."

"He's a chieftain, not a thief. And Kalin, priest of the sacred oak, will be here tonight like the midnight owl."

"Who's Kalin?"

"The druid who advises our clan. He fought your Romans in the sacred grove."

"Why is he coming here?"

"To see *you*, of course."

"Am I to be ransomed?" It was a polite way to ask if she was going to be killed.

"You're asking as if it were my decision to make," the Celtic woman said, not unkindly. "Or Cassius, or Arden, or Kalin. But you're north of the Wall now, Roman. Maybe it will be you who decides your fate. You and your goddess. Maybe your future is already cast by the runes and the stars."

"Or by the one true god, the Lord Jesus," Savia spoke up.

"Who?" Brisa asked.

"The Savior of us all," the maidservant said.

"I haven't heard of this god."

"He's the new god of the Roman world. Even the emperor worships him."

"And what kind of god is he?"

"A good and meek one," Savia said. "He was killed by Roman soldiers."

The woman laughed. "This is your savior? A god who can't save himself?"

"He rose from the dead."

At this she showed more respect. "When was this?"

"More than three hundred years ago."

Now she looked skeptical. "And where is he now?"

"In heaven."

"Well." She looked at them with doubt. "Each woman finds her own goddess or god who speaks to her heart in a special way, like a lover or brother or husband. So you can have this alive-and-dead-and-remote god if you wish, it matters not to me. But our gods are all around us, in the rocks and the trees and the flowers, in every spring and every cloud, and they've kept my people free of you Romans for that same three hundred years. In Caledonia it's these gods that have power. My advice is to listen for the god that sings to your heart and ask him or her, not me, what will become of you."

"You suggest this," Valeria objected, "after we've been abducted and brought here against our will and shown to this small room."

"But perhaps not against your god's will." Brisa gave them a slight smile. "You're of our clan now, Roman lady, and your fate is linked to ours. You can spend your days wishing you were somewhere else if you want, but I say you should eat and sleep and weave and hunt and wait for gods, not men, to tell us what to do."

A hundred people ate in the Great Hall, women shocking Valeria by sitting casually on the benches alongside their men. Both sexes helped cook and serve, children fought and crawled underfoot, dogs prowled for scraps and nipped each other's flanks, and the hearth fires cast a red, wavering light. A great iron kettle was filled with water and warmed by heated stones for the company to wash there before eating, the Celts surprising her with their fastidiousness. Contrary to what she'd been warned in Rome, they cared how they looked and smelled! For this celebration of Arden's return, the men and women had carefully combed their hair and chosen their best jewelry, some men painting the stripes of war on their faces, and some women using berry juice and ash to accent their lips and highlight their eyes. Yet just when she was ready to admit that Romans had some things in common with these rough people, and hope that she might understand them, a common cup was passed down their rank, and Valeria realized to her horror that the cup was in fact the crown of a skull, hacked from some victim, given two handles and plated with yellow gold.

"You drink from the dead?"

"We honor the spirit of our enemies by venerating their heads," Brisa explained matter-of-factly. "The head is the seat of the soul."

The Celts paid their prisoners no particular mind, neither honoring a Roman lady with proper seat and deference nor putting her in shackles or bonds. Savia was drafted to help with the serving, but Valeria was spared that indignity, the rough warriors glancing almost shyly at her beauty while their tall chieftain pretended indifference. Their lack of watchfulness astounded and somewhat heartened her. I could thrust this carving knife right into one of their eyes, she thought. Yet she also feared that such an assault would be more difficult than it seemed in the genial chaos of supper, that a strong arm would be quick to deflect her blow or a maid to cry warning, and then she herself would be dead. So she did nothing, eating an embarrassing amount because she was so famished, and watched with fascination the pride and equality that the women assumed with their men, challenging their boasts and braying their own jokes and offering their own opinions on the pasturing of the clan herd, the tyrannies of weather, or the impotence of Romans. A single turma of disciplined cavalry could slice through the lot like a pin through a grape, she knew, and yet the warriors who'd captured her boasted yet again of its prowess at the spring, and the haplessness of her doomed rescuers.

The forced memory brought to mind the death of Clodius and the waste of his young life, depressing Valeria anew. The barbarian had slain her best friend, the man she'd ridden to protect! He'd belittled the power of her husband! He was a sworn enemy of Rome! She glanced at his handsome figure at the head of the table, hating his triumph. Should she endure existence among them and wait for fate, as Brisa had suggested? Somehow try to signal the soldiers she was certain must be searching? Or escape to find a way home?

While the men seemed less threatening than she'd feared, one of the women seemed more so. She was a Celtic beauty with a proud and watchful manner and flame-red hair who periodically would cast a glance of distaste at Valeria and then look past to give a covetous stare at Arden. Well, that was plain enough. You can have him! Yet the chieftain seemed to pay no mind to her, either. If the maid hoped to cast a spell with her eye, the chieftain just as assiduously avoided it. Valeria asked Brisa who she was.

"That's Asa." She speared a piece of pork. "A lover of Caratacus but not betrothed as she'd hoped. She's as skilled with weapons as I am, and dangerous to cross. Stay friends with Brisa, Roman, if Asa becomes your enemy."

"She's very beautiful."

"She's used to having men's eyes on her, not you. Don't be alone with her."

The songs turned from skirmishes with the Romans to older and grander tales of great raids and foggy voyages, of dragon hoards and mythic beasts. While the company lingered at table, they ate sparingly, Valeria realized, avoiding the intentional gluttony she'd seen at Roman banquets. Savia kept munching contentedly, as starved by the recent adventures as Valeria was, and Brisa began looking disapprovingly at the maidservant's steady consumption. Finally she spoke sharply.

"Leave off, freed Roman, or you'll owe the table the fatgelt."

Savia looked up with her mouth full. "The what?"

"It's a useless Celt that can't run and fight. We levy a tax on anyone who gets too fat. A body's form is a reflection of the gods. Eat too much, and you'll pay for it until you lose enough to earn it back."

"But I'm not a Celt."

"You are if you prove yourself useful. Turned out to starve if you don't."

Savia glanced around at the others and reluctantly sat back from her plate. "Yours is a cruel country, to prepare all this food and not eat it."

"Only Romans eat everything. We eat only what we need. That is why your side of the Wall is so poor, all cut over and the earth sliced open and streams impounded, while on ours it is more like the gods intended it, where flowers still sing to the sun."

"If you farmed better, you could eat more."

"If I built a fire twenty feet high, I could sit farther away, but where's the sense in that?"

At length it was late, and Valeria longed for sleep, yet the assembly showed no sign of breaking up. She could hear a hiss of rain and guessed that most of the clan had decided to sleep through the coming wet morning. Perhaps time had less meaning here.

There was also a camaraderie that made clan members linger. Most of these Celts were related, and all had a role to play in their small society: the storyteller, the jokester, the warrior, the mother hen, the tippler, the magician, the singer, the cook. They knew each other's strengths, weaknesses, skills, feelings, and past, and interacted without rank. Valeria herself felt isolated, defeated, and homesick, and wanted only to crawl between the woolens and furs of her bed. She began to watch for an opportunity to creep off and do so, but before it came, there were shouts, the opening of a door that let in a blast of wet wind, and then its slamming shut behind a newly entered guest, hooded and mud-splattered. It was a man, Valeria saw, stamping and wet, his frame tall and gaunt, his features shrouded. At his arrival the crowd grew quiet.

The newcomer lingered in shadow a moment, his gaze briefly holding every eye, and Valeria felt chilled at realizing who this must be, this figure of dark gods and blood sacrifice. Would she be given to him for his magic?

"You've come to us like the midnight owl, Kalin!" Arden called.

"An owl, yes, but not wise enough to stay out of the rain." The self-deprecation surprised her. "It's wet as a crannog in a spring freshet out there. Cold as the butt of a bony woman. Dark as the hole in a centurion's ass."

The assembly laughed.

The druid put back his hood, and Valeria could see he was balding on top, his hair cut short, his nose like a beak, and his eyes sly and inquisitive. The man's flickering gaze picked her out, too. He came through the group, making quiet greeting, working his way to the head of the plank table while occasionally glancing at her, and finally came to Arden with his eye still fixed on the Roman. "Well, Carata-cus. Is that piece of downy fluff your latest capture?"

Valeria felt physically and emotionally ragged but still carried her Italian beauty and Roman poise: her complexion unblemished, her stola stained but fine, her figure trim, her carriage delicate. Unconsciously, she held herself straighter.

"Our highborn guest," Arden replied.

"Welcome to the north, Roman lady," the druid said. "Refuge of the free, home of the unconquered, where we give no tribute to distant emperors and honor the gods of the oak. I've heard your tale. You've Celtic spirit to ride to save a friend."

"And yet he wasn't saved," Valeria replied more coolly than she felt, startled at the sound of her own voice in the quiet. "And I'm not really free."

"A temporary situation. Soon all Britannia will be free. When it is, you will be too."

His smug confidence annoyed her. "No, soon this fort will be burned by the Roman cavalry, and you'll cook in its flames. *That's* when I'll be free."

The assembly cheered this boldness.

"You haven't won her over yet," Kalin observed to Arden.

"She's not an easy one to win."

"Do you fear her?"

"I respect her."

"And will her husband come after her?"

"We can hope, but I've no word of it yet."

This news stung. Surely the men of the Petriana were looking by now! Perhaps they were waiting for Marcus to hurry back from his meeting with the duke. Perhaps this conversation was a trick to make her give up hope. "He'll come," Valeria promised.

"No," the druid said. "He'll bluster, but he'll not risk your death or his own career by challenging us so deep in Cale-donii territory. We're letting him know that it would be your dying throes we'd use to forecast the course of battle." Savia took sharp breath at this threat. "Unless your husband is a very stupid man, lady, you'll be our guest for some time. As a water girl, perhaps. Or a grinder."

"Absolutely not! Treat me nobly or suffer the consequences!"

"She likes to make threats," Arden said, as if he had to explain for her.

"Threats that are laughable unless you have the power to carry them out," the druid said. And indeed, the men were laughing at her! They were treating her like a fool! Even Asa, still watching from the end, was smirking.

"Send me home so we can avert a war," Valeria tried miserably.

"The war has started, lady, with your husband's burning. The drums and pipes have been sounded all along the Highlands ever since to bear the tale. Caratacus here invited Roman miscalculation, and your husband had only two choices in the grove: to be destroyed by ambush or, failing that, to provoke wider war. Now we wait for the right moment. You're our guarantee of safety until that moment comes."

"Then I'll run away, long before you use me in this war of yours!"

The druid smiled and gestured at the shadows of the Great Hall, larger and blacker as the coals died. "Where would you run? How would you find your way home? Before you go back to your old world, why don't you open your eyes to this one? Then report back to the Romans. Make them understand."

"Understand what?"

"That for the first time in your life you're free, and thus truly alive. Give thanks, because the alternative is to be like them." He pointed.

It was then she realized that the corner shadows were not as empty as she'd assumed them to be, that four faces were watching her, and that the four were the mournful, shut-eyed, severed heads of the Romans that had dangled from a pony, now mounted on spear points and posted in the murk of the four corners of the hall.

*   *   *

Valeria sat up near dawn.

As Brisa said, there was no lock at her chamber. Savia was snoring gently, overcome by exhaustion, but her mistress had been too distraught to sleep. It wasn't just her own plight that was agonizing. Her capture could paralyze her husband and destroy his career. There would never be a better time to escape. She must take advantage of their arrogance.

Stealthily, she opened her door and peered out. There were a few drunk and satiated Celts passed out in the banquet hall, but none stirred when she emerged. There was no guard to issue a challenge. Did they really think her so helpless? The Roman crept along to a side door and slipped outside, pressing herself against the wood of the Great House. She regretting leaving Savia, but the slave would only slow her down.

A light rain still fell, obscuring the moon. The only glow she saw was from a watchfire at the guardhouse near the main gate. No escape that way, and no chance of taking her mare Boudicca. Yet she remembered the horses corralled in the dell below. She ran lightly across the wet mud of the courtyard between two of the round dwellings. A dog barked to no one. She scrambled up the dike that formed the lower part of the fort wall and peered over the log palisade. The night was ink. She couldn't see the bottom of the surrounding ditch or the slope of the hill beyond. Good. No one would see her, either. She hoisted herself, balanced a moment on the rough logs while fearing a cry or arrow, and then jumped, slithering down into the ditch and its puddles. Then up the other side and down the grassy hill, breathless and exultant.

No one saw her. No one called.

She was soaked, cold, and free.

XXVII

The euphoria didn't last long.

It was past noon the next day, and Valeria was bewildered, depressed, and increasingly afraid. The forest she found herself in was still and deep, without lane or trail, trunk ranked behind trunk as densely as a phalanx. All vision was blocked. All navigation was impossible. It was too drizzly to see the sun, and her sense of direction had become muddled. Just hours after her bold escape, the Roman fugitive was thoroughly lost.

At first her flight had gone well. She'd slid to the bottom of the fortress hill, grateful that the rain shrouded her movements. Dawn had been a sullen lightening of grays that neither awakened the settlement nor silhouetted her against the trees. She'd crept past farm fields of young grain, darted through an orchard, and found horses grazing in a long-grass meadow. Squirming through a brushwood fence that scratched her face and arms, she'd managed to approach a brown mare without spooking it. Valeria's soft murmurs had gotten her close enough to reach the animal's mane, and even as the horse began to sidestep, she'd hauled herself up and on, feeling precarious but bold for riding bareback. A kick got the horse moving, and a cry from a watchboy helped urge it to run. She'd closed her eyes as they neared the brushwood boundary; the horse bunched and leaped, and they were breathlessly over, weaving through a natural park of trees as the lowing bleat of a cattle horn gave first warning.

She'd feared immediate pursuit, but there'd been no sign of one.

Maybe she'd truly outrun the drunken, snoring barbarians.

The horse had slowed after a while, its flanks heaving as it blew great clouds of vapor after its dash. Clucking to urge it forward, Valeria had angled upward along the slope of a ridge until gaining the grass-and-rock crest, trying to aim south. Then fearing pursuit along so direct a course, she'd left the ridge after two miles and ridden down into a narrow valley to cross a stream and gain another ridge on the far side. She'd angle east while making for the Wall. More ridges, across a small wood and smaller clearing, up a hill and over, down into a much larger forest, picking her way through dense trees . . .

Now she was lost.

It wasn't simply that she didn't know the best way home through these woods. She didn't even know how to find her way out of them. They seemed endless, like that forest where Caratacus had almost captured her before the marriage. It was summer by the calendar, cold but leafy, and the green canopy was so thick and dark that her way was a labyrinth of sylvan tunnels. Valeria was fiercely hungry; her escape had been so sudden and impulsive that she'd forgotten to bring food. She was cold because she'd fled without her cloak. She'd counted on sun that wouldn't appear and a swift route she couldn't find. Worse, she was dispirited and lonely. She hadn't enough sleep since leaving the Petriana, and was operating on fear.

Hours passed, a blur of trees and bogs and blind, tiny meadows. She came finally to a small stream winding through the forest, its steel gleam reflecting leaden sky. This brook was marshy and surrounded by dead alder, the sticklike trees drowned by dark water. It was a desolate place. Following the boggy waterway might mire her horse, so she decided to cross in hopes of finding firmer ground on the other side. She'd have to hurry because the day was waning. The thought of spending a night alone in the woods terrified her.

She started down the muddy bank, no different from a dozen others, and then stopped in confusion.

There were hoof prints in the mud, filled with water.

Valeria looked around. The woods were quiet, with no

sign that other humans had ever passed here. And yet there was something familiar about this crossing, that leaning trunk, this sunken log . . .

Her heart sank as she realized the truth. She was riding in circles.

Valeria looked at her tracks in stupefaction, then slid from her horse to cry.

There was a boulder on the bank, and she sat miserably on that, weeping in frustration and cursing herself for not having remained on the ridges. Cursing herself for having come to Britannia at all! Clodius had been right. It was a hideous country of barbarians and swamps. Her decision to follow Marcus to Britannia had been a disaster, and her decision to find him on her own was disaster compounded. Her own girlish impulsiveness had finally doomed her. Animals would pick at her bones. And now she'd fled and left behind her closest remaining friend, Savia.

She wanted to go forward but had no idea how to find Hadrian's Wall, and wanted to retreat but had no idea how to find Arden's fort again. She wanted to sleep but was too wet and cold, and wanted to eat but had no food. Her horse looked as forlorn and soaked as she felt, and she supposed that if anyone from Rome were to see her right now, they would pass by a particularly dirty, bedraggled, drowned cat of a woman, a beggar, a leper, an orphan . . .

"It's easy country to get lost in, isn't it?"

Her head jerked up in surprise, alarm, and sudden outrage. Caratacus! Arden had somehow crept up on her and now was standing not twenty feet away, calmly taking a bite of sausage and looking perfectly at home. The thick woolen cloak he was wearing was drawn over his head and beaded with rain. His sword was sheathed, and his hands were weaponless. He made no move to come closer and looked as calm as she felt despairing, as if their reunion was the most inevitable thing in the world.

"What are you doing here?"

"Following you, of course, since no sane man would come into Iola Wood unless a particularly fine stag had run this way—and maybe not even then. It's a tangle. Do you know that when you haven't been traveling in circles, you've been riding northeast, away from that Roman wall of yours?"

"I most certainly have not!"

"You're farther from your rescuing cavalry than ever."

She whirled around to find evidence to contradict him, but there was none, of course. The sun hid, the sky was slate gray, the forest a maze.

"How did you find me?" she finally asked.

"I've been following you for hours."

"Hours! Then why didn't you recapture me?"

"So we wouldn't have to do this again. I don't want to cage you, lady, but you need to realize how hopeless it is to try to reach this wall of yours. You can't find your way. Even if you could, we wouldn't let you. Your only luck is that you didn't do slightly better, because that would have meant the hounds, not me. They might have chewed on you for a bit before I could call them off." He took another bite himself, which made her stomach growl. "Now come. I'm tired of this game."

"Why don't you just kill me?" she pleaded miserably.

He appeared to consider this. "Because you're entirely too valuable. Because poor Savia is at wit's end, furious that you left her behind. Because I enjoy watching the choices you make, even the stupid ones. Because you've got some spark to you."

"I'm too wet to have any spark left."

He grinned. "I don't think so. We'll turn you into a Celt yet."

They led their horses into the trees and tied them. Arden gave her a cloak he'd rolled behind his saddle, as if anticipating her recapture from the moment he'd called for his horse. His confidence infuriated her. Yet she took the garment with gratitude, her body thoroughly chilled, and watched dumbly as he gathered wood for a fire, picking dry scraps from under a log and flicking shavings with a knife. Flint and steel struck a spark. Despite her annoyance at recapture, his quiet efficiency at this vital task couldn't help but reassure her. A flame caught in the nest of duff, and he added twigs and then branches to nurse it to size, a reassuring pop sending sparks wafting upward. The heat was hypnotizing. She stood near, opening the cloak to dry her sodden clothes underneath.

"My thanks for the fire."

"It's not for you. The smoke signals that I found you." He handed her bread and sausage. "It lets everyone else go back inside and get warm."

"Oh."

"But it's true I don't want you dead of exposure. What use would you be then?"

"Oh." Was he mocking? Or afraid to admit kindness? The bread was ambrosia, the sausage a different kind of heat.

"I was lost," she admitted.

"Obviously."

"I thought you'd kill me if you caught me."

"Well, it might have saved me a piece of bread. But then why catch you?"

So he wasn't going to kill her. He gave no sign he intended to molest her, either. Despite all her dire expectations she suddenly felt strangely safe with this man, this barbarian, this murderer, this awful hunter of heads and consorter with witches and leader of brigands: not imprisoned but rescued, as if rescued from herself. The feeling was so unexpected that it confused her. She'd felt so bold and clever to escape, and now so foolish.

"I would have found my way eventually," she impulsively insisted.

"Your way where?"

"To my husband."

He grunted. Mention of Marcus irked him. "Who you barely know."

"He's where my heart lies. Sooner or later, it would lead me to him."

Arden shook his head. "You've yet to feel your heart, I think. Yet to feel love. You're nothing like your husband at all."

"You don't know that!"

"Everyone along the Wall knows that."

"How dare you say such a thing!"

"Everyone knows about the marriage, and his appointment because of it, and the fact that you're three times braver than your husband and five times smarter. The Romans fear you, and the Celts admire you. You've come to a better place, believe me."

She didn't believe him, not for a moment, and yet his comment about the longings of her heart disturbed her. Secretly she suspected there was some tiny truth in his presumptions, and yet he was also maddening. Who was he to say what her heart had felt, or how deeply she'd loved? Still, there was a yearning in her breast that remained unfulfilled, a formality to her marriage that seemed to belie the promises that the seer had made in Londinium. Perhaps deep love would develop, but this brigand had stolen some of her complacency. "I know my husband is looking for me right now, at the head of five hundred armed men," she said.

"And I know he isn't." Arden had seated himself on a log and was ripping off great chunks of bread with his teeth, gulping them down like a wolf. The man was disgusting! And yet there was something compelling about his lack of self-consciousness, his freedom from doubt.

"He'll catch you unawares," she argued doggedly.

"No, he won't."

"Why are you so certain?"

"Because we've already sent him one of the heads of the soldiers we killed, preserved in cedar oil, with a warning that yours will come next if he dares try to rescue you. If he truly loves you, he'll leave you, with me."

"No, you didn't. I saw the four heads in your Great House."

"You saw four of what were five."

Her heart chilled.

"Hool stayed behind for a while to package the head of the man who first tried to save you. We've sent it to the Romans."

"Clodius? You're a monster!"

"I'm a warrior and a realist."

Furious at herself for showing weakness, she began to weep again.

"Oh, come, lady, it's not as bad as all that. Your young soldier died in battle, the best fate of all men, and his head is being honored. It means his soul is still protecting you. I'd be flattered if our fortunes were reversed." He reached in a leather bag. "Here, have some dried fruit." He held up shriveled apple and pear.

She was still hungry enough to want it but instead refused, sitting across the fire to fume. She couldn't believe Marcus wouldn't try rescue. Clodius's poor head would spur him on, not deter him!

Yet where was he?

Perhaps she should just wait for her husband. Wait in the warmth of Arden's fort.

She hated men and their cruelties.

"So," Caratacus went on, "the question is what to do with you in the meantime. Everything I've heard and seen suggests that you're a natural horsewoman, a Morrigan of the Romans."

"Who's Morrigan?"

"How ignorant you Romans are about the island you've conquered! She's the goddess of war and the hunt. Her symbol is the horse."

"I simply like horses. They seem as noble as men are base."

"So we agree on something after all. Will you go riding with me, then?"

"Back to the fort?"

"Yes, on your stolen mare, and we need to go before darkness falls. But beyond that, will you ride with me on a hunt?"

"A hunt?"

"We've got one planned for sport and necessity."

"A woman on a hunt?"

"A woman can do what she wants."

"Not in Rome, she can't."

"You're not in Rome. You're in a place, unlike your country, where a woman can own property and wield a spear and choose who she wants for her bed and who for her marriage.

Believe me, they're not always the same person. Come with me. It's exciting."

"You're trying to enlist me."

"I'm trying to calm you."

"Why, after I've escaped? Why don't you lock me in a cage?"

"But you didn't escape, did you? Here you are, still my prisoner. And if you try again, it will only give me an excuse to abduct you once more." He was grinning.

She said nothing, not wanting to give him satisfaction.

"Are you recovered enough to ride at least?"

She nodded glumly.

"Then let's make our way home. My home, and temporarily yours."

They rode on faint game trails that Valeria had been too anxious and inexperienced to see, Arden making no effort to tie or restrain her. While he was leading her to what he called his home, his hill fort called Tiranen, it occurred to her that he seemed even more at home *here*, in this forest. If there were willow gods and dark shrines, he showed no fear.

"How can you find your way so easily?" She needed to talk about something, because she kept thinking about the persistence of his pursuit and abduction. The result was unsettling in ways she didn't want to admit.

"I grew up in this country. But Iola Wood is confusing even to those of us who know it well. It's no embarrassment you were lost."

"One of my husband's soldiers told me that you Celts believe the woods are haunted. That trees like the willow can pull people underground."

"We believe that the woods are inhabited by spirits, or rather that the trees are spirits themselves, but that doesn't mean they're haunted. The willow story is just for children." He turned in his saddle to look at her. "Not that I'd sleep under one, mind you."

"Titus talked about Esus, some woodman's god, who demands a tribute of blood."

"Esus must be placated, it's true. A god should be honored with sacrifice, giving back to her some small portion of what she has given to us. But there's also Dagda, the good god, who walks through these trees as a Roman walks through his garden. The groves of oak are places of both darkness and of light, just like the world as a whole."

"Savia believes there's only one god."

"I've heard this. And the Christians eat their god and drink his blood to be made strong by him, which sounds far more savage to me than sacrificing a captive to Esus. The Christians talk of a father and a son and a spirit as well, and argue among themselves whether the three are one or the one is three. Is this not true? I listened when I soldiered in your world. That's not so different from us Celts. Three is our most sacred number, and our gods are often trinities, like Morrigan, Babd, and Nemhain, separate and yet the same."

"If they are the same, then why three?"

"Three is a sacred number. Three can surround itself, each member flanked by two others. Druids believe that the educated mind requires, first, knowledge, second, nature, and third, truth. All these are the same, and yet they're different as well."

"Perhaps you should become a Christian, then."

"Theirs is a very weak god, a humble man killed so easily that none even remember what he looked like. In our world we worship strength. Besides, how can one god do the work of dozens? How silly to have different people, with different needs, all worship the same god. That defies common sense."

"Christ is the god of civilization. The god, now, of Rome."

"And what good is civilization? Your poor are worked like animals, and your rich become tyrants. In our world men and women alike are more equal, and we share in toil, and we move with the wind and season and allow ourselves to enjoy life. We care nothing for monuments but only for deeds, nothing for power but only for friendship, nothing for death—which is only sweet release—but only for life. We care for the deer and the oak and the brook and the stone. Christians are proud their god walked among them, but our Celtic gods are with us all the time, in everything we see and touch. The Christian god has gone away, but ours speak to us with wind and thunder and sometimes, more softly, in the call of birds."

"And yet it is Rome that rules the world."

"Not this world. Not this warrior." He glanced upward into the trees and pointed. "Let me show you." Reaching up, he grabbed the limb of an oak and swung himself off his horse as easily as an acrobat. Climbing to the topmost bough, he sawed at something with his dagger and then descended, his catlike drop to the ground reminding her of the time he'd surprised the mule pulling her cart. Then he remounted and walked his horse over.

"Here."

It was a branch of polished leaves and white berry, very different from the oak it came from. "What is it?"

"The sacred mistletoe. It's a magic plant that grows at the crown of trees. Wear a sprig in your hair, and it will protect you from evil spirits. Keep it at hand, and it will ward off death and disfigurement. Put it over a cradle, and it will prevent a baby from being abducted by faeries. This is the most powerful plant the gods have put on Earth, and it's free for the taking. It symbolizes the truth of the world, that wood and water give us all we really need."

She looked skeptical. "And yet you barbarians sneak into Roman territory to steal, so you can live as Romans do."

He laughed. "How clever you are! Some do, I don't deny it. But there's more to the magic of this mistletoe." His arm stretched, and he held it near her face, dangling from his hand, and then leaned and kissed her, a kiss as swift and fleeting as one of Brisa's arrows. "There!"

She leaned back in consternation. "Why did you do that?"

"Because the mistletoe is also our plant of friendship and conciliation. Our plant of love. Because you're pretty. Because I felt like doing it."

Her face was aflame. "Well, I did not feel like it, and I'll not let any man take liberties without permission." It reminded her of Galba. "I'll, I'll . . ." She thought desperately for a threat. "I'll stick you with a brooch again!"

He roared with laughter and backed his horse away. "It's

only a Celtic custom, girl! But if you're threatening with your brooch, then I'll throw my charm away." He raised his arm to toss the mistletoe aside.

"No!" she relented. "No, no. Don't kiss me, but I want a sprig for protection like you said. Please give me one."

So he plucked a piece and gave it to her. She put it in her hair.

Then they turned and rode again, finally breaking free of Iola Wood just as the sun broke clear of ragged cloud, setting toward crags in the west. They galloped up a steep ridge to a place from where it seemed they could see the entire world . . . all of it, perhaps, except the distant wall. Lakes, painted gold by the late fire, lay in every hollow. Mist swirled along the ridge crests like wool combed from the sky. Rainbows arced like portals to the heavens. Rocks glistened from the recent rain, their veins a raiment of diamonds. The raw beauty took her breath away.

"How wondrous the world," she murmured, as much to herself as him. Then, remembering her plight, "Will we get back before dark?"

"There, Tiranen." He pointed, and she saw the cone of his hill and its fort, just two ridges away. "Come, race me there!" Then he cried like an eagle, a wild screech, and rode like the wind without even bothering to look behind, Valeria following as gamely as she could, clinging to her racing mare.

She'd not come very far from the fort at all, she admitted to herself. Yet Arden had made her curious about his world. Maybe she could learn something useful from these strange people. Something important to take back to her Romans. Back to her Marcus.

XVIII

The prospect of a boar hunt filled Valeria with excitement, apprehension, and resolve. It was clearly a test of her fortitude. She'd already endured jests about "escaping" to Iola Wood and becoming lost, but she'd also noticed an undercurrent of respect among the Celts for her courage at running off. She was not quite the Roman kitten she looked, they whispered; perhaps there was some cat to her as well. She felt she was representing not just herself but the empire. So this time she took her own mare, Boudicca, as well as a Roman saddle, leather boots, and woolen trousers.

Savia regarded the mannish garb with mourning, convinced the barbarians represented a particularly corrupting kind of hell. "Your mother would die if she could see you."

Caratacus gave her a more approving eye as the hunting party gathered. "You've dressed smartly this time. Are you ready to risk Attacotti adventure?"

"The risk is yours, barbarian. Take me on enough hunting trips, and sooner or later I'll be able to find my way home."

The other hunters cheered with approval at her boldness.

"I'm wagering that by that time you won't want to leave," Arden countered.

"You're very confident about your charms."

"Not *my* charms, lady. The charm of wood and fen, moor and meadow."

The chieftain had given the boar the name Erebus, after the Greek station of the underworld: a classical reference again betraying the mystery of her captor's background. Their quarry was described as a bristling, black, monstrous hummock of an animal, all shoulder and hoof, as deadly as a bear and as swift as a bull. It stole out of the forest at night with red eye and yellow tusk, goring and furrowing, and two watchdogs had already been killed. Caratacus had finally directed the clan's hunt master, an old and leathery woodsman named Mael, to track the beast to its hiding place. He had done so.

Now a dozen men and women rode out of Tiranen in high anticipation, heavily armed with spear and bow. A dozen hounds ran with them, loping through high green grass that scraped their bellies. It was early summer, birds flushed as the horses galloped, meadows had erupted with flower, and the morning seemed fresh with promise.

Valeria had neither the experience nor trust to have a real weapon and so was given only a silver dagger. Brisa rode alongside her with bow and quiver. Proud Asa had come too, her long red hair rippling in the morning's breeze and three light javelins holstered on her saddle. Arden had a lance, Hool a shorter and sturdier spear, and Luca a sword. Each of their weapons had names, Valeria had learned, as well as druidic blessings, a complicated history, and intricate decoration. The spear shafts were finely carved, the arrows fletched with feathers of different birds, and the bows studded with silver.

Brisa had adopted the captive Roman like a puppy and had set out to teach her Celtic ways. Valeria had never known a woman so mannish, and yet the barbarian archer commented frequently, favorably, and sometimes lewdly on the attributes of men in the tribe: she cheerfully admitted to frequent lovemaking. Unlike the females of Valeria's class, she seemed in no particular hurry to marry anyone, and didn't seem to have the need of a man for completion. She was also comely enough to draw suggestions, both polite and vulgar, from the single men. She laughed at them unless whim and fancy took her, and then she'd lead one to her bed. This independence of emotion fascinated the Roman, whose society valued careful relationships and formal alliances above all else. She asked Brisa once why she resisted betrothal, and the woman replied simply, "I've yet to find a man who would let me be me. But I will." So she stayed in her parents' hut, dissuading serious suitors and living life as a boy.

As they rode, the Celts boasted of other hunts. An orbiting hawk called to mind some past bit of falconry, the flashing rump of a disappearing deer provoked the memory of a great stag, and the dart of a rabbit recalled the wiles of a fox. Every rock and tree represented some peculiar piece of clan history, and every dale and hillock recalled the wanderings of gods and spirits. Valeria realized that these rough people saw the landscape differently than she did; it was alive to them in a way the Romans had never considered. Behind the visual world was a second universe of vision, legend, and memorized song that was somehow as real to these barbarians as stone, bark, and leaf. Every object had its spirit. Every event had its magic. The waking world was merely a brief dream, and their lusty and violent lives a quick hallucination, before passing through to something more substantial and lasting.

Because of that, their carefree, undisciplined, war-crazy life was beginning to make a kind of sense to her. She'd explored Tiranen after returning with Arden, and decided they were not the simple, ignorant people she'd assumed. Their round huts were cramped and dim, smelling of smoke and musk, but also cozier and more richly furnished than she had imagined, each occupying family exhibiting a communal unity very different from the stiff hierarchy of an upper-class house in Rome: three generations sharing chores, food, sleeping loft, and the fire. Their chests and furs and woolens were often of fine quality and elaborate, with time and work lavished upon them. Yet there was no concept of duty or discipline. The Celts would start a hundred projects with the enthusiasm of children and abandon them just as swiftly to go riding, wrestle in mock fights, shoot arrows, or make love, their passion audible from the round walls of their houses. The lusty noise intrigued Valeria. What were they doing? What was she missing? The cries of the women were especially loud, but she was too shy to ask about their experiences. These people fought as casually as they made love, and didn't put too much importance on either. They washed together at the heated tubs at night and splashed in cold barrels of rainwater in the morning, howling at the cold with brisk roaring pleasure, and they loved perfumes, fine clothes, bright jewelry, and intricate tattoos: they were as fastidious about their persons as they were oblivious to the rude dirt of their hamlets. Their long hair was ornament, some male warriors stiffening their locks with lye to make it arc upright like the mane of a horse. They took great delight in costume, their ceremonial helmets fitted with wings or horns, and they were as craven about superstition as they were bold in combat, wearing amulets, and as fearful of thunder as they were indifferent to pain.

Nothing ever seemed to get quite done, and yet they were satisfied with the half-doing, and happiest in some reckless venture that promised fresh bruises and cuts. Their children were even wilder, running half naked while they invented mischief that drew only the mildest reprimand. Only in their animals did the Celts expect discipline, the dogs kept in order with the kick of a boot and the horses ridden so constantly and hard that they melded through thigh and fist and heel into the mind of their riders. They galloped across the rough and wooded country with reckless abandon, whooping like loons.

When the barbarians met the Petriana cavalry, the Romans would certainly have the edge in any battle, Valeria guessed. But the chase after victory, when the Celts fled, would be like trying to catch the wind.

Their way to the hunt was cross-country and rambling, seemingly as aimless as an exploring dog. Arden chose this ridge for its fine view and that hollow for its sweet spring, his course a total antithesis to the practical straightness of a Roman road. The air warmed as the sun rose higher, each breath rich with the scent of heather, and there was a brilliance in the low light of the north that seemed to pick out every hue of blossom and every sparkle in rock. The air made you drunk. Valeria felt strangely alive with these people. Their enthusiasms made her heart beat faster.

"I'm surprised the clan can spare so many to go on a mere hunt," she said somewhat breathlessly to Brisa as they cantered along. "How does the work get done?"

"This *is* the work, Roman. This Erebus has been terrorizing our livestock and rooting our fields. His kill will feed the clan for three days."

"But so many?"

"It may take this many to slay the boar. He's a huge one, according to Mael."

"So it's dangerous?" She'd heard of boar hunts, of course, but had never known anyone who'd been on one. In Rome all the wild animals she'd seen had been in the arena, where they were swiftly slain for the amusement of the mob.

"That's what makes it fun."

"You can stay to the rear," Asa called back. "The women of the Attacotti will show Rome how it's done." The Celt's antipathy toward Valeria had grown since the Roman had ridden back to Tiranen with Arden.

Bitch, Valeria thought. "I didn't say I was afraid, Asa."

"You will be. And Arden will be too busy, Roman, to look after you this time."

They rode down the slope of a cirque into a narrow defile and then into another forested valley, reining up at the edge of the wood. Mael jumped down and unwrapped a bloody fleece, taken from a sheep that the boar had killed, and gave their quarry's scent to the dogs. "Hunt!" The pack set off in frenzied tumult, baying to the wind, and Arden gave a great cry and led the hunters in pursuit.

So fast and disorienting was the chase through the trees that it was like tumbling down a hill. Valeria's mare kept pace with the others, hooves pounding, but it ran outside her own control, branches flashing wickedly past, the Roman clinging desperately just to keep to her saddle. The men yipped, the Celtic women added a high, wavering warble, eerie and foreboding, and the blur of the chase was like being caught up in an unstoppable wave.

Surely the boar would hear them and flee.

Yet the barbarians hollered as if the animal was waiting for them.

She glanced in wonder at the people riding with her, their faces flushed, their eyes bright, their mouths open, their hair rippling in the wind, and realized they'd become the boar in their own minds. Their thoughts echoed the beast's thoughts, imagining it rousing itself sleepily out of the mud, grunting in perplexity at the approaching thunder, shaking its fat, bristled head at the baying of the dogs, pawing the earth with its sharp hooves, and then trotting tentatively up and down the tunnels of its thicket, wondering who dared disturb its bloated slumber. And somehow the boar heard the human thoughts as the Celts heard his, both taking the measure of the other. Valeria suddenly knew, as certainly as the Celts did, that the animal wouldn't try to escape.

That it was seeking them as they sought it.

They slowed as the ground dipped and the trees became denser. The hounds were bunched at a thicket, howling in confusion, and the party halted so weapons could be readied. Brisa strung her bow and notched an arrow. Asa unsheathed one of her javelins, balancing it lightly in her slim fist. Arden rested the butt of his lance on the ground as if to anchor his horse, his hand near the weapon's head.

Hool leaped down with his stout spear. "It was my cow that was gutted a fortnight ago. Give me first call, Caratacus."

"Don't you want your horse?"

"Horses panic. I trust my own feet, where I can meet the pig eye to eye."

Mael was shouting at the dogs, urging them into the thicket. The animals hesitated a moment, milling like an uncertain mob, and then finally the lead hound charged in, giving the rest enough courage to follow. They were bred to hunt! The pack's frantic barking echoed as they raced down the labyrinth of tunnels, fading with distance and then falling to strange silence for a moment. Then Valeria heard a snort and low grunt, drowned out immediately by renewed furious barking. The dogs had found the boar! There was a yelp, the sound cut short as if a sword had sliced it off, and then a pounding as something huge and heavy ran through the thicket, dogs howling in pursuit. The top of the brambles quaked as the quarry moved, the disturbance coming in a long, rolling wave. Hool tensed, peering down a dark tunnel, and then with unworldly speed something huge and black exploded from the tangle.

It was Erebus! Valeria gasped, and her mare sidestepped in alarm. The monster was far bigger than she'd expected, its shoulder almost waist-high and its upright tusks as long as a man's hand. It seemed all head and shoulder and long shaggy tail, like something hurled from a catapult. There was a curdling human cry of revenge as Hool moved to block it, but the boar was quicker, and wily. Swerving from Hool's lunge and then cutting back faster than her eye could follow, the beast turned under the warrior's spear and plowed into Hool's legs as powerfully as a rolling log. The Celt was butted up and over, flipping a neat somersault, and when he came down his legs were bloody and the boar was careening past Arden's horse, the chieftain cursing as he threw his lance too late. Brisa shot an arrow that also missed, and she swore like a decurion when it whickered uselessly into the brush. Then the animal was gone.

"This way!" The riders were in motion now, pounding after the boar, the surviving dogs pouring out to add to the furious chase. Their quarry was far ahead, saplings rocking from its passage, and then all of them disappeared into the trees.

Valeria, shaken by the animal's ferocious speed, didn't follow. She struggled to get her shuddering mare under control and finally trotted Boudicca over to the stunned Hool, worried that the man was seriously hurt. There was a red gash on one thigh, and the other leg was bent peculiarly, as if broken. He was grimacing.

"Are you all right?" she asked unnecessarily.

"Angry as a wolverine and foolish as a goat," he gasped. "By Taranis and Esus, I don't think I've ever seen one that big. Or that fast."

"It's a wonder you're still alive." She jumped down from her horse and used her dagger to cut a strip of cloth from her tunic. "I've got to get that bound before you bleed to death." He winced as she bandaged the wound. "And we must splint that leg. You're lucky you aren't dead, Hool."

"If I were, I'd have already seen the worst the underworld could frighten me with. I've never faced an uglier snout, not even on Luca's homely daughters."

"His eyes were like coals. His tusks like knives." She glanced around for something to splint him with. "Maybe we can use the shaft of your spear to set your leg."

The weapon had fallen to the ground, and she picked it up. Valeria was surprised at how heavy and yet how balanced a spear was. She'd never hoisted one before. She could still feel the warmth and sweat from Hool's hands on the shaft's grip. The head was blue iron, filed and sharp. "It's too long, though."

"Don't break my spear!"

"Maybe we could strap it along your body."

"Wait for Arden and Mael. They'll know what to do."

"How long before they come back?"

"When the boar's dead." He lay back on the leaves of the forest floor, resting.

They waited in companionable silence, grateful for each other's company in the green dimness of the forest. They could still hear the others, but the sound was distant and faint. Perhaps the boar had slipped away. Valeria hoped they'd give up soon and come help their companion.

They didn't. Time drifted.

Finally something cracked in the bushes. Were the hunters finally returning? She looked up, following the sound to the brambles, and saw a dark shape watching, panting heavily. One of the injured dogs? No, it seemed too big . . .

Her breath caught, her heart stalled.

It was the boar.

Hool saw it too and sat painfully upright. "Get on your horse," he ordered.

She took a step backward. What was the boar doing here? Somehow it had circled through the forest well ahead of its pursuers, come back to its home thicket, and then followed the scent of human blood . . .

"Go get help, as quickly as you can!"

The animal was very near, as big as a bear, its snout hideous, its back a hedge of upright, quivering bristles, a drool of blood and saliva dripping from its tusks. She could smell its rankness as it eyed them.

She still had the spear. Should she give it to the man?

The boar pawed, snorting.

"Hurry!" Hool shouted.

It charged. Valeria sprang for her horse, the mount already starting to bolt in terror. The mare screamed. Or was that her scream? She glimpsed bunched fury, and then the boar ran over the wounded Celt like a careening chariot, the two tumbling as Hool roared in pain. The pig butted at the man with its snout, the tusks cutting at him again and again as he was rolled along the ground. Hool howled with frustration and helpless rage, beating at the animal with his arms as it shook him like a doll. She had to do something!

Valeria was in the saddle now, sawing at the reins with one hand and the spear in her other. Her mare was dancing frantically. Finally she managed to drag Boudicca's head around and kicked as hard as she could, driving her mount toward the boar before the horse knew what it was doing. That got her close enough to lean and jab with the spear, hard, at the creature's skinny hindquarter.

The boar jerked as if stung, and turned. Now the mare was sidestepping, eyes rolling in fear and head too high to choose intelligent direction.

The boar charged again, this time at Valeria.

She yanked up her leg to avoid the slicing tusk, and the beast struck the mare's side with concussive force. It was as if an ocean wave had picked the horse up with her astride, shoving them sideways against a tree, Boudicca screaming for sure now as the mare was eviscerated. Valeria jabbed desperately at the monster's enormous shoulder, but the hide and cartilage was so tough, it was like stabbing chain mail. The three of them crashed together against an oak, and the tree quivered from the impact. The boar was frantic to get at her, but the butt end of Hool's spear had been accidentally driven into the oak by its furious charge, the animal's shoulder against its point. The ashwood shaft bowed as if to shatter, yet just before it must do so, the boar's furious energy pierced the spearhead through its plate of shoulder cartilage, and it sliced deep. The wild pig squealed in surprise, a new scream that mingled with the screams of woman and horse, and then all three crashed over, Valeria caught in the saddle and slamming hard onto the ground over the body of both horse and boar.

She waited for its head to come round and gore her.

Instead, the pig grunted, sighed, and shuddered. Finally it was still.

She laid her cheek on the damp earth, her vision blurred, her mind stunned. Then she heard shouts, a baying of hounds, and suddenly she was surrounded by a circle of barking and snarling dogs, nipping at the dead boar even as Arden and Mael strode angrily through them, shouting commands and pulling the pack off. The chieftain probed the monster with his lance, but it was already dead, Hool's spear jutting from its heart. The tiny forest arena was spattered with gore, and the woman was sprawled awkwardly as if dead.

"Good Dagda, have you killed my lady?" Arden lifted her face from the mud, his own stricken with fear. Her eyes were closed, a tendril of hair in her mouth.

"I'm caught," she mumbled dully.

"Help me get her clear of this horse!"

Strong arms lifted the bulk of the animal to work her legs free. She winced from a dazzling kind of pain. Boudicca was wheezing in agony, her guts spilling over the pig. Luca took his own spear and thrust it into the horse to put the mare out of her misery.

"Hool's still alive!" Brisa called. The man was groaning.

"The trickster circled to finish him off," Mael marveled, piecing together the fight. "If your Roman girl hadn't been here, it would have gored him and then trotted on its way, to terrorize us again."

Arden sat on the ground, cradling her in his arms. She felt faint and floating against the comfort of his body, astonished she was still alive.

"She killed the biggest boar I've ever seen," the chieftain murmured. "She saved poor Hool."

Asa was looking at the Roman woman in wonder and

envy. "How could that puny thing get the spear through the animal's shoulder?"

Mael pointed to the trunk of the tree. "She braced her weapon, and the boar did the rest. It's as brave an act of hunting as I've seen in all my life."

There was no courage at all, Valeria wanted to say, but she was so stunned by the horror that she couldn't speak. The boar looked like some shaggy black mountain beside her, its snout tipped with two bright beads of blood.

"The Roman got him off me," Hool gasped in pain. Then he fainted.

Arden looked at the others. "No one knows the thinking of the gods," he said. "No one knows why things happen the way they do. But I say that this woman came into our lives for a reason, and part of that reason we've seen here today. This will be a song that will be sung for generations."

"She was lucky," Asa insisted. "Look at her. She's almost dead from fright."

"She's an arrow from the sacred," Brisa contradicted. "Look at Hool's legs, she tried to bandage them! This, after we captured her, when she could have slit his throat! This Roman has the spirit of a Celt, Arden Caratacus. The heart of a Morrigan."

"Our Morrigan, then, she shall be."

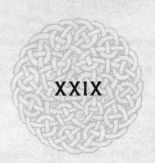

XXIX

Valeria woke to the sound of lapping water. She was inside, she sensed dimly, but the murmur of waves and play of sun still filtered through the woven wattle of an undaubed wall. Light ignited dust motes in the air. The roof was lost in shadow but smelled of damp thatch. She was lying on a straw mattress—she could hear it crinkle beneath her—and covered with thick wool blankets. She also ached so much that she could barely move. Half her body felt like it had been drummed with hammers. Her ankle throbbed, and cuts and scratches added a slighter but sharper discomfort.

Only the water was soothing.

She was thirsty, but it would hurt too much to turn her head and look for something to drink, so she concentrated on noises instead. A faint sough of wind. The cries of waterfowl. The splash of water as if she were on a boat, except her boat wasn't rocking. And the gentle breathing . . .

Of a man.

She forced herself to turn then, gasping at the pain. There was someone sitting in the dimness of what appeared to be a crude hut. Even in shadow his profile was unmistakable. Arden Caratacus had been watching her sleep.

"Morrigan has come back," he whispered.

She was confused by the name. "Where am I?"

"A safe place. A healing place."

She lay back. "I hurt so much."

"That's because the best bear the most pain."

"Oh."

Then she fell asleep again.

*   *   *

When she came awake a second time, her entire body felt like a vast, rotting bruise. It was dark, the hut still. She could hear Arden's soft breathing on the other side of the enclosure, asleep. Pale moonlight filtered through the wattle, weaving a silver tartan on the floor, and again there was that odd sound of wavelets rippling. Trying not to groan, she stiffly sat up and put her eye to the wall. There was water on the other side, a lake or bay. A corridor of white, reflected light led across it: the hall of the moon. Maybe they were on a boat, a boat gone aground. Maybe she wasn't alive after all.

Something touched her lightly. A hand.

"Here, something to drink," he whispered.

Then he left her alone again.

When Valeria awakened the next time, she was hungry. Sunlight again, a small window open to scrubbed blue sky. Arden was gone. She stood and staggered, momentarily dizzy, her bare feet on rough wood. She was wearing a woolen tunic that came to her calves.

A window revealed a small lake, its surface reaching under the floor where she stood. Reeds grew in nearby shadows, and bright birds, red and black, darted there. Shuffling to the other side of the little hut, she found a door and opened it. A wooden ramp led to a grassy shore, a curtain of alder riffling in the wind. Geese were feeding in the shallows. She was on a dock, suspended on pilings. The hut was like a little island, the water making a moat. A catwalk connected it to another hut on pilings, a short distance away.

She wondered, illogically, if she'd been abandoned. Then she saw Arden walking along the lakeshore, a pole over one shoulder and two fish hanging from the pole. He waved to her—as if this strange habitation were the most natural thing in the world—and in moments he was treading good-naturedly across the boards of the ramp to join her, his cheerful stride making the planks thump.

"You're up!" he greeted. "And sooner than we hoped. You've got the stamina of a Brigantia. The mettle of a Morrigan."

"I've got the bones of an old woman and the muscles of a baby," she replied softly. "I feel like raw meat. Where are we, Arden?"

"A crannog. My people like the protection of water, so we build small islands or platforms for refuge. You were too badly injured to take back to Tiranen, so we brought you here."

"How long have I been here?"

"Three days."

"Three days!"

"That boar gave you a beating. Have you looked at yourself?"

"No."

"Your entire side is purple."

Valeria nodded, beginning to remember now. "I thought he was going to kill me. Such a vicious—" She stopped. "And how did you see my side?"

"We had to get your bloody clothes off you."

"We?"

"Kalin helped too."

"Kalin!"

"He's a healer, Valeria. It's his broth that's brought you around."

She didn't remember any broth. "It's not right for you two to be looking."

"We couldn't bear the stink of you."

She was embarrassed, grateful, and resentful at her dependency. She changed the subject. "Where's Savia?"

"Taking over Tiranen, I suppose. When she heard you'd been hurt, she told me exactly what she thought of me, which you can well imagine. I think you'll recover faster away from her, so in her boredom she's got the rest of the clan under siege. She wants to convert and reform us at the same time."

"That sounds like Savia." She was beginning to remember. "And Hool?"

He looked at her gently, reaching up to touch her cheek as softly as the fox cape that had wrapped her neck on her wedding night. She shivered.

"Alive, Valeria." So startling, that touch. Her name on his lips. He caressed her skin. "Saved by your courage. He's in the hut next door, taking strength from your own healing. You will get well together."

She blinked. "Can I see him?"

The Celtic hunter was on the same kind of straw mattress she had found herself, his skin pale and his frame shrunken, as if the near passage of death had collapsed him in on himself. At first he seemed confused by his visitors in the shadows, but then he recognized the young woman and cracked a smile. "Morrigan," he croaked.

She knelt by him. "It's Valeria, Hool."

His hand reached out and grasped her forearm, the grip still surprisingly strong. "The others told me what you did."

"Let you get trampled, it looks like."

He coughed a slight laugh and then lay back, still in pain. "I owe you my life, lady. Saved by a woman! For that, I give you my spear."

"Don't be silly—"

"I give you my spear in debt for my living. It marks you as a Celt."

She blushed. "I'm only a Roman."

"Not now. You're one of us."

Valeria shook her head. "That will only be when you're well, Hool. When you can take your place in the hunt again. Let me help you to get better."

"You are here. It's enough—" He was drifting off, slipping back to sleep.

"And your survival helps me."

He lay still, breathing slowly.

She stood, shakily. "I'm tired now, Arden."

He took her elbow. "Yes. Rest some more."

Valeria was young, and impatient to heal. The next day she began to move about, appalled at her discoloration but relieved she was still alive. She dipped into the lake, the shock of cold water countering the pain of her injuries. She'd had an adventure! In time she'd be well. Then she visited Hool, checking his dressings. He too seemed to be healing, without infection, and had lost none of his good humor. These were a tough people.

The crannog's ramp could be raised like a drawbridge, and now that Valeria had strength enough to lift and lower it, Caratacus instructed she do so. As a result she felt curiously safe in her hut: the ramp up, a gap of water between herself and the shore, and herself sitting gratefully in the summer's sun. How peaceful it was here! How removed from the cares of the world, after the recent tumultuous days of fear and emotion! She liked to watch the alder as it was riffled by the wind, or study how the trees lent their green color to the water. The crannog let her stop thinking. This, she knew, was why the man had brought her there.

He wanted her to think less and feel more.

He wanted her to understand the Celts.

A day and a night went by, and then she saw someone approach again, strange and yet familiar. She touched the rough hemp of the drawbridge rope, uncertain what to do.

It was the druid, Kalin. She still feared the priesthood's reputation.

"Will you make me swim, Roman lady?" His hood was back, his smile disarming.

"Where's Arden?"

"He'll be along soon enough. I've brought you some gifts, but if you want them, you'll have to let down your little bridge."

She stalled by teasing him. "I thought druids could walk on water and fly through the air."

"Alas, I get just as wet as you, lady. Don't you remember seeing me, soaked and shiny as a crow, when I came into the Great House?"

"I remember how frightening you were. So how do I know you don't want to burn me in a wicker man now, or put me in a pot, or drown me in a bog with a golden cord around my neck?"

"I'd not waste something as valuable as a golden cord, I don't have a pot, and I've never seen a wicker man. Besides, you seem to know less about the future than any of us: I don't think you're much use as a portent. The killing of that boar was a sign of some other purpose. Just what, we don't know."

"You're healing me for this purpose?"

"I'm healing you so I can stop making the walk from Tiranen."

"You don't have a horse?"

"I can't see what I need to see from a horse."

"What do you need to see?"

"Fern and flower, herb and sprig. My plants for healing."

She was far from Roman medicine, and this herbalist was as good as she was going to get. Besides, he could also check on Hool. "Come across, then."

Kalin's medical manner proved gentler than she expected. He had her unpin her tunic on the sunlit porch so he could briskly inspect her bruises while she clutched it around her private places to give herself dignity. He touched lightly, murmuring approval at her progress, and then turned discreetly to let her redress.

There was a raised hearthstone inside the hut, and Kalin stoked the embers, added fuel, and put water on to boil. Then he sorted through what he'd brought.

"First, a package from Savia." He handed over a leather pouch. "A comb, pins for your hair, some perfume. She said it will make you feel Roman."

Valeria was delighted. "It will make me feel human!" She held up a sweet-smelling bar that puzzled her, however. "What's this?"

"Soap. It's an essence of animals that cleans the skin. We scent it with berry."

"What essence?"

"Their fat."

"Ugh!" She dropped the bar.

"It works better than Roman oils."

"I can't imagine how."

"You don't have to scrape it off. It rinses with water."

"How does the dirt come off, then?"

"With the soap and the water, in a trinity."

She looked at the brown bar dubiously. "Then why hasn't Rome adopted it?"

"You live in a primitive world, lady." Now he was teasing her.

"What else?" she demanded. She liked presents!

"This is from Arden." He unfolded what seemed like a shimmering curtain of water, and she gasped. It was a tunic of emerald green that would reach to her calves, made out of silk as thick and fine as anything available in the markets of Rome. Such a prize was worth its weight in gold, and only the richest could afford it. "It comes from somewhere beyond your empire, as you know. Caravans carried it thousands of miles. It's surprisingly tough and warm."

"How smooth it feels!"

"He said it would be a salve for your bruises."

She held it against herself. "So soft, in so hard a place."

"Is it really so hard, Valeria?" He handed her a lock of hair that was bound with a twist of grass. "This is from the clan, cut from the mane of the horse you rode to the hunt. It's a promise to find you another."

She was flattered, and surprised. "I hope I can take better care of the next one."

"It's obvious you have a love of horses. Like a Morrigan."

That name, again. "And your own present, priest?"

"My knowledge." He untied a bundle of herbs. "The forest balances all things, and is thus eternal. Each danger is countered by a remedy. All that you and Hool need to recover, lady, is in the wood." He began adding flakes from his packages to the heating water. "You're both young and strong, but these drugs will speed the healing. We'll bring the broth to him when it's ready."

A scented steam began to arise. "How do you know which plant to pick?"

"It's lore that dates to the dawn of time. Our elders teach our acolytes. We don't put things down on dead tablets; we carry them in our hearts and sing the truth like birds. Each generation memorizes anew." He gave her a sip of the tea.

"Generations of druids?"

"Yes. Memory is our job, as well as healing and ceremony."

"And sacrifice."

"Any wise man gives back to the world a token of what he receives. Arden showed me the cones you brought."

"My stone pine? Where are they?"

"He burned them to Dagda shortly before he captured you."

The idea chilled her. Had her own offering been turned against her? It seemed a blasphemous thing for Arden to have done. "And now you're calling your people to war."

Kalin shook his head. "War is coming, but not at our call. The proper sign hasn't arrived yet. All we druids have done is give the oak's strength to our warriors and remind them of ancient ways. They know your wall is an abomination against nature that must be swept aside. Whether your husband and his men will be swept aside with it is up to them, not us. We are tools of the gods."

"*Your* gods."

"Britannia's gods. Your Roman ones are half forgotten, your temples weed-grown, your beliefs changing as frequently as the hairstyle of the empress. Ours endure."

She sipped, feeling the medicine ease through her bruised body. "Yet for all your confidence you find it necessary to keep me, a woman, a helpless captive."

He laughed. "How helpless, boar-slayer? How captive, when the control of your little drawbridge is in your hands, not mine? It's not chains or cages that's keeping you here, and we both know it."

"What, then?"

"The man who captured you, of course."

"You mean Arden. That I'm *his* prisoner."

"No. I mean he's yours. That you won't leave until you've taken his heart."

After Kalin left, Valeria was tempted to flee again, just to prove the druid wrong. She didn't need to wait for cocky and carefree Arden Caratacus! He was thief, spy, traitor, killer, and barbarian, and the idea that she cared a bronze coin for him or his feelings was ridiculous. He'd abducted her! He'd threatened all her plans! All her dreams of home, career, children, and status had been overthrown by his ruthlessness! It was simply that she must use Arden as he was using

her, trick Arden as he'd tricked her, so she could report his
vulnerabilities.

But only when she had the spirit to go. Only when she'd
learned enough. It still felt good to be in this isolated refuge,
her choices simple, her life placid.

Arden came at sunset, the sky a soft rose against the enclosing hills and the lake molten glass. He was triumphant
at having killed two ducks with his arrows. "I shot them on
the wing, breast and neck. The second one was a lucky hit.
Here's wild carrots and bread from Tiranen, as well. And
wine, stolen from Rome."

So, her stomach growling, they prepared the simple meal
together. While he cleaned the birds, she built up the fire and
put on water for the carrots. Then she began roasting the
fowl on a spit, their fat spattering to erupt in little spouts of
flame. Arden stood close to help. He was like another wall,
enclosing her.

As evening came, she lit a candle.

Her captor, or caretaker—she was no longer sure which—
had brought his wine in a leather bag and showed how she
could jet a stream into her mouth. Her laughter at the trick
made the liquid splash her chin. The domesticity was so typical of the lower classes that her mother would be shocked,
yet it left Valeria strangely content. They were alone in the
wild and yet not alone, because they had each other. She had
to remind herself not to trust him too much. He was still a
barbarian. But he was also becoming a kind of friend, like
Brisa.

She could hear and feel the silk whispering against her
body and knew he could see its borders peeking from beneath her Gallic coat. He didn't mention it, however, and she
was too shy to thank him.

"You can walk," he commented instead.

"I can hobble."

"Savia suspects me of torturing you. Tomorrow I'll bring
my horse, and you can ride behind me back to Tiranen.
There's a meeting of the clans I've got to go to, and you're
strong enough now to finish your recovery there."

She was surprised at her own disappointment. She liked

the quiet of the crannog. She liked being alone with Arden outside the crowded and noisy hill fort. But certainly her place was back where she could be found and rescued, wasn't it? "Planning another abduction?"

He didn't rise to her provocation. "There's rumor of trouble."

"What kind of trouble?"

"None that concerns you, yet."

"You haven't heard from my husband?" She was annoyed he wouldn't confide in her and couldn't resist asking it.

"I told you he won't move against us."

"Marcus isn't afraid of you." She insisted on it without knowing why.

"But he's afraid for you, Valeria, and because of that he's afraid for himself. As long as you stay alive, he retains his office. If you die, his future is in peril. By capturing you, we've captured him."

The thought depressed her. "You pick on a woman to defeat a man?"

"What kind of man is so easily defeated?"

She had nothing to say to that.

"Is it really so bad, my clan and my crannog?" he persisted.

"It's not my home."

"What if it was?"

Here was *his* weakness, and it gave her an opportunity to sting him. "You know I could never belong here. Never belong to you." There. She'd said it. ·

"Celtic women belong to no man. And yet you *do* belong here, among the free. It relaxes you, I can see it. I know we don't have your fine things, but we do have great spirit. We have each other."

"So do Romans."

"I admire your loyalty, but you have to be realistic. Your husband might worry for you, be embarrassed by your capture, even miss your company. But he won't risk his career when he doesn't love you."

"You don't know my husband's heart!"

"I know the emptiness of yours. He's not in love with you because you aren't with him."

"The presumption of you!"

"Why are you always upset by simple truth? I didn't abduct you, I rescued you, from an arranged marriage and Roman ambition."

"Now I should thank you?" She was flushing.

"You enjoy this crannog. I can see it on your face."

She turned away. "This is dinner, not a lifetime."

"Sometimes a dinner is all a lifetime allows." He stood close, lightly touching her arms. She trembled. "Come, you know I've treated you well. Let's eat, not argue, and let the Wall take care of itself for an evening."

The simple food was good, her body ravenous. How could such a meal taste better than an elaborate banquet? How could a rude hut seem as comfortable as a Roman mansion? They chatted for a while of simpler things, of the hunt and horses and history of his clan, and let the wine numb their frustration and desire.

At length they pushed themselves back from the food. He was watching her more lazily now, seemingly content to drink in her features in the candlelight. It both flattered her and made her nervous. She still looked like a bruised pear and wished she was prettier, and yet also wished he wouldn't look at her at all. She'd promised her fidelity to Marcus! Yet she wanted Arden to want her, if for no other reason than to turn him down.

How mixed-up she felt.

"You pretend to know a lot about love," she said finally.

His smile was wistful. "That's because I've been in love and know how terrible it can be, this thing that all young women long for."

Suddenly she saw it. There'd been a romance. "When?"

"Before, when I was in the Roman army." His gaze was lost in memory.

"Please tell me what happened."

He shook his head. "I don't tell it to anyone. It's bitter, not sweet."

"But you must to me."

"Why?"

"You must trust me."

He was amused. "Why must I trust you?"

"Because I must trust you, the two of us alone, a thousand miles from Rome." Each the other's prisoner, Kalin had said.

He knew what she meant: the price of friendship, or something deeper. He considered, then shrugged. "Her name was Alesia."

"A pretty name."

"Just why I first noticed her I can't truly say. By the time I saw her, I'd marched past a thousand women, or ten times a thousand women. She was pretty, almost as pretty as you, and had a kind look, and yet that doesn't fully explain it. I'd seen other women equally pretty, and equally kind. There was simply a peculiar radiance to that moment, a trick of light that made me feel directed by the gods. Have you ever experienced it?"

"No."

"The setting sun had backlit clouds beyond the Danube, turning them black, and the Roman shore was golden. Alesia was fetching water, her back straight and neck erect, the jar balanced on her head, and the light turned her shift white and translucent. I remember her steps, small and careful, the slim silhouette of her form, and her manner, graceful and chaste. I walked past without stopping, on an errand to buy some wine for my comrades, but something made me look back."

"You fell in love." She was envious.

"We hadn't said a word, and yet I lost my heart. I wanted not just to possess her but to know her, to protect her, to besiege her heart."

Valeria swallowed.

"She glanced back at me," he continued, "and with that our fates were sealed."

Where was this woman? She couldn't ask that yet. "Why were you in the army?"

"My family was rich and had come to partial accommodation with the Romans. We had lands south of the Wall. We tried your civilization, but it trapped us in debt. When my father couldn't pay the Bite, he was arrested, and our lands were confiscated. When he went to Rome for justice, he was ignored and died of illness. My mother died of grief. I was left with revenge. So I joined the legions."

"You joined the empire you hated?"

"Not hate, not at first. I was young enough to think that perhaps it had been my father's fault, because he wasn't Roman enough. I Latinized my name to Ardentius and marched where the army told me. At first, everything Roman seemed grand. I heard the roar of the mob at the Coliseum. I guarded generals who dined at the villas of Italian millionaires. I prowled the wharves of Ostia, where all the wealth of the world comes and goes. My first impression was yours. Rome was universal and eternal and necessary."

He made it seem false. "It's brought order to the world."

"And slavery, poverty, and hollowness. Cities so great they can't feed themselves. Taxes no one can afford to pay. Army life was callous, and the Romans I met were a soft, spoiled people, ignorant of who they ruled and unwilling to fight. They got tribute from places they couldn't name."

"Yet you took their pay and wore their clothes and slept in their barracks."

"For a while. When I knew enough to beat you, I wanted out."

"With an Alesia, after your twenty-year enlistment?"

"No, I wanted Alesia then, when I saw her on the grassy bank of the Danube. Not that part between a woman's thighs, which can be bought by soldiers for a coin, but her, to end the loneliness of the legions. I found her owner, Criton the leather maker, and began bargaining for her freedom. I trailed her to the market and to the river, finding excuses to talk and help carry her things. She was frightened of disappointment but alive with hope. I told her about life here, how the sun in summer seems to linger half the night and stars in winter are thick as snow. I told her we'd never be treated as equals within the empire—I an alien and she a slave—but that here we could make a free and happy life."

"She believed this?"

"Her eyes, Valeria! How they ignited with the promise of it!"

The woman said nothing. Was she herself some kind of replacement for this slave woman? Had she been captured to replace a memory?

"What I hadn't anticipated was the jealousy of Lucullus, the centurion who commanded my unit. He hated happiness because he was incapable of it himself. The man was piggish, with that kind of animal cunning that thrives in the army. He'd tried a particularly insidious form of the Bite, demanding that his soldiers give him a portion of their pay to be granted any leave. Their families, crops, and financial affairs were hostage to his greed. This went too far, and the others persuaded me to speak for them to the cohort commander. Lucullus was reprimanded, his pay fined, and his power curbed. I was a hero for a day. Then my comrades forgot. Lucullus didn't."

"You're an idealist!" Arden was the kind of man her politician father had always disparaged. The senator said empires were sustained by accommodation and that self-righteous men caused grief. Valeria had secretly disagreed. She thought people should believe in something, but her father would have called her foolish.

"I see things clearly," Arden went on, "which is a curse. Anyway, word of my intentions toward Alesia came to Lucullus, as it must. Nothing is secret in the army. Reports that Ardentius the troublemaker was about to spend all his savings to buy a slave's freedom caused my commander much amusement, and then much thought. He went to Criton and bribed him to tell when and how I was going to buy the girl. Then he came to a grove of poplar where Alesia waited, arriving before I did. He seized her, embraced her, whipped her, raped her, and burned her—all to get back at me."

"Oh, Arden . . ."

"She hanged herself for shame. I'd come with a wedding present and found a corpse." His voice was hollow.

"What present?"

He swallowed, looking away from her eyes. "That silk you're wearing."

She blushed, suddenly alarmed at the gift. Horrified. Flattered. Confused. It felt as if it were on fire.

"I won it for a deed in battle. I've had no one else worthy of it until now."

"Arden . . ."

"I didn't have an instant's doubt who killed her," he cut her off.

He was like that probatio who she'd watched training in the courtyard, letting his shield drift and exposing his heart. "So *you* killed *him*."

"No man had ever beaten Lucullus in a fight, fair or foul. But I found him that night, knocked away the dagger he kept at the small of his back, and strangled him with my own hands. I killed Criton, too, and took both the money I'd paid for Alesia and the bribe Lucullus had left and threw it to the beggars. I dumped my Roman armor into the river and swam for Germania. Eventually I made my way back here."

"To drag others into revenge."

"To warn others of Rome. It took my father. My mother. The woman I loved. So I took you."

"To get back at the empire," she whispered.

"That *was* my motive, at first."

She looked away. She must not fall under his spell. "But you can't mean to sweep all of Rome away from Britannia for—" She gestured around the hut. "This."

"This is all I need."

"Except for that wine you brought. I, too, am a product of the empire you despise. If Rome is so worthless, why do barbarians try to plunder it? And if you plunder too much, where will your sons and daughters get their goods?"

"And if you Romans conquer too much, who will you ever learn from but yourselves? Why does one nation need to own the entire world?"

"The world is that nation now!"

"Not my world. Not my life."

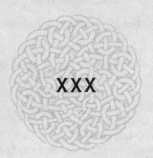

XXX

I realize, when Savia is brought before me again, that our relationship has subtly changed. I had her moved to better quarters and quietly inquired about her purchase price. It was low, as expected. Some word of my interest must have filtered back to her. She sits before me with new confidence.

Certainly we seem not so much master and slave, or interrogator and witness, as tentative allies trying to understand what happened at Hadrian's Wall. I don't find this assumption of equality entirely disturbing because I realize that I look forward to her company. This is the woman closest to the heart of Valeria, and thus most vital to my own understanding. I also find some strange comfort in her presence, as if we know each other better than we do. She's a little thinner than when I saw her last, but not disagreeably so, and in fact has an attractiveness that I didn't entirely recognize before. It is the serene beauty of the good mother or the longtime companion. It occurs to me that the beauty of another person increases with affection. Is it possible that I feel something for this woman? What does that say about my habit of solitude? I have roamed the Roman world and met thousands of people. Who, in the end, do I really feel close to? This is a question that seemed trivial in my youth. It is of increasing importance as I age.

She sits before me less anxious this time, knowing there's some unspoken understanding between us. Perhaps she thinks the story I'm piecing together has subtly affected me. Certainly I have become more at home in this tale of Britannia, less the skeptical sophisticate sent by Rome. My imagination has smelled the acrid smoke of the burning grove and the rank *musk of a dead boar. What seems inexplicable at long range sometimes seems inevitable when explained in context. We share a history now, she by experience and I by understanding, and are bound to each other by what happened and what must happen next.*

I greet her politely and relate what I have learned from the druid Kalin, who nursed Valeria on that crannog. I ask Savia to think back to her captivity in Caledonia with the clan of Arden Caratacus, prince of the Attacotti. What developed between this Celtic warrior and this Roman woman who had been ripped so quickly from her new marriage?

"I have been told of this boar hunt, for example. It changed things, did it not?"

"It changed Valeria." Savia looks at me now with hope.

"How?" My tone is gentler than the first time we met.

"She was almost killed, and thus never more alive. I saw the huge gorgon she'd killed when it was brought back to Tiranen for feasting, so heavy it had to be suspended between horses instead of men. Yet this Roman girl had slain the boar."

"The Celts were impressed?"

"The Celts thought it a sign. When she rode back from the crannog with Arden and passed between the wooden gate towers of Tiranen, they sang her powers as if she were an Amazon. Hool rode back with them, still bandaged with splints to his leg and torso, but everyone knew she had saved his life, and helped nurse him afterward. He shouted her praises. Cassius, her former bodyguard, gave her the polished tusks to wear on her neck. She had a look of stunned radiance. She'd felt the fire of being a barbarian."

"She liked it."

"She told me later that she'd never felt such fear. Or such exaltation at having survived. That hut on the lake where she'd healed had seduced her as well."

"So she and Arden came together."

"Oh, no. She remained a chaste married woman. You could tell by his longing."

"She felt loyalty to her husband?"

"Loyalty is everything. The question is how much loyalty her husband felt toward her."

"She gave up on the idea of rescue?"

Savia thinks about this for a moment. "She felt the rescuers had given up on her. Both of us felt that way, master. We
still waited to hear the bleat of the Celtic warning horn that
would signal her husband's approach in his golden armor,
determined to wrest her away. This is the way it is in the old
stories, like Agamemnon sailing to Troy to win back stolen
Helen. Yet day after day went by without even word of nego-
tiations. Then week after week, month after month. We didn't
understand what was happening in the Empire, nor how
Galba plied Marcus's fears. None of this would be made
clear until the winter."

"And so Valeria, despite her chastity, felt doubt."

"We felt abandoned."

Abandoned. And adopted, I think. "What was your life
like among the Celts?"

"Simpler. In Rome, everything was strategic: marriage,
career, children, assignment, house, neighborhood, entertainment. One measured the progress of one's life by money
and station. The barbarians, in contrast, were like animals,
or children. It was hard to get them to commit to anything
tomorrow, let alone months or years ahead. Time had less
meaning. You'd set a meeting, and they might ignore it completely. Or show hours late with no apology. They were wonderful craftsmen who could carve a piece of wood into a
song—but would also put off the repair of a leaky roof for
weeks."

"Surely they had to pay attention to the seasons."

"That's what the druids were for. The priests would watch
the sun and stars and tell them when to plant and reap.
They'd also divine the future."

"With blood sacrifice?"

"Of animals. Yet I didn't doubt it might be with Roman
captives, too."

"Was it clear that war was coming?"

"The raid on the grove had aroused the tribes, but the
Wall was still too strong and the barbarians too divided.
Uniting the Picts and Attacotti and Scotti and Saxons into
one great army was Arden's goal, but it was an almost

impossible one. There was no strategy. Arden understood planning because he'd lived among the Romans, but it was difficult to explain to his people. To them, time was circular and life was brief."

"A rather aimless existence."

"Not aimless. Simply that every deed was aimed at that day, not the next. It's a way of life not entirely unpleasant. They measure happiness by feelings more than achievement. Their homes are cruder than a tenement in Rome, their heat is more spotty, a proper bath is nonexistent, their clothes are rougher to the skin, their cooking is plain, their mud is everywhere, and they are more apt to have a cow in their dining room than an aristocrat. Yet why was there more laughter in Tiranen than at Petrianis, or even the Roman house of Senator Valens? Because they had so little, they worried less about keeping it. Because they had so little to be proud of, they seemed less poisoned by the sin of pride."

"Surely Valeria longed for Roman comforts—"

"Their barbarism meant that our own worries receded as well. I'd never noticed as many flowers and as many birds as I did that summer. I enjoyed rain, and the sewing that it meant inside, and then sun because it meant we'd roam the meadows. Valeria rode almost every day on the new mare that had been given her, and Brisa began to teach her the bow and arrow. The archer had taken my lady under her wing, finding a kind of sibling that she'd missed since the deaths of her brothers. As Valeria improved her Celtic, Brisa learned some Latin. We were so dependent on our captors that we developed a strange fondness for them, the natural surrender of child to parent, or slave to master, or legionary to centurion. We still expected rescue and return, of course, so we regarded it all as an interlude. Almost a dream."

"The barbarians were kind to you?"

"The barbarians were people. Some were kind, and some were vulgar. None molested us except Asa, who resented Valeria and would play her little tricks. Once it was a burr under the saddle that caused her new horse to buck her off. The bitch would slip salt into a serving of honey or vinegar into a draught

of wine. Petty things and catty gossip. It was annoying, and Valeria's protests did no good."

"Why did Asa resent her so much?"

"Because Asa was in love with Arden, and he'd forgotten the Celtic girl's existence. He'd been blinded by Valeria. She can do that, you know; the pretty minx has known how to manipulate and get her way since she was a young child. She'd flirt with him even while clinging to her married purity, and enjoy his torture without admitting it to herself. He'd warned others to leave her be and so felt he had to do so, too, and feared she'd lose her value as a hostage if despoiled. Yet it tormented him. Despite his professed hatred of Rome, he viewed her as exotic, somehow better than the women in Caledonia. I think he wanted Rome as much as he wanted to destroy it: his hatred and fascination came in part from a conviction of inferiority. The awkwardness was made worse because she was attracted to him. She tried to hide it, but I knew. Everyone did."

"He was more her own age than her husband was."

"And handsome, daring, and commanding. Every woman felt a tremor when he went by. And yet it was more than that, I believe. The two fit naturally together like the halves of a broken coin. Despite his protestations, he was Roman enough to understand her world, and she wild enough to understand his. Yet they kept apart as if they'd burn if they touched. Both seemed haunted, and it worried the warriors. There were rumblings that he should either couple with the Roman vixen or get rid of her."

"What did you advise?"

"That she remain loyal to Marcus, of course. But when he didn't come and didn't come, I could see the child's doubt. Each evening we'd go to the palisade, and the country to the south would be empty of rescue. She'd never really been married; the man was too remote. Now this barbarian was at her side. My counsel was duty, but my secret question was, Where did her happiness lie? Finally I went to see Kalin."

"What a meeting that must have been! The Christian and the Celtic mystic!"

"We'd talked before. He feared my god because I didn't fear his. I told him the old gods were dead and that he'd see as much if he tried to attack the Wall; that Rome had the protection of the Jesus it had once crucified. My warning made him wary. For men to sacrifice to the gods, this he understood, but for a god to be sacrificed for men: this, he complained, was almost impossible to believe. How could people follow such nonsense? And yet I'd describe how the Christian martyrs had in turn sacrificed themselves. He was fascinated by a Rome he could scarcely imagine, and I was intrigued by his herbs and roots to ward off sickness and heal wounds."

"So you were friends?"

Savia laughs. "I was determined he not sacrifice me!"

I smile. I'm not the first man Savia has manipulated. "What did he suggest for Arden and Valeria?"

"The new year's feast comes after the leaves fall from the trees. The Celts date their year from the end of harvest and the start of winter, and call it Samhain. They believe the spirits of their dead ancestors wake to walk the earth that night, and that the festival grants strange powers and unusual liberties. There's a fertility rite that involves two Celtic gods, the male Dagda and the female Morrigan. Each year a different man and a different woman are chosen by lot to play the roles. Kalin draws the lots."

"He decided to draw Arden and Valeria."

"He said it is a night of that other world, not this one, and that what happened between them on Samhain would be in the hands of gods, not men."

XXXI

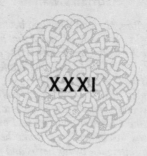

Samhain was the first night of winter, the end and the beginning of the Celtic year, and thus a night outside the normal cycle of time. The world stopped, the dead rose to dance in the glens, and reality became a dream.

Valeria never imagined she'd still be at Tiranen so late in the Roman year, and so enmeshed in a world not her own.

She existed that long northern summer without any news of rescue, enjoying days in which dusk would linger past bedtime and the east would blush before the wheel of stars had barely turned. It was as if night were near repeal. Cattle fattened, crops ripened, and the clan celebrated the festival of the god Lugh-the-Many-Talented near high summer. Valeria had never spent so much time outside, hardening to the weather and invigorated by the smell of sea and heather. She rode, she gathered, she walked, she weaved, she waited, and she learned skills a patrician would never learn in Rome. She was in a carefree limbo of captivity, past and future having disappeared. While her entire life was held captive, many of her ordinary worries had disappeared because of her own initial helplessness and, later, a reluctance to recognize and confront her own confused feelings.

It was easier to drift.

Then the sun began slipping south, the night began to lengthen, and eventually it was time for Harvest Home, the gathering of the autumn equinox. Every clan member from child to chief took part in the great harvest, and the captive Romans were no exception.

Valeria and Savia found themselves with the other women

one dawn at the fringe of yellow wheat, a bag on one shoulder and a leather flask of spring water at their waist. A drum and flute began, a song arose, and the line of women began moving through the high grain with hands outstretched, nimble fingers breaking loose the fat and brittle heads. The kernels sifted past their bright metal rings like a tumble of coins, cascading into shoulder sacks with a whisper. The harvesters swayed as they worked, forming a slow dance of Celtic females in blue, yellow, and scarlet tunics who moved across the fields like feasting songbirds. Their men came in rhythmic line behind, stroking with their scythes to cut the stalks for winter straw and hay. Mice ran from the stubble and so hawks orbited overhead, picking them off.

It was the first time Valeria had harvested the bread she ate. At midday the women sat in the shade together, gossiping and eating a lunch brought from the huts by the youngest children. Her labor made her a part of them, and she enjoyed this strange new camaraderie of shared work. At day's end her hands were raw, her back stooped, her feet aching, and yet when her bag of grain cascaded into its storage hole, she felt it was filling her as well, even before she ate it. She tried to share her enthusiasm with Brisa.

"It's still a novelty to you," grumbled the archer, groaning as she massaged her feet. "I've been harvesting since I could walk. I'd rather practice archery."

"It's astonishing to work together. Rome is so crowded that you're never together with anyone."

"That makes no sense."

"Cities don't, sometimes."

"I've never been to one, and from your description, I don't care to."

Valeria found herself eating like a wolf and never gaining any girth. Her skin tanned a common, scandalous brown; her endurance increased. She noticed things she'd never really seen before: the curve of windswept grass that signaled a change to rain or sun, the progressive migration of birds, the heaviness of dew, the twin half-moons of a deer print in the mud, the hiss of rain on straw. After harvest, Arden took her riding up into highlands so windswept that they were stripped at their tops to raw rock, the lichen like spilled paint. The view seemed endless, and yet never a glimpse of the Wall! Then he took her down into narrow, shadowed valleys to fish. She caught some, their scales slick as oil and their muscles jumping.

He never touched her, yet never stopped looking at her.

She was haunted by him.

Brisa continued to teach her to shoot. Valeria's fingertips callused to pull the bowstring, and her aim became good enough to hit a target. Once, in a meadow, her rival Asa set a sewing basket on a rock, and Valeria impulsively put an arrow through it, pinioning the wicker against the ground and making her tormentor jump. The Roman didn't say a word, but her message was plain enough. She was becoming dangerous.

Asa's tricks stopped.

Inside the hill fort, Valeria weaved tartan on the clan looms and traded recipes with her captors. At night she listened to the stories of their gods and heroes, and told her own of Hercules and Ulysses and the court of Jupiter.

At Harvest Home, the animals came down from high pastures to winter barns. Vegetables were pickled and meat salted. Fruit was stacked in fat casks. New beer was fermented in vats smelling of malt and barley. Night overtook the day, the first frosts and bitter winds came, and leaves came showering down from the trees. Here was a breath of winter far deeper and more enduring than Italy's, and, despairing of rescue, she braced herself for a harsh season. Now, at Samhain—the end of autumn and beginning of winter, that time when the dead can walk and the faery kings emerge from their barrows—the clan would celebrate the New Year.

She'd been chosen by lot to play the central role.

At Kalin's command, each young woman had woven a tassel of individual pattern. Brisa taught Valeria a swirling Celtic design of saffron and cobalt. As they wove, the Roman admitted to herself that by now she was captive in name only; she could ride away at any time with a rough understanding of which direction the Wall must be. Yet the failure of Marcus to rescue her, the seasonal cycle, and her interest in Arden had all conspired to still impatience.

She was still gathering intelligence on these Celts!

She was still disturbed by her abductor.

Her tassel went with the others in a covered wicker basket.

Three nights before Samhain, Kalin stood before the clan to choose the woman who would play the role of the good and terrible Morrigan, and drew Valeria.

There was a confused and knowing murmur.

"She doesn't even believe in the goddess she's to represent!" Asa protested.

"How can a Roman play a Celt?" added Luca.

Kalin listened judiciously to their complaints. Valeria was horrified at her selection; she'd planned to watch the ceremony from the shadows! Why had fortune selected her for a central role? She glanced at her maidservant. Savia's eye avoided hers.

"The goddess herself guides my hand," Kalin said. "This year, for whatever reason, Morrigan has decided to be danced by the Roman."

Valeria felt trapped. This new honor picked her out again just as she was fitting in. She feared she'd embarrass herself at the pagan festival, or make new jealousies.

Brisa tried to reassure her. "Morrigan will inhabit and guide you. She's honoring you because of the boar."

"You must tell me what to do!"

"Ask the goddess."

"I'm asking you!"

"Calm yourself. I'll come the evening before Samhain and make things plain."

Brisa came as promised and found Valeria worriedly combing her long dark hair before a mirror of polished bronze.

"I don't want to dance the part, Brisa."

"Kalin believes you touched with magic. As Asa said, it's peculiar the goddess would pick you. Maybe she wants you to understand the ways of the Caledonii, should you ever go back to your wall."

"Of course I'll go back! Soon! I must!"

"Yet will you?"

Valeria wasn't sure of the answer anymore. Tiranen was a cruder place: its rooms colder, its courtyard mud, its latrines mere pits in the ground, its food plainer, its conversations less witty and knowledgeable. She missed many things. And yet all the restrictions that had bound her old life had fallen away. Instead of feeling captive she felt strangely liberated. A woman was more equal with these people. Her life could be less calculated. Friendship simpler. Pleasure quicker. Worries less complicated. And yet this wasn't her. Was it?

"Look." Brisa held up a carefully selected and polished apple. "To tap Morrigan's magic, you need the fruit of the gods. Slice this with your dagger to reveal your future."

"My future? I paid for that in Londinium, and little of it has come true."

"Sometimes the future takes time. Slice it."

Valeria reluctantly started to.

"Not that way! Crossways, the blade level."

She cut horizontally as directed, and Brisa gestured at the five-pointed star that the core made in the severed halves. "Here is a fruit of the earth that reflects the stars. It's one more sign that all is one. Can you see it?"

"Yes."

"Now take a bite as you look in the mirror. Legend has it that over your shoulder you'll see the image of your future husband."

"Future husband?"

"It's Celtic custom."

"Brisa, I have a husband."

"Then what are you hesitating for? Take a bite."

Valeria lifted the apple to her lips. There was no one in the mirror but herself and the warrior woman, of course. No Marcus, just as he'd been absent all summer. No husband at all. Was that what the goddess meant? She bit. "I see nothing."

"Swallow."

She did so. The fruit was crisp and sweet. Her eyes closed to remember her soldier husband, and she was surprised that her picture of Marcus had become cloudy. She remembered the stolid sense of him more than his appearance. So odd . . .

"Valeria?" It was a male voice.

Her eyelids fluttered open in alarm.

There was a figure in her mirror, she realized, dimly reflected from the doorway, but it wasn't her Roman. She whirled around in her seat.

Arden.

His mouth was open to speak, but he'd stopped in surprise at her shocked expression. He noticed she was holding something shiny in her hand.

"I didn't mean to surprise you," he said, looking confused. "I came to speak about Samhain. It's important for the clan that it goes well. Are you all right?"

Valeria turned away in alarm.

Brisa spoke softly. "It's all right, Arden Caratacus. Valeria will play her part well. Leave now, for you've done what you must. We'll see you at the fire."

Valeria wouldn't look back at him. She dropped what she was holding, and he saw it was half an apple, a bite taken. It rolled under her stool.

He swiftly disappeared.

"I saw *him*," Valeria whispered.

"You saw what Morrigan wanted you to see."

The celebration would take place at midnight on the horse meadows below the hill fort. It would give time for a banquet in the Great House by the legions of the dead, who could return this one night from the realm of Tirnan Og and feast as if still living. Oakwood platters, eating knives, and pewter cups were set in neat ranks for the restless ghosts, the cups filled with milk and the platters graced with an apple and a sheaf of barley. The benches were empty, the shadows deep. If the dead truly came—on this one night between past and future when time became meaningless and distant events could be foretold—then they'd celebrate in Tiranen and leave the living, who would be dancing in the meadow, alone.

The clan left the hill fort in procession, descending to the waiting bonfire that would keep them safe. Every third member held a torch, the march of light reminding Valeria of her impossibly distant wedding. How different and yet alike the two worlds were! Instead of stern cavalrymen lining their way, there were horn lanterns stuck on upright poles, each frame carved into a grotesque face, grinning or hideous. Candles lit them with an eerie glow, making the succession of lanterns like an arc of orange fireflies, or a tendril of glowing salmon eggs.

"What do all these images mean?" Valeria asked Brisa as they walked together. Savia, just ahead, was crossing herself.

"These lanterns become our guardians this night, lighting our way to Samhain and frightening away roaming spirits. They're the luck to see us through to the next year that comes at dawn, when the old crone Cailleach strikes the ground with her hammer and makes it hard with frost."

"We Romans believe the year begins with the spring."

"And we Celts believe the spring begins with the triumph of winter. Death is a necessary prelude to birth, and darkness the herald of the coming sun."

It was frosty this night. A full moon was up, making plain the shapes of the hills that surrounded them. Great trees lifted bare beseeching branches to heaven, and all color was leached from the world. Valeria had come to like the forest, but on this night she could once more imagine ghosts marching through it, the stone dolmens of the dead yawning open and slain warriors issuing forth. Old women would be reborn as young maidens. Drowned children would be given the adult bodies they'd never enjoyed. All would glide across the ground and up the mist to the hill fort, there to sit in the banquet hall and feast for one night in the world of the living.

She shivered, wrapping her cloak more tightly against the cold.

The Celts sang a song as they marched, a saga of a legendary chieftain who sought the gold of the dragon Brengatha, and the warrior queen he freed from the dragon's lair. Then a song of thanks to the gods for giving the clan another year, another harvest, another cycle of life. And then a ribald song about the maiden Rowena, so beautiful and tempting that she'd made fools of three men, and lover of a fourth.

In the clearing was stacked an immense cone of wood, ready for firing. The procession circled, stopped, and looked back up the hill at Tiranen. Gurn, who at the ceremony of Lugh had passed from boy to man and was thus, at fourteen, their youngest warrior, was still up there watching them—a test of his young courage against the imminent approach of ghosts. At their halt he disappeared from the gate and hurriedly went into the emptied Great House, the hair on his neck rising at its strange chill. A burning fire seemed to give little heat, casting a dance of shadow on the peaked ceiling. He lit the final torch from its flame and then sprinted in relief from the deserted hill fort, running to the others below. They watched his descending flame draw gold filigree against the night, its arc like the vine and rainbow of Celtic artisans. Finally the youth came dashing into their circle, breathless and triumphant, a young maiden named Alita already watching him with covetous eyes. He thrust the torch into the base of the pyramid of wood, its tinder caught, and fire began reaching up the cone.

The clan held hands, singing a song of the departing and returning sun as flames licked the cold sky.

Then there was quiet again, the Celts tensely waiting as the fire heated them on one side and the approaching winter chilled them on the other. Finally the circle broke to let in Kalin, his hood back, his eyes bright, and his arms bearing a trembling animal.

It was a sheep, black as winter night.

The druid stood inside the circle of Celts, the column of sparks behind him a roiling funnel. His face beaded with sweat, he called in a deep and steady voice. "Who speaks for the clan of Caratacus, of the tribe of the Attacotti and alliance of Caledonia?"

"I do!" Arden replied. He stood straight, his sword by his side, his cloak thrown back, his hair plaited, and his tunic open to the golden torque at his throat. "I'm chieftain of this clan, confirmed by combat and acclamation."

"Does your clan appreciate what the gods of wood and

water have given them, chieftain Caratacus? Do they have thanks and humility in their hearts?"

"The clan thanks the good god Dagda, who knows all crafts and all hearts, and who gave us the harvest to see us through the coming winter."

"And who speaks for the great god Dagda?"

"I do," Arden replied.

"And will the god accept sacrifice from the Caledonii?"

"The god demands it. The god desires it."

With surprising strength, Kalin lifted the trussed sheep up above his head. The Celts roared their approval. Then the druid lowered the animal to the dry grass at his feet and took out a golden dagger.

"Accept back some of the fruit you have given us, Dagda!" The knife plunged; the sheep kicked and was still. The blade came out red, and Kalin turned the animal to efficiently slit its throat. Then he walked in stately circle around the fire so that the drain of the animal's neck left a splattered circle of blood.

Finally he came back to where he'd started and hurled the carcass into the fire.

A great shout went up. "To Dagda and all the gods!"

Then, amid the acrid smell of burning wool and flesh, the celebration began.

There was sour-sweet mead scooped by cups out of cauldrons, the skull drinking bowls passed from lip to lip. There was wine, traded or stolen from the Romans. There was beer in oaken casks. Cooking pits were uncovered and meat unwrapped from steaming leaves. Pork and beef were stabbed by daggers, dribbles of grease wiped clean by warm bread. There were fresh-picked apples, late-autumn greens, and honeyed cakes, all consumed under moon, stars, and sparks, laughter making white clouds in the night. Occasionally they'd glance more apprehensively at their fortress on its hill, wondering at the dark banquet going on there.

Arden kept a careful distance from Valeria, but his eye was almost always on her, watching her eat with the others, a kiss on her cheek here, a cheerful insult about her Roman origins there. She moved with quiet aura like the goddess she was about to play. What did she think of them now, in her secret heart? What would she do when her husband finally came for her, as someday he surely must?

She had her own goblet. "I'm learning to like their mead and beer," Valeria confessed to Savia, even while discreetly keeping her own eye on Arden.

"Don't drink so much that you forget who you are."

At length, Brisa touched Valeria's arm to escort her away. Arden disappeared as well. The merriment and feasting went on in their absence, more logs hurled onto the fire. Finally there was the low, long call of a horn, echoing down the pasture, and the crowd quieted somewhat, most of them drunk now.

Kalin's voice came out of the dark. "Make way for the good god Dagda!"

Music began, the beat of drums and swirl of pipes, men and women tapping and swaying to its rhythm. Out of the darkness a stag appeared: five-pointed antlers, muzzled head, shoulders draped with dressed deerskin. It was a stag with two legs, human and yet not human, quick and strong. The animal darted, stopped, stepped hesitantly, and stopped again—and then, its head up, it recognized the clan and the fire that welcomed it every year, and danced ahead. Blue human eyes looked out from the holes in its head, the great rack of antlers dipping up and down like a god in rut.

It was looking for its mate.

"Dagda!" the assembly cried. "Lord of all the gods!"

Round the fire the stag danced, three times. Then the horn sounded again.

"Morrigan of the horse roams free on the pasture," Brisa cried. "Now she comes into the circle of fire!"

The goddess ran headlong into the circle as if pushed, rearing to a halt just before crashing into the flames. The horse-goddess whirled in confusion as if bewildered or intoxicated. In truth, of course, she was both. Her head was that of the horse, a framework of hide and free-flowing mane, and her body, freed of its cloak, showed a goddess's form. A light dress was belted in an X across her breasts, and the firelight through the tunic silhouetted slim, muscular legs. A belt of gold cinched her narrow waist, its ends tied over and dropping into the grotto between her thighs. The tusks of a boar gleamed at her neck. The goddess-pony dashed this way and that, every attempt at escape blocked by the surrounding corral of laughing humans. Giving up, she danced light and carefree as a filly around the tower of flames, the antlered stag following half a circle behind, the drums pounding harder and the pipes swirling toward some kind of climax.

"Morrigan of the horse! Her belly promises spring!"

Fearing that something irrevocable was about to happen, the goddess kept darting ahead. She'd pause, allow Dagda to approach, and then bolt. Around and around they danced, Dagda ducking and rearing in feigned impatience, Morrigan whirling to give a glimpse of her thighs. The heat made them sweat, and the night made them shiver.

The drums were accompanied by pounding feet and clapping hands in rhythmic thunder, the pace accelerating as Dagda drew ever nearer to the goddess whose fecundity would bring back light and food. She was slowing from exhaustion, looking over her shoulder at the antlered buck, her movements becoming more liquid and seductive as her soul was swallowed by her costume. Her hips were in rhythm with the music, her bare feet skipping on heat-curled grass. The sweat and heat picked out the points of her breasts, the geometry of her hips. The stag's arms were bare and powerfully muscled, a bone necklace rattling on his chest as he danced.

"Catch her, good god! Give us promise for the end of winter!"

Yet still she darted away. It seemed the tension of the dance might never end.

Then Dagda suddenly stopped, crouched, and whirled, darting swiftly around the fire the other way. He met a surprised and dazed Morrigan on the other side before she realized he'd changed direction. He grasped her with his arms and swept her around in great, dizzying, dancing turns, the two animal heads muzzle to muzzle, his horns like the branches of the bare trees that reached for the moon. He'd

captured her! Or had she allowed herself to be captured?
And even as the goddess stumbled, exhausted, he swept her
off her feet and into his arms, her horse's head falling off.
Valeria looked up at the beast who held her with dazed, surrendering eyes.

The Celts howled.

Then the stag ran off into the dark, still carrying her.

Savia was weeping.

Arden's horse was waiting, and he cast his own headdress
aside, the antlers tumbling away on the meadow. Valeria was
lifted up onto the stallion's back, and he vaulted up behind
her. "Let's reclaim our home from the dead," he whispered.
They pounded toward the sentry line of lighted lanterns,
their candles guttering, the moon orange as it set in the west.
The horse galloped up the winding line of light as the others
watched from the meadow below, and then it disappeared
into the hill fort.

It was dark and silent inside Tiranen. Arden slipped from
the horse and caught Valeria as she slid down, holding her
tight to keep her bare feet out of the frosty mud. Then he
strode toward the Great House where the dead had feasted,
banging open the doors with the confidence of the greatest
of all the gods. He saw with satisfaction that the mugs of
milk had been drained and the platters had been emptied of
their apple and barley. Their ancestors had been satiated.
The ghosts were gone.

He carried her past the fire pit, his boot kicking a fresh log
onto the embers of a fire. Then through a tapestry of winged
birds to a chamber she'd never seen before.

There was a winding wooden stair, its balustrade carved
with the scales of a snake. At its top was a sleeping loft. Thin
windows looked out over moors and mountains silvered
with starlight. Valeria had swooned as he'd carried her, not
entirely sure if she were goddess or mortal woman, alive or
dead, in a dream or reality. Now Arden laid her on a bed
piled high with bear and fox fur, closed the chamber's shutters, and lit a fire on its hearth. She watched him dazedly,
and all she knew was that she wanted the arms, chest, and
heart of Dagda.

He knelt to whisper. "Let's tear down the Wall, Valeria."

He grasped her hand and gently slipped off her silver wedding ring with its intaglio of Fortuna, goddess of Fortune. She'd forgotten she even wore it. Then he produced the sea-horse brooch she'd abandoned in the forest so long ago. "I've kept this since I first saw you. For Samhain we join these in a golden goblet."

The ring and brooch rang as he dropped them into a cup.

She was trembling. "I don't know where I am. Who I am."

"You're one of us."

He came to her then, the warmth of his skin a renewed fire, and kissed with a tenderness she'd never known. Instead of the rough urgency of the stag, he was gentle as he undressed her, murmuring words and stroking her skin in transcendent wonder.

She was more beautiful than he'd imagined, her breasts high and full, her nipples roseate, her hips like the curve of the polished apple that had fallen from her hand.

His body was hard and hot like sanded wood, and as they continued to kiss, his passion and urgency grew.

She opened to him like a flower.

The gods joined and cried out even as the setting moon sent beams of radiance through the cracks of the shutters. Then the east glowed with promise, and the last of the grinning gourds, in the smoky line far below, finally burned out.

The New Year had been achieved.

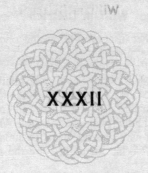

XXXII

Valeria woke at midafternoon to a world that seemed utterly changed and newly magical. She stretched her drowsy body in its nest of fur and woolens with languid laziness, physically satiated. What joy, followed by what an odd combination of depletion and fulfillment! Who'd known her body could be made to feel like that? Their beings had joined like flash and thunder, every nerve on fire, and now it was the aftermath of a vast and wonderful storm, everything wet and glistening in its wake.

She and Arden had made love well into morning before falling into exhausted sleep. At some point he'd awakened, kissed her tenderly, and left to attend to the clan. She'd lain in a cocoon of heat and musk, drifting randomly, dreaming of forest gods and a gourd-glow moon and the swirling stars of a winter's night. Now she came awake as if from a spell. How magical Samhain had been!

And then, as she remembered where and who she was, her contentment began to be polluted with guilt.

She had betrayed her husband.

Everything seemed turned upside down. She was in love with a man she once thought of as a dangerous and uncouth barbarian, and impossibly distant from a man she'd traveled more than a thousand miles to wed. She felt more at home in this timbered building than in the commander's house that was a reminder of Rome. She had more freedom and authority in the wilderness than she'd ever had in civilization, and thus more power with this poor tribe than she'd had in the Roman Empire. She was happier than she'd ever been, but only because everything she once scorned she now accepted.

How strange life had turned out to be!

Now she dreaded seeing Savia. The maidservant would no doubt start lecturing her about Christian ideas of sin.

Where was Arden? Suddenly she felt lonely with her doubts. Why had he left her like Marcus? Was this the way of all men? And why was her heart so suddenly and miserably confused? What mischief were the gods inflicting on her?

She got up, filled now with disquiet and a premonition that something was more deeply awry than she knew. It was wrong to have danced as a Celtic goddess, of course, no matter how weirdly thrilling it had been. Wrong to have gone to the bed of Arden Caratacus, sworn enemy of Rome. Yet how she savored the memory of his embrace, sometimes gentle, sometimes rough! Never with Marcus had she felt the passion and ecstasy she'd felt with Arden. It made her half dizzy even to remember it. So was the greatest moment of her life a mistake? Had she lost all sense? What did that foretell for future happiness?

What if she became heavy with child, hidden here away from her husband?

Why hadn't Marcus ever come for her?

The room was cold outside the coverings of the bed, and the sky had clouded over. It was already dim, slipping again toward long winter night. She looked outside and saw men leading strange horses toward the hill-fort corral. Who would come so late in the year? Or rather, so early in the next? Smoke rose from cooking fires, and she could hear the squeal of children and cackle of chickens. Everything was normal and yet strangely warped, as if viewed in a mirror. Her life had irrevocably changed.

She dressed hurriedly and crept downstairs. The Great House was being readied for supper, and Valeria realized she was famished again. She'd never been very hungry in Rome but always seemed that way here, where food was so simple. It wasn't just her mind that had changed, it was her very body, the buds of taste, the memory of smell. How disoriented she felt, as if still drunk!

She almost bumped into Asa, the redhead looking at her warily. Valeria's position in the clan had changed. By surrendering to the chieftain, she'd gained his power, so now Asa exhibited toward Valeria the surly deference of a disciplined dog. These were people who lived at extremes, overbearing in victory and downcast in defeat.

"Where's Arden?" Valeria asked.

"In the Council Hut with a visitor." The question allowed Asa a small victory. "He's not to be disturbed."

The Council Hut was one of the round and peaked Celtic houses inside the hill fort, used for meetings when there were issues that were not for all ears. No doubt the horses Valeria had seen were from another chief. Was there some business that went with the dawn of the Celtic New Year? She'd have to ask Arden.

"Where's Savia?"

"Who knows?" Asa sniffed. "She scurries like a lizard from rock to rock."

Valeria got her cloak and went outside. She wore the high Celtic boots, but the mire had stiffened anyway: Cailleach had indeed struck with her staff. The overcast was low, its color sword-steel, and Valeria's breath made quick puffs of cloud. She wanted to find her maidservant, so much like a mother, and explain what had happened. Or have Savia explain it to her. She wanted, unconsciously, her slave's blessing.

Yet Savia was not at the gate, nor at the well. The corral? Valeria walked there and noticed that saddles had been taken from the tired mounts and placed on the rail. She was about to walk by, paying no mind, when she stopped and turned.

They were Roman.

The angle of horns, stitching of leather, and embedment of small coins were as distinctive as a face. These horses had come from the Wall.

Her heart skipped a beat. Was it Marcus, come to bargain for her release? Had she fallen in love with Arden Caratacus only to leave because of ransom?

But she should leave him, of course, out of loyalty to her husband!

She should, but she didn't want to.

She went to the railing of the corral and looked at the horses. They whinnied, trotting this way and that, fearful they'd be made to ride again before resting. But no, she only wanted to see if she could tell which horses they were. . . .

"The black one. Recognize him?"

She turned. It was Savia, the older woman hiding her face with the hood of her cloak. She'd stolen up on Valeria from behind.

"Go on, look," the maidservant urged.

The black one? Yes, there he was, big and proud, head uplifted, nostrils wide. "Galba!"

"Yes, my lady, Galba. Or rather, Galba's horse."

"Is the senior tribune here, too?"

"Like an apparition of the devil."

"Why?"

"Come to negotiate our release, I suspect."

"After all this time?"

"Before anything worse can happen. Before we forget where we came from and who we are."

Valeria felt sick. If it were Marcus, her feelings might be more mixed. But to have to ride back to the Wall with Galba . . .

"Why now? Why him?"

"I don't know. But if this concerns our fate, then I suggest we do what we slaves do best, which is listen. There's a hayrick in back of the hut where two women might hide while peering through a chink in the wall."

"A chink?"

Savia held up a stick. "When I saw Galba ride through the gate, as bold as an emperor and as wary as a wolf, I made one."

Two Roman cavalrymen guarded the door, Valeria recognizing the posture and profile of Galba's closest decurions. A third was in the rear of the hut, squatting in boredom. The women burrowed through the hayrick and lay not four paces away, invisible to his eyes.

Savia's slit in the daub-and-wattle wall revealed Arden and Galba sitting by the charcoal heat of a small fire, each holding wine cups but regarding each other with the stiff courtliness of men who are allies but never friends. Behind them, listening like an owl and swaddled in robes, was Kalin.

The Roman's boots were spattered with mud, and his tunic was wet from sweat, evidence of a hard ride. Galba looked all business. So did Arden. The gentle and passionate lover of Samhain had been replaced by the warrior. He was unarmed but tense, military, alert, his features chiseled. Galba's face was darker and more sunken, as if caving in on itself.

"Are you here for the woman?" Arden's question was carefully flat.

"Who?" Galba seemed uncertain for a moment what the barbarian was talking about. "Oh, her. Of course not."

Arden stayed expressionless. "She's our hostage against attack, you know."

Galba nodded. "The situation has been more than a little frustrating for Marcus Flavius. I pretend ignorance about the girl's whereabouts while he fears to even hunt for her. He's wretched about doing nothing and wretched about doing something. He vacillates and broods and blames me, while ignoring letters from Rome seeking news of her plight. What a coward the man is! Given enough time, the duke would relieve him. But events on the Continent mean we don't have that time."

"What do you mean?"

"It's I who am about to be transferred. To Gaul or Spain."

"You?"

"It's the work of the praefectus. He's never trusted me and secretly blames me for the loss of his wife. Never mind that I lost four good men trying to save her."

"From a rendezvous you engineered, Brassidias."

"At your suggestion, Caratacus."

"You didn't warn us those four would come after her."

He shrugged. "I didn't know. There happened to be a conscientious duplicarius that night. When they didn't succeed, I had to punish him for his diligence. I had to pretend surprise."

Arden looked at the tribune curiously. "It doesn't bother

you to be ruthless, does it?" It was as if he only now fully realized the menace of the man he was treating with.

"It doesn't bother me to be effective, forced by the jealousies and preferment of lesser men. Marcus hates that I've forgotten more about running the Petriana than he'll ever learn. He's as afraid of me as he is envious. So he's trying to get rid of me, and now, with events changing, the duke seems inclined to listen."

"What events?"

Galba leaned back, savoring his announcement. "The emperor is ill."

"Valentinian? He's been sick for a year."

"But now near death. The appointment of his son Gratian as co-emperor has divided the court. The Germans sense opportunity. Generals are taking the child under their wing and filling his ears with nonsense. Troops are being moved into Gaul as a precaution against invasion or civil war."

"How does this change things for us?"

"I'm to go there because soldiers are being taken from Britannia."

There was a long quiet. Kalin, who'd been so still that Valeria wondered if he'd fallen asleep, had straightened.

"Where from Britannia?" Arden asked with quiet intensity, his posture taut.

"The Wall."

The Celts absorbed the news. "They'd risk that?"

"The duke thinks it insane, but commanders in the south have more influence to hold their troops. The difference is being made up from the Sixth Victrix. Marcus contributed by claiming his raid on the grove suppressed chances of a northern uprising. He even cites the hostage of his wife as evidence of truce! As a reward, the Petriana is being depleted and given twice the length of wall to patrol."

"They think that little of us?"

"You know better than I that the tribes and clans have never acted in concert. The Romans think they can bluff you until the succession is settled. They regard you as a fool, Arden Caratacus."

Arden smiled grimly. "I hope you encourage them to continue that view, tribune."

"Continental transfer be damned! I'm too old, and I've worked too hard, to give up Britannia. By the gods, I gave my *life* to Britannia, my blood and my sweat, and they've rewarded me with second-place spit. I tried working with that plodding praefectus and buttering his little bitch, and they both disdained me. So I'm half tempted to take their transfer to Gaul and leave Marcus Flavius to roast in one of your wicker cages, screaming as he recognizes his own stupidity."

"We don't roast anybody anymore, Galba."

"Pity. I've persuaded him that you do. But while such a fire would satisfy my emotions, it won't fulfill my goals. So listen. The empire is weak and divided. You've a once-in-a-lifetime chance to wrest Britannia away from Rome. Rally the tribes, advance on the Wall, and you'll cut like a knife through cheese. You can loot your way to Londinium and crown yourself king."

"He's a traitor!" Savia hissed in the hay. Valeria pinched her maid's shoulder. The men didn't hear.

"You'll help us do that?" Arden asked.

"I'll make sure the Petriana doesn't oppose you too strongly."

Arden added charcoal to the fire. "What do you want in return?"

"My own little kingdom, of course."

"The Wall?"

"South of it, among the Brigante tribe. I know those people and can keep them from turning on you Attacotti. I can tell you how to beat the legions. What I want is northern Britannia and a quarter share of the gold you'll loot in Londinium."

"You don't care about your fellow soldiers?"

"The ones I care about will stick to me."

There was silence then, the men regarding each other. Bound by necessity, mistrustful by experience. "How do I know you're telling the truth?"

"The news about the emperor is no secret, and the transfer of troops not much more of one," Galba said. "Ask your allies. Query your spies. They'll confirm what I've told you. Believe me, Caratacus, at one time I'd have opposed you with all my might. But I've learned that the empire is a place where the best men are passed over and the least rewarded. I despise Marcus Flavius, and I despise the Roman bitch who allowed herself to be used by him for advancement. I want to build a—"

"Stop calling her that." It was flat warning.

"What?"

"Don't call Valeria a bitch."

Galba paused in surprise. Then he grinned. "Ah. I see. That little beauty has gotten to you, too. Why am I surprised? Too bad that initial ambush we arranged on the way to the wedding didn't work as intended. If you'd ambushed them before we were near, you wouldn't have vows in your way."

Valeria sucked in her breath. Galba had intended her abduction all along? He'd conspired with the brigands in the forest from the beginning? Of course! That was how the Celts had known when and where she'd be. That she could ride a horse. He'd maneuvered Clodius into being her lone escort. Had Titus known?

"The gods work in their own strange way," Arden said. "If I'd captured her then, Marcus would have likely lost his posting, and I'd be preparing to fight you, Galba."

"True enough. Still, the wedding—"

"Empty vows are no vows at all. She lives here now."

The tribune snorted. "Until she gets a chance to betray you. Wake up, man! Rut her if you wish, but never forget she's Roman. The purebloods live for intrigue."

"I don't think she's Roman anymore."

"Then you're naive."

"Look. She gave me this." Arden took from a pouch something small and bright. Valeria stiffened and felt Savia do the same.

It was her ring, the one given to her on her wedding night by Marcus. She'd forgotten she'd let him slip it off at Samhain and put it in the golden cup.

Galba recognized it. "By the gods, you've bedded her, haven't you? And she's driven you crazy as a result! Does she taste as good as she looks?"

"Shut up, Thracian pig, or you'll not leave my fort alive." This time the low warning was unmistakable and deadly.

Galba held his hands up in mock apology. "I'm just saying she's an eyeful."

"She has more courage than most men."

"And how many men have courage?" The tribune looked at the ring with interest. "I don't care what you do with her. I wish I had that bauble, though. I'm missing one from my chain of trophies." Valeria heard the clink of his waist belt.

"You're a bastard, Brassidias."

"I'm a survivor. And you'll learn her nature soon enough. Don't be a fool."

"It's you who are the fool, Galba. You who have never loved."

"And how do you know I've never loved?" There was a silence of surprise at the tribune's hurt expression. Indeed, who knew anything about Galba's past?

"I don't," the chieftain conceded. "I just know I love this woman."

Galba burst out laughing. Any tenderness had been a pretense. "Love, love! Fair enough. It's all the Christians talk about, you know, this love they claim."

"It's a powerful thing."

"Yes." He laughed again. "And now you'll go to kill her husband!"

Savia tugged on Valeria to pull her away, taking advantage of the noise of Galba's laughter. The women crept away to leave the conspirators to talk into the night.

"The men in your life have all betrayed and abandoned you, lady," her slave whispered angrily. "You've been married off for money and position by your father, abandoned by your husband, seduced, mocked, and now plotted against."

"Where's the Arden I knew last night?" Valeria mourned. "He's nothing but a conspirator with Galba! Men use love like a cheap coin!"

Savia sighed. "Who knows what he really wants or thinks? Did you really give him your ring?"

"Just in a cup, for a moment. Was last night false, Savia?"

"Fleeting."

"I thought my life had changed forever."

"Don't you think every young heart believes that?"

She groaned. "I don't know what I believe."

"Believe in law and duty, mistress. Because when men fail you, as they eventually must, order is all that's left."

They crept back to their chamber, Valeria tortured. What just the night before had seemed impossibly distant—Rome!—had come crashing back into her life with Galba's arrival. The man was a traitor! An enemy of her husband! An ally of her lover! And that made Arden . . .

She threw herself down on her bed. Where did her emotions lie?

Where did her loyalty lie?

Beware the one you trust, the seer had said in Londinium. Trust the one you beware. What did that mean? Who was who, which side was which?

She was sleepless, in an agony of indecision. Finally she slipped on her cloak and went back outside. It was late night, Galba's horse still waiting. Yet already signal fires were being lit on surrounding hills. Messengers were saddling up to ride to the four winds. Military opportunity wouldn't last long. Arden would call a gathering of the clans for a march against the Wall. A march against Rome.

Thousands would die.

Including, possibly, Marcus and Arden.

Yet the barbarian plan hinged on surprise. If she could reach Marcus before the northern tribes struck, he in turn could warn the duke. Reinforcements could be sent. Faced with the full assembly of Roman power, the Celts could do nothing but retreat.

Marcus would be saved.

Arden would be saved.

And once more she'd be with her husband. It was what she should want, shouldn't she? Surely it was where her duty lay.

Duty! How many times she had scorned that word! Now she understood its importance. In following it, she would save the two men in her life, and save Rome. Yet in following it she would put behind her the happiest moment of her life.

Why, then, was her heart like a stone after resolving to carry out this plan? Why did she feel that she, too, was being forced into some kind of treachery?

She loathed leaving Arden. She ached for his touch. Yet she must get back to the Wall before Galba and spread the alarm.

She summoned Savia.

PART THREE

XXXIII

*Valeria left you behind?"

I am surprised. Throughout this narrative Savia has been portraying herself as the lady's closest confidant and steadfast friend. It seems strange that Valeria would ride off alone. I feel some sympathy for the loneliness the slave must have felt, like a dog abandoned by its master.

"It was the only way to buy time before they started pursuit," Savia explains matter-of-factly. Having won my alliance, she is not inclined to pity herself. "She slipped out of the hill fort shortly before dawn as she had before, her months in Caledonia giving her a better notion of which way to go this time. Arden had gambled that he'd win her heart by the time she knew enough to find her way, but he hadn't reckoned with her loyalties. She had to beat Galba to Petrianis."

"So you somehow persuaded them that she was still at Tiranen?"

"I pretended that Valeria was sick after Samhain and that I was tending the woman in her room. It helped that she'd slept with Arden. The other women were hesitant about pushing their way in because she had rank and power now. I also hinted that Valeria's heart was confused because she was already married. I suggested she was trying to sort out her choices and wished to be left alone while she did it."

"This worked?"

"For a day. By then it was too late to catch her."

"Did not Arden want to see her?"

"He was busy making preparations for war. But yes, of*

*course he came looking for her. The man was in love. It was
plain in his face and in his bearing."*

"A happy foolishness," I suggest.

*"Well put, inspector. You know from your own experience,
perhaps?"*

I admit such experience only to myself, a scabbed memory of hope and pain. "I have seen it in other men." My authority is maintained by solitude, I remind myself: by never
confiding weakness, by never caring too much. There's some
Galba in me, I suppose. "I'm surprised he accepted your excuses."

*"He was confused and hurt that she wouldn't let him in. I
told him that Valeria was confused herself, an explanation
men readily swallow because of their low opinion of women
and exalted opinion of themselves."*

I let this pass without correction.

*"He was also frantic with haste. It was late in the year,
not the traditional warring season, but it was also past the
harvest so men could ready quickly. If the barbarians were
to take advantage of Roman weakness, they had to strike before the Wall was reinforced or winter became too deep.
Their plan was to attack everywhere at once to keep garrisons from reinforcing each other. Whichever chieftain
broke through first would fall upon the rear of the Romans
at the next assault point."*

"You seem to have a grasp of strategy."

*"The Celts don't command, they lead. Arden had to ex-
plain the plan to the assembly in the Great House if anyone
was to follow him. It didn't really matter if word reached the
Romans. The question was exactly where the attacks would
come, and exactly when."*

"Of course. Still, the barbarians seem to have had more
cunning and organization than I assumed. Perhaps my report can lay the blame for what happened on Celtic strategy,
not Roman jealousies."

She shrugs. *"They are brave and smart. But as an army . . ."*

"Disorganized?"

*"Independent. Individualistic. They join together, but in
his heart each warrior is his own general. They fight not for*

an empire but for themselves. Not for victory so much as glory. Not for land but for loot. I listened to their boasting as weapons were sharpened and shields uncovered. They each wanted to be the hero."

"Which is why Rome has beaten them again and again."

"And why they are beaten but never conquered."

I pause, pondering her point. Then: "How did they finally discover that Valeria was gone?"

"Asa was suspicious and stole in while I slept. She sounded the alarm, and men came with swords drawn, dragging me out of bed."

"You must have been terrified."

"I wept and begged." She recounts this without shame, slaves allowed honesty denied their betters. Again, I envy them.

"Did you tell them that Valeria had gone to warn Marcus?"

"I told them that she'd left without telling. I suggested she was confused about love. Arden might have believed this, but none of the others were so blind. Galba wanted to roast me until I told the truth."

"Yet you are here, unroasted." It is a little joke, and draws only a little smile.

"Arden intervened. He said that even if she'd fled to the Wall, the Romans had no time to get more troops, and that frantic vigilance against impending attack would only tire them. He said he'd pledged no harm to me and was keeping that pledge. The men grumbled, but none dared challenge him. They thought that in everything else he was sensible, but on the issue of Valeria he was insane. It had become a fact of clan life. Galba left for the Wall, and the rest speeded their preparations."

"Kalin had tolerated and even fostered Arden's infatuation. What did he say?"

"He cast the future. He cut out the entrails of a sheep and studied them for signs. He threw the bones of fortune. He looked through one of those hollowed stones, a Keek Stane. He said Valeria's departure was the sign that they'd waited for; that her return to the Wall meant final war. He foresaw a great battle, the death of the enemies of the Caledonii, and a return to the old ways after a dark and bloody time."

"Did you believe him?"

"I didn't want to, but his troubled expression made me wonder. Prophets who only tell people what they want to hear are frauds because the future is never entirely in our favor. Those who admit uneasiness are more convincing. He'd seen something that confused him, and in the march south I had a chance to ask him. He told me he'd seen not just the oak but the cross. He asked me about my god again and how a holy man like Jesus, who seemed so weak, had become, in the retelling, so strong."

"He feared Christians."

"More than legionaries, I think. Kalin had the curse of knowing too much."

"It was foolish to assault Rome." I sound more arrogant than I feel, but it is a confidence based on a thousand years of history, an arrogance we Romans are born to. Savia looks at me in disbelief. "Of course, the barbarian horde was just barely turned back," I concede.

"And yet you seek to blame a single young woman." Her tone is disapproving.

"For her bewitchments," I justify myself. "She frustrated Galba. She was faithless to her husband. She broke the heart of her lover."

"It was they who abandoned and betrayed her," Savia counters. "All she was doing was to try to save them from themselves."

I ponder this view. This slave remains too loyal to her mistress, perhaps, but I'm intrigued by her perspective. Certainly I'm intrigued by Savia herself, as intrigued as a man can be by a woman.

"She provoked disloyalty," I insist.

Savia shakes her head. "She was the only one loyal. She was the one who tried to save them all. . . ."

XXXIV

The drums and signal fires started with the Roman woman's disappearance. The Wall was weak, and Valeria had fled with warning. The tribes must strike before the Romans could prepare.

Galba and his guards pounded out of Tiranen in hot pursuit of the fugitive, even as great Celtic war horns blew from the hill-fort towers to signal any who were away to return and join the approach of war. Young Gurn rode too, sent to give final word to the Picts and the Scotti to join with the Attacotti in the great assault. All across the empire's northwestern frontiers the host was mustering, not just in Caledonia but on the shores of Eiru and Friesland and Germania. Longboats were slid into the cold winter sea, and horses were brought from stables, their nostrils steaming in the cold. On a hundred hills the watchfires burned, and in a hundred hill forts warriors oiled mail, sharpened sword and spearhead, bundled arrows, tucked bowstrings in their tunics for protection from the weather, ground ax heads, studded clubs, and packed bread, dried fruit, and dried meat in bundled cloaks. The air was electric, voices pitched higher and louder than normal from the anticipation of assault. Only Brisa, the arrow maid, went about her preparations in a mood of sorrow.

"I thought she'd become one of us," she mourned. "I thought Morrigan had chosen her." She felt the bitterness of having been abandoned by a friend. "She didn't even say good-bye."

A barbarian clan had none of the baggage, animal train, or heavy artillery of a Roman army. If less disciplined, it was also less burdened. Arden's contingent of one hundred warriors, with another hundred women and children and old men following to cook and clean and help scavenge for booty, streamed down from Tiranen in loose formation like water finding its own course, quick and opportunistic. A few of the richest and noblest rode warhorses, but Arden, who could have done so, chose to accompany the majority who marched south on foot, each armed as best he could afford, shields strapped to backs, spears shouldered with a bag of rations suspended hanging just back of the tip, waterskins slung, and cloaks tied back that each could wrap himself in when they paused for the long winter nights. Weaponry was as individualistic as its owners, a mix of decorated spear, sword, lance, javelin, ax, club, sling, bow, and stave. Hounds sprang in and out of the procession or loped alongside, children tagged on the edges to herd a few goats and sheep that would make early provisions, and a few chickens clucked from the wicker cages that the camp wives bore on their backs. The high grass was frosted like an old man's beard, the streams ran like molten lead between skins of new ice, and the pine and fir were dull against the flanks of snow-crested hills. The mud of the track had hardened, crystals frozen in its fissures, and the sky was like a cowl.

Plumes of signal smoke rose from ridge after ridge into the gray overcast, calling the clans to war. Kalin the druid strode in the soldiers' midst, his countenance so grim that he kept his face half hidden within his hood. He bore the burden of the future, of course, and no warrior envied him that: better to live for now. Walking her pony next to him was the freed Roman that the high lady had abandoned, the former slave Savia. She looked just as unhappy at this swelling tide.

As Arden's modest contingent marched in a long brown line down the valley that led to the south, other bands began to join like the tributaries of a river. The union was always a similar pattern. A single figure would be silhouetted on a ridge above at first, watching the growing army and flashing greeting with a mirror if the sun had broken, or waving a banner if it had not.

Then other heads would appear, looking from below as if they were rising from the ground: two, six, a dozen, until suddenly there were scores of warriors lining the horizon, assembled as if for inspection. Great shouts would go up, from above and below, a mixture of greeting and genial insult as each group boasted that its warriors were the bravest, its blades the sharpest, its women the most beautiful, its horses the swiftest, its dogs the hardiest, and its leaders the craftiest. Then the newcomers would spill down the slope hooting their cheers, waving spear and battle-ax, sword and bow, and collide with Arden's force in a mixture of hugs and good-natured pummeling, finally finding place in the growing host that marched toward the Wall. This was happening not just along Arden's course but in half a dozen other vales that led from Caledonia's mountains toward the border of Britannia. The entire north was awake, and every able spear and sword was moving toward the Roman barrier. Here came Caldo Twin-Axe, his namesake weapons strapped in an X pattern on his back, leading twenty horsemen and fifty infantry. Waiting at the Dell of Beech was Rufus Braxus and forty companions, a dozen of them good bowmen. Giles Darren and Soren Longsword joined the advance with their clans, and then Owen Spearpony, the north's best wrestler, came striding in with an iron mace on his shoulder. The warrior woman Brigantia the Brave arrived with a new subtly curved sword, as lovely as a waterfall, that she brandished gleefully while galloping on her horse. Soon the horde had swelled to more than a thousand, and then two thousand, with a thousand camp followers besides. Still they poured from the hills, an eruption of might and pent-up passion to sweep aside Hadrian's millions of stones and let the island be whole again.

"There are more spears than the stars of Caledonia," Luca marveled to Brisa.

And this was solely the contingent of Arden Caratacus. Other armies were marching, and fast fleets of seaborne raiders were setting out to strike the southern coasts of Britannia and the fringes of Gaul. The long months of talks, threats, and promises had at last paid off. For once, the barbarians were acting in concert. Never had they managed such a numerical advantage. Never had they set out to attack so many places at once.

Even the sky seemed in league. Scudding cloud blew southward, against the Wall. The rain and sleet were at their backs, and into the teeth of the Romans.

XXXV

This time Valeria knew the way. Time had allowed her to associate landmarks with the daily path of the sun. She knew which direction must lead to the Wall.

After slipping out of Tiranen before dawn, she saddled her mare in the valley below and started south in sorrow, blinking back tears. The barbarians couldn't win, she knew; Rome was too strong. Arden was reckless to conspire with Galba. So now she must lose the only man she'd ever truly loved in order to save him, by warning the Romans of the attack so it could never happen. She'd ride back to the Wall. Back to her husband. Back to a lifetime of regret, as Galba had once warned her.

The gods were cruel, and Savia's new god seemed just as indifferent to her prayers as the old ones.

To avoid pursuit she followed high ridges and empty moors, riding all that lonely day and on through the lonelier night. This time she'd had the sense to bring proper clothing and food, including oats for her mount, but anxiety and the lack of rest exacted a mounting toll. The landscape was gray and cheerless, the wind sharp, the heather brown. Once she heard the distant howl of wolves.

Always she turned to look for pursuit. The tension slowly drained her.

Near the second morning she restlessly snatched two hours sleep in a grove of barren birch, wrapped in her cloak against the cold. She woke to a day cloudy and still, without sun or shadow, and had to use her own rough sense of geography to go on. Her months among the Celts had given knowledge enough that she was able to keep the Highlands at her back and retain a rough sense of direction, but she dared not use road or trail. Her meandering course added many miles.

In the afternoon of the second day it began to snow lightly, small flakes kissing the cheeks where her tears had been. She was too weary to be excited about weather she'd once dreamed of seeing. The snow was wet, soaking her cloak, and made it hard to see. Valeria noticed dully that her horse left a trail of tracks in the snow as it padded across the moors, helping any pursuers, but that when night fell again and the snow stopped, the thin coverlet also brightened the gloom and made it easier to find her way. It was thus both curse and blessing. Mostly, though, the snow simply made her feel colder and lonelier than ever. She felt lost between two worlds.

As she rode south and the number of farmsteads thickened, she'd sometimes hear the barking of dogs or the faint call of human voices, rising from a hollow and echoing across the moors. She'd wearily and carefully veer away. The detours might force her to drive through a thicket or circle a bog or climb an otherwise unnecessary hill, devouring time, but she couldn't risk capture. Finally Valeria would be alone on empty moorland again, making better progress, with the cold north wind at her back and endless rolling hills before her. She was sore to the core of her bones, her rump and thighs blistered, reeling in the saddle from exhaustion. Still she pushed on.

On the morning of the third day the dawn broke on a cold sky of pale blue studded with clouds. At long last, the pale line of the Wall! How endless it looked. It crowned the crest of Britannia's boundary like a great white worm, perched atop an escarpment here, plugging a narrow ravine there. How could the Celts hope to prevail against a civilization capable of building such a thing? How could Rome muster enough soldiers to adequately defend it? She saw legionary pennants flying from each milecastle where a contubernium of soldiers would live and stand guard: isolated, bored, quarreling, gambling, and dreaming. The sight gave her relief and disquiet.

How would Marcus receive her?

How would she respond to him?

She'd encountered the Wall at a place she was unfamiliar with. Rolling, windswept hills led down to a wet valley of small lakes and bogs. Dark volcanic cliffs on the far side of the marshes were fortified at their top by the stone barrier, making this a place impossible to attack or even approach. What a view the clifftop must have! Had the barrier's builders stood there once, proudly imagining the line they were about to impose upon the earth? Guessing in her fog of exhaustion that Petrianis must lie to the west, she rode slowly in that direction, paralleling the fortification. The muscles of her horse were shuddering.

"Just to the Wall," she whispered, "and then you'll have feed and shelter. Just to the Wall, and then you'll be a Roman horse. Then it will be over."

After two miles the ground in front of the Wall rose out of marsh and grew firmer. She picked her way toward a milecastle, its base marked by a gate. It looked uninhabited. No helmeted heads watched her. No trumpets of recognition rang out.

Up close, the barrier seemed even more impregnable. Its V-shaped ditch exaggerated the effective height of the parapet, and all brush and trees had been chopped away for four hundred paces, the distance of a ballista shot. Even a Roman like herself felt naked and vulnerable when crossing that final stretch of ground. She felt watched, even though she could see no one.

There was a wisp of smoke from a cooking fire rising from behind the crenellations of the milecastle, but still she saw no sentry. They must be huddled inside because of cold. The absence of any visible soldiers made it seem as if the barrier was patrolled by ghosts, but no, that was Samhain, and this was the frontier of Rome: a place of stone and discipline and crisp reality.

It was simply early.

"Is anyone here?" she shouted across the ditch and its bridging causeway.

No answer. She was salivating at the scent of their breakfast.

Valeria got down from the mare, the horse sighing in gratitude. Wearily, she took out the spear she'd slipped into a holster at the rear of the saddle. It was the spear that Hool had given her, the one she'd used to kill the boar. The weapon had been presented to her in honor, and she wasn't about to leave it behind at Tiranen; it was her reminder of that vibrant, lusty, rough-textured, rank, colorful, and communal world, now left behind. She hefted the spear experimentally, her arms having gained a surprising and unaccustomed strength, and aimed at the gray and pitted oaken gate. Then she threw.

It thudded home smartly, the shaft quivering after it stuck, its knock booming inside the milecastle. "Hallo! Open this gate!"

The hurled weapon finally brought oaths and a rattle of footsteps. "Who's there?" someone shouted angrily. She looked up. A Roman infantryman was leaning over the parapet. "This gate is closed to passage, barbarian!" he said in Latin-accented Celtic. "Go down to Aesica if you want through! We're having breakfast!"

"Please! I'm Valeria of the House of Valens, daughter of a Roman senator and wife of the commander of the Petriana cavalry! I'm too exhausted to go anywhere! I've just escaped from the Caledonii!"

The man looked bewildered. "You're a woman?"

She realized what she must look like: Celtic trousers and mud-stained boots, her hair tucked beneath a woolen cap, her cloak hiding any hint of figure. She wore a raw tapestry of stains and spatters and bits of burr and leaf. She'd just hurled a spear.

"I'm a pig after riding two nights and three days, but yes, underneath all this I'm a daughter of Rome! Please open, before I faint!"

He shouted orders, and she heard the pounding of hobnailed infantry boots. The gate was unbolted and swung inward, creaking from disuse. She stepped into the milecastle archway, her horse pushing anxiously in behind her in hopes of food. Beyond was a small courtyard and barracks building where the soldiers slept, with a second gate on the far side. These entrances were traps. Anyone charging through the first gate could be blocked by the second and killed by Roman soldiers firing down from parapets on all four sides.

The barbarians stood no chance without Galba.

"Are you really the lady Valeria?" a decurion asked. This woman looked so wretched. Her face was filthy, her eyes red from lack of sleep and hopelessness, her hair like string. She looked haunted.

"I've come to warn of an attack on the Wall," she whispered.

Then she collapsed.

Valeria had struck Hadrian's Wall ten miles east of the fort of the Petriana. She was revived with cider and put to bed over her own exhausted protests, clearly in no condition to push on. Signal flags sent a message to her husband while she slumbered, and before long an answering communication came back: *Bring her to me.* In early afternoon she was roused and taken to a chariot. She stood in the vehicle numbly, her clothes still filthy, her hair a tangle, her anxiety dulled by emotional depletion, her finger barren of any ring. She gripped the chariot rim tightly.

"Are you all right?" the driver asked doubtfully.

"Just take me home."

The driver cracked his whip, and they jolted forward along the military road, swiftly picking up speed. The wind helped revive her. Tower after tower and milecastle after milecastle flashed by. They dipped down into gullies and up onto panoramic bluffs. After an hour they came down into the river valley behind Petrianis, giving her the same view she'd seen on first arrival. They passed the house of Falco and Lucinda, where she'd been married, crossed the river, and clattered up the winding lane that led through the clinging village. Their route brought back a flood of memories and even more emotional confusion. They rode through the same southern gate she'd first ridden through on her wedding night—once more standing in a chariot, once more uncertain of her husband. It was as if her life had become a wheel, repeating itself. A sentry trumpeted an alert, and then they were in the paved courtyard of the fortress, men relaying shouts, the chariot team snorting and pawing, horses in the stables whinnying in reply. The familiar smell of charcoal fires, stables, fish oil, and olives washed over her.

She was back.

She realized she'd forgotten Hool's spear.

It was almost evening. Marcus was like a statue on the steps of their house, making no move to greet her but waiting instead for his wife to come to him. What must he think? She got wearily down from the vehicle and walked toward him stiffly, feeling the eyes of the sentries upon her. None gave her greeting. None offered help. Then she stood two steps down from her husband and looked up, their positions ensuring that he towered over her. His assumption of male authority, apparent in his bearing and stance, took her by surprise. It was an unquestioned superiority that Arden had never pretended to, even when she was simply a captive. What a change of worlds!

"I've come back, Marcus." She waited, shivering, for an embrace.

"You're dressed like a man." It was not a question.

"For riding."

"You're dressed like a barbarian."

"I rode three days and nights to get here."

"So I've been told. Well." He looked away as if it made him uneasy to meet her eye. Was he embarrassed by her return? Angry at her absence? "I didn't even know you were alive." His tone was remote.

She took a breath and said what she'd rehearsed. "I've escaped to warn you of approaching war. If you act quickly, you can stop it. Even as we speak the tribes are gathering."

"Escaped from where?"

"From the hill fort of Arden Caratacus, the man who told us about the druids in the grove. Everyone's playing a double game, husband, and the Petriana is in peril."

"Everyone?" His mouth twisted. "I'd have thought better, until I was posted here."

And then, as if conceding her despair, he reached out a hand for her to finally, gratefully, take. Perhaps his hesitation was his habitual shyness. Marcus was quiet, she remembered, and undemonstrative. So different from the

Celts! So different from Arden. "Come inside, woman, to bathe and eat and tell me what you know."

The warmth of the house enveloped her like a familiar blanket, and suddenly she had a rush of longing for the Roman baths and for everything that Rome stood for. The security! The stability! The predictability! She longed to surrender to order. The furniture and architecture was a reminder of where she'd come from and where she truly belonged. Her sudden nostalgia for the empire caught her by surprise. It was a dizzying attraction, leaving her more confused than ever.

With which man did she truly belong?

Which side of the Wall was native to her heart?

Marcus looked at her clothes with distaste. "Go, discard that filth and wash. I've ordered supper from Marta. There we'll discuss this adventure of yours."

"You need to alert the garrison now! Send a message to the duke now!"

"The men are already alerted. Wash first, it will help calm you. There's time enough for you to become presentable while the slaves make our meal."

"Marcus, you don't understand—"

"I *do* understand, wife. I understand I want you out of those rags and back in the proper dress of a Roman matron. So go, *now*!" It was an order.

She went to the baths at the rear of the house without calling for a slave. Their help seemed curiously superfluous. Her clothes, damp with sweat and snow, were peeled off and cast in a corner to corral their smell. Something caught at her neck, and she realized she still had the boar tusks. What must Marcus think? Adorned like a savage! He probably believed barbarians didn't wash at all and that she'd been dirty for half a year. No wonder he was remote. She gratefully but briskly bathed, not lingering as she'd have liked. With no maidservant, she had nobody to help with makeup and no time. Her hair was roughly tied back with a circlet of gold, and the stola she chose was a warm woolen one without style or seduction. The last thing she felt like doing was sharing her husband's bed! A mere half hour after she'd left

Marcus, she was back and eating, once more famished by her adventures.

You'll have a bottom like Savia, she scolded herself. And yet her exploits just gave her more muscle. She supposed her husband would not entirely approve of her new fitness. It was unwomanly.

Marcus watched silently as she ate, chewing his own food more absently. It was as if he were trying to decide something about her. The continued remoteness of his gaze, even more pronounced than she remembered, made her uneasy. Why was he so distant? "Marcus, the Celts are gathering against you," she tried again.

"So you've said," he remembered, as if she'd commented on the weather.

"I overheard it being discussed in the hill fort of Arden Caratacus, the man who captured me."

"You spied on him." It was more accusation than praise, which puzzled her.

"With my maidservant. We suspected something was amiss and hid in a hayrick to hear their talking." She paused, trying to find some diplomatic way to say what she must confide next, but finally gave up. Their senior tribune wasn't just rogue, he was traitor. "Arden was plotting with Galba."

"Was he really?" Her husband's tone was mild.

"Brassidias rode in with some soldiers to meet the barbarians. He said he was going to be transferred to Gaul, and there is a question of imperial succession, and soldiers are being drawn from the Wall for possible civil war on the Continent."

Marcus said nothing. Valeria's uneasiness increased. What did he already know? Had she ridden like the wind to warn him of nothing?

"The barbarian plan is to overthrow all Roman rule in Britannia," she went on. "If you can muster reinforcements from the south, you can stop them when they attack. Probably you can forestall any attack at all."

He looked at the tapestry covering the battle mural. "Where's Savia?"

It seemed an odd digression, given the weight of her news. "I had to leave her behind to delay their pursuit."

"The Celts freed her, didn't they?"

"Yes, but she didn't seek such freedom—"

"What did they do for you?"

She flushed. "Kept me prisoner for six months—"

"Stop it." His voice was ice.

She was bewildered. "Marcus? What's wrong?"

"Stop your lies. I'm humiliated enough."

"Lies?"

"You didn't spy on Arden Caratacus, did you?"

"I did!"

"You heard what you're telling me in his bed."

"That's not true!"

"Isn't it? Then answer me this. Did you, or did you not, sleep with that conniving, treacherous, double-dealing piece of donkey offal who abducted you?"

How could he know? She couldn't speak.

Her husband stood to loom over her again, now a pillar of humiliation and rage. "Did you, or did you not, shame me and mock me and ruin me before every respectable man and woman of Rome?"

"How can you say these things?" All appetite had left her.

"Did you, or did you not, play the part of one of their pagan gods, and dance at their sacrificial ceremonies, and ride and hunt like a man, and work in the dirt like a peasant, and eat like a Hun as you've just done, and disgrace your own family's name for a hundred generations?" His voice was rising.

Furious at her own emotion, she began crying. "I rode here to warn you—"

"You rode here to betray me!"

"No, Marcus, no! You've got everything all wrong!"

"Where is Caratacus going to attack, Valeria?"

"Here!"

"I should concentrate my forces here, at the strongest part of the Wall?"

"Yes, yes!" she sobbed. "Here! I think so. He's coming to attack, and I want to save your life—"

"Save whose life, Valeria?"

She looked at him mutely, not understanding.

"Save your husband?"

She nodded, dumbly.

"Or save your lover?"

"Marcus, please . . ."

"You didn't ride fast enough, Valeria. Galba reached me first."

She closed her eyes in despair. "Don't listen to Galba! He's your enemy!"

"He outpaced you and told me of your lust for a barbarian. Did you like the roughness of this so-called Caratacus, Valeria, who names himself for a famous Roman enemy? Did you enjoy his crudity?"

"Marcus, don't believe—"

"Shouldn't I? Brassidias!" He roared the summons.

Boots rang across the stone floor of the commander's house, and Galba made an entrance in full armor, sword at his side, his chain of finger rings jingling at his waist, his bearing ready for war. He snapped to stern attention. "Yes, commander?" There was no surprise in his eyes.

"Is this the woman that you were told of at the hill fort of Arden Caratacus?"

"The same, commander."

"The woman who fled my house in the middle of the night to attempt an assignation with the tribune Clodius?"

"The same, commander."

"The woman who shamed Rome by becoming the lover of a barbarian?"

Galba bowed his head. "So I was told, commander."

"And who told you of this?"

"Arden Caratacus. He boasted of possessing the body of a daughter of Rome."

"What proof did he have for this boast?"

"A trophy, commander."

"Would I recognize this trophy?"

"You gave it to your bride on the night of your wedding."

"A ring, you mean? And how do I know you're telling the truth?"

"Because I brought it back with me. Because I have it here." Galba reached in a pouch at his belt and tossed something that rang as it bounced across the table, coming to rest near the praefectus. It was her ring with the intaglio of Fortuna.

Had Arden given it to Galba to betray her? Certainly fortune had deserted her.

"No!" she protested wildly. "Galba came to Tiranen to plot with Arden. It's been a plot from the beginning to manipulate and discredit you, Marcus—"

"Answer me! Did you sleep with that Caledonii animal?"

"He's not an animal."

"Answer me!"

Her voice was small. "Yes." She struggled for explanation. "We were drunk from a ceremony, and it was a meaningless thing, and I came back to warn you—"

"It was *not* a meaningless thing!" His fist came down on the table with a bang, and its leg buckled. Valeria shrank, fearing a beating. He was in a rage. "By the gods, betrayed already! Our marriage bed scarcely warmed!"

"You don't understand. I was a prisoner—"

Marta appeared, summoned by the clamor. Her eyes darted from one aristocrat to another, her expression a combination of curiosity and smirk. This scene would be all over the fort within an hour.

"Get out," Marcus snapped at her.

The slave disappeared.

The praefectus turned back to his wife. "And yet somehow you found the freedom, the moment it entered your head, to ride blithely back to the Wall. To tell me how to dispose of my forces."

"To warn you!"

"I've had my warning. From Galba Brassidias."

"He's the traitor!"

"He's our agent, Valeria. He's been treating with this Caratacus bastard for years. He fills the barbarian's head with foolishness and keeps the Celts off balance. You had no idea what was going on in that fort. No idea what your secrets meant."

His contempt stung. Now she was getting angry. "Isn't the emperor ill? Aren't powerful men choosing between him and his son?"

Marcus didn't reply.

"Aren't troops being sent to the Continent?"

"What of it?"

"You're in peril!"

"From you! *You* betrayed me!"

"I was confused! I came back—"

"To betray me with your words!"

"No!"

"Caratacus sent you to mislead me about the attack. To seduce me with your sex. To make us ready for an attack in one place while he strikes at another. All this he boasted about to our senior tribune, Galba Brassidias."

"No . . ." It was a moan.

"He's used you, Valeria. Caratacus seduced you, and persuaded you to betray Rome. To engineer the death of your husband. To serve as an agent of confusion—"

She was shaking her head in despair.

"And breach the Wall."

"Galba has twisted everything all around."

"Galba set a trap. For Caratacus and for you. And now it has snapped shut on the first one of you."

Valeria looked at him in disbelief.

"We can beat the Celts if we're ready," Galba rumbled. "It's persuading a pitched battle in a favorable place that's difficult. I've convinced Caratacus that I'll help him get through the Wall, but we'll pinch him off and destroy him when he does."

"See!" Valeria exclaimed. "Galba's going to let Caratacus through the Wall! Let me go to Arden, Marcus! None of this bloodshed will be necessary! I'll warn him, and no one will have to die!"

Marcus laughed, the bitter laugh of a man who sees his marriage and its political influence in ruins. His wife had shamed him, and what had he ever given her but love and honor? His only chance now was victory in battle. "Let you go to Arden? How you must wish it! You'll rue the day you left his protection. You're a traitor to the Roman state and the destroyer of our marriage, and after the battle I'll deal with you in accordance to ancient law."

"Ancient law?"

"A Roman husband has the right of divorce. Of discipline. Of taking the life of an adulteress if her treachery is grave enough, as Cato and Augustus and Constantine have said. You know that. You've risked that. Of losing your life by stoning or drowning or a noose around the neck."

She was dizzy with fear. This couldn't be happening. "Marcus—"

"You might wish to use a dagger or poison to assuage your shame, but I'm not going to give you that chance. You'll wait here, in locked confinement, for my final decision after the battle. And the next time I let you out, it will be to watch the torture and death of your barbarian lover."

XXXVI

As I did in the beginning, once more I depend on the crisp and soldierly memory of the centurion Longinus. He hobbles to me on a crutch, a good sign that infection of his smashed foot has not advanced up his leg. I remember his challenge to me when I chose him as the first to be interviewed. He demanded that I understand Hadrian's Wall. Am I any closer now than I was before?

"My congratulations, centurion. You appear to be recovering."

"I'm too old to recover. The best a warhorse can hope for is to endure. So I endure the pain of this damned foot, I endure the bureaucracy of the retirement list, I endure the prattle of nurses, and I endure the dirty jokes of decurions that I first heard two decades ago."

"It sounds like my interview might be an improvement."

His smile is wry. "When an imperial inspector becomes amusement, you know life isn't worth piss. It's time to get out of Eburacum."

"To your farm?"

He collapses, without invitation, onto a stool. "No, I'd never be able to work it, not as a cripple. I'm selling it. An old trumpeter named Decinus has opened a wheelwright shop and has offered to teach me the parts I can do sitting down. We'll fart and drink and curse together and keep each other from being too lonely. It's not a bad fate."

Sunset, sunset. Each of us must come to an end, and why isn't the way better prepared? A warrior's death is not so terrible, perhaps, compared to retirement. And yet how *ready would I ever be for a soldier's death?* "You are a brave man, centurion."

"You learn in the army to do what you have to do. Afterward, some call it courage." He stretched out his injured leg.

I make a note to acknowledge his professionalism. This man is Rome. "I want to go back to when the barbarians attacked. I know the outcome of the battle, of course, but not its course. Was Galba really in league with the barbarians? What did he intend?"

Longinus considers a moment. "Galba was in league with himself."

"He did not really let the Celts through the Wall?"

"Of course he did! But he had a grander plan. Galba knew he couldn't beat Rome, not in the long run. Galba knew that even though the woman had been jailed, her return had seeded her husband with confusion and doubt. So he devised a battle plan that betrayed everyone but himself."

"You approved of this plan?"

"All the officers did, including Marcus, because it seemed brilliant. It had just one flaw, which didn't become apparent until the fighting."

"What flaw?"

He laughs. "There were more of them than we thought!"

"So it was not Valeria's fault. It was all imperial politics and the shifting of legions and the conspiracies of the tribes."

Longinus shakes his head. He's not a man to forgive or forget, not with his foot crushed. He's not a man to blame human failings on the maneuverings of armies. "The woman brought Marcus. The praefectus ignited the war and tried to transfer Galba. She inflamed the barbarian Caratacus. And Galba outwitted us all."

I sigh. "Galba would do well at imperial court." *It's an impolitic statement to make to a near stranger, but I cannot resist it. One either plots to survive in Rome, or one stays on its fringes, as I have done. In a sense, my job is a form of hiding. Galba, in contrast, chafed at being on the fringe.* "What was Marcus thinking?"

"That it was he who would win the battle and the glory.

That was the genius of Galba's plan. Caratacus, Marcus Flavius, and Galba himself all felt they were on the path to victory."

"It was a trap for both Arden and Marcus."

"Engineered by Galba Brassidias." Longinus smiles thinly. "I rode with Marcus and got to see it play out. It's a beautiful spectacle, battle, until it's over and you're left with the stink of the dead and the screams of the wounded."

I look at his foot. "Did you scream?"

"Do you think I remember?"

We sit in silence for a moment. The gulf between us that he hinted at in our first meeting seems less deniable now. It is the gulf between virgin and harlot, or play and work. I have been around soldiers my entire career, but always afterward: questioning decisions, plumbing motives, and passing judgment on an experience I don't understand.

What do my reports really matter?

"What is it like getting ready for battle?" I impulsively ask.

Longinus isn't impatient with my question. He understands that I truly want to know. "Like prayer," he replies. "Not just that you're praying, though all sensible men do so, but that your preparation for combat is a ritual itself, a form of meditation. I don't know what it's like for others, but my mind is always full. I sharpen all my weapons. I eat sparingly, for quickness and to avoid infection from a stab in the gut. I order and reassure my men, taking their measure, and go over in my head what we must do as a unit and what I must do individually if faced with open combat: each thrust, each parry, and every fighting trick I've ever learned and taught. I dream the battle before I fight it. There's this solemn rasping of blades being honed, and the smell of oil being wiped from steel and applied to leather. The talk is quiet."

"You are not afraid?"

"Any sensible man is afraid. But soldiers have chosen their lot long ago and are far too busy trying to survive to let fear overmaster them. Besides, you have your comrades,

and you share your fate with theirs. *That's a kind of friendship a civilian can never know. We depend on each for our lives, and there's bittersweet love in that."*

"Love? In a battle?"

"War isn't about hate, inspector. It's about communion."

XXXVII

The Wall, Caratacus."

The ground had frozen brittle. A skin of ice had formed on the shallow river Ilibrium, which meandered in a swale below Hadrian's Wall. Gray cloud had covered the stars, and dawn saw a few scattered snowflakes drift down, sticking and then evaporating on the brown grass. The Wall itself materialized slowly, surfacing out of ground fog like the back of an undulating sea monster, its serpentine crest marking the horizon. The heads of a few Roman sentries were silhouetted against the sky, but as Galba had promised, there didn't seem to be any concentration of strength here.

"A good morning for fighting," Luca went on as he stretched and grunted, his breath forming a light cloud. "The kind of morning to hunt or ride."

"Can we beat them?" Arden asked softly.

Luca glanced at him. "A fine time to be asking."

"None in the world has ever beaten them permanently."

"Battle is no time for doubt."

"Every man has doubts."

"And real men don't voice them. It's that woman who's drained you of certainty, Arden, and you won't get it back until you get her back. Get through that Wall and find her. Kill her or marry her, but set things to right."

"Yes. To right." Could he find her? And if he did, what would she say? Had she fled him or this war? It was as useless to speculate as to spit upon a fire.

He reviewed their strategy. There were two gates to force open at each milecastle, one in the wall that he could plainly see, the other at the rear of the small fortlet that jutted from the southern side of the Wall like a boxed pimple. Get through those two gates, and all Britannia lay before them. Then wheel . . .

"The druids say the Roman time is over," Luca went on. "They've never been so weak, and we've never been so united. Worry if you wish, but I'll eat off Roman flatware tonight."

Arden thought such confidence tempted disaster. Better to worry. "The cavalry is ready?" The Celtic aristocracy had gathered as a reserve, their heads crowned with fantastically crested helmets, their swords inscribed with runes, their lances carved and beaded with gold.

"Yes. Everything is happening as Galba promised."

So: at long last it was time. None respected and feared Roman prowess at war more than Caratacus did. None had more confidence in Celtic courage than he did. At full charge, his clan was unstoppable.

Now the two would be tested, each against the other.

Arden wore chain mail but had rejected a helmet, preferring unencumbered sight. Some of his infantry disdained any protection at all, waiting naked or nearly so under their cloaks in the cold, as patient and dangerous as wolves. They squatted by the hundreds, staring at the stone barrier with predatory hunger, the ex-gladiator Cassius among them. They lived for war.

The bowmen waited nearby, their bows nearly as tall as a man and able to kill at three hundred paces. They'd provide covering fire. Each arrow had been shaped smooth over long winter evenings, given a name, marked with that name, and fitted with a slim iron arrowhead that could punch through armor. The war-maiden Brisa was among them, and Arden would trust her to find a fat target before anyone.

Still another group were the Scotti, who'd sailed from Eiru. They'd marched in only the night before, painted blue and garbed for war, grim and anxious. He'd never fought with their kind, but they said they wanted Roman blood to avenge a captured prince of theirs, a man named Odocullin of the Dal Riasta. Murdered, they said.

He envied their grim passion.

His own excitement, so long anticipated, was curiously absent. The world seemed a plain of ashes, its taste like sand. He'd opened his heart to two women in his life, and both times it had been squeezed like a rag, wrung dry of blood. He'd thought that after Alesia his sorrow had scabbed over and that he could never be hurt that badly again, but then he'd dropped from the oak to see Valeria on her mule cart, frightened and brave and wily enough to use her brooch pin to unhorse him, and with that he'd been lost.

So he hunted her again, captured her, and introduced her to his world. And just when Arden needed her most, trusted her most, desired her most, Valeria had deserted him for her husband. Chosen an empty marriage over love! She'd even taken her wedding ring back with her. She'd run to warn the Romans and ensure his defeat, to set up his death. And indeed, he longed to die after this betrayal.

First, he would do all he could to injure Rome.

And then die, with a Celtic cry in his throat.

"You really hate them, don't you, Arden?" Luca asked. "That's how you're different from us, who just want gold and wine and silk and cotton and horses."

"I know them. That's how I'm different."

He turned and walked to Savia, who had trailed him for protection like a dog ever since Tiranen. He'd tolerated it because, strangely, she reminded him of Valeria. She'd given some of her strength to the girl. Any good Roman would choose duty over love, she'd told him. And any Celt would choose passion, he'd replied.

"Where will your lady be?"

"In the fort of the Petriana, I suppose." She looked at him sadly. She knew Valeria had broken his heart, just as he had broken Valeria's with this senseless war.

"If we get through the Wall and overwhelm the garrison, I want you to find her, protect her, and bring her to me."

"What will happen to her if I do?"

What *would* happen? He didn't know. He feared the moment, even as he desired it. Dread, and anticipation. "By then my sword will be slick with gore and my arms weary from killing. I'll look into her eyes and heart—look at the woman who made love and then left me—and let us both decide, together, what our fate must be."

Savia closed her eyes.

Now he must lead them to it.

Arden walked out in front, where the druid Kalin waited with a raven-headed staff. The barbarians stood as one when he did so, a great host rising up out of the dry and frosted grass like a crop of death. What must it look like from the Wall, this host materializing in the mist?

They were ready.

Caratacus raised his sword and faced his men. He'd no doubt of their courage. "For Dagda!" he shouted. His voice floated in the winter air.

Kalin raised his own staff. "For the gods of the oaken wood!"

The warriors roared their reply. "For Dagda!" Their shaking spears were like a field of wheat in the wind, their howls that of the pack. "For the sacred wood!" Neck torques and silver armlets gleamed in the pale light. Muscles, greased against the cold, shone like bronze. Celtic cattle horns were lifted and blown to add to the din, a clamor like the trumpeting of geese.

We're coming, the horns promised. Stop us if you can.

Then they charged, hard ground rumbling under their running feet.

XXXVIII

The Celts raced toward the Wall in a streaming pack, shattering the thin ice of the Ilibrium as they crashed across its shallows and yelling at the cold. Then they surged up its far bank and scrambled toward the Wall like a cresting wave. Twenty carried a pointed log of forest pine to batter the gate, its snout a great brown phallus of revenge. Dozens more had grappling hooks on the end of coils of line.

A handful of Romans could be seen at the parapets above the gate now, running this way and that and shouting alarms. A trumpet sounded. Arrows began to sail out toward the attackers, most thunking into shields or sticking harmlessly into the ground. One found flesh, however, and a warrior grunted and went down. Then another Celt caught a shaft in the eye and whirled, screaming. There was a bang and a scorching sizzle in the chill air. The huge arrow of a cocked ballista rocketed into the barbarian charge, crashing into a tier of barbarians and bowling them over like crockery, their shields splintering under the impact.

It had started.

The attackers howled and shot arrows in turn, the woman Brisa among them. The steady rain of barbarian shafts took one catapult operator squarely in the chest, pitching him backward, and helped clear the parapet of Roman heads.

"Rapid aim!" Arden roared. "Don't give them time!"

One Roman soldier got a shaft through the throat, gurgled, and pitched violently over the wall, landing in a heap in the ditch at its base. A chieftain howled and dashed forward and in an instant the Roman's head was chopped off and thrown down the slope toward the river, bouncing like a ball. A woman of the Attacotti chased it, caught it, and danced by the Ilibrium, holding it aloft.

A Roman arrow shot the decapitator down.

The ballista fired again, but this time its range was long and the missile sizzled over the head of the first wave of attackers.

"We're under their fire! It's safest at the Wall!"

The defending arrow fire began to slacken and grow inaccurate. Romans who leaned out from the Wall to shoot or hurl stones became instant targets, reeling backward with five or six shafts jutting from their bodies. A grappling hook soared up, caught a defender, and jerked him over the lip of the parapet. Other hooks caught on the crenellations, and the barbarians began climbing the barrier hand-over-hand.

The dirt causeway that led over the defensive ditch hadn't been dug away, and so the Celts with the battering ram had an easy time of it, trotting across to hurl the end of the log against the gate. Its boom reverberated under the stone archway, shaking the entire milecastle. The oak ominously cracked. Then another slam and another, even as a few javelins and arrows dropped from above.

"Keep shooting! Rain arrows! Throw hooks!"

The line of the grappling hooks made a shrill whine as they cut neat parabolas in the winter air, the ropes cinching the face of the Wall in an entangling web. A Roman leaned out to chop a line with his sword, and Brisa coolly shot an arrow that punched through his ear. He screamed and disappeared. First one Celt, then two, then three scrambled up to struggle with the defenders. At a dozen different points now the barbarians were scaling the Wall like flies. The defenders were desperate.

The ram crashed again, and then again, and finally the crossbeam broke and the gate burst, collapsing in a tangle of timber. Barbarians bounded over the top of their discarded ram. A few legionaries tried to stem the tide but were hopelessly outnumbered and swiftly cut down. Up on the top of the wall the Romans simply broke and ran, fleeing east and west along the crest of the barrier. Triumphant Celts streamed up their ropes and dropped down into the courtyard of the mile-

castle. The barracks was hurriedly ransacked, the second gate
that led south was thrown open, and Arden led a throng of
warriors through the milecastle and into the grassy military
zone beyond.

Hadrian's Wall had been pierced! As Galba had promised, it
was a shell, as easily breached as a sword through parchment.
Ahead was the earthen dike of the fossatum, and beyond that
all the riches of Britannia. Even as the Celtic army behind
bunched to squeeze through the milecastle, the first barbarians
were whooping as they spread between wall and dike.

Galba grimly watched the attacking breakthrough from his
hiding place on the crest of the fossatum's earthen dike, three
hundred paces away. The barbarians poured out like angry
bees, half naked and triumphant, and only Galba's firm dis-
ciplinary grip had kept his cavalry from bolting immediately
to meet them. His men were in an agony of impatience to
help their comrades dying in the early defense, but he held
them in line.

"You'll get your blood," he'd promised them. "Mount
when I tell you to."

Now it was time. He slipped down the dike and bounded
up on Imperium, the black stallion dancing with excitement.
A hundred cavalry swung onto their horses with him, their
lances rotating to the sky. His chain of blood-won rings jan-
gled at his waist, his gloved fist seized the reins, and his
other hand pulled out his wicked spatha, its hilt carved,
rumor held, from the bone of an enemy.

"Remember! I want Caratacus alive!"

Then he trotted to the lip of the grassy dike, calmly counting the barbarians to judge the perfect time. He was a sudden silhouette, posed like a marble effigy.

"Now!" he finally shouted.

A flaming arrow shot from behind the dike and soared
above the Wall, giving the signal. A quarter mile from each
side of the captured milecastle, on the six-foot-wide path-
way atop the undulating Wall, two centuries of Roman infantry rose in unison from where they'd been lying prone in
hiding. Their grove of spears rose with them. Silently, but

with rehearsed urgency, the two units ran back along the top of the Wall toward the fortlet the Romans had just abandoned, boots ringing on the stonework. New Roman bowmen followed and spread out along the Wall to fire at the barbarians below. The trap was being sprung.

A few Celts saw the danger. Brisa sent missiles at the charging Romans and watched in frustration as they stuck harmlessly in shields. Then she herself was hit in the arm, the impact throwing her onto her bow and breaking it. She cursed in pain.

Arden's spearhead of tribesmen hadn't yet noticed the envelopment of new Romans on the Wall behind them. They were still fanning out between Wall and dike, losing any sense of formation even as their chieftain shouted at them to maintain some kind of order. How many times had he lectured on the importance of discipline? Now they thought the battle was over.

"Not yet." Galba was watching their cohesion dissipate. "Not yet . . ."

The two charging columns of Romans atop the wall converged on the milecastle with crushing speed, slamming into the handful of Celts on the parapet between them like angry rams. Spears sliced through bodies, and Caledonii went over like pins, survivors spilling in confusion back down the milecastle stairs. They cried alarm, trying to warn Arden and his warriors of this fresh attack, but it was too late. The Roman columns met atop a litter of bodies over the archway of the outer gate, and quick commands brought heavy pots forward. These were upended, and their black contents spilled through firing portals onto the Celts milling in confusion in the passageway below.

The barbarians began to panic.

A torch was passed, and the sticky fluid exploded. Greek fire!

The passageway flashed into an oily inferno, setting aflame the warriors who were trying to press forward through it. The ignited men lurched and ran screaming back down the slope toward the river, blindly seeking relief. As they burned, Celtic fervor began to waver.

A disciplined Roman fire of missiles from atop the fortification began to grow again. Barbarian after barbarian pitched over in agony, the charms of the druids failing to save them from Roman ashwood shafts. The charging legionaries retook the ballista once more and began firing its heavy missiles as well, each bolt cutting down a file of attackers like a scythe. Other Romans ran to the rear wall of the milecastle and slammed shut the second gate there, sealing Arden's wave of barbarians off from retreat.

The Celtic army had been cut in two. The Wall was closed, its outer portal on fire, its inner one shut, its crest manned more heavily than ever. Caratacus and two hundred of his followers were suddenly trapped south of the barrier.

"Annihilation!" Galba roared.

A shout went up, there was a blare of trumpets, and suddenly the Roman cavalry surged up and over the earthen dike as if they were the dead of Samhain leaping out of the ground. They used the dike's downslope to accelerate their charge as they rode for the winded enemy.

"Betrayal!" Arden cried out in warning. It was too late.

There was a huge splintering of shields and lances as cavalry and Celtic infantry met, the screams of skewered men and disemboweled horses, and then a melee of combat, the senior tribune slashing with his spatha as he kicked his horse toward Arden.

"I want him alive, remember! He's no use to me dead!"

More trumpets, and then cheers from the Romans on the Wall.

Outside and to the north, Marcus and two hundred additional troopers of the Petriana had just swept out of the trees and were attacking as well. Just as Galba was about to pin part of the barbarian army against the southern side of the Wall, Marcus was going to pin the remainder against the north.

Lucius Marcus Flavius, his wife in prison and his career in probable ruin, was going to win glory this day. Glory, or die in the attempt. Rome was built on bloody conquest, and its history had proved that military victory could relieve every embarrassment, erase every humiliation. Rome was built on sacrifice, and a dead warrior could reclaim any honor lost while living.

This was his moment of redemption.

Marcus and his men had issued from the fort of the Petrianis at dusk the previous night, two hundred of his cavalry on a desperate swing through enemy territory to take the attacking barbarians in the rear. His garrison had been stripped bare of soldiers by the sortie, and miles of the Wall were hollow, but Galba had persuaded his praefectus to take this gamble, that the barbarians would concentrate where he'd told Caratacus to attack. How else could the Petriana prevail against overwhelming numbers?

The Roman cavalry had drawn up in a grove of beech to the north of the Wall before dawn, watching the attack unfold and waiting impatiently for the flaming arrow that would be Galba's signal. Now the Celtic army had been neatly snipped in two, as the senior tribune had promised, and Marcus had the opportunity to destroy its rearward portion. If they could crush the barbarians between them and kill Caratacus—bring Valeria the man's bloody, dirtied head—maybe he could salvage something of his career and his marriage. And if he died in the attempt, well, there was a peace in that too. Certainly life had come to seem more burden than joy. His wife's abduction had been humiliation, and her infidelity a crushing betrayal. His tenure on the Wall had turned to chaos. His future had dissolved into recriminations.

So he'd oil his sword with the blood of the Caledonii this day, these Picts and Attacotti and Scotti and Saxons, and give back to them some of the sorrow they'd inflicted on him. That, or perish in the attempt.

"We take them from behind!" he cried. "For Mars and Mithras, charge!"

The line of Roman cavalry burst from the trees as if the forest had exploded, shields on the left arm, lances leveling on the right, the sound of hooves on frozen ground thundering like barbarian drums. The hundreds of Celts before them were milling in confusion in front of Hadrian's Wall after being hurled back from the burning gateway. Warnings were shouted, warriors turned, and they looked at his cavalry charge at their rear in horrified wonder, each individual barbarian deciding whether to fight or run.

Run where? The Wall and its rain of arrows were at their backs.

Marcus's own line widened as each trooper picked a target and aimed his lance.

Many Celts howled defiance, of course, running to meet this new threat with the fatalism of the condemned. Shields were raised and swords brandished. Their tactical hopelessness was perversely giving them maniacal courage. They'd fight as berserk individuals, and that, the Roman knew, would prove their undoing. They fought with bravery, but not with thought. And so they were doomed, or so Marcus hoped.

The cavalry first ran down some camp followers and wounded at the rear of the barbarian mass, the victims screaming in terror as the thrashing mill of hooves chewed over them. Then came a ragged line of defiant warriors, shields up, axes poised, a few of their arrows striking home and spilling some of Marcus's cavalry from their saddles. Brisa had pulled the shaft from her own arm and found another bow. Now, desperate and heedless of the flow of her own blood, she was firing as fast as she was able.

It wasn't enough. The Romans simply ran over them. The woman saw a blur of horseflesh, a maelstrom of hooves, and then she was under and trampled, blacking out. There was another concussive collision, its sound like a clap of thunder, and the two armies north of the Wall were shredded together as they were to the south, lances impaling the Celts who didn't dodge fast enough, horses screaming and toppling, men butted aside like dolls. The power and weight of the cavalry shattered the barbarian formation, and the Romans shouted fierce satisfaction as they wheeled their horses to work with their swords. The blades rose and fell in awful rhythm, like the arms of a primitive machine.

Marcus expertly guided his horse through the confusing combat, its horror more familiar now after the battle in the grove. He feinted as if to pass to the right of a painted barbarian carrying a two-handed broadsword, then cut his

horse to take the man by surprise on his left. The praefectus's shield arm went out to fend off the barbarian's blow
even as his own spatha swung in a great deadly arc. The
handle stung as it chopped into muscle and bone. The barbarian screamed and went down. Then Marcus was beyond
him, using the prancing hooves of his excited horse to push
more of the barbarians into the cold river, trampling some
underfoot. He saw a javelin catch one young cavalryman in
the back, spilling him, but then another Roman rode up and
cleaved the thrower's head.

The Romans on the Wall were roaring encouragement
and firing arrows. On both sides now the Roman cavalry
was chopping up the split attack. Soon the Celts must surrender into slavery or be met with certain death. Some of the
demoralized barbarians sought shelter toward the smoking
ruins of the gate archway, only to meet Roman legionaries
dropping down from the crest above.

"Victory, Marcus Flavius!" the centurion Longinus
called. "We have them!"

And then Celtic horns sounded again.

More than a thousand men and women had followed Arden
Caratacus in the first assault at what he'd been assured
would be a weakly defended gate. It was this thousand that
was in desperate straits, cut in two and fighting for their lives
against a smaller but far more disciplined and better-posi-
tioned Roman force. Hundreds were already dead and
wounded, and annihilation seemed a real possibility.

But a thousand more Celtic warriors had been secreted in
a nearby ravine, including almost all the horsemen who represented the best and wealthiest of barbarian warriors. Galba
hadn't told Arden of the ambush he'd meet after breaking
through the Wall, but he had told the barbarian about the
flanking attack by Marcus, explaining that the praefectus intended to fall upon their rear. The charge by that wing of the
Petriana was no surprise.

This rear was bait, in other words, and the Celts were determined to make the Roman trap a trap of their own. Now
out of the trees to the north came the barbarian horses in

wild attack against the rear of the preoccupied Roman cavalry, followed by hundreds of additional infantry on foot. They were going to surround the Petriana as it had tried to surround them.

The soldiers on the Wall sent up shouts of warning at the approach of this new onslaught, but most of Marcus's cavalry were fighting too desperately to pay attention. There was a wild wavering cry, a call to their gods as chilling as death itself, and then the Celtic horses crashed into the Latins like an avalanche, toppling Romans from their mounts before they had a chance to turn or form or escape.

In an instant the barbarian foot soldiers, who'd been overmatched by Roman cavalry, turned on their dismounted foes and chopped in a frenzied spray of blood.

Marcus's own horse was driven into the bloody river Ilibrium by the impact of the attack. He was confused as to what was happening. Where had all the barbarians come from? At one moment victory had been in his grasp. A moment later his cavalry seemed mired in a sea of Celts, arrows and spears whistling past and horses screaming in terror as they were gutted. The barbarians who'd been demoralized only moments ago were now hoisting weapons for revenge. Even some of the wounded were picking themselves off the ground to fall on the Romans again.

"Marcus, we've got to retreat!" cried Longinus, hauling the head of his horse around to bolt. Yet even as he did so a red-haired chieftain in horned helmet galloped by and hit the centurion's horse with a two-bladed ax, knocking animal and rider into the cold water of the river. With a splash, they went under.

Longinus struggled to get out from under his dying horse, kicked free, and surged up onto the bank, sputtering. His spatha was gone. The barbarian came at him again, missing the centurion with his main blow but chopping into his foot, and so he screamed and went down once more, sliding into the water. A red plume ran off his wound.

Marcus rode up and took off the barbarian attacker's arm with his sword, its artery spewing like a fountain. The Celt bellowed, reeled, and lurched off his saddle.

Then the praefectus jumped off his horse into the icy river and seized the half-drowned centurion, pulling Longinus across the Ilibrium and onto the bank nearest the Wall. The battle had become a nightmare. His men were being unhorsed. The pennants and standards of the Petriana were falling like toppled trees into a mob of screaming, excited Celts. The tide of battle had reversed once more. Arrows were falling everywhere, each side hitting both foes and comrades in the confusion.

Then his own deserted horse was down, a spear in Homer's side, and any chance of escape was gone. "We need to get under the Wall! We'll seek protection there!"

He began dragging the wounded Longinus up the bloody slope. It was littered with bodies, Celtic and Roman, and the centurion left his own trail of blood from a foot half severed. A few Romans saw what their commander was doing and formed a protective ring around him to help, but this concentration only drew more enemy fire. The guards began to topple over as arrows struck home.

Marcus was dragging Longinus with one hand, hacking with another. There was a blow to his thigh, and he stumbled, dimly realizing that he was wounded. It was surprising that it didn't yet hurt. He panted from the labor.

Finally the stonework of Hadrian's Wall loomed above him. Cavalrymen were fighting desperately with Celts who'd taken their own shelter in the burnt passageway, both sides wrestling for the refuge.

Where was Galba? Why wasn't he helping?

Now the Celts were surging up the slope again, and it was time to make a stand. Marcus threw a protesting Longinus behind the broken gate in hopes he'd remain undetected, then turned to fight his enemies. Something clawed viciously at his side, the scrape of a spear. An arrow thudded into his shoulder. He staggered backward.

I'm dying, he thought dimly.

The thought gave him a surprising peace.

Suddenly he remembered the Celt in the grove, the one who'd tied his torso to a tree. The one who didn't want to die lying down.

Marcus battled his way forward to grasp a line hanging

from a grappling hook and cut a length free. Then he backed
to a blackened, smoldering post. He was losing blood, and
his vision was beginning to blur. He didn't have much time.

"Someone tie me!" he roared. "Someone tie so I can die
standing like a man!"

As if they understood what he was trying to do, the Celts
hung back for a moment. Small hands seized the line, and the
rope was tightened against his chest. Gratefully he sagged
against it, letting his last strength flow to his arms. He glanced
aside a moment to give a visual thanks to his benefactor and
realized with a start it was a woman—not just surprisingly
female, but a woman vaguely recognizable.

"Savia?"

It was his wife's maidservant, her eyes wide with fear but
mouth set in determination and sympathy. What was she
doing in the blood and filth?

"Good-bye, Marcus."

Was she a hallucination?

"Take him, Cassius!" Marcus heard barbarians shouting.
"Finish the Roman and confirm your freedom!" Then something cold as fire pierced into his side, robbing him of air. A
sword thrust.

"Valeria!" He didn't know he screamed it.

Would his father approve of him now?

Then more blows, and he was dead.

Trapped on the southern side of the Wall, Arden ducked
beneath the jab of a cavalryman's lance and swung his own
sword at the horse's knee. It chopped through and the animal went down in agony, falling on its rider. Before the
man could pull himself out, the chieftain had shoved his
sword through the Roman's throat, feeling the crush of
neck cartilage. Then he whirled and chopped at the back of
another rider, and that man fell too, roaring in pain. Two
barbarian warriors stabbed at him with their spears until
he, too, was still.

Then a Roman arrow took one of the warriors in the chest,
freezing him in place, and a lancer rode down the other.
Everywhere his men were stumbling under the onslaught of

horse and falling like timber. Galba's cavalry had height and hundreds of pounds of rearing horse to their advantage, and arrows were decimating Arden's men from the stonework behind. It was as ruthless a massacre as it was rank treachery.

"Retreat! Form by the Wall!"

The barbarians backed toward the southern gate of the milecastle they'd surged through just half an hour before, but it was a ragged rout toward a rain of arrows. The gate had been shut against them. Man after man grunted and went over, shot before they could even match blades with the Roman cavalry. As the horses pressed, the Celts were squeezed so tightly that some couldn't raise their swords. They were stuck at with lances like squealing pigs, pinned by their own dying comrades. Some, preferring death to slavery, thrust daggers into their own hearts.

Yet no arrow grazed Arden, no spear came close. Did the gods protect him?

No, it was Galba, trying to get to him. "Remember, that one stays alive, or the man who kills him is himself dead!"

What confusing conspiracy had isolated him here? What had happened to the Attacotti and Picts on the other side of the Wall? Why weren't they pouring through in support? Why hadn't Galba turned on the Romans, as promised? Brassidias had betrayed him, just as the woman had! Were they working together? Arden desperately picked up a loose helmet and hurled it at the senior tribune, hitting his shoulder.

If nothing else, he'd take the damned Thracian with him. He charged.

Galba acknowledged the challenge, his black horse bucking toward Caratacus. The Celt planned to strike at the underbelly to dismount the tribune and kill him on the ground. Yet even as he crouched to attack, he noticed that Galba had sheathed his sword and drawn something else. What? Then there was a sizzling buzz, and a whip cracked and wrapped on Arden's forearm, jerking him to his knees. "Now! The net!" Something entangling fell to ensnare Arden's arms. Two troopers had hurled the gladiatorial prop as if he were in the arena. He tried to struggle upward, but they pulled on the netting and he lost his footing again.

"Give me a chance to fight!" he cried.

The reply was harsh laughter. "See his tattoo! We've caught a deserter!"

Through the mesh he could see the last of his men pushed against the inner stone of the Wall, lances impaling them, arrows cutting them down, stones dropping on them from above. Luca fell, bleeding from twenty wounds. The Celts were singing their death songs, trying to take as many Romans as they could with them.

Then something hit his own head, and everything went black.

XXXIX

Stillness settled over the battlefield. To the south of the Wall, the Romans had won. Galba's cavalry had overwhelmed the Celts who'd broken through the gate and killed or enslaved every one of them. Arden Caratacus was unconscious and in chains. They'd even bagged a lean and defiant druid, caught in the conspiracy he'd spun. Kalin, the barbarians called him, clubbed to the ground and hog-tied to corral his magic. A priest to minister to the dungeon of Eburacum! The Romans spat on him and jeered, in fear.

To the north of the Wall the Celtic cavalry had triumphed. Marcus's force had been overwhelmed by a flood of numbers, and he and all his men killed, except for a handful who fought their way to the burned-out gate archway and finally gotten reinforcements from the Romans above. Longinus had survived, but the heart and the flower of the Petriana had been destroyed. His companions were dead.

The Celts, howling with triumph and wailing with grief, had retreated into the trees a mile away, taking most of their dead with them.

The stripped bodies of the Romans were left lying in the trampled and frozen mud. It began to snow harder, fogging the field.

The inner gate of the milecastle had been slammed shut against Arden's column of warriors, denying escape, and their bodies were heaped against it like a windrow of leaves. The pile was prickled with arrows and leaking a delta of blood. Now Galba ordered the corpses dragged aside and the gate opened, its lower half mottled with the stain of the dead. Eventually the heavy door swung wide, revealing the carnage of the milecastle courtyard beyond. Galba strode through in gruesome triumph, the dead the price of his victory. He stepped around the Roman bodies. He trod on the Celtic ones.

From the archway of the other side came the stink of ashes and burned flesh. Its barrel roof framed the other battlefield and its scattering of dead Romans and horses. From far away, through the gauze of snow, came the mournful drumming of the Celts.

Galba's expression was one of tight satisfaction. Everything had happened as he'd planned. He was the savior of Rome.

Huddled against the stone were the surviving men who'd ridden with the Petriana's flanking attack—a dozen in all, muddy, spattered with blood, exhausted. They were his now.

"Marcus Flavius?" he asked no one in particular.

They pointed. "A hero's death. He died standing up."

The praefectus hung from a loop of rope around his chest, his chin down, eyes closed, bloody arms dangling, one foot turned abjectly inward. Galba's face betrayed no emotion. "Indeed. We'll burn him with honors."

The Celts wouldn't come again, the tribune judged. Not for a while, at least, giving him the time needed to complete his scheme. The barbarians were headless, their leader captured. He'd won. Won everything in a morning! The praefectus dead, Caratacus in chains, the woman imprisoned and helpless, the victory his to claim alone. Now he'd see to the Roman beauty, and—

A familiar voice spoke to him from the shadows. "What's become of Valeria?"

He started in surprise. It was her slave woman, Savia! Huddled like the others against the blackened stones of the archway, a cloak around her trembling shoulders, her face black with soot. What was the maidservant doing here?

"Stand up, woman."

The familiar figure stood. A bit leaner, perhaps, swaying with exhaustion, but the same kind, stupid, cowlike face. That doggish loyalty he despised. "I'm servant to the lady," she reminded unnecessarily.

"And what are you doing here, handmaid, in the dung of battle?"

"I followed the Celts in hopes of rejoining Valeria. I was swept up in the attack—"

"Valeria's in prison. Locked there by her dead husband for adultery."

Savia looked at him with sorrow but not surprise. She knew, he realized. Knew he'd planned it this way from the beginning. Maybe he should just run her through now and be done with it, but no, what did he care what a slave thought? Besides, this mother hen might help persuade Valeria what her only choice must be. Savia, like everyone, had her uses. "That means your future is in my hands."

"Are you going to kill Valeria, too?" The question was a quiet one.

Galba walked close to her then so that the others couldn't hear. Spattered with blood and rank with sweat, he leaned close, the scar in his beard like a vast canyon. "Listen to me, slave," he whispered hoarsely. "Your mistress has one chance. One chance only. If you help me, then I can help you. If you oppose me, then I'll destroy you, just as I've destroyed everyone else who's ever challenged me. Do you understand?"

She nodded dumbly.

"Only I can save Valeria now. Do you agree?"

Savia said nothing, looking at him in wonder.

"Then come. We're going to see your mistress."

Galba burst through the entryway of the commander's house like a man who once more regards it as his, his black battle cape rippling behind to punctuate his urgency, Savia scuttling in his wake. "I'm here to see Valeria!" Slaves scurried out of his way and peered with apprehensive wonder from doorways. His skin was speckled with blood, hewn from his enemies. There was mud on his boots. Grim triumph on his face. And haste in his manner. He marched with a tramp as steady as a galley drum to the sleeping chamber where she was confined, the blood rings of his waist chain jangling of victory, his sheathed spatha rocking in rhythm. Two soldiers posted by the chamber's door snapped to attention.

"Unbolt the door!"

They did so, and it opened inward. Valeria stood at the sound, her back to the wall, unable to hide the worry on her face. She'd no idea who next would open that door, and thus who'd survived the battle. At the sight of Galba she tensed. He stepped inside.

His nostrils creased. The room had no window and was stuffy from the lack of air. Its lone oil lamp had created a haze of smoke, and its chamber pot added an acrid odor. Valeria hadn't been allowed to wash and again looked haggard, her eyes red from crying and her clothes sagging. She looked nothing like a Roman lady.

How he relished that fact.

"What news of the fighting?" she whispered.

"Shut the door," Galba told the sentries behind him.

It closed behind the tribune and Savia, leaving the trio in gloom. Valeria glanced past Galba for reassurance, but the maidservant leaned back against the door with her eyes shut in sorrow.

"Your husband is dead," Galba said.

Valeria groaned, bending as if punched.

"He died honorably, fighting the Celts. He'll join my fallen warriors in the pyre."

She drew breath. "*His* warriors."

Galba shook his head. "No, mine. They were never his, and he knew it."

"You're a cruel man to make such a remark, Galba Brassidias."

"And you're a faithless wife."

"You're the faithless one!"

"I'm a soldier, lady, who has won his campaign. Won everything."

She looked bleak. "The Celts lost, then?"

"Of course."

"And Arden?"

"Caratacus is in chains. He'll be executed when I order."

She slumped against the stucco. Just a few nights ago at Samhain, she'd known supreme happiness. In horrible payment ever since, her life had become a nightmare.

She'd tried to save them all, and hadn't even saved herself.

"If I'd been given rightful command, this war would have never happened," Galba went on. "The Celts would never have dared rise, and hundreds of good men would be alive. It's you who put all this in motion, lady. You who almost destroyed the Wall."

Valeria looked bleakly past him to Savia. "What are you doing here?"

"I don't know. He found me among the survivors and brought me here."

"She's here to make you see reason," Galba said. "Your husband is dead and your lover captured, and because of that all protection has been stripped. Your family in Rome is a thousand miles away, and your usefulness to your father is at an end. I have it in my power to ruin you with scandal, a widow with no prospects, an adulteress who lay with a barbarian. You'll be disgraced and impoverished the rest of your life."

She looked at him in bewilderment. "Why do you hate me so?"

"I hate your class, lady. I hate its pretensions, I hate its unearned privileges, I hate its ignorance, I hate its joy. It lives behind my shield and gives no more thought to men like me than to a cur in an alley."

"Rome has rewarded you with career and station—"

"Rome has rewarded me with nothing! Nothing! I took what I have!"

"You'd never have had the opportunity—"

"Enough!" It was a shout. "From this moment forward you will speak to me only when I wish it, or I'll beat you within an inch of your life!"

Instead of cowing her, this sparked her own anger. "I'll speak to you as the provincial you are and will always remain—"

His blow cuffed her like that of a bear, slapping her back against the stucco. She bounced and slid down, mouth bloody and abruptly shut. Savia screamed but didn't move, fearing a beating herself.

"Listen to me," Galba growled, standing over Valeria. "You

have *one* chance to regain your station. One chance to have a life! I can let the world know your sluttish ways; the humiliation of having coupled with a barbarian. Or . . . I can save and enhance your reputation in an instant."

He waited until she asked it, mumbling past her pain and bleeding. "How?"

"By marrying you."

She gave a quick gasp. "You're joking!"

He shook his head. "I'm as earnest about this as any battle. Marry me, Valeria, and no scandal will be heard. Marry me, and you retain your status. Marry me, and bring no shame on your family or yourself."

"You're a provincial!"

"So, originally, were half the emperors of Rome. Marry me, and I have entry into the patrician class."

"For your own advancement!"

"You'll rise as I rise. Enjoy what I attain. Unlike your late husband, I have ability, and have only lacked birth. You have birth, but you're a woman. We're not as different as you think. Together we could triumph."

"This is insane."

"It's the only logical course for you now."

"I'd never go to bed with you! I told you that before!"

"It is *I* who may never bed *you*. I'm seeking marriage, not love. Alliance, not sex. I'll satisfy myself with other women. Only if the mood strikes me will I take you. But I *will* take you, if I wish, as a husband's right."

"So I refuse."

"You'd rather have public humiliation as adulteress and traitor?"

"I'd rather have self-respect and freedom."

"Not freedom, lady. I'll leave you here to rot."

"You wouldn't dare. I'm a senator's daughter!"

"If word reaches your father of your conduct across the border, he'll disown you to save his own position. You know that better than I do."

"You don't know my father!"

"I know he sold you to a mediocrity to advance his own career."

She shook her head with new determination. "The answer is no, Brassidias."

"So." He nodded. "The plaything has some fire after all. Did you find it north of the Wall?"

"Get out of here. Leave me alone."

"But if you refuse me, you doom Rome as well."

"Rome?"

"If you don't marry me, woman, and give me the chance at advancement I deserve, I'll throw open the gates to the Celts. You heard me promise that cretin Arden before. I'll do it this time for real, and throw in my lot with the barbarians. I'll watch Londinium burn and make myself a king."

"You'll be hunted down and hanged if you dare that."

"I'll be a little man with thwarted ambitions if I don't."

He'd take the gamble, she realized. He was insane with frustration. And yet that was Rome's issue, not her own. "I still don't care. I'm not going to marry you, Galba. I once married a man I didn't love. I'm not going to marry a man I hate."

"Yes, you will." His look was confident. "Because there's one more reason to seek my protection. If you don't marry me, Roman bitch, you doom the man you *do* love."

"What do you mean?" she whispered, knowing full well what he meant.

"Arden Caratacus is known, falsely or not, as an agent of Rome. He worked, in a sense, for me. He could, arguably, be spared. I will in fact spare him, if you consent to marry me. But if you don't—"

"You'll kill him." It was a whisper.

"He'll be crucified on the parapet of Petrianis."

"That's inhuman! It will infuriate the Christians! No one uses that method anymore!"

"I will, and in a way that will take him days to die. And I'll tie you to a catapult next to it so you can watch him suffer."

She covered her face with her hands.

"I don't love you, and I never will," he went on. "I simply require you. Marry me, Valeria, and both our problems are solved in an instant. Defy me, and I'll destroy you, Arden Caratacus, and Roman Britannia."

Savia was weeping.

Galba grinned at them. "Think of all the gods. Think of all the druids. Think of all the priests, and then think of me, who believes *none* of it, and consider that *I'm* the one who has won."

"Can't you just kill me and free him?" Her question was a whisper.

"That would be too easy." He ran his hand along his waist chain, making it jingle.

Savia watched the rings of dead men dance at his stroke.

The home of Falco and Lucinda was in quiet turmoil, the slave saw to her surprise. It was midnight, the countryside of Roman Britannia dark, and yet here candles burned as household slaves ran back and forth to pile bundles of belongings on carts. Horses were being hitched to harnesses. Litter and garbage were feeding a fire burning incongruously in the garden courtyard. The family was packing to flee.

"Who goes there? What do you want?" It was Galen, Falco's servant. He blocked her entry to the villa with drawn sword.

"I come from the lady Valeria. I need to see centurion Falco."

"Savia?" He squinted at her in the dark. "I thought you prisoner in Caledonia."

"I got back in the fighting. I was in the battle at the Wall. Please! My mistress is in peril."

"As are we all. There's a war on. My master has no time to see you now."

"What's happening?" She looked past him to the tumult of packing. "Is Lucinda leaving? Rome won the battle."

"The battle, but not the war. The Wall has been broken in other places, and each hour brings a worse dispatch. The duke is missing. It's not just the Picts and Attacotti. The Scotti, the Franks, and the Saxons are also attacking. My mistress is fleeing to Eburacum. Maybe Londinium."

"That defeat is what I'm here to prevent! Lady Valeria is in peril, as is the fort and everyone in it! I need to talk to Falco about Galba!"

"He's no time for Galba anymore, no more than Galba had time for his praefectus," Galen spat. "My master is tired of treachery. We've become a divided and dispirited command, each officer looking to himself. If the Celts come again, my master won't guarantee the outcome."

"That's what I need to talk to Falco about! That, and Roman justice!"

"Justice?" He laughed. "Where do you find that these days?"

"It's about a murder. The murder of his slave, Odo."

"Odo? That's an old matter, long buried." But Galen was curious.

"No, he was exhumed by the druids and spirited north of the Wall. When they carried him, he spoke a final time, naming his murderer. The killer wasn't young Clodius, as everyone believes."

"What are you saying?"

"That the Petriana is falling under the control of a man not just ruthless, but a criminal. Your own master is just. Let me explain to him."

They found the centurion in his office, instructing the foreman to drive the cattle into the nearby woods. An anxious Lucinda was bustling from room to room, issuing instructions like a general.

"What's this?" Falco said to Galen in annoyance.

"This slave has urgent news about Odo."

"Urgent? All Britannia is under assault. Odo and his killer are long dead."

"That's where you're wrong, centurion," Savia spoke up. "I've come because you're the last chance for my mistress. You remember the handle of the knife that killed your slave—"

"From my own dinnerware, which tribune Clodius was using."

"As was every other dinner guest, including Galba."

"You're accusing our new commander? Odo and Galba had no quarrel."

"He murdered Odo to cast doubt on Clodius. To provoke the attack on the grove. To maneuver lady Valeria to a place where she might be captured—"

"That's absurd!"

"The senior tribune dishonored you by misleading you, centurion."

Falco was impatient. "I've no love for Galba Brassidias, but you have no proof."

"Unless a dead man talks."

"What?"

"Did you know the Celts exhumed Odo's body?"

"There was report of this."

"They carried it north for return to the Scotti. A druid named Kalin oversaw this, and in the north, I met him. Now he's a prisoner, so I went to him and was reminded of a very strange thing. It seems that when they bathed and prepared the body of poor Odo and tried to place a coin in his mouth, something was already there."

"What thing?"

She held up a warrior's ring, heavy gold with red stone. "Do you recognize it?"

Falco looked puzzled. "The foray in support of old Cato. Galba took that ring from a Scotti chieftain he killed. It was the fight where Odo was captured."

"If you count the rings on Galba's lorica of chain mail, you'll find one missing."

"So?"

"Odo must have seized it as he died."

"He clutched Galba's belt?"

"The rings spilled like coins. In the dark and haste of having to prepare for the wedding processional, Galba couldn't find one. Instead, the druid Kalin eventually did, in the victim's mouth. The slave named his killer."

Falco was grim. "So Galba lied to all of us about poor young Clodius." He sighed. "Well, what of it in this catastrophe? What's one more victim?" He began to turn away. "Galba's in command now. If I challenge him, he'll simply have me arrested, or worse, put in battle to be killed. There's nothing to do except try to save what I can."

"But there's something you *can* do, centurion. Something before Galba weds the widow of your dead commander, Marcus Flavius."

"Weds Valeria!"

"Something before he creates a new tyranny over the wall that your family has defended for generations. Something before he betrays more armies, as he surely will do. Something before you and the last of the Petriana are sacrificed to his ambition."

"What, slave woman?"

"Help me free Arden Caratacus. And let him seek Roman justice for you."

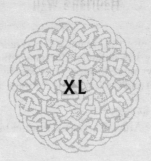

XL

The wedding of Galba Brassidias, senior tribune of Rome and de facto commander of the Petriana cavalry—soldier of the empire, winner of thirteen battles, killer of every man who'd ever opposed him, man of the border—and the lady Valeria, widow of the praefectus Marcus Flavius and daughter of Rome, was to be neither a formal nor a leisurely affair. A wounded but still-dangerous barbarian army was camped somewhere in the forest beyond the Wall. Signal flags warned of continuing assaults, feints, and partial breakthroughs elsewhere along the barrier's eighty-mile length. The north was in full revolt, and all Britannia was threatened. Galba had triumphed, but his orders for transfer to the Continent still stood. Both the imperial succession and the barbarian war were far from decided. His garrison was drastically depleted. The future could change in a moment. He wanted to triumph over his last opponent now, during that predawn quiet that marked the exhaustion of his garrison. He wanted to vanquish the woman by marrying her, thus tying her fate to his. He wanted the political protection she represented.

"Pin the rag, and let's begin," he muttered. "Where's that fat maid to help?"

Valeria was sullenly arranging the same wedding dress she'd worn to marry Marcus only half a year before. Galba had insisted she put it on.

"I don't think she wants to witness this."

"She doesn't approve?"

"She hasn't approved of me for a long time."

He grinned. "That, at least, we have in common."

Galba had ordered the rousing of Sextus, the soldier who'd married Valeria the first time. He liked symmetry in his conquests. The man appeared sleepy, sore, and confused, having received a sword cut over one eye in the recent fighting. The entire side of his head was purple and black, and the blow had left him befuddled.

"I want you to marry again, Sextus," Galba instructed brusquely. "Marry the lady Valeria and me."

Sextus blinked. "But the lady is already married."

"Her husband is dead, dolt."

"Oh. Yes." He tilted his head as if to clear it. "When will the ceremony occur?"

"Now, you dull-headed shit! Now! There's a war on!"

"Now? With a war?"

"Yes, now." It was a growl.

"Here? In this house?" They were in the dining triclinium of the commander's house, Valeria standing stiff and pale and Galba wearing grubby chain mail over a simple woolen tunic, ready for quick battle should another assault come. His belt of rings once more numbered forty, the last in the chain the wedding ring his dead commander had given his new bride. The slave Marta had been pressed into service as witness, the tribune taking perverse pleasure in forcing the wench into the role. It was near dawn, a cock crowing from the village outside the fortress walls, oil lamps providing a dim, smoky illumination. There was no feast, no decoration, and no other guests. Just the mural of Roman triumph over Celtic chariots, which Galba had once more uncovered by ripping Valeria's tapestry down. He liked the cruel triumph the mural represented.

"Yes, here, unless you care to object."

"Here would be good," Sextus agreed, finally recognizing the impatience of his commander. He fingered the wound on his brow. "It's a splendid time for a wedding."

"Just get on with it."

Sextus glanced around as if for guidance. "Which gods shall we use?"

"The good god Dagda," Valeria suddenly spoke up. "The god of the wood."

The soldier blinked in confusion.

"A Roman god, you fool," Galba corrected. "No blasphemy, and nothing to challenge the union later. Jupiter. Jupiter and cake. Isn't that a Roman custom? Marta, do we have some cake?"

"Not really, lord."

"Then use Mars, the god of war."

"A wedding is not war, tribune," Sextus ventured.

"This one is."

Marta was dispatched to fetch a figurine of Mars from Galba's old quarters. Sextus took a wax tablet and scratched the outline of a blessing so he'd not stumble under his commander's stare.

While they waited, the groom leaned toward his bride. "I've decided I'm going to have you after all," he told her hoarsely. "Take you until you bear me a son and thus consummate our marriage."

"I'll neither take nor give any pleasure from it."

"Nor will I. After you start fattening with child, I'm going to put you aside for the rest of your life. If any other man so much as touches you, I'll kill you both."

She closed her eyes. "What will become of Arden?"

"He'll live, but finish his days as a slave."

"If you don't keep your word to spare him, then *I'll* kill *you.*"

He smiled. "I don't doubt you would, given the chance. But I never give anyone the chance."

Marta brought the small clay figure of the god Mars back and Sextus set it in an alcove of the wall alongside a candle. "Galba's god," the soldier observed.

"The sword spatha," Valeria corrected, remembering the senior tribune's comment on that day in Londinium so many months ago.

"What?"

"He told us he worshiped the sword."

"Enough! Enough! Begin!"

Sextus turned to them. "Take her hand, please."

She refused to give it.

"Don't hesitate, Sextus!"

"But why does she withhold her hand?"

Galba grabbed her arm and jerked it to him. "Begin!"

The soldier took a breath. "Very well. I call on Mars to witness—"

He got no further. Suddenly something large and heavy sailed through the doorway and hit the central dining table with a bang, making everyone jump. It skidded to a stop, gleaming dully.

"Look," Sextus said in wonder. "Galba's god."

It was Galba's unsheathed cavalry sword, recognizable to everyone by its white hilt and gold pommel and edge nicked in the recent fighting. In respect and custom to his own wedding, he'd left it sheathed and hanging on a peg in the entryway. Yet here it was, thrown as if in challenge.

The centurion Falco stepped after it. He had his own sword and armor on.

The wedding party had frozen.

"What's this, Falco?" Galba growled, uncharacteristically taken aback by this intrusion. "Can't you see I'm getting married?"

"You might need your sword, tribune. Arden Caratacus has escaped."

Valeria gasped and jerked her hand away from Galba.

"Escaped? When?"

"Just now. He's in the entry hall at this very moment, waiting to kill you."

"What! How did he get here?"

"I let him."

Galba, slowly understanding, darkened like a cloud. "So you've betrayed me, Falco."

"It's you who are the traitor, Galba Brassidias, you who let a unit of the Petriana perish outside the Wall and your commander with it. You who conspired to abduct his wife. You who murdered my slave Odo and blamed it on another soldier, setting into motion his death as well. If Caratacus doesn't kill you, I just might."

"Are you insane? It was the stripling clown who killed Odo, not me!"

"Then why, Galba, did my property have *this* secreted in his mouth?"

Falco tossed again, this time an object tiny and bright. It too hit the table and bounced, finally skittering to a stop. It was a ring of heavy gold bearing a red stone.

The tribune blinked in surprise, recognizing his own tactic for betraying Valeria.

"I remember you with this trophy on a bloody finger after we ambushed the Scotti for Cato Cunedda," Falco said. "What I can't remember is seeing it since the wedding. Why did the dead Odo have it, and why is it missing from your belt?"

Galba involuntarily glanced down, and as he did so, Valeria and Sextus stepped away from him. Suddenly he seemed very much alone.

"He pulled it from your waist, didn't he? He named you from the grave."

"By the gods, I'll slay you too," Galba slowly muttered. "You'll beg not to have me as an enemy. I'll spit on your corpse and possess this bitch anyway!"

"No, Galba," Valeria calmly told him. "If you kill Arden and Falco, then I'll kill myself."

And even as they turned to the entrance hall that Falco had come from, looking for Caratacus, Marta took the back way and darted from the house to give alarm.

Arden was waiting for Galba in the broad entry. He was as still as a statue, resting on the long sword of the Celts. It made Valeria remember that awful moment by the spring of Bormo when young Clodius had charged to save her and been slain by this man she now knew she desperately loved. She could hardly breathe.

Could Arden win? Galba Brassidias was no Clodius. He'd never been beaten in battle. Never been bested by the sword. The Thracian walked in with unsheathed spatha and without fear, his forearms roped with muscle, his eyes dark and wary, his torso erect, his manner deliberate. Would he kill the Celt as easily as he'd killed everyone else?

Arden, by contrast, looked dirty and tired, dressed in the ragged tunic left to him after capture. The chieftain's ankles and wrists had the chafe marks of chains, his body was scratched, and his hair was a tangled mane. What remained bright were his sword and the bold blue eyes that regarded Galba with icy malevolence. It was different from any look that Valeria had seen in the Celt, even in previous combat. It was a look not just of hatred, but of final judgment. Involuntarily, she shivered.

"So you crawled from the pit, Britlet," Galba growled.

"Falco ordered me out under pretext of interrogation." Arden glanced just a moment at Valeria, his eyes softening, and a lifetime of explanation flashed between them. Then his cold focus was once more on his opponent.

Galba snorted. "If you'd let me marry your bitch, I'd have let you live, Caratacus, and maybe even made you a petty king. I've always been your best chance."

"What a habitual liar you've become."

"I told you I'd let you through the gate! I just didn't tell you what you'd find on the other side." Galba grinned. "I played with your dreams of independence, Britlet. But I gave you those dreams, as well."

"I've realized I can't even fully kill you, Galba. You're already half-dead, rotting from the inside out. Your self-pity lives on, but whatever heart you had died long ago."

"But I can kill you, barbarian. And I will!"

Galba sprang, and their blades clashed in the entry chamber's dimness, sparks flying as the metal rang. Their arms bulged, pushing and testing each other's strength, and then they repelled with a grunt, leaping apart, each armed with some knowledge of his opponent's power. They circled warily, looking for weaknesses or mistakes.

"You didn't even dress for your wedding," Arden said, his feet light on the boards of the room. "You look as though you feared she'd stab you."

Galba's circle was smaller and more solid, his guard high. "Maybe instinct told me to dress for war. Better instinct than you." Galba charged, his spatha flicking back and forth in a blur, and before Arden could fully knock it away, the sword found fabric and ripped, cutting a slash on the Briton's chest. Valeria screamed and wished she hadn't.

The barbarian danced back, Galba tracking him. "Poor armor, boy!" It hung on Arden with a bloody fold.

"Then I'll fight in the armor of my ancestors. I'll fight with the shield of the gods and the oak." With his free hand he gripped the tunic and wrenched until it ripped and fell away, leaving him naked. "This is how my people first went into battle against the Romans, murderer, and this is how we'll fight the last battle as well." His body was lean and sculpted and his act both challenge and insult, a tactic as old as the Greeks of Olympia and the Gauls who'd charged Caesar.

Galba smirked. "Then you'll leave the world as naked as you came into it!"

The tribune lunged again, missing, and Arden took the moment's space to utter a high, wavering cry that echoed in the room, an eerie reminder of earlier times and older gods. "Dagggggggdaaaaaa!" Then he lifted his tall sword and closed with his opponent in earnest, both hands on his weapon now as it beat furiously toward Galba, the churning of their blades so swift that it made a subtle wind Valeria felt on her cheek. She could feel the sweat of the antagonists, the room hot and close. The suspense was suffocating. She longed for a weapon if Galba triumphed, to kill him or herself.

The swords danced and clanged like flashing beams of light, stroke and counterstroke so quick it couldn't be followed, like the beat of raptor wings. Both men were grunting, taking harsh breath.

The cavalry officer was trying to get under Arden's guard as the barbarian had gotten under Clodius's, but the ferocity of the Celt's attack wouldn't let him. The barbarian sword was longer and heavier, designed to cleave a man in two, and the pounding of its weight was twisting the tribune's wrists. Galba's sword was chipping under the pounding, bits from its edge flying like fire. The tribune was snarling and backing, beginning to pant, sweat beading as he realized this wouldn't be the easy kill he was accustomed to.

"You're carrying your murders on your back," Arden taunted him. "You're wheezing like a crone."

Galba began to give ground in a circle. In response the chieftain shifted his relentless assault to the other side, so Galba had to back the other way. Then Arden reversed

again, and then again. Thus the tribune found himself being
forced into a corner, hemmed by the ceaseless rain of blows.

"Damn you!"

Arden's attack seemed as tireless as it was relentless.
Valeria remembered the Roman probatio exhausting himself
against the post in the training courtyard and wondered if
that would happen here. Yet there was no slowing, no
respite, and no opportunity for Galba to duck in and under.
Instead the Thracian was being pounded downward, shrinking under the barrage of steel, his spatha darting near
Arden's flesh but never striking as it was parried.

Caratacus, Galba realized with incredulous dread, was the
stronger. "You're going to tire, scumlet!" he gasped, as if the
threat might make it true. Yet the opposite was occurring.

The corner of the room was against Galba's back, trapping him, and for the first time the officer's dark eyes
showed fear. There was something supernatural about this
assault, he thought, a combination of strength and fury he'd
never faced before. Were there really gods? And had this
barbarian oaf somehow summoned them? Had that fat cow
Savia summoned hers?

It was time for something desperate.

As Arden swung, the Roman suddenly dove to one side,
sacrificing his own balance to put the Celt off aim. The tip
of the barbarian sword slammed into stucco and stone and
sheared off with a shrill ring, the broken piece spinning
backward and narrowly missing Arden's face. Plaster
exploded in a puff of smoke. Galba's knee hit the floor, but
he managed to stab as he fell, his spatha finding his opponent's thigh. It sank in an inch, and Arden saved himself
only by recoiling, falling onto his back.

It was enough!

In an instant Galba was up like a cat, his sword swinging
overhead for a final cleaving blow at the man sprawled
beneath him. The spatha made an audible whistle as it cut an
arc through the air. Yet at the last moment Arden spun desperately on his back, and the death slash missed by inches,
thunking disastrously into the wood floor. It stuck there,
imprisoned.

It's my blunder against the Scotti chieftain all over again, Galba realized with a curious detachment. Then Arden's own long sword swept horizontally like a scythe and struck the Thracian in the ankle, severing tendons.

Brassidias roared with fury and toppled, wrenching at his sword.

It broke too, snapping off a hand's-breadth from its tip.

The men reared up, both limping and desperate now, Galba managing to make a thrust toward Arden's throat before the Celt could get his guard up.

His sword stopped harmlessly, however, missing by a finger's width because the Thracian hadn't adjusted to his shortened sword. Even as he missed, his severed ankle buckled beneath him.

"Dung of Plut—"

The curse was cut off as Arden's sword, its tip gone too, whipped down and chopped at the joint between head and neck, slicing into Galba's shoulder, chest, and chain mail with a sickening thud of connection. It struck like an ax into a block of wood, and the tribune quivered as the force reverberated through every fiber of his being to confirm his mortality. His own sword dropped.

Arden wrenched his bloody blade free, chest heaving, arms trembling. "Look your last on my woman, Roman pig."

Then he swung horizontally, and with a crack of severed spine Galba's head came neatly off, its expression locked in stunned surprise, the skull flying to whap against the wall with a wet crack. It and Galba's torso hit the floor at the same time, the latter ejecting a great gout of blood.

. In a corner, the head rocked like a spilled pot.

The barbarian staggered back, his body shaking from the violent exertion, muscles dancing, his great sword wavering.

"Arden!"

Then his own sword dropped, and he collapsed into Valeria's arms.

Even as the barbarian chieftain gasped for breath, bloodied and naked, the locked door of the commander's house boomed dully as Roman soldiers roused by Marta hammered against it. "Open up!"

Falco, frozen in fascination by the fight, jerked to action. "Come!" he shouted to the couple. "Onto the roof!"

"Wait." Arden broke from Valeria, stooped for something, and then came back to seize her hand. The rhythmic pounding followed the fugitives as they clambered upstairs to the building's loft. Below they could hear the front door splintering.

"What now?" Valeria asked when they reached the rafters. They seemed trapped.

"Across the rooftops to the parapet!" Falco explained. "You'll find a horse waiting on the far side."

"A horse?" Arden asked.

"My slaves, it seems, have friends among your people." It was a grim, almost regretful smile.

"You're a Celt yourself, aren't you, Falco?"

"Aye, loyalties have become blurred. Who's a Roman and who's not? Who a Briton and who an invader? We sort it out with blood and thunder."

Falco used his shoulder to butt the underside of the roof. Clay tile broke loose and skittered to the pavement below, making enough of a hole to let Arden scramble out onto the roof's slippery surface, his torn tunic now tied haphazardly around his waist. He reached down and pulled Valeria up after him. They could hear the front door caving in far below, the shouts of anxious Roman soldiers, and then their sudden stunned silence at the sight of the decapitated body of Galba Brassidias.

What had happened to his head?

"Go!" Falco called up at them. "I'll misdirect them. The moat has been dammed and filled with recent rainwater as a defense. It may be enough to break your fall."

"They'll kill you, centurion."

"No, I'm the only commander they have left. Get over the Wall, and they'll stop worrying about you and start worrying about their own survival. Run!" He disappeared to intercept the soldiers climbing the stairs.

The couple looked around. It was cool and clean up on the

roof. There was a rosy glow to the east from the rising sun, a promise of renewal, and yet the longer they lingered, the surer the light would make them targets. They could hear argument in the house below, Falco's voice among them, and knew they had only moments before discovery.

Arden grasped Valeria's hand. "Can you jump?"

She took breath, and with it, courage. "I'll not leave you again."

"Run now, as hard as you can!"

They sprinted on the tiles, the edge of the house a yawning pit, and then leaped, legs churning, bodies falling, and in salvation sprawled on the stable roof across an alley, skidding to safe purchase. They could hear the horses neighing in consternation below. Loose tiles slipped off the building, breaking with a bang. Soldiers were shouting. Then they were up and running lightly along the stable peak, hearing like music the confusion of sleepy sentries.

Another edge and another wild leap, this time into a canvas awning that spilled them into a hayrick. Even before Valeria had time to understand what they'd done, Arden was hauling her up once more, and they sprang over a low fence and made for one of the stone stairways leading to the top of the wall.

It was all a wild blur.

A decurion loomed to block their way, his sword out, his look desperate and undecided. Arden had no weapon! But then suddenly the Roman looked at Valeria in startled recognition and lowered his blade.

She recognized that it was Titus, their guide in the forest, long since promoted by Galba. He'd avoided her after the ambush. Now he bowed his head in shame.

"I betrayed you once, lady. I won't again."

Even as she gasped thanks, they rushed past, hurtling up the stairs to the parapet and gaining a glimpse of the lightening countryside beyond.

Caledonia! Freedom!

"There they are! Stop them!"

An arrow whizzed by their heads, and then another. Boot steps rang on the paving below, a horse was screaming, and somewhere a trumpet called an alarm.

"Now!" Arden shouted in her ear. "The water!"

"Not yet! We need to slow them!"

She pulled free and bent to a rack of weapons. Another arrow hissed by. But then she had a bow too, hastily strung. As Brisa had done to her long ago, she swiftly notched, pulled, and shot. There was a cry in the dark and yells of warning. The next Roman arrow went wide.

"Now!" she agreed.

He jerked her off the edge of the wall.

Valeria's heart seemed to stop as they plunged into a void. Then she saw the glint of water. She was slowly rotating backward, looking back up at helmeted heads popping over the edge of the wall to look for them, and then with a titanic splash they hit the water rump first and, an instant later, the muddy bottom.

They recoiled upward, and before she could even notice the shock of cold, they were scrambling up the muddy bank. There'd been just enough water to break their fall.

"Where are they?" soldiers were shouting. Shadows briefly hid them. A random arrow plopped into the mud with a sucking sound, and they tumbled down the outer hill, running wildly from the fort and its white wall.

Arden's hand gripped hers as if welded. Valeria's decision was irrevocable, and it felt good. Tremendously right.

A horse whinnied. "Over here!" someone called.

It was Galen, Falco's slave, who'd crept over the Wall as his master freed Caratacus. He'd found some barbarians, and a conscious Brisa, her arm and head bandaged after the recent battle, had come to lend a horse.

The chieftain vaulted onto the stallion's back and pulled Valeria up behind him. She was breathless, sore, dizzy, and as wildly triumphant as she'd ever been in her life, grasping her man like a tree in a storm. Brisa mounted another horse as well.

"Come with us, lad!" Arden urged Galen. "Come to freedom!"

The slave, lying on the ground to escape detection and Roman fire, shook his head. "My life is with my master. Ride quickly now. Ride with the gods!"

An arrow arced down and slunk into the ground not far from them. Then another and another. It was at an extreme range, but the Romans were trying. Soldiers were aiming a ballista.

"Soon!" Arden promised. "Soon a free Britannia!"

"Tell Savia I love her!" Valeria added, her voice breaking.

Then he kicked and, riding like the wind, made a wild race for the trees.

One of his hands was on the horse's mane, guiding it.

The other held the wet, bloody head and soul of Galba Brassidias.

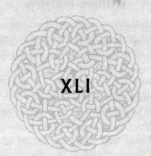

XLI

"You let a rebel loose to kill your commanding officer and abduct a daughter of Rome?" As I put this question to Falco, my tone is more incredulous than my actual surprise—my informants have, after all, been leading up to this—but still, how am I to explain all this in my report to the Senate? A deserter and brigand escaped, an aristocratic woman gone, a senior tribune dead. Everyone talks of religion in an age when nothing seems sacred.

Falco answers me without apology. "My commanding officer, Marcus Flavius, who married in my own house, was already dead because of treachery. Valeria was a widow, and Galba a murderer." He doesn't display the least fear of me. Why should he? What am I going to do to him that life hasn't already done? His estate eventually burned in the fighting. His slaves scattered. His livestock was eaten. The Wall is a sieve, half wrecked and half manned. The empire needs men like Falco more than he needs the empire. More than the empire needs my reports.

"Yet surely you see the disaster I'm dealing with here," I nonetheless grumble.

"It was the emperor who pulled troops from Britannia and tempted the barbarians, not me. And Galba who sacrificed a wing of the Petriana for his own ends. He didn't want to wed Valeria, he wanted to destroy her, as he felt he'd been destroyed. He'd ceased being a soldier and started being an opportunist. He deserved to die."

I look out at the damnable gray sky. "Yet even with Galba gone, she chose to go north of the Wall again."

"And not come back."

I nod. *My entire life has been about sustaining Rome's walls. So why am I not more sorry that this one, eighty miles long and made of millions of stones, has proved so permeable?*

"What happened after their escape?"

"Our military situation was already precarious. One of the Caledonii chieftains, Thorin, had already broken the Wall to the east and was raiding toward Eburacum. Scotti were landing on the west coast, Saxons on the east. We were depleted, wounded, and in danger of being cut off. With Galba gone, the Petriana came together. We retreated toward Eburacum but learned the duke had been killed. So then we fell back to Londinium, taking the captive druid with us. We could see the smoke from the burning of Petrianis for two days."

"Where were the legions to the south?"

"Tardy and afraid," Falco sums up contemptuously. He's a man who lost his home to pillage, and there's bitterness in his reply. "No rally took place until the remnants of the Wall garrison assembled in Londinium. Then the other two legions marched in support. By that time the barbarian attacks were beginning to falter. We managed to ambush some that came that far south."

"Did not Caratacus dream of driving the Romans out of Britannia entirely?"

"He was just one rebel. One dreamer. They had no king, only a council, and the offshore looters were interested only in booty. Caratacus understood the kind of organization required to permanently resist Rome, but none of the others did. Then the imperial succession was stabilized, Theodosius landed with fresh troops, and the barbarians were driven back north of the Wall."

"So the empire is saved again."

He looks at me steadily. "Yes. For how long this time, Inspector Draco?"

This is the kind of man the empire has relied on for centuries to sustain its borders, and even he has lost heart. I look away. "What do you intend to do?"

"Rebuild my farm as best I can. I have no desire to soldier on. I'll live by the Wall and make my living there, as generations have before me, and make my peace with whoever finally wins. There was a time when we only looked south for guidance. Now we look north, as well."

"But there's nothing in the north!" It bursts from me in frustration, this central mystery of my entire investigation. "The north is wilderness! Why would she go north?"

"It's full of free and hard men, with restless new energy. Someday they'll come across that wall to stay, and bring a different kind of world with them."

It is an ominous prophecy to make in the wake of Roman victory, and yet our triumph was so bloody and prolonged as to be exhausting. It is not that people can't sustain the empire; it is that they barely wish to. The old gods are dimming, and this new one, this Jewish mystic, is a god of women and slaves. I like the sound of the Celtic gods better, I think: Taranis and Esus and the good god Dagda. These are gods of songs and men. "Someday," I concede. "Someday."

"And what will you do, Inspector Draco? Travel to some warmer place and make your report?"

"I suppose so." I say it without thinking. Indeed, what will I do? What exactly is it that I am going to report? The imperial court and Senator Valens already know about the barbarian conspiracy and the recent war. My mission is to explain something more baffling: the passions of women and the yearnings of men.

I could write it in four words: She fell in love. But in love with what? A man? Or a place outside the suffocation of my own empire?

"But only when I finish," I amend. "Only when I understand."

He laughs. "If you understand Britannia and the Wall, inspector, you'll be the first. And if you claim to understand young women, you'll be a liar."

I dismiss him so that I can think in solitude for a while. I brood as I listen to the heavy tread of soldiers in the corridor outside. My world suddenly seems a tired one, of ancient traditions and musty laws. Rome is old, almost indescribably old. The woman I seek is young, and in an entirely new place. What do I really know about her, even now?

I suddenly realize that I am profoundly lonely.

I send again for Savia.

She comes and sits quietly. She senses that the end of our interviews is near and that I am going to move on. What will be her fate? And yet instead of the anxiety I detected when we first met, there is calm. As if she thinks I understand more than I realize.

"Why did you not go with her?" I now ask.

She smiles. "Leap from the Wall?"

"In the confusion afterward, perhaps. She was still your mistress, whatever this Caratacus proclaimed."

"I tried, inspector. I was arrested at midnight, trying to unbolt the gate. They made me a cook for their camp and took me to Londinium and then here. As maidservant to a senator's daughter I wasn't an ordinary slave. They thought she might come to me. They thought they should keep me for you."

"To be interrogated for my report."

She nods.

"What is it really like up there?"

Now she cocks her head, thinking of a suitable reply. "Rugged. Yet the air is clearer, somehow. Happiness simpler."

I shake my head. "I do not really understand what's happening."

"About the empire?"

"About everything."

She nods, and we sit in silence some more. It is an oddly companionable quiet. I feel we are communicating even when we don't speak. Is this what long-married couples do? But then she does speak. "I think the Christ is coming, master. Coming everywhere. And that his coming is accomplished in mysterious ways. Priests like Kalin feel the wind as much as you do. The druids are dying too, I think. The world is holding its breath."

"The wind has blown against the empire for a thousand years."

"Every tree must fall."

I turn to look at her. *"What should I do, Savia?"* It is the first time I've used this slave's name, and it seems thick on my tongue, but not unpleasant. *"How can I make sense of what happened here?"*

"Find her, master."

"Not master. Not inspector."

She looks at me a long time, her eyes deep and kind. *"Find her, Draco."*

Of course. If I am to understand the walls of the empire, I must go beyond them. I must see for myself this new world that presses like a wave against our shores. I must talk to the one person I've not yet talked to, the woman herself. Valeria.

"Will you guide me?"

"I, and Kalin."

"The druid?"

"He's dying down there from lack of light, as doomed as a flower. Free him, Draco, and take us both. You'd be an excuse for the garrison to get rid of him. He'll be our guide and guarantee of safety. I was terrified to go north the first time, but it's only there that you'll understand what's happening to the empire."

"I am an old man, Savia."

"And I'm an old woman. But not too old to search for new things." She pauses, embarrassed to admit all her motives. *"I want to go north and tell them more about the Christ. They sense his wisdom. It might put an end to their feuds and cruelties."*

"You're going to preach your faith? You—" I am about to say slave, but I check my tongue—*"a woman?"*

"Yes. And I want to go with you." She is saying what I already know, and still it comes as a thrill. Who has wanted to go with me anywhere before? Who has not dreaded my arrival and been relieved by my departure?

"It will be as a freed woman, not a slave," I say thickly. *"Caratacus gave you your freedom up there. So will I."*

"I know." She expected this manumission all along, I realize. She knew these stories of freedom would infect me.

"And what is it that you think I'll find up there?" I ask her.

"Yourself."

No, no, it is impossible. The north! I must make my report to the emperor.

Yet not until I am ready. Not until I understand.

I realize I've made this decision long ago, made it somewhere in the course of these interviews and the course of my travels, made it because of the weary rot of the imperial court I represent.

Where is she now, this Valeria? What tower does she watch from? What has she seen? What is she learning? What does she think?

A senator's daughter!

We go north, starting tomorrow.

We go to find what she found.

EPILOGUE

Thirty-nine years after the battle of the Wall, on the last day of the Year of Our Lord 406, the Rhine River froze solid during the coldest winter in memory. Hundreds of thousands of waiting Vandals, Alans, Suevi, and Burgundians emerged from the forests of Germania and marched across the ice into Gaul.

A thin and dispirited Roman and Frankish army mustered to meet them but was easily brushed aside. With that, the world was open to pillage.

Some of the barbarian invaders claimed new lands in Gaul. Others struck south toward Italy, Spain, and Africa. In 410, the Gothic warlord Alaric sacked Rome. It was the first conquest of the city in eight centuries.

In that same year as the sacking, the province of Britannia sent an urgent plea to the emperor Honorius to seek military assistance against barbarian invasion.

The inheritor of Caesar replied that the island would have to look to itself.

No other communication from the empire was ever received.

HISTORICAL NOTE

Hadrian's Wall is a work of fiction based on real events. There was a "Great Barbarian Uprising" in A.D. 367 that convulsed northern Britain, though the details of this war are obscure. There was a famed cavalry called the Petriana. There was a great tidal mixing of migrating tribes, religious faiths, new ideas, and old dissatisfactions in both Roman Britain and the empire as a whole in the fourth century, a prelude to the storm that would break in the fifth century. Above all there was Hadrian's Wall, today one of the most evocative ruins of Rome's imperial glory. Some have declared that a walk along its length is the greatest hike in Britain.

Despite the fame of what is today a World Heritage Site, many of the most basic questions about Hadrian's Wall remain unanswered. Because it has been mined for building stone for more than a millennium, all that remains in most places are its foundations. While its thickness of six to ten feet can be deduced from the surviving stone stump, its height can only be estimated. Most authorities believe—based on the angle of fragmentary steps found at one spot, the wall's necessary height at another place to join a bridge top, and so on—that the Wall averaged about thirteen to fifteen feet high, its dimensions likely varying with location and terrain. This would not have included any protective crenellations that soldiers could have stood behind, which would have added several feet more to its imposing appearance from the Celtic side. This is only an estimate, however. While there are re-creations of the Wall's gates and towers in the English city of Newcastle, and numerous speculative drawings, they represent only educated guesses. They are based on Roman architecture elsewhere in the empire and a couple of crude depictions of the Wall found on a Roman bowl and cup uncovered by archaeologists. Simply put, we moderns don't know exactly what the Wall looked like or how it changed over its three centuries of use. The white-washing of the structure described in this novel is based on the findings of a lime paint on some stones, but whether Hadrian's Wall was truly painted for its entire length—Roman construction was often colorfully painted—remains a matter of speculation for historians. We do know its western half began as a turf wall that was later mostly replaced with stone.

There is no written record of an actual assault on the Wall, though it certainly could have happened. As barrier and landmark, it undoubtedly figured in periodic conflicts such as the A.D. 367 uprising, since any invading army would have had to cross it. There is little evidence, however, of the kind of fire or destruction that might have accompanied an Alamo-like attack. Did the Wall deter all assault? Was it so easily pierced that invaders left no mark? Or has time erased all evidence of past battles?

Above all, experts are uncertain how the wall functioned. It seems impossible that the estimated five thousand Roman soldiers who permanently manned the Wall—stretched out for eighty Roman miles, or seventy-three modern miles—could have hoped to defeat a determined attack at any one point. They were simply spread too thin. What was the Wall's purpose, then? Simply to mark civilization's boundary in an emphatic way? To control trade and immigration, like the Iron Curtain of our recent times? To collect tariffs and taxes by funneling travelers through gates? Or was the Wall and its forts a mixture of all these things, a barrier that was both physical and psychological? The only thing we can surmise with confidence is that to a certain extent it worked at protecting Roman Britannia from raid and invasion and at sustaining different cultures south and north. The historic division between England and Scotland (Britannia and Caledonia in this book) was set by this Wall.

It is unlikely the Romans would have referred to the fortification as "Hadrian's" Wall. We don't know what name they gave it. Still, modern-day attribution to that energetic, gifted, eccentric, generous, ruthless, rugged, and sensual emperor is accurate. The Wall was started during Hadrian's reign, after he visited the province of Britannia, and a scene much like that of the prologue may indeed have occurred. Remains of a fifty-room wooden "palace" have been found at the Roman fort of Vindolanda that date from Hadrian's visit to Britain, and archaeologists think it may have been constructed for his entourage. We can only guess at what the emperor said or ordered, however: the only specific line in ancient literature that refers to the Wall's construction is a much later fourth-century imperial history by Aelius Spartianus that states, "Having reformed the army (in Gaul) in the manner of a monarch, Hadrian set out for Britain. There he corrected many faults and was the first to build a wall, eighty miles long, to separate the Romans from the barbarians."

This is not the only ancient writing I relied on. Many of the Roman aphorisms in this novel are taken from history. The poem of Florus in the prologue is close to one that has actually come down to us from antiquity. So is Clodius's poem from the emperor Julian, about the dubious merits of British beer.

The Romans were aware of the great civilizations of India and China far to the east, trading with both: Valeria's silk gown would have originated in China and is based on the fact that Rome imported such luxuries. Historians thus believe it is possible that Hadrian would have heard of the Great Wall of China, which had taken continuous shape about three centuries before Hadrian's Wall was started. Did China's wall inspire his idea to protect the Roman Empire behind permanent fortifications? We don't know.

One of the challenges of this novel was to convey the prejudices Romans had toward the world outside their empire while suggesting that Celtic tribes were not quite the troglodytes that Roman commentators would have us believe. First of all, the word *barbarian* did not carry to the

Romans the rather savage, uncouth, and filthy image that Hollywood movies give us today. It more accurately meant "outsider," and to apply it to the Celts or Germans creates an image in the modern mind that is not altogether fair. There is no question that the Mediterranean civilizations were for centuries militarily and culturally superior to the peoples of the north, but it was superiority of social organization more than advanced technology. The Romans were supremely disciplined and had centuries of experience in military strategy and governing conquered peoples. But the Celts were farmers of equal skill, superb artisans, ferocious fighters, and had an intricate religion and complex oral literature. The Romans borrowed from them some techniques of wagon-making, metalworking, and plowing. They incorporated many Celtic weapons. The outlying tribes did lag behind the Romans in writing, tactics, strategy, architecture, engineering, and ancient artillery, but appear to have been in no hurry to adopt such advances. The slow progress of ideas—including Christianity—in the ancient world is one of its most alien features, so accustomed are we to mass communication and quick change.

The Celts were a very old people, with a culture that stretched from the Black Sea to Ireland. They sacked Rome early in the city's history and at one time occupied northern Italy before being conquered there by the Romans shortly before the Punic Wars with Carthage. The fact that their remnants were ultimately pushed into Wales, Ireland, and Scotland should not negate the fact that they resisted the Romans for eight centuries. Portrayals we have of them come entirely from Latin sources, and some—such as Caesar's account of his conquest of Gaul—are part history and part deliberate political propaganda. Depictions of the "barbarism" of non-Roman outsiders should thus be taken with a grain of salt, given the incredible artistry of Celtic works that have been uncovered. Whether a Roman of Valeria's station would have reacted favorably to Celtic culture is debatable, of course, but intriguing to speculate about. In the American West, white captives of Indian tribes frequently preferred to stay with their captors when "rescued" by the cavalry. I have imagined a somewhat similar reaction in this novel. Nor should we forget that Rome, ultimately, was overcome in its western half by the very barbarians it disdained, for reasons still vigorously debated. While in many ways the fall of the empire was a catastrophe for civilization, it also cleared away the encrustation of a classical Mediterranean culture that had fossilized. The Dark Ages, however miserable they must have been to live in, were a necessary prelude to a new kind of light: an eventual marriage of northern energy and southern ideas.

None of the characters in this novel are based on real people, except for brief mention of such high-ranking figures as the emperor Hadrian and his governors, the emperor Valentinian, Duke (or Dux, in Roman usage) Fullofaudes at Eburacum (or modern-day York), and Theodosius, the Roman general who landed reinforcements and eventually drove the A.D. 367 uprising back. So is Valeria a probable figure? Would we even find Roman women at so remote a place as Hadrian's Wall?

The answer is certainly yes. A remarkable find of writing scraps in a Roman dump at the military fortress of Vindolanda, about midway along Hadrian's Wall, includes letters between military wives of commanding officers stationed at nearby forts. Also found have been children's shoes in the vicinity of the commander's residence, and we know commanders were allowed to live with their families during their standard three-year tour of duty. Julia Lucilla was a senator's daughter married to a commanding officer at High Rochester. And while Rome was in general a patriarchal society based on military power, with wives legally subordinate to their husbands, upper-class women received some education, generally led comfortable lives, and sometimes wielded considerable political influence through their mates.

While soldiers below the rank of centurion were not allowed officially to marry until after an edict of A.D. 197—a change made to combat lagging recruitment—even before that time there is documentary evidence of legionaries being accompanied by unofficially recognized "wives." There were also brothels, of course, and male-female relationships were undoubtedly as complicated then as they are now. Any reading of surviving Roman correspondence suggests that while technology has changed greatly in the past two millennia, human nature has not changed at all.

Though movies and books have given us a mental picture of the Roman Empire at its height, Rome's incredibly long history means that artistic and archaeological records represent a few surviving snapshots of a long scrapbook that has been mostly lost. The period from the legendary founding of Rome to the city's sack by Alaric in A.D. 410 is an astounding 1,163 years. We can add another thousand years for the persistence of the Byzantine successor to Rome's eastern empire. Simply the time span between the assassination of Julius Caesar and the events in this book is 411 years, or longer than the period between the founding of the English colony at Jamestown, Virginia, and the present day. While technological and social change was incredibly slow by modern standards, change nonetheless took place, and the Rome of *Hadrian's Wall* was different from the Rome of such films as *Cleopatra*, *Spartacus*, or *Gladiator.* The widespread adoption of more flexible chain mail and the mobility of the horse anticipated the dress and armor of the early Middle Ages, far from the classic Roman soldier we are so familiar with. The horse gave the Roman army the mobility to meet fast-moving barbarian raiding parties, and the height of a horse meant that the short stabbing gladius sword was gradually eclipsed by longer slashing swords, eventually evolving from the cavalry spatha of Galba to Excalibur-type weapons. Exactly when and how these transitions took place is unclear. Our mental picture is blurry because ancient literary and archaeological sources decline sharply after about A.D. 200. The late 300s present an author with both a paucity of detail and considerable room for novelistic imagination. The next few centuries in Britain—the probable time of King Arthur, if he really existed—are even foggier.

We do know that Hadrian's Wall provided a three-centuries-long solution to a vexing military and technological problem that Rome continually struggled with: defending an empire 3,000 miles long and 1,750 miles wide. Despite the superb construction of 48,500 miles of Roman roads, transportation in ancient times was extremely difficult. At the time of Valeria's journey, the stirrup had not been invented, horseshoes were mostly unknown, wagons had no suspension to even out bumps, and "horsepower"—horses, mules, donkeys, and oxen—had to be fed. The practical limit of economical land transport away from water was about seventy-five miles, which helps explain why the empire was oriented around the Mediterranean and why major new cities grew up along such waterways as the Danube, the Rhine, the Seine, and the Thames. Yet the empire's land area was the size of the United States. Hadrian's revolutionary solution was to halt the expansion that his predecessors had pushed and establish a defensible boundary. In Britain it was Hadrian's Wall, in Germany it was a log palisade two hundred miles long between the Danube and Rhine, and in North Africa and Arabia it was a series of forts in trackless desert. Where possible, the Romans used rivers, canyons, and ridges to make their stopping point as defensible as possible. A precipitous gorge near the headwaters of the Middle East's Euphrates River was one such barrier.

Still, the Roman army, even with as many as 300,000 men, never had sufficient numbers to firmly guard such lengthy boundaries. As time went on, the Romans were increasingly forced to recruit the barbarians they had conquered into their army to sustain its numbers. These new warriors brought new methods, such as heavy cavalry and long swords, with them. While border fortifications provided bases and a fixed boundary, it was relatively easy for a determined barbarian horde to pierce Rome's long line. The solution was infantry that could march quickly on Roman roads to crisis points, or cavalry that could run raiders to ground. The analogy between the Petriana and the U.S. cavalry that patrolled the American West is obvious. Hadrian's Wall was not just a fixed fortification but a base for patrol.

While Petrianis may have been a real fort, I have moved it in my imagination from its likely flatland location near modern-day Carlisle (Uxello durum), where cavalry would have been most effective, to a more evocative but fictional setting of hill and river: a place that borrows from the geography of the Roman fort at today's Birdoswald, called Banna by the Romans, and that near Corbridge, called Onnum. Arden's fort of Tiranen is not based on any specific Celtic hill fort, but its design is typical of those found across Britain, and its described terrain is typical of the increasingly rugged Scottish countryside north of Hadrian's Wall.

The Scotti, incidentally, came—at the time of this story—from the isle that the Celts called Eiru and the Romans called Hibernia: modern-day Ireland. It was later that they gave their name to Scotland as part of that back-and-forth tide of conquest that ultimately made Great Britain the product of Celt, Viking, German, French, Irish, and Roman invaders, a melting pot of sword and blood. Thus a distant and ancient empire, Rome, helped seed a much later and even bigger one. Though Hadrian's Wall did not last forever, both the political boundaries it set and the elusive dream it represented—of permanent security, behind some kind of impregnable defense—remain with us to this day.

Please turn the page for an early look at the next
novel of epic struggle from
William Dietrich

THE SCOURGE OF GOD

Available in hardcover from HarperCollins

BROTHER AND SISTER

Ravenna, A.D. 449

"My sister is a wicked woman, bishop, and we are here to save her from herself," the emperor of the Western Roman Empire said.

His name was Valentinian III, and his character was unfortunate evidence of dynastic decay. He was of only middling intelligence, without martial courage, and with little interest in governance. Valentinian preferred to spend his time in sport, pleasure, and the company of magicians, courtesans, and whichever senatorial wives he could seduce in order to gain the greater pleasure of humiliating their husbands. He knew his talents did not match those of his ancestors, and his private admission of inferiority produced feelings of resentment and fear. Jealous and spiteful men and women, he believed, were always conspiring against him. So he had brought along the prelate for tonight's execution because he needed the church's moral approval as much as his soldiers' protection. Valentinian relied on the beliefs of others in order to believe in himself.

It was important for his sister Honoria to recognize that she had no champions in either the religious realm or the secular, the emperor had argued to the bishop. She was rutting with a steward like some base kitchen trollop, and her just punishment and proper salvation would be an abrupt end to the affair and forced marriage to an aging senator she'd never met.

This little surprise was really a gift, Valentinian reasoned.

He was saving his sister from a trial as traitor in this world, and from damnation in the next.

"No child is beyond salvation, Caesar," Bishop Milo assured. He shared complicity in this rude surprise because he and the girl's wily mother, Galla Placidia, needed money to complete a new church in Ravenna that would help guarantee their own ascent into heaven. Placidia was as embarrassed by her daughter's indiscretion as Valentinian was fearful of it, and support of the emperor's decision would be repaid by a generous donation to the church from the imperial treasury. God, the bishop believed, worked in mysterious ways. Placidia simply assumed that God's wishes and her own were the same.

The emperor was supposed to be in musty and decaying Rome, conferring with the Senate, receiving ambassadors, and participating in hunts and social gatherings. Instead he had galloped out four nights ago unannounced, accompanied by a dozen soldiers hand-picked by his chamberlain Heraclius. They would strike at Honoria before her plans ripened. It was the chamberlain's spies who had brought word that the emperor's sister was not just sleeping with her palace steward—a reckless fool named Eugenius—but was plotting with him to murder her brother and seize power herself. Was the story true? It was no secret that Honoria considered her brother indolent and stupid, and that she believed she could run imperial affairs more ably than he could, on the model of their vigorous mother. Now, the story went, she intended to put her lover on the throne with herself as Augusta, or queen. It was all rumor, of course, but rumor that smacked of the truth: the vain Honoria had never liked her sibling. If Valentinian could catch them in bed together, a princess and a servant, it would certainly be proof of immorality and bad judgment. Perhaps it implied treason as well. In any event, it would be excuse enough to marry her off and be rid of her.

The emperor excused his own romantic conquests as casually as he condemned those of his sister. He was a man and she was a woman and thus her lustfulness, in the eyes of man and God, was more offensive and shameful than his.

Valentinian's entourage had crossed the Apennine spine of Italy and now approached the palaces of Ravenna in the dark, pounding down the long causeway that was the only land access to this marshy refuge. While easy to defend from barbarian attack, the new capital always struck Valentinian as a dreamlike place, divorced from the land and yet not quite of the sea. It floated separately from normal industry or agriculture, and the bureaucracy that had taken refuge there often had only the most tenuous grip on reality. The water was too shallow to sail on and the mud unstable, requiring countless pilings and fill. The wit Apollinaris had thus claimed the laws of nature were repealed in Ravenna, "where walls fall flat and waters stand, towers float and ships are seated." The wetland was brown and fetid, the marsh produced a miasma of mist, and canals cut a labyrinth. The one advantage of the new city was that it was nominally safe, and that was no small thing in today's world. Treacheries were everywhere.

The life of the great was a risky one, Valentinian knew. Julius Caesar himself had been assassinated, five hundred years before. The gruesome endings of emperors since was a list almost too long to memorize: Clodius poisoned, Nero and Otho both suicides, Caracalla a murderer of his brother who was assassinated in turn, Constantine's half-brothers and nephews virtually wiped out, Gratian murdered, Valentinian II found mysteriously hanged. Emperors had died of battle, disease, debauchery, and even from the fumes of newly applied plaster, but most of all from the plottings of the family, friends, and officers closest to them. It would have been a shock if his cunning sister had *not* conspired against him. The emperor had been more than ready to hear his chamberlain's whisperings of a plot, because he had expected no less since being elevated to the purple at the age of four. He had reached his present age of twenty-eight only by fearful caution, constant suspicion, and necessary ruthlessness. An emperor struck, or was struck down. He had consulted his astrologers and they had warned that those closest to him could be least trusted, a prophecy that, in confirming his worst fears, left the seers richly rewarded.

So now the arresting party dismounted in the shadow of the gate, not wanting the clatter of horses to give warning. They drew long swords but held them tight to their legs to minimize their glint in the night. Cloaked and hooded, they moved toward Honoria's palace like wraiths, Ravenna's streets dark, its canals gleaming dully, and a half moon teasing behind a moving veil of cloud far overhead. As a town of government instead of commerce, the capital always seemed desultory and half-deserted.

The authority of the leading tribune and then the emperor's own countenance made possible a swift passage past startled sentries.

"Caesar! We didn't expect . . ."

"Get out of the way."

Her palace was mostly asleep, the tapestries and curtains bleached of color by the night and the oil lamps largely extinguished. Its domes and vaults bore tile mosaics of saints who looked serenely down at the sins below, the air languid with incense and perfume. The emperor's entourage strode down dark marble hallways too swiftly for any challenge, and Honoria's chamber guardian, a huge Nubian named Goar, went down with a grunt from a crossbow bolt fired from twenty paces before he even understood who was approaching. He struck the marble with a meaty thud. A wine boy who startled awake, and who might have cried warning, had his neck snapped like a chicken's. Then the soldiers burst into the princess's quarters, knocking aside tables with dishes of honeyed sweets, kicking a cushion into the shallow pool of the bath, and butting open the door of her sleeping chamber.

The couple jerked awake, clutching and crying out behind the gauze of the curtains as a dozen dark shapes surrounded their vast bed. Was this assassination? Why had there not been more warning?

"Light them," Valentinian ordered.

His men had brought torches and the wick of an oil lamp was used to ignite them into flame, turning the scene bright and lurid. The steward Eugenius slid away on his backside until he bumped against the headboard wall, his hands seeking to cover himself. He had that look of a man who has stumbled off a cliff and, in one last moment of crystalline dread, knows there is nothing he can do to save himself. Honoria was crawling on her stomach toward the other side of the bed, naked except for the silken sheet draped over her form, her hip bewitching even in her terror, clawing away as if distance from her commoner lover would provide some kind of deniability.

"So it is true," the emperor breathed.

"How dare you break into my bedchamber!"

"We have come to save you, child," the bishop said.

The exposure of his sister strangely excited the emperor. He had been insulted by her mockery, but now who looked the fool? She was on humiliating display for a dozen men, her sins apparent to all, her shoulder bare, her hair undone, her breasts dragging on the sheet. The situation gave him a heady satisfaction. He glanced back. Goar's prostate form was just visible in the entry, his blood pooling on the marble like a little lake. It was his sister's vanity and ambition which had doomed those around her. As she had doomed herself! Valentinian spied a golden cord holding the drapery of linens around the bed and yanked, pulling it free. The diaphanous shelter dropped to the floor, exposing the couple even more, and then he stepped forward and began flailing at Honoria's hips and buttocks as they flinched under the sheet, his breath quick and anxious as she howled in outrage.

"You're rutting with a servant and plotting to elevate him above me!" he accused.

She writhed and protested, pulling the covering away from poor Eugenius in order to wrap herself. "Damn you! I'll tell mother!"

"Mother told *me,* when and where I'd find you!" He took satisfaction in the way that betrayal stung. They had always competed for Placidia's affection. He whipped and whipped, humiliating more than injuring her, until finally he was out of breath and had to stop, panting. Both he and his sister were flushed.

The soldiers dragged the steward out of bed and wrenched his arms behind his back, forcing him to his knees. His manhood was limp and he'd not had time to muster a defense. He looked in beseeching horror toward the princess as if she could save him, but all she had were dreams, not power. She was a woman! And now, in gambling for her affections, Eugenius had doomed himself.

Valentinian turned to study the would-be emperor of Ravenna and Rome. Honoria's lover was handsome, yes, and no doubt intelligent to have risen to palace steward, but a fool to try to climb above his station. Lust had bred opportunity and ambition had encouraged pride, but in the end it was a pathetic infatuation. "Look at him," Valentinian mocked, "the next Caesar." His gaze shifted downward. "We should cut it off."

Eugenius' voice broke. "Don't harm Honoria. It was I who . . ."

"Harm Honoria?" Valentinian's laugh was contemptuous. "She is royalty, steward, her bloodline purple, and has no need of a plea from you. She deserves a spanking, but will come to no real harm because she's incapable of giving it. See how helpless she is?"

'She never thought of betraying you . . ."

"Silence!" He slashed with the cord again, this time across the steward's mouth. "Stop worrying about my slut of a sister and start pleading for yourself! Do you think I don't know what you two were planning?"

"Valentinian, stop!" Honoria begged. "It's not what you think. It's not what you've been told. Your advisers and magicians have made you insane."

"Have they? Yet what I expected to find I found, is that not right, bishop?"

"Yours is a brother's duty," Milo said.

"As is this," the emperor said. He nodded to the tribune. "Do it."

The big soldier stepped behind the steward and knotted a scarf around his neck.

"Please," the woman groaned. "I love him."

"That's why it's necessary."

The tribune pulled, his forearms bulging. Eugenius began to kick, struggling uselessly against the men who held him.

Honoria began screaming. The man's face purpled, his
tongue erupting in a vain search for breath, his eyes bulging,
his muscles shuddering. Then his look glazed, he slumped,
and after several long minutes that made sure he was dead,
his body was allowed to fall to the floor.

Honoria was sobbing.

"You have been brought back to God, daughter," the
bishop said.

"Damn all of you to Hell."

The soldiers laughed.

"Sister, I bring you good news," Valentinian said. "Your
days of spinsterhood are over. Since you've been unable to
find a proper suitor yourself, I've arranged for your marriage
to Flavius Bassus Herculanus in Rome."

"Herculanus! He's fat and old! I'll never marry him!" It
was as hideous a fate as she could imagine.

"You'll rot in Ravenna until you do."

Honoria refused to marry and Valentinian held to his
word to confine her, despite her begging. Her pleas to her
mother were ignored. What torture to be locked in her
palace! What humiliation to gain release only through marrying a decrepit aristocrat! Her lover's death had killed a
part of *her,* she believed; her brother had strangled not just
Eugenius but her own pride, her belief in family, and any
loyalty to Valentinian's regency. He had strangled her heart!
So early in the following year, when the nights were long
and Honoria had entirely despaired of her future, she sent
for her eunuch.

Hyacinth had been castrated as a slave child, placed in a
hot bath where his testicles were crushed. It had been cruel,
of course, and yet the mutilation that had denied him marriage and fatherhood had allowed him to win a position of
trust in the imperial household. The eunuch had often mused
on his fate, sometimes relieved that he had been exempted
from the physical passions of those around him. If he felt
less like a man because he'd been gelded, he suffered less
too, he believed. The pain of emasculation was a distant
memory, and his privileged position a daily satisfaction. He

could not be perceived as a threat like Eugenius. As a result, eunuchs often lived far longer than the nobles they served.

Hyacinth had become not just Honoria's servant but also her friend and confidant. In the days after the strangulation of her lover, his arms had comforted her as she had sobbed uncontrollably, his beardless cheek against hers, murmuring agreement as she stoked the flames of hatred for her brother. The emperor was a beast, his heart a stone, and the prospect of the princess's marriage to an aging senator in tired Rome was as appalling to the eunuch as it was to his mistress.

Now she had summoned him in the night. "Hyacinth, I am sending you away."

He blanched. He could no more survive in the outside world than a domestic pet. "Please, my lady. Yours is the only kindness I have known."

"And sometimes your kindness seems the only that I have. Even my mother, who aspires to sainthood, ignores me until I submit. So we are both prisoners here, dear eunuch, are we not?"

"Until you marry Herculanus."

"And is that not a prison of another sort?"

He sighed. "I would miss the fine new buildings of Ravenna, my lady. But perhaps the marriage in Rome is a fate we must accept. It might not be so bad."

Honoria shook her head. She was very beautiful, and enjoyed the pleasures of the bed too much to throw her life away on an old patriarch. The reputation of Herculanus was of a man stern, humorless, and cold. Valentinian's plan to marry her off would snuff out her own life as effectively as he had snuffed out Eugenius. She was desperate. She needed a companion, someone powerful enough to oppose her brother, and she knew just the man to do it. "Hyacinth, do you recall how my mother Galla Placidia was taken by the Goths after the sack of Rome, when she was young, and married to their chieftain Athaulf?"

"Before I was born, princess."

"When Athaulf died Mother returned to Rome, but in the meantime she had helped civilize the Visigoths. She said once that her few years with them were not too terrible, and I think she has some spicy memories of her first husband. The barbarian men are strong, you know: stronger than the breed we now have in Italy."

"Your mother had many strange travels and adventures before assuring the elevation of your brother and yourself."

"She is a woman of the world who sailed with armies, married two men, and now devotes herself to the church. She looked beyond the palace walls as she now looks to Heaven. She always urged me to do the same."

"All revere the Augusta."

Honoria gripped her eunuch's shoulders, her gaze intense. "This is why we must follow her brave example, Hyacinth. There is a barbarian even stronger than the Goths. He is a barbarian stronger than my brother—a barbarian who is the strongest man in the world. You know of whom I speak?"

Now the eunuch felt the slow dawning of dread. "You mean the king of the Huns." Hyacinth's voice was a whisper, as if they were speaking of Satan. The entire world feared Attila, and prayed that his plundering eye would fall on some other part of the Empire. Reports said that he looked like a monkey, bathed in blood, and killed anyone who dared stand up to him—except for his wives. He enjoyed, they said, hundreds of wives, each as lovely as he was grotesque.

"I want you to go to Attila, Hyacinth." Honoria's eyes gleamed. Dreams of revenge consumed her. She knew that ever since the days of the dictator Sulla, nearly six centuries before, power in Rome had depended on force of arms. Strong women accordingly relied not just on their wits, but their alliances with strong men. The Huns had the most terrifying army in the world, and mere word from their leader would make her brother quail. If Attila asked for her, Valentinian would have to let her go. If Attila forbade the marriage to Herculanus, Valentinian would have to accede. Wouldn't he?

"Go to Attila!" Hyacinth gasped. "My lady, I scarcely go from one end of Ravenna to the other. I'm not a traveler. Nor an ambassador. I'm not even a man."

"I'll give you men as escort. No one will miss *you*. I want you to find your courage and find *him*, because both of our futures depend on it. I want you to explain what has happened to me. Carry my signet ring to him as proof of what you say. Hyacinth, my dearest slave: I want you to ask Attila the Hun to rescue me."

Dark mayhem and foul murder in the Middle Ages—
THE KNIGHTS TEMPLAR MYSTERIES BY
MICHAEL JECKS

> *They were warrior monks dedicated to the protection*
> *of pilgrims in the Holy Land—until stories spread by*
> *an avaricious king destroyed the order.*
> *There was one knight, however, who escaped the stake,*
> *vowing justice as he watched his innocent brothers die.*

THE LAST TEMPLAR
0-06-076344-2 • $7.50 US

In the year 1316, Simon Puttock, bailiff of Lydford Castle is called to a nearby village to examine a burned-out cottage and the dead body within. But it is the newly arrived knight, Sir Baldwin Furnshill who discerns the deceased was, in fact, murdered prior to the blaze.

THE MERCHANT'S PARTNER
0-06-076346-9 • $7.50 US

When the mutilated body of a midwife and healer is discovered, a frightened local youth is suspected. But Sir Baldwin Furnshill, once a Knight Templar, has doubts about the boy's guilt and enlists his friend Simon Puttock in the hunt for a murderer.

A MOORLAND HANGING
0-06-076347-7 • $7.50 US

Cold-blooded murder has transformed Simon Puttock's official obligation into something horrid—and he will need the able assistance of his friend Sir Baldwin Furnshill to draw a criminal out, even if their search exposes extortion, foul corruption and killers eager to shed still more blood.